I0635155

Copyright © 2006 by Young Films & Publishing LLC

Cover design by Young Films & Publishing LLC

Editing by:
Jill Pomerantz

Printed in the United States of America

ISBN 0-9774328-1-5

I

This book is dedicated to my wife, Connie Jean Young

After twenty five years of marriage and two wonderful children, I have learned the real importance of family. And on our 25th Anniversary, I dedicate this book to her, for without her, I would be a lost soul.

A Special Thanks to:

All of the wonderful writers that contributed and to the hard working staff at Young Films and Publishing that made this book possible.

CONTENTS

CONTENTS CONT'D

THE PENNY
By Sheila Brothers & Roxanne Marchand

BACKSTORY

The story started off like most other ideas. . . just a thought. Sheila was watering her garden when the idea came to mind: What if you had a magical penny that allowed you to follow the lives of everyone who touched it? Then Roxanne realized, as they started writing, it wasn't the penny that held the magic. The magic was found within the everyday people who touched it - and thus came the story you know. As for cast suggestions, we were thinking of Kate Hudson in the role of Cecilia

CHAPTER ONE
The Road to Grampa's

It's a beautiful day on Main Street. Nestled in the center of the thoroughfare is a small park. It's landscaped to the finest detail with abundant flowers blooming on bushes that surround a large fountain. Young children play near the cascading water as their parents converse nearby.

Passing along the rooftops, a schoolyard is busy with laughter and play. Middle school children congregate during recess. Some girls play hopscotch and others jump rope as the boys horseplay or engage in a ball game.

Suddenly a boy cries out, "Fight! Fight!"

Children turn in the direction of the voice and run to the tight cluster of other children who have already gathered. Eleven-year-old Harrison "Harry" Talbott, a thin brunette, and Ralph, an older stocky redhead, wrestle on the ground. They are surrounded by a pack of screaming kids who egg them on. The fighters are covered with grass and mud. Ralph has Harry pinned to the ground.

Ralph whines in his most annoying baby voice. "Looks like your mommy had to teach you how to fight since your daddy couldn't stand the sight of you."

Harry's eyes grow dark and anger rejuvenates his resolve. Ralph nearly crumples over with Harry's kick to the gut. A left hook to the chin knocks him to the ground.

Harry winces as he tries to shake the pain from his hand. "At least my mama knows how to fight. All your mama knows how to do is sit on her fat ass and eat!"

The schoolyard children's eyes go wide. "Ooooh!"

A beautiful eleven-year-old, Sarah, a bit disgusted, turns away. She scurries to the outer edge of the crowd and looks up to see the headmaster coming out of the school. He looks at the huddle and starts their way. Sarah runs back into the crowd. She pushes her way to the front and pokes her head into the circle.

"Harry, the headmaster! He's coming!" she exclaims.

Just as Harry looks at Sarah, Ralph charges him and drops him to the ground.

"Nobody talks about my mama like that you stupid piece of —" Ralph sees the headmaster and quickly rolls off Harry onto his back. He pretends to cry. "Don't make fun of my mom, Harry. What kinda person says mean things like that?"

Harry looks bewildered at Ralph until the headmaster penetrates the circle and the kids quickly disperse. Sarah lingers behind and watches sympathetically.

"Harrison Talbott, come with me," the headmaster demands.

Ralph laughs as the headmaster lifts Harry off the ground. The children watch as he's marched into the school building, the headmaster holding firmly to his ear as he takes him to the waiting area to his office. Harry is filthy with mud and grass not only tangled firmly in his hair but also stained eternally in his clothes.

A young secretary stands behind the counter situated in front of a multitude of file cabinets. "Harrison, what happened this time?" she asks sympathetically as she collates papers. Harry shrugs. "It was that bully Ralph again, wasn't it?"

Harry nods.

"I know. I've seen him do some mean things around this school."

"Then how come I always get in trouble?" Harry asks.

"I don't know," she says with a sigh. "I guess you were an easy target today. You let him get to you. You're giving him what he wants; a chance to beat on some kid half his size. Once you open the door, you can't expect him not to come in."

"But he said—"

"Doesn't matter what he said. They're just words, Harrison. Don't give in to his manipulative ways. He wins every time you do."

Harry nods pathetically. "I know."

The door to the headmaster's office opens. "Harrison Talbott?" The secretary smiles softly. "Good luck."

Harry nods and slowly shuffles into the office.

An hour later, Harry's mom, Cecilia, an attractive woman in her late twenties, digs in her purse as she quickly walks out of the front entrance of the school with Harry on her heels. She looks overworked and angry.

"I pay good money and work three jobs to keep you at this school," Cecilia protests, "and this is the thanks I get!"

"But Mom—"

"Don't but mom me. A suspension? Really, Harrison, what am I gonna do now?

"But, it wasn't my fault!" Harry says desperately.

"I know. I've heard it before. It's never your fault. When are you gonna learn to accept responsibility for your actions? I can't believe this. What am I supposed to do with you for three days? I've got to work."

"I don't need a baby-sitter, Mom. I can stay by myself," Harry says attempting to sound mature.

"Alone? Ha! How can I trust you to stay at home by yourself when I can't even trust you to behave in school?"

Cecilia mutters to herself and Harry rolls his eyes. She finally pulls her keys from her purse and heads to the parking lot. Harry quickly follows with his hands in his pockets.

"Mom—"

"No."

"But, Mom—"

"Harrison, I don't—"

"MOM!" Harry exclaims, loud enough for the whole neighborhood to hear.

"WHAT!" she answers just as loudly.

Both go silent for a moment. Harry looks into her eyes. "He was making fun of our family, Mom. About me not having a dad."

Cecilia looks at him, really looks at him. She can see the hurt in his eyes and can hear the pain in his voice. She stoops down to look into his eyes.

"Harrison, look at me. I love you very much and I'm sorry I have to be your mother and your father. I wish things could be different. I wish you had the perfect life. I wish that everyday. But things are the way they are, and our situation is something that I just can't change. Do you understand, honey?"

"Yeah," he says softly.

"Maybe in a few years things will be different, but right now, this is our life. This is just the only way it can be."

She stands up and opens the door of the old beat up Pinto. Harry gets in, then stares at the school through the open window and sees Sarah on the steps looking back at him.

At the Talbott home, Cecilia talks on the phone in the kitchen while Harry watches television in the living room. "I see," Cecilia says. "OK. No, no. We'll figure out something." She listens to the other end, then, "We'll manage, Sophie. We always do. Yes, thank you. Bye-bye." She hangs up, rubs her forehead as she thinks for a moment, then goes in the living room and turns off the television.

"All right, get up. Go to your room and pack a suitcase."

"Am I going to Aunt Sophie's?" Harry asks.

"No, now, let's go!"

"Well, where am—"

Cecilia cuts him off. "I said move it!"

Harry jumps up and runs up the stairs.

A few minutes later, Cecilia throws Harry's suitcase inside the trunk of the Pinto, and slams it shut. "You're going to Grampa's!"

With Harry sulking in the backseat of the car, Cecilia drives out of the neighborhood and heads into the steady traffic on the outskirts of the city limits.

After pondering their destination for the past half hour, he finally has the nerve to speak. "Grampa? You gotta be kidding me. I don't even know him!"

"Well, this is the perfect opportunity for you to do so," Cecilia says with the attempt of putting a positive twist on the situation.

"Mom, you can't be serious. Cousin Charlie told me stories about him and it gave me nightmares for a week."

"Harrison," Cecilia says rolling her eyes, "if you believe anything your cousin Charlie says, than who's the bigger fool? Besides, it's not that bad. Kinda peaceful."

"Then how come we never visit? Like, ever!" Harry says desperately.

"Not another word from you," Cecilia scolds. "I told you that is none of your business."

"It is, especially if you leave me there to rot and die," Harry says dramatically. "Don't I have any say in this at all?"

"Don't you sass me, young man. You're in enough trouble as it is. And no, you don't. Not this time."

Harry finally gives up. For the next three hours, he gazes out the window brooding on what's in store for him. With the city far behind them, they drive through large open fields where tractors push through crops and cows are at their daily ritual of chewing grass and staring blankly at the passing traffic.

As the sun sets, Cecilia turns off the highway onto a road that parts acres of fields. After a mile's stretch, an old house appears, a bit of light stream from within. Open fields extend from the side of the house to a wooded area in the back. Cecilia's car makes a noisy stop in front of the aged house. Harry reluctantly opens his car door and stares at the monstrosity someone calls a home.

Cecilia doesn't waste anytime getting everything out of the overheated vehicle.

Harry slowly lags behind his mother, dragging his huge suitcase up the walk.

"C'mon, Harry," Cecilia urges. She steps onto the porch, looking nervous as she forces her hand to knock on the door.

"I'm trying," Harry says straining, "but this suitcase is too heavy."

"Well, I told you not to pack so much. You're not moving to Alaska, ya know."

"Might not be a bad idea," Harry says under his breath.

She knocks on the door again as Harry makes his way up the stairs. She seems impatient and quickly knocks once more. Mumbling to herself, she says, "Come on, come on, I know you are in there. Oh, you better be in there." She moves to the dusty window and tries to look in. She then returns to knock once more at the door.

"Maybe he's not home," Harry says wishing it were true. Harry's face brightens at the thought.

"Oh, he's home all right."

"Maybe he's dead."

"He's not dead!"

"Maybe he can't hear us because he's burying a dead body in the back yard."

"Harrison! I swear if you say one more thing about dead anything, I'm gonna—"

The door swings open and Grampa looks straight faced at Cecilia. His gaze slowly diverts to Harry who has now taken a step back.

"Hi, Dad," Cecilia says with an awkward tone.

"Cecilia," Grampa grumbles flatly. An awkward silence increases the tension. "What are you doing here?" he asks.

Trying to remain calm and in control she says, "Well, you can at least ask us in. Where are your manners?"

Grampa stares at Cecilia for a long moment then opens the screen door just wide enough for her to enter.

"Thank you," she says too politely. "Come along, Harrison."

Harry reluctantly trails behind his mother. He leaves his suitcase behind and tries to stay as far as he possibly can from Grampa as he walks through the door.

Cecilia looks around the simple living room. She glides her finger on an end table and examines it. Clean. She raises an eyebrow in surprise. The living room is in perfect order. "Looks like nothing's changed since … since the last time I was here," she says trying to avoid the sensitive subject.

"That was a long time ago."

"Yes, well, I have been busy with work and, as you know, trying to keep Harrison at that school."

Grampa's stare is cold and distant. "What do you want, Celia?"

Cecilia is taken aback by the question. "Harry, go to the kitchen and find something to drink, I need to talk to Grampa for a second, honey."

Harry looks around and slowly makes his way to the kitchen.

"Don't touch anything on the top shelf," Grampa barks, "that's definitely not yours." He stares Harry down until he is out of view.

"OK, so here's the thing. I need Harry to stay with you for a few days until—"

"Out of the question," Grampa says firmly, but Cecilia continues her pleading.

"I wouldn't be here if I weren't desperate."

"I got enough to do around here without some kid messing things up."

"Please, Dad," Cecilia says raising her voice, "just hear me out!" She lets out a deep breath to calm herself. "You are still such a stubborn old man."

"Remind me why I let you into my house again?"

Harry steps out from the kitchen. Cecilia looks at Harry then at Grampa, at her watch and back to Grampa. She gives him a pleading look.

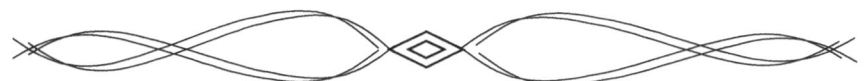

CHAPTER TWO
Life with Grampa

Grampa and Harry sit in the living room in front of the fireplace. An old radio plays music from yesteryear. Grampa smokes a pipe and reads a newspaper.

Harry slouches on the sofa, bored out of his mind. "When did Mom say she was coming back?"

Grampa sits very proper, still reading his paper as if he did not hear Harry. He turns the page and takes his pipe out of his mouth. "The day after tomorrow," he answers nonchalantly and then continues to read.

Harry rolls his eyes at the old man, sinks back further into the couch and folds his arms. "Can I use the phone?"

"Don't got one," Grampa says frankly.

Harry's eyes go wide. "You don't have a phone? How do you call someone if there is an emergency?"

"I don't have emergencies," Grampa says plainly.

"What about someone else?"

"They can use their own phone," Grampa says keeping his eyes on his paper.

"Well, can I at least watch TV?"

"Never did see a use for that either."

Panic ensues for Harry. "No TV! Well, how do you have any fun around here?"

"Oh, there's plenty of fun. Tomorrow." Grampa puts his paper down and slowly gets up from his chair. "Let's get you settled in." He motions for Harry to follow him. Grampa goes to the front door and lifts Harry's suitcase. "Follow me." Harry follows him up the creaky steps. The stairway is dark. "Watch your step."

They turn down a dim hallway and come to a half opened door. As Grampa pushes, it squeaks loudly on its hinges. Harry looks at the rundown appearance of the bedroom.

"Here's your room." Grampa looks at Harry's expression. "What did you expect? This ain't no Holiday Inn, boy, and the maid's on permanent vacation." He clears his throat. "So, the bathroom's down the hall on the right. Next to that, is where I sleep."

Harry points to a closed door at the end of the hall. "Where does that door go to?"

Grampa's jaw tightens and he quickly answers. "That door is off limits. You understand? No one goes up there including myself. Got it?"

Harry sighs. "Got it."

"Supper will be on in thirty minutes, so wash up."

"I'm not hungry," Harry gripes.

"Suit yourself. See ya in the morning, then."

Harry turns around and enters his bedroom. He closes the door harder than he meant to.

"And no slamming doors, either!" Grampa yells from the hallway.

Harry looks around. The hardwood floors are worn and the area rug in the center of the floor is tattered around the edges. The walls are sun beaten with broken cobwebs in the corners.

He lies on his bed and puts his hands behind his head. "Why did she have to stick me here? He's probably some psycho killer, and I'll probably die 'cause I have no phone to call 911. Great. Dead at a mere eleven years old. That's just grand!"

He hops off the bed and awkwardly lifts his suitcase onto the mattress. He opens it, digs under his clothes and pulls out two Snickers bars and a Capri Sun. He takes a sip, goes to the tall bureau, and looks into each drawer. He pulls the top drawer last and hears a clank. He reaches up, but he is too short to see. He pulls a chair up and peers inside to find an old rusty skeleton key. Harry picks it up, eyes it for a moment, then looks mischievously at his bedroom door. He puts the skeleton key in his pocket as he steps down from the chair. He lies down on the bed and rests his eyes, falling into a dream.

Harry enjoys the company of his mother and his father, John, on a beautiful day in the park. John picks Harry up and lifts him to the sky, turning him in circles. "I love you, son."

Harry laughs. "I love you, too, Dad."

Cecilia comes in for a group hug. Harry savors the moment with his parents surrounding him with love. John's face unexpectedly turns from joyous to sad and puts Harry back down on the ground. John slowly backs up from him, then walks away. Cecilia crouches next to Harry and puts her arms around him.

"Dad! Dad!" Harry cries out. "Where are you going?" Harry wrenches free and runs after him. When he catches up, his dad turns around. But he is no longer the man who just swung him around. It's Ralph, the bully from school.

"What's the matter?" Ralph teases. "Lost your daddy again? Poor baby, Harrison, your daddy doesn't even want to play with you. You know it's all your fault." As Harry wells up with tears, Ralph continues with his sing-songy taunt. "It's all your fault. It's all your fault."

"It's not my fault!" Harry cries. "It's not my fault!"

Early in the morning, Harry yells out from his bed, still in his dream. "It's not my fault. It's not my fault." He shakes his head from side to side. Suddenly, a loud banging on the door startles Harry to a sitting position. He's dressed in his clothes from the day before.

"Time to get up, boy," Grampa yells from the hallway. "We got chores to do!"

Harry is disoriented. It is still dark outside. In his morning stupor, he stares wildly around the room to figure out where he is.

"Did you hear me, boy? You up?"

"Yeah, yeah. I'm up," Harry says as he lies back down on his pillow.

Ten minutes later, another knock on the door alarms Harry into an upright position again.

"Breakfast in ten minutes," Grampa barks.

"OK, OK," Harry says rudely to the door. "Weird old man," he says to himself. He closes his eyes and falls back asleep.

11

Moments later, Harry is surprised by a rude awakening, as cold water gushes over his body from head to toe. He jolts up, sputters and gasps as the water hits him. He looks up to see Grampa standing over him holding a bucket, a stern look on his face.

"I only like to say things once." Harry gives him an evil look as he wipes the water from his face. Grampa motions to the wet sheets. "Your first chore is to change them sheets." He leaves the room.

Harry roughly throws the wet sheets off and stands up. He looks at the open door and then pulls his wet shirt over his head. "Ya know, cousin Charlie was right about you. You are crazy!"

Grampa pops his head into the room. "What was that?"

Harry jumps with surprise. Harry quickly balls up the wet sheets. "Nothing, just pulling these sheets off the bed and stubbed my toe."

Ten minutes later, Harry stares cautiously down at a plate of greasy, fatty bacon, runny eggs and lumpy grits. A look of disgust is displayed on his face as he plays with the food with his fork.

Grampa notices. "Ya gonna eat it or have a conversation with it?"

Harry lies. "I'm not hungry."

"You a little young to be on one of them city diets. You better eat. You got a long day ahead of you." Grampa shoves a mouthful of runny eggs in his mouth. A string of yellow yolk runs from his bottom lip to his chin, but Grampa doesn't seem to notice.

Harry looks sickened as Grampa smacks loudly. "Gotta eat so you can grow up tall like me. Ain't too many tall genes on your father's side, but by the looks of you, you take after your mama."

Harry looks up surprised at the mention of his dad. "You knew my dad?"

Grampa eyes Harry for a moment. "Like I said, long day, better get a move on."

Grampa shoves another fork full of eggs in his mouth as he gets up from the table to avoid Harry's question. Harry's eyes follow Grampa, and then stare back down at his plate of greasy food.

Meanwhile, back in the city, Cecilia picks up a plate of greasy eggs and bacon from under the warming lamps. She wears a light blue waitress uniform with a white apron. She quickly moves behind a counter with a full bar of barking customers. Cecilia turns to the short order cook in the kitchen and slides a plate back to him. "She said no onions, Earl."

A customer shouts as she passes, "Miss? My coffee?"

"Excuse me, isn't that my order?" another questions rudely.

"Ma'am, I need a menu," another customer demands.

Cecilia refills the coffee, grabs the order from under the heat lamps and hands a menu to the customer at the counter. As she walks, she unties the bow on her apron. She stops at the end of the counter where an older waitress stands. Cecilia hands the apron to her. "They're all yours, girl."

She continues to the back of the restaurant and punches her time card. As she walks to the back door, she yells to Earl. "Good luck with order number fifty-six, Earl. You're gonna have it coming back three or four times at least."

Earl smiles at her. "Thanks for the warning. Where you off to? Job number eight?"

"Sounds about right. See you back here at six."

"If you make it," Earl says concerned. "You better slow down Cecilia or you're gonna give yourself a heart attack."

"That will be the day I finally get some rest." Cecilia winks at him, then walks out the back door and out to her car. A light mist of rain fills the air as she gets in her car. She tries to start it, but it doesn't turn over. Cecilia frowns and tries again. Nothing.

"Come on baby, don't do this to me now! Come on." She incessantly tries, but to no avail. "Great."

She runs to the end of the block as a city bus approaches. The rain starts to pour. She puts her purse over her head and tries to run faster. "Wait, wait. I'm coming." Out of breath and soaking wet, she steps up into the bus. Cecilia puts her money in. She goes a few rows back, sits down and settles into her seat. She finds a handkerchief in her purse and dries her face. She lifts her body off the seat and unzips her waitress uniform. She has a cute yet obviously worn skirt and blouse underneath. She fixes herself and then looks out the window, deep in thought about Harry.

Harry, covered in dirt, works in the front garden. He yanks on a stubborn root that just won't budge. Grampa sits in the rocking chair on the porch and sips on a tall glass of iced tea.

"Put some muscle in it, boy."

Harry pauses for a moment and looks at Grampa. "My name is not boy. It's Harrison and isn't there some type of child labor law?"

"Not in these parts. And what kinda name is Harrison?"

"I dunno. Mom got it from some Indiana Jones movie or something. Just call me Harry."

Grampa motions to the shovel. "Well, Harry, use the shovel to pry up underneath it." Harry refuses to take Grampa's advice and continues to struggle with the root. "So, I see you get your stubbornness from your mother, too." Grampa takes another sip of his iced tea and gets up from the rocking chair. "You need a glass of water or something?"

"Help would be nice," Harry says with annoyance.

"I'll get you that glass of water, then." Grampa goes into the house and the screen door slams behind him. Harry stares after him for a moment and then mutters to himself while he pulls on the root.

Harry's glare pierces the back of Grampa's head. "Just use the shovel while I sit here in the shade drinking my ice-cold tea, boy," Harry mimics. He wipes the dirt and sweat from his face with his sleeve. "I'm gonna die out here and he's gonna bury me with the rest of 'em." Harry yanks hard on the root, loses his balance and falls to the ground with a thud.

In a small office, Cecilia sits behind a desk piled high with papers. She quickly moves papers from different piles and puts them into file folders. Her eyes gaze into nowhere remembering a time she so desperately tried to forget.

Sparse living room furniture is laid out in a disorganized fashion of a small run-down apartment. Cecilia's husband, John, sits at a small folding table wearing a dingy undershirt and boxer shorts. Cecilia, dressed in a waitress uniform, rushes around the small kitchen, opens and closes cabinets, searching for something.

"I just need a little more time," John grumbles.

"A little more time?" Cecilia shoots back. "You've had almost three years, John. I'm working two jobs and it's getting harder to pay the bills, especially now that Harry will be starting school this year." Cecilia stops and leans on the counter, deep in a sudden revelation. "John, have you seen a white envelope with money in it that I had in the cabinet?"

John moves in his seat awkwardly and takes a gulp of coffee. "I, uh, I needed it for— "

"John, you didn't. That was Harry's registration money for school."

"I don't know why he has to go to that bratty school, anyway."

Cecilia is now on the verge of tears. "Because I want him to have a better life than we've been able to give him. Or actually than I've been able to give him."

John looks insulted. "Hey, I've contributed."

Cecilia shakes her head, a look of desperation across her face. "Did you spend all of it?" she asks stern, but calmly.

"Well, yeah."

"Damn it, John! You had no right to touch that money."

"You don't tell me. I stay home every day and take care of your kid for you and I think I've done my share," he says satisfied with himself.

"My kid? We're married. He's our child, John. Ours!"

John sarcastically takes a sip of his coffee. "So, you say."

"That's it!" She zips around the kitchen counter and knocks the cup of coffee out of John's hand. She points at the door. "You're right. Get out! He's never been your son and you shouldn't be tied down to us anymore. Go live your life. We'll be fine."

John appears amused, but his demeanor is lined with a tinge of anger as he gets up from the table. "You'll never survive without me."

"You're right," Cecilia says boldly. "I'll finally live!"

John passes five-year-old Harry, who peeks around the corner. He has heard everything. Cecilia looks at him, her expression changes and bursts with love for this scared little boy. She goes to him, picks him up and squeezes him tightly. Cecilia sits him down on the counter and smiles really big. "So, handsome, you get to come with mama to work today. You'll get to help Earl in the kitchen and Ms. Jane with the cash

15

registers and if you are really good you can have a big bowl of ice cream."

Harry's face brightens at the mention of ice cream. As Cecilia hugs him tightly, he says, "I love you, Mama."

"I love you, too, Harry Bug."

Returning from her memory, Cecilia sits in her office chair and looks over at a framed photo on her desk of her and the five-year-old Harry. They look happy.

Harry stands sweaty and dirty in the finished front garden. A huge pile of weeds, dead plants and roots stand in piles. Grampa comes around the side of the house with a wheelbarrow. He walks over to the porch and looks at his garden.

Harry grins with satisfaction. "All done."

Grampa looks sincerely impressed for a moment, then points to an area of the garden. "Looks like you need some more dirt to fill in some of those holes." He points to another area. "And it looks a little shallow there."

Harry's grin fades at the thought of more work. His shoulders fall in defeat as he walks slowly to the wheelbarrow.

"You can find some loose dirt at the back of the house by the big oak tree," Grampa says as he points. "Don't you be digging too deep now, take it only from the top."

Harry slowly pushes the wheelbarrow around the side of the house with a forward vacant stare. He sees two raised mounds of dirt, resembling fresh graves, parallel to each other. With some trepidation Harry digs scoops of mud into the wheelbarrow. He hits something hard. He crouches and moves the dirt aside. A white colored object appears. A closer glance proves it to be bone. Harry jumps up, shovel in hand, screams and runs into the woods.

Grampa nonchalantly walks around the side of the house with a toothpick in his mouth. He watches a screaming Harry disappear into the woods. "That boy sure is a nervous one," Grampa says slowly to himself following Harry's path into the woods behind the house.

Harry runs with his shovel. He trips over broken branches, large tree roots and rocks, but continues to scramble for a place to hide.

Grampa calls to Harry in the near distance. "What you doing back here, boy? We got work to do."

"We? You aren't doing any work. I am. You think I don't know what you're doing?" Harry finds a large tree and crouches behind it. He holds tightly to the shovel. "You stay away from me you ... you ... murderer."

Grampa nears the tree. "What craziness are you talking, boy? Come on out before you get lost in there."

Grampa takes a few steps and Harry jumps out from behind the tree, poking the air with the shovel. "You don't fool me, you quack. I saw what you did. I'm gonna call the cops and they're going to put you away for life."

"Didn't your mama teach you manners? Give me that shovel before you hurt somebody." Grampa tries to take a step toward Harry.

"Don't even think about it ... Hannibal!" Harry pokes his shovel toward Grampa again.

Grampa looks slightly amused. "Harry, what is this all about?"

"The graves," Harry says. "You've got dead bodies in your yard. Cousin Charlie was right about you."

"Graves? You mean the piles of dirt? That was just extra dirt I had from the last time I gardened."

"Yeah, tell it to a judge, Manson. We both know you haven't weeded that garden in like twenty years."

"Not the front, the back." Grampa motions through the trees to a newly weeded garden at the back of the house.

"Oh ...well ... It still doesn't explain the bone I found!"

Grampa changes his tune and looks at Harry with great seriousness. "Oh, so I see you've met Chester."

Harry looks at Grampa in disbelief. "Chester! Who was that, your last gardener?"

Grampa smiles but tries not to laugh. "Actually, Chester was my sixteen-year-old hound dog, may he rest in peace."

Harry lowers the shovel but still keeps an eye on Grampa. "You mean you buried him in your backyard?"

"Yep, along with a pet rabbit."

Harry lowers the shovel with a look of relief. Grampa takes the shovel from him. They exit the woods to the backyard where Harry eyes the graves again. "So, there aren't any human bodies buried back there?"

"Nope. But there's always a first time for everything." Grampa lets out a hearty laugh at his joke. Harry is not sure how to react and slows his steps behind Grampa. "And let me tell you a thing or two about cousin Charlie ... "

An hour later, back at the front of the house, Harry continues with yet another chore he does not agree with. His feelings are clearly painted on his face. He dips a brush into a bucket and sloppily splats white paint on the picket fence. White paint streaks across his muddy forehead and drips down his dirty arm. He re-dips and pulls out the brush without scraping the excess off. Paint drips down the side of the bucket. Grampa is amused yet again by Harry. "Boy, you are wasting more paint than you're putting on the fence."

"I've never painted before," Harry says completely frustrated. "I told you that."

Grampa walks over and kneels beside him. He pulls the paintbrush from Harry's hand and demonstrates how to wet the brush and paint the fence in smooth strokes. "It's not rocket science, son." He hands the paintbrush back to Harry and pulls another from his back pocket. Grampa dips his brush and paints beside Harry, who watches and tries to emulate his grandfather's movements. "That's it. Nice and easy strokes. Up and down and up and down."

Harry eyes Grampa's paintbrush and then checks his own work. "How come you and Mom don't talk?"

"Guess that's a question for your mother."

"OK, well then how come you never come to visit?" Harry continues.

"You and your mom are very busy people. Plus, with everything to do around here, guess the time just slips by too quickly."

"Cat's in the cradle," Harry says quickly.

"What?" Grampa asks.

"That's what Aunt Sophie says every time we cancel when she asks us to come to dinner."

"Oh, like the song." Grampa nods. "I see. Yes, well I suppose she's right. You have grown up to be quite a little man already."

"So, you still haven't really answered my question." Harry is persistent. "Aunt Sophie says that's circular reasoning."

"Yeah, well Aunt Sophie says a lot of things," Grampa says laughing. "You think you got this under control?"

"Sure, why not. I seem to be doing everything around here anyway."

CHAPTER THREE
Treasures in the Attic

Grampa and Harry sit at the kitchen table, dishes still in front of them. Grampa reads a newspaper, which is worn and old. Harry stares at the front page.

"Um, the date on the paper is January 18, 1985."

Grampa pulls back the paper to read the front page. "Yep, so it is."

Still puzzled, Harry replies, "But that was a long time ago? Why are you reading it now?"

"Nothing's really changed that much, just the names."

Harry raises his eyebrows. Before he can probe Grampa again, thunder rumbles from an oncoming storm. The lights flicker. Harry looks up, startled as the lights waver in the kitchen. Grampa calmly folds his paper as he glances at the ceiling. He takes his reading glasses off and gets up from his chair. He leaves the room, followed by Harry to the living room where he grabs an oil lantern from the fireplace mantle, places it on the coffee table and lights the wick.

"Looks like we have a storm a brewing."

Harry looks nervous. "You think it's gonna be big?"

"My knees have been telling me all day it is."

"Huh?"

"Finish your dinner and then we'll make sure all the windows are down and locked and turn in for the night. Lots to do tomorrow."

"There's more? What else can ... never mind. I don't wanna know."

After securing all the dusty windows in the house, Harry turns in for the night. He closes the door behind him and digs into his suitcase. He finds a candy bar and a Capri Sun. He takes a big bite and lies on his bed. He looks at his candy bar.

"Thank God I brought you or I would have starved to death." Thinking about the night before, he jumps off the bed and looks around. He digs in his pants pocket and finds the skeleton key. Harry finishes off his Snickers and jumps back on the bed, holding the key eye level. "Tonight, we explore uncharted waters."

When midnight approaches, Harry's face peeks through the crack of his door. He shudders at the creaking sound as he slowly opens it. He looks both ways then scurries quietly to the attic entrance. He turns the knob on the attic door. Locked. He slowly puts the key into the lock.

"Perfect fit. OK, Grampa, what're you hiding?" Harry whispers.

He turns the key and the lock pops so loud, he jumps. He quickly looks to the stairs, holding his breath. Certain Grampa did not hear the noise, he lets out his breath. Harry turns the knob and slowly opens the creaky, old door. "Anybody ever heard of WD-40 around here?" He opens it just enough for his thin body to get through and closes it behind him.

As Harry sneaks off, Grampa reaches in the refrigerator and grabs a beer. He walks around to the living room and stops at the bottom of the stairs. He takes a swig of it as his eyes visit the banister. He takes only a moment to find a memory. He had played it too many times over the years so it wasn't far from the front of his mind. It was one of the last memories he had of his daughter.

She stood at the bottom of the stairs, much younger than she was now. A frown completed her outfit, which consisted of a tank top labeled with a rock band logo and a pair of stonewashed jeans that hugged his daughter's figure too well. His stern face hardened even more at the thought of his little girl growing up, especially this way.

She was stubborn; she'd gotten that from him. And even though her sweet face and beautiful smile had gotten her a lot as a child he looks his daughter over with new eyes. *She isn't that little girl anymore*," he thinks as he dramatically crosses his arms over his chest.

"Absolutely not. This discussion is over."

Cecilia's hands fly quickly to her hips in defiance as she begins her rebuttal, "But Dad, everyone is going and—"

"It is improper for a young lady to go away for the weekend with her boyfriend. Period. Your mother would never have done such a thing. I won't allow it." He nods his head at Cecilia as if to say conversation over, but she was not even close. Her eyes darkened as she met her father's stare. "I'm tired of hearing what's proper and what Mama would've done." She pulls her shoulders back and stands a little taller. "I'm a grown woman—"

"You're seventeen years old and still living under my roof," her father interjects loudly. "You'll abide by my rules. I will NOT have my daughter running around like the town whore!"

Cecilia's face turns ashen, as if she'd just been slapped in the face by his words. But he couldn't take them back even if in some ways he had meant them.

"Well, if that's how you feel then maybe I should go," Cecilia almost whispers.

"Yes, maybe you should," he says as he sits back down in his chair and picks up his folded newspaper. "Just be home by curfew."

Cecilia stands in silence. She stares at her father as tears fill her eyes, and then takes a deep breath. "No. I mean maybe it's time for me to leave and start my own life."

Grampa's hands stiffen as he opens his paper. Without looking at her, he nods. "You do what you feel is best, Cecilia. I won't try to stop you."

"Yeah, you gave up on me a long time ago." He lifts the paper to hide the anguish on his face as Cecilia's footsteps pound quickly up the stairs.

Thunder rumbles outside, shaking the memory from the old man's thoughts. A sad look adorns his face as he sits in his chair with nothing to do except think.

Apprehension covers Harry's face, yet he summons up the courage to walk up the old worn wooden steps to the attic in the darkness. The storm is getting stronger and the lightening provides just enough light for him to see how many steps he has to climb. He uses his hands to feel what's ahead of him. Harry reaches the top, sticks out his hands and finds the attic floor. He pulls himself into the musty room.

As he looks around, a loud roar of thunder shakes the house and then lightening strikes again. A figure appears in the strobes of light. He gasps and darkness envelops him again. He crouches to the floor, debating whether he should move or play dead like some defenseless animal when another strobe of light flashes. The figure stands tall before him. It turns out not to be a phantom, but an old bodice used for the making and hemming of dresses. He exhales with relief and gets up.

Another streak of light flickers and something catches his eye. It's a light bulb hanging from a wire. He waits for another wave of lightening, runs, jumps and pulls the cord on the light. The dim light reveals a mouse scurrying across the floor toward a wall layered with framed art pieces and odd-shaped furniture draped with sheets. Spiders have created their artistic masterpieces in every corner, the only backdrop being the dusty color of the room.

None of this looks alluring to Harry and he frowns in disappointment, until he sees a large chest against the wall. He rushes over, grabs the handle and drags it under the dangling light bulb. The chest is made of brown leather and metal and a thick layer of dust covers the outside.

"Pirate's treasure?" Harry says out loud to no one. "So, that's what the old kook is stashing away up here." His excitement boils as he quickly reaches for the latch. It's locked. "Oh, great." Harry looks around for something to force the lock open. "There's got to be something around here." Then, realization crosses the boy's face as he slowly digs in his pocket. "Oh yeah! The key." Harry looks at it and smiles. "Come on old key. Be my friend again." Harry puts the key into the lock and turns it. He struggles for a moment, jiggling the key roughly. "Come on. Turn. Turn!" He argues with the inanimate object as he twists the key as hard as he can. Finally, he hears a metal pop and the latch opens. "Yes!" he cries. "Let there be gold and I swear I will be good for the rest of my life!" Harry slowly lifts the top of the chest. It creaks loudly and Harry's eyes are fixated on the treasure inside.

"Didn't I tell you not to come up here?"

Harry jumps back from the chest, the top slamming down loudly. He slides back across the floor awkwardly on his butt until his back hits the wall. Harry squints into the beam of the flashlight in Grampa's hand. He holds his hand up to shade his eyes and looks up at the man.

Grampa stands tall before him, looking more intimidating then ever, especially with the special effects of the weather crawling across his angry face. Harry huddles petrified against the wall, wishing the same death upon Ralph that he is surely about to experience himself.

"Answer me, boy!" Grampa growled at the creature quivering on the floor.

"Y-yes sir."

"Then why the hell are you up here? You got problems with your hearin'?"

Harry's lip quivers uncontrollably, and his chest feeling like a ton of bricks lay upon him. "I-I-I don't know, sir. I …just … just … " Harry looks down.

Grampa hears the fear in the boy's voice. "Just what?" he asks with less authority.

"Just bored, I guess," Harry shrugs.

Grampa moves a step or two closer to Harry. "Son, when I was your age, we couldn't afford to be bored. If we slacked off we wouldn't have food for a week or clothes to wear in the winter. If you're bored, then you don't know the meaning of hard work and dedication. Well, until today, that is."

Harry's face smears into a frown; he's heard these words before. "I know, I know, you sound like my mom."

"Well, where'd ya think she got that from?"

Harry looks up, a sigh escaping from his lips. "It's just the same thing everyday–school, homework, chores, bed, day after day. I just wanted something different for a change. Not like all the time or anything, just—"

"What do you call today, a day at the beach?" Grampa smirks briefly, but in the darkness Harry misses it. "You should be exhausted by now."

"I am. Well, kinda. It's just ... I've never stayed here before and you've got all this cool stuff." Harry motions toward the chest still sitting shut on the attic floor.

Grampa's face softens a little more. He raises a bushy eyebrow at the boy and squints his eyes mysteriously. "Ah, so you are a seeker?" he questions just before a roll of thunder shakes the house.

"A what?" Harry twists his face in confusion.

"Lookin' for an adventure?" The old man steps closer to Harry who still sits huddled against the wall.

At the mention of adventure, Harry sits up straight, his eyes wide with excitement. "Yeah, that's it. I just want some adventure."

"So you think breaking all my house rules is an adventure?"

"No," Harry says sheepishly. "But you do have some great stuff up here." He eyes the chest again and looks back at Grampa. "Can I see what's in it?" Harry looks up with a twinkle in his eyes Grampa had not yet seen.

He looked down at the small boy so full of excitement and nods. "Go ahead," he consents. Harry scrambles across the floor to the front of the chest as Grampa comes to sit down on the floor beside him.

The storm is in full force, the rain pounds on the old house with a fury but the two don't notice the rain or the thunder and lightening. Both pairs of eyes are fixated on the old chest. Harry shines the flashlight on it as he opens the lid.

Dust flies into the air as the lid creaks to an open position and Harry peeks his head into the chest.

"Grampa, look at this!" Harry pulls out a ribbon with a metal attached to it.

"Yeah, back in the day I was quite a swimmer."

"You competed?" Harry questions with a little disbelief. "Hey, I compete, too."

"Is that so?" The old man smiles proudly.

"Yeah, I got four golds and a silver last summer."

Grampa eyes him for a moment and then asks, "What's your strong suit?"

"Freestyle," they both say together. Grampa chuckles. It was an unusually nice sound coming from the old man and he knew Harry must have thought so too because when he looked over at the boy his eyes held a bit of admiration.

"Well, isn't that something? I shouldn't be surprised though, it's in your blood."

A slight glimpse of a smile appears on Harry's face as Grampa continues, "You see this chest? Everything inside is everything I have ever loved." Grampa's brow wrinkles in distress. "Don't really come up here anymore, though."

"Why would you lock up all the things you love and never look at them again?"

"It hurts too much to see what I have lost." Grampa shakes his head and Harry sincerely sees the hurt his grandfather feels. The moment is cut short when Harry's eye catches sight of something inside the chest. A questioning look appears on his face as he leans in for a closer look.

"You say everything you love is in here?"

"Everything," Grampa says confidently.

Harry peers deeper into the chest, reaches to the bottom and pulls something out.

"Even this?" Harry opens his tiny hand to reveal a penny. It is old, worn and dented in the center. He smirks as if he's made a funny, not understanding how something like this could be loved. But the old man slowly reaches out and takes the coin with care, lifts it to the light, and cautiously turns it as he becomes lost in his own world.

Harry scowls. "It's just a penny, Grampa. What's so interesting about that?"

"Sometimes, something so small, something with so little value to one person, can be someone else's treasure for a lifetime." He lets his eyes stray away from the penny to meet Harry's gaze. "To you, boy, it might be small, old and dull, but underneath the surface lays a hidden power, something special."

Harry is not convinced. "Yeah, but, it's just a penny. How could a penny be worth more than a penny?"

The old man snaps quickly at Harry. "Don't be a fool boy! Never judge a book by its cover. If you do, you might miss something that could change you for life." Realizing his harshness he calms his voice to a mystical whisper. "Maybe you should take a closer look," he says as he leans closer to Harry.

Harry leans in. He continues to stare at it and then at Grampa in a confused wonderment and back at the penny once more. Another roar of thunder hits and a flash of lightning lights up the entire room as Grampa's story begins.

"Ya see, my boy, this fellow's journey began a long time ago, in 1926. Back in those days a penny was worth much more than just a thought."

Grampa's story travels back through time to an assembly line of workers at the U.S. Mint who are busy printing pennies with the date 1926. The coins roll like waves onto conveyor belts and drop by the thousands into a bin. A worker grabs the weighty bin and moves it to another part of the plant where several more workers sort them into heavy moneybags. The bags are put into yet another bin where another worker pushes it near a large door next to more filled bins.

When the door opens into the busy city of Chicago, the bright sunshine pours into the dimly lit building. An armored truck is parked just outside the door; its rear doors already open. Two security guards stand ready on either side of the vehicle's doors as the workers load the money into the rear of the armored truck.

"Come on, boys, pick up the pace," a superior calls out to the younger workers loading the truck.

The last of the bags are loaded into the back of the vehicle. But just before they close the doors a worker sees one more bag at the bottom of a bin.

"Hold on!" he shouts and grabs the bag. He rushes to the truck, knocking the bag on the edge of the door as he places it inside. No one notices the tiny tear in the bottom of the bag or the single coin that falls onto the bumper of the truck as the doors close.

The car takes off and as it nears the gates of the mint, the penny bounces off the bumper and into the street where it rolls on its side for a moment before finally landing flat in a puddle, shining brightly in the dirty water.

Vito, a decent looking man in his thirties, with wire-rimmed glasses, crosses the street hurriedly. His suit fits him nicely and his shoes are polished to a flawless shine. But his disposition shows a nervous, anxious man. His mind elsewhere, he steps directly into the puddle and onto the shiny penny.

The puddle doesn't distract him even though his foot and the cuff of his pant leg are soaked. He crosses the street, turns into an old apartment complex and heads quickly up the stairs to apartment 2B.

He opens the door to the neat but plain apartment. It's alive with the sound of children. The baby cries in the other room. Audry, his wife, rushes past him so engrossed in finding something that she doesn't even notice his quiet entrance.

His middle child, eight-year-old Maria, sits at the small kitchen table concentrating on a picture she is drawing. He smiles at her just as his twelve-year-old daughter, Gabriella, who is the eldest, heads toward him from the back bedroom with Leo. Although his face is tear-stained, he manages a smile as his daddy closes the door to the outside world.

Maria looks up. "Daddy! I'm drawing a picture for you." Audry quickly stops and turns her attention to Vito, a questioning look upon her face. He smiles at Maria then meets Audry's stare.

"I can't wait to see it, sweetheart," he says as he heads over to his wife.

"Well?" Audry asks.

Vito hesitates. "This is the last time, Audry. I swear."

Audry's face turns from questioning to anger and fear. "That's what you said the last three times." She shakes her head. "That's it. I can't take it anymore, Vito, I just can't."

Vito grabs her lovingly but forcefully by the shoulders and looks into her eyes. She won't meet his stare. "Look at me, Audry. I mean it. It's the last one. If I don't do this, we won't have anything to live off of. I'm doing this for us."

"Us?" Her eyes begin to fill with tears as she glances over at her baby boy. "All I keep seeing is little Leo dead in the gutter somewhere. Is this the kind of life you want for your only son? This is wrong; you gotta get out, Vito. We can't live like this anymore. People are dying everyday around us. Good people." Audry pauses for a moment and then meets Vito's eyes straight on. "WE used to be good people. I love you, but we just can't live another day like this ."

"I promise tonight, and that's it." He grasps her hands in his. "Please, Audry, please understand." She sighs deeply and nods her head, her tears hanging precariously.

He looks away, he can't bear to see her cry, but his gaze falls upon his children. They are huddled together near the kitchen table listening intently to the conversation. Vito smiles widely, walks over and squats down next to them.

"Family hug for Daddy?"

His children hug him tightly. He looks at Gabriella and thinks to himself how she has always seemed to be the wise one. Since the day she was born he knew she was smarter then her years should allow. Her face fills with worry as he pulls her in tighter, holding all of them as if he will never see them again. He gives one extra tight squeeze and kisses them each on their heads, leaving Leo for last. He looks into his tiny little face and then lightly rubs his head.

"OK, my little ones. You be good for Mommy." He smiles and winks at them as he turns around to find Audry lugging a packed bag to the front door.

"You know where we'll be." She stands tall, but her bottom lip begins to quiver as she tries to stay tough. Nevertheless, she quickly breaks down and runs to Vito. They embrace. She passionately caresses his neck, runs her hands through his hair and then strokes his face as if to remember his features. Her eyes fill again with tears but they still do not fall.

"Tomorrow morning. I better see you tomorrow morning on my mother's doorstep. Do you hear me?"

"You will, Audry. You will."

Anthony 'The Boss' Rosario, a man in his forties, exits the mint. His chiseled good looks match his intellectual mind. He is a fine dresser and his confidence exudes through every pore in his body. He stops to take in the hustle and bustle of his town. A smile slowly appears on his face as he repeats "my town" in his head. He signals his driver to pull the car up to the curb. Anthony steps to the edge, looks down and notices the penny. Leaning over, he pulls the penny from the dirty water, shakes it off and takes a long look at the shiny treasure in his fingers.

"I just might have a job for you tonight," he says to the penny. Anthony puts the coin in his vest pocket as the well-dressed young driver promptly opens the car door for him.

While the sun sets over the windy city, Vito pushes open the door to a dark office and carefully slips inside. He stops and listens then turns on his flashlight to begin his search of the room. He starts with the desk drawers, then the file cabinets. Frustrated he stops and whispers to himself, "Where is it? It's got to be here."

Finally, he notices a book slightly out of place on a bookshelf. He pulls the big book from its shelf and places it on the desk. Shining the light on it, he opens it and finds what he was looking for. The hollowed book contains stacks of crisp one hundred dollar bills. He pulls the money out and shoves it into the pockets of his jacket. Suddenly, he's interrupted by the sound of two men talking; their footsteps approach the office door. Vito rushes and puts the empty book back on the shelf and turns off the flashlight.

Just outside the door, the men stop as one of them motions to the slightly open door. Without words, one of them reaches for something inside his coat pocket and nods at the other to open the door.

Vito scurries under the desk just as the overhead light comes on. He twists up like a pretzel. One move, one noise and he knows he's dead.

The men enter the office and look around.

"What do you think?" one of them asks the other. Before he can answer another guy calls from the hallway.

"Come on, let's go. You know how he gets when we're late."

"The door was open. We think somebody's been in here."

"Well, there ain't nobody there now unless they stuffed themselves in one of those drawers. Let's go. Remember what happened the last time Junior was late? He ain't been walkin' right since."

The two men look at each other, then start moving to the door. The light goes out and the door closes.

Vito sweats profusely and lets out a big relieved breath. He comes out from under the desk, the money falling from his pockets as he wipes his face on his sleeve. He looks around and spies an empty black bag in the corner. Grabbing it, he stuffs the money inside, locks it and heads cautiously out the door.

The three men make their way to a speakeasy. The place is hopping. A woman on stage sings seductively and swoons her audience as they engage in conversation. A working girl makes her way through the crowd. "Cigars, cigarettes, ten cents." She heads to a VIP table with gangster types, including Anthony Rosario.

"Come here, sugar," he says. The girl sits on Anthony's lap and giggles. "Now, ya see this." Anthony makes a gesture at her body. "This is a woman. As sweet as candy and as hot as a pepper."

"You always know how to make a girl smile, Anthony." She giggles again.

"That ain't all I know how to do," Anthony says with a cocky grin.

"Is that an offer or just a line?" The girl cocks her eyebrow seductively.

"Oh, so you're a hell cat?" Anthony grabs the girl's thigh seductively. "It's whatever you want it to be, sweetheart."

The girl gets up and Anthony slaps her backside as she walks away. She lets out another loud giggle and gives him a look of approval.

Another member of his family, Tony, walks up to the table. "You wanted to see me, Boss?" Anthony flicks a penny to Tony. His playful self fades away as business always comes first. Tony catches it. "Who's this for?"

"I want you to go and have that talk with Vito."

"Tonight?"

"No, yesterday," Anthony says annoyed by Tony's stupidity. "And get it right this time or the next penny will be for you."

"Boss—" Tony attempts to chime in, but Anthony gives him a look of finality. Tony knows he is on thin ice and smiles uneasily at Anthony. "Sure thing, Boss. I'll take care of it right now." Tony walks out of the speakeasy past two large, well dressed bouncers. Tony looks angry.

"Hey, Tony," a bouncer calls out. "How ya been?"

Tony lights his cigarette as he steps onto the street, ignoring him. He walks across the damp pavement and stops next to his car. He takes another deep drag from his cigarette, flicks it away and gets into his car.

Vito sits on a bench at the train station, smoking a cigarette. He looks around nervously at the vacant depot, his foot tapping the pavement. He takes a long drag as Tony appears behind him from out of the shadows.

"Hello, Vito," Tony says. Vito coughs and chokes on the smoke. "You oughta quit those things, Vito. They'll kill you."

Vito replies with a nervous laugh. "Yeah. Been thinking about it."

"So, whatcha doing here? You going somewhere?" Tony asks casually, but his stare is anything but relaxed.

"I-I, uh, I'm waiting for my cousin Maria to come in on the next train."

"Oh, Maria, I hear she's a nice girl. I think I'll sit with you. Mind the company?"

Vito tries to control his fear. "No, no, that's fine." Vito sweats. He takes another drag from his cigarette, discards it and tries to avoid eye contact. "Sure is a hot one tonight."

"Not as hot as your cousin Maria, I'm sure," Tony says with a dirty smile.

Vito nods his head and gives a fake laugh. Tony notices the bag next to the bench. "Oh, look at this. Is this yours, 'cause if I didn't know any better I'd think this was your bag and you was leaving."

Vito, looking nervous, shakes his head in denial. "Oh, I didn't notice. It must have been there before I got here."

Tony gives a quizzical look. "So somebody left their luggage here in the middle of the night. Now, how could somebody forget such a nice bag as this? I wonder what's inside."

"Oh, Tony, nah, leave the bag alone. I'm sure it belongs to a nice lady who just forgot it."

"Now, now. Where's your sense of adventure?" Tony pushes the bag toward Vito and his face turns cold. "Open it."

Vito knows he's busted. "S-sure thing, Tony." Vito reluctantly opens it and puts on a fake smile. "Nothing but clothes in here."

"Really? Let me take a closer look." Tony grabs the bag and pulls out a man's shirt. "Nice threads. Well, we can rule out your nice lady theory. Hmmm, I think it's your size. Why don't you try it on?"

"No, no, I don't think—"

"Suit yourself, I just think it's a nice color for you," Tony says pretending not to care. He digs and finds a large amount of money at the bottom. "Whoa, looks like somebody's really gonna miss this bag. And comes to think of it, this looks really familiar to me."

"Tony listen, I can explain, please!"

Tony pulls a gun from inside his jacket and stands up. "Don't you think the big fella might resent the fact that you made vacation plans without telling nobody?"

Vito looks at the gun. Sweat pours down his face. He swallows hard. "Tony, please, I'm just going to see my Aunt Verda, she's real sick and she can't afford no doctors where she is. I was coming right back."

"Aunt Verda? Oh, is she sick? Send her my regards."

Vito stands up, pleading with Tony. "Please, Tony, I swear! I just needed a little cash up front. I'm gonna pay it back, every last cent. Please Tony!"

"You swear you're coming right back?"

"Four days tops, no more. It's the truth."

Tony looks around then back to Vito. "Make sure nobody knows about this, Vito."

Vito, sweating, exhales a sigh of thankfulness. "Tony, I swear, nobody. Thank you. Thank you so much."

Tony pulls Vito into him and embraces him. He pats him on the back and pulls away. Tony flicks the penny at Vito. "For good luck. Give Aunt Verda my love."

Vito catches it. "Sure thing, Tony. And thanks again."

Tony walks off into the darkness of the train station. Relieved, Vito pulls out a handkerchief from his pants pocket and wipes the sweat from his face. Then, he slips a flask from his breast pocket, takes a long swig and returns it. He looks down at the penny one more time before he slips it into his breast pocket next to the flask.

"Vito? One more thing."

Vito, wide-eyed, quickly turns to find Tony standing behind him, his gun aimed at him. Tony smirks as he pulls the trigger. In a loud blast and a puff of smoke, Vito falls to the ground. Tony casually walks and stops beside Vito's still body. He points his gun at Vito's head. Just as he's about to pull the trigger he's illuminated by a powerful white light and a train whistle pierces the darkness.

The station worker calls out from inside the ticket booth, "Train!"

Tony puts his gun back inside his jacket as the train pulls into the station. The faces of those inside stare at him as they pass. He looks in both directions and walks away as the train comes to a screeching halt.

Vito lays lifeless on the ground. Then, a subtle flinch of his fingers, a flicker of his eyes and after a moment, he slowly picks his head up. He strains to sit up but with a few grunts and groans he manages.

"I'm not dead?" he asks incredulously to himself.

His hands pat his chest as he searches for a wound. He feels a cool sensation near his breast pocket and his fingers find the wet hole. He looks down and sees a dark spot on his jacket growing larger. He's been shot. But there's no pain. He pulls his fingers from the hole and doesn't find any blood there either. Vito reaches into the inside of his jacket and pulls his flask out. There's a hole through and through. "It can't be," he says under his breath. He digs into his pocket and pulls out the bullet, his ticket and the penny. The penny has a dent in the center where the bullet stopped after going through his flask. He stares down at the penny in disbelief for a moment, then lets out a hysterical laugh that echoes throughout the station.

The people begin to exit the train. A kind looking young man steps up beside him. "Excuse me, sir, are you all right? Do you need help?"

Vito can't find the words. He shakes his head, then a burst of laughter makes its way out as he gets to his feet.

Another voice calls out to him. "Is this yours, sir?" Vito looks down at what the young man is holding in his hand.

Vito can't believe what he sees. "The bag! Tony forgot the bag!" he thinks elatedly to himself. He nods and takes the bag with a smile, then walks to the train. For the first time he's relaxed, happy, giddy. For the first time, he's free. Vito approaches the conductor as he steps up to the train.

"Ticket?" the conductor requests.

Vito pulls out the ticket and unknowingly the penny falls out of his pocket and onto the tracks. He hands his ticket to the conductor, tips his hat and then walks to the back of the train, chuckling loudly the entire way. The conductor stares after him as the loud horn of the train blows like thunder in the night.

THE PENNY

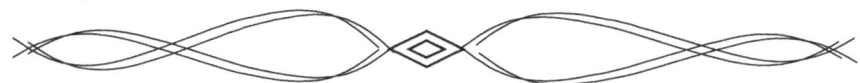

CHAPTER FOUR
Lives of the Penny

"Ya see. If he hadn't had the penny he might have died." Grampa stares out the window of the grungy attic as he adds the finishing touch to his story. "It was destiny, it was fate. Ever heard of that?"

Harry leans comfortably back on the chest, engrossed in the words that pour out of the man's mouth. "I think so. Is it the same thing as karma?"

"Well, karma's a little different," Grampa says as he looks over at the boy.

"Mom always says karma's a bitch."

Grampa lets out a little chuckle, amused by his grandson. "Karma is something that people believe in so that the bad things that others do to them, well, they know they don't have to get even because karma will." Harry squints in thought as Grampa continues. "It's like an unseen avenger of the good. Destiny is more like a storyteller who's already written your story and is just waiting for you to live it out. A higher force we have no control over, that shapes the life of a person in ways we will never understand."

Harry's mind whirls with thoughts. "So you think I was supposed to get into that fight at school?"

Grampa shrugs. "Well, I suppose if you didn't get into that fight, you wouldn't be here right now."

"Yeah, I guess so." Harry bites his bottom lip in thought again. "Grampa?"

"Yes, Harry?"

Harry's eyes look to the floor uncomfortably as he tries to manage his words. "I kinda like it here."

Grampa clears his throat, not sure what to do with the compliment. "Well, Harry, I hope we can spend some more time together in the future, but on good terms instead of you being in trouble."

An awkward silence falls over them. Harry looks down at the penny in his hand and rubs the indentation with his thumb and then quickly looks up at Grampa, eager to continue. "Well, what happened to the penny?"

Grampa smiles and nods his head slowly. "Ah. That penny was waiting." Harry closes his eyes as Grampa's words flow through his mind. "Waiting for someone very special to come along."

It's now 1941. The train station walls are covered with WWII posters. Rosie the Riveter and Uncle Sam greet the crowd of soldiers dressed in their uniforms, and their loved ones who pave the platform.

"Who?" Harry asks impatiently.

"You'll see," Grampa whispers back.

A young boy leans precariously over the tracks, his greedy eyes look at something near the rails. He springs happily onto the tracks and picks up the dirty, soot covered penny. He curiously observes the small dent in the center.

The boy's mother looks from the platform and screams in shock. "Lewis!" She runs to the tracks and grabs the boy by the ear. He let's out a cry and drops the penny on the platform as he is dragged back into the crowd of people. "If I have to tell you one more time, you are going to lose this ear." The mother scolds her son as they pass other ticket holders to get back into line. "Do you understand me? Now you stay right next to me until we arrive in New York."

"Yes, ma'am," the boy whines and accidentally bumps a couple headed toward the train. Lewis' mother pulls him closer with a scowl as Tom and Susan pass them engrossed in their own conversation.

"Don't worry I'll be back before you know it." Tom looks at his little blonde wife and lifts her chin with his hand. "I'm coming home, you know that, right?"

Susan doesn't want to think about it. "I'm going to miss you so much. Maybe when you get back, we can try again."

Tom smirks. "Darlin', when I get back, you know I'll give it my all! Four times a day if necessary!"

Susan looks embarrassed and she playfully slaps his arm. "Tom!"

"I never met a woman who couldn't wait to get fat." Susan's face shows her disappointment. "No worries, Suzie. It will happen for us, too."

"You keep reassuring me, but it's been almost two years. I'm beginning to think we'll never have a family of our own." Susan wipes a tear from her cheek but another one follows.

Tom leans in close and kisses the tears from her cheek. "You just wait. Everything will be fine and we'll have a baker's dozen," he whispers with a smile.

Susan smiles back and then something on the ground catches her eye. "Tom, look! You can't get any luckier than this," she exclaims as she picks up the penny. She kisses it and places it in Tom's hand, closing his fingers over it as she softly says, "May luck be with us all the way."

Tom puts it in his pocket as he jokes, "How 'bout a kiss for me, too."

Susan smiles and drapes her arms around his neck. They kiss passionately. The train whistle sounds loudly, startling Susan. Tom pulls her close as her tears reemerge. He kisses her forehead and they pull apart. Susan whispers, "This is it."

"I'll be home before you know it," he replies as he grabs his bag and runs for the train. The whistle blows loudly as the train begins to slowly pull away from the station. Tom holds the railing and watches his beauty as she stares up at him, tears streaming down her face.

"I'll write you everyday. I love you, Tom," she calls out over the noise of the train.

"I love you, too."

Susan watches the train roll away as Tom leans out and waves. He blows her one last kiss and she pretends to catch it in her hand, placing her closed fist over her heart.

In the six long weeks that have passed since Tom's departure, Susan keeps herself busy with cleaning the house and helping some of the elderly in the neighborhood with their mending. She sits on the sofa with Mrs. Dewster's red dress, which is just a stitch away from being finished. The radio plays Benny Goodman. While he plays his serenade Susan stands with the dress and dances around the room. She is interrupted by her best friend, who pops her head in through the open window.

"Caught ya!"

Susan jumps and drops the dress on the floor. "Fanny Mae Darlington, you'll be the death of me yet," she scolds playfully.

Fanny lets out a big laugh then climbs through the window. Susan quickly picks up the dress and drapes it over the ironing board.

"Now what would your mother say? 'Cotillion never did you a bit of good.' That's what!"

Fanny contorts her face and mimics her own mother. "Fanny Mae, just look at you. You are such a disgrace to the family name. You dress like a tomboy and you chew with your mouth open and laugh like a horse. Girls should be dainty and have pleasant voices."

Susan laughs along with Fanny. "Oh, I love this song!" she exclaims as she rushes to the radio to turn up the volume. Fanny grabs hold of Susan's hands and they dance. Fanny spins Susan and they move their feet in time with the beat of the music. The song ends and they fall onto the couch in a laughing heap. Susan changes her expression and looks a little disoriented as she puts her hand to her head. Her face turns pale.

"Are you all right?" Fanny asks, worried.

"Yeah, yeah. Just a little dizzy I guess."

"Well, that's what you get for not coming out with us girls for a night on the town once in a while. You forgot how to have fun. Thank goodness I'm around or you would blend into the wall paper."

Susan sits up, excited. "Oh! I got a letter from Tom today."

Fanny flicks her eyebrows up and down. "Do tell. What has lover boy written you this time?"

Susan opens a drawer in the end table next to the sofa and pulls out Tom's letter. She carefully slides the letter out of the envelope and reads.

"'My dearest, Suzie. It has already been too long being without you. I think about you everyday. Thoughts of coming home to you lift my spirit when things get tough … '" Susan continues to read the beautiful love letter to Fanny but in her mind she hears her husband's voice vividly.

Tom sits on a cot under his covers with a flashlight as he writes a letter to Susan. His face has changed. He's a little thinner and has a lot more hair, but he's still the handsome Tom. He writes,

> *By the time you get this letter I will be on foreign soil. I will continue to write to you every chance I get. It's after midnight and we have to be up in just a few hours. But I can't sleep without telling you how much I love and miss you. I want you to know that I am with a good unit. There is this one guy we call Joker. He's from Texas. Joker keeps our spirits light when things get tough. We have a lot in common. He left his wife and three kids back home and painfully misses them. I think he writes to them almost as much as I write to you. We will stick together and be at each other's side until our fight is won. I hate saying good-bye, so I will say goodnight until tomorrow.*

"You are a lucky girl, Suz," Fanny interjects. "How did he end it?"

"'I love you, my darling. Tom.'" Susan finishes and then lingers at the sight of Tom's handwriting for a moment.

"So, you think Tom will bring some handsome soldiers back when he comes home?"

"If he comes home."

"Suz! Don't talk like that. He's coming home."

Susan shakes her head and shrugs. "You're right, you're right. That's my loneliness talking. This house has just been much quieter with Tom gone."

"Not anymore. Tonight you're coming with us."

"Who's us?"

"Just a small group of friends. There's a dance at the hall tonight."

Susan looks unsure. "I don't know what Tom would say about that. I mean, really Fanny Mae. A married woman going to a dance without her husband? What will people think?"

"Oh, for goodness sakes! It's a fund-raiser. And if you didn't go, what kind of person would you be to not help a charitable cause? If you don't go, people will say, 'did you hear about Susan? Yes, that's the girl who wouldn't help raise money for the needy.'"

"Well … "

"The wells run dry if you wait any longer," Fanny adds.

"OK, I'll go."

Susan laughs as Fanny hoots, hollers and dances around the room. "That's my girl. Now, my dear … " Fanny looks Susan up and down, "what will you wear? 'Cause what you're wearing now does not accentuate your girlish figure."

Susan playfully smacks Fanny's head with the letter and the girls fall over onto the sofa in another fit of laughter.

That night, Susan and Fanny arrive at the crowded hall with four other girls. All but Susan are single and the walk was filled with talk of the kind of gentlemen they hoped to meet that night.

A swing band plays on a large stage at the front of the hall and the whole place is decorated in red, white and blue. Balloons, colorful paper cut-outs and other decorations adorn every inch of the large room.

"You, Suz, are going to have fun tonight if it kills me!"

Susan forces an uncomfortable smile as they work their way over to a table and sit down. One of the girls, Colleen, immediately points to a dark-haired soldier who stands against the wall with a few other soldiers. The girls look and look again.

"That's the one I was telling you about!" she exclaims.

And just at that moment he notices her and grins. Colleen returns a smile.

"Go over and talk to him." Fanny nudges her elbow as she talks.

Colleen looks at Fanny in horror. "Fanny Mae! I'd rather die than embarrass myself like that." Colleen has a matter-of-fact look on her face as she talks to the other girls. "I have to remain calm and not look interested. If you look too interested—"

"Don't look now but he's coming over here …. with his friends," one of the girls interjects. They all, not so casually, look up to find the dark-haired soldier and three of his buddies walking toward them. The four men stop at the front of the table.

The soldier smiles again at Colleen while the other three smile at the rest of the girls. "We were wondering if you ladies care to dance?"

Colleen enthusiastically nods her head and jumps up from her seat. The soldier grabs her hand and they walk onto the dance floor, an excited bounce in Colleen's step.

"So much for not looking too interested," Fanny whispers to Susan.

Susan laughs as she watches the other girls being escorted onto the dance floor.

Fanny turns to Susan with excitement in her eyes. "Are you going to be OK here for a moment? I see someone I'd like to say hello to."

Susan nods. "Sure, I'll be fine. Go on." Fanny smiles and pops up from her seat and heads to the refreshment table where a young man hugs her tightly. A few words are exchanged then they walk away and get lost in the crowd.

Susan looks around the room. Couples dance cheek to cheek, some laugh and others seem to be lost in their own world together. Susan watches one couple who hold each other very close. The girl's head is buried in the soldier's shoulder and his hand caresses her back gently. The girl lifts her head to look at him and tears fill her eyes. He softly kisses her forehead and then pulls her close again as they continue to move to the music.

Susan cannot take her eyes away from the couple as her eyes, too, build up with tears. Even though the band changes the tempo of the music and a fast swing begins, the couple does not seem to notice as they continue to hold onto each other.

A handsome young soldier walks up to Susan, blocking her view of the couple. She looks up into his face. He resembles Tom and she's taken aback for a moment.

"Excuse me? I was wondering if you might do me the honor of this dance?"

He smiles big and offers his hand to Susan. Susan takes a deep breath and bites her bottom lip as she forces a weak smile. "I'm sorry. I'm married. I just came out with my girlfriends tonight and—"

"That's OK." He offers her a bigger smile. "It's just a dance. I'm not asking you to run away with me."

Susan laughs quietly at the soldier's sweet and genuine humor, but shakes her head. "You seem like a really nice gentleman, but I'm going to decline. Thank you."

"Well, you let me know if you change your mind," he says. He turns to leave as Fanny walks up. He nods to her politely and continues on. She turns to look at him as he walks away and then sits back down at the table.

"Well, now, he was handsome. He looks familiar, though."

"He looks like Tom," Susan states.

Fanny sees the hurt in Susan's eyes and grabs her hand. She squeezes it lightly as she talks. "C'mon. Let's go out there and wear out our dancing shoes. You and me." Fanny stands up along with Susan.

"It's time for me to go." Susan smiles tightly and tries to hold back tears.

"You're leaving?"

"This isn't for me anymore, Fanny. I don't belong here."

"Just because you are married doesn't mean you can't go out and have some fun. If anyone has a problem with it they can come talk to me," Fanny says matter-of-factly.

Susan looks at her friend. "I have a problem with it. I look at these men and they just remind me that Tom isn't here. It reminds me that these men are someone's brother, friend, husband, boyfriend, son, and most of them will leave and won't come back." Susan takes a deep breath to hold back her emotions. "I can't imagine what the rest of my life will be like if he doesn't come home."

Fanny doesn't say a word, she just grabs her friend and hugs her tightly. Susan sobs quietly into her shoulder.

"You'll never have to know what that feels like. He's coming home, Susan. Believe that, let that be what keeps you living each day. I'm sure he's somewhere thinking about you and that's what keeps him going, too."

Susan wipes her eyes and smiles at Fanny. "I just need to go home. I'll be fine."

"You know if you need anything—"

"I know. You go have fun. Don't worry about your old married friend."

"How about I come over tomorrow? We'll have lunch and I can tell you all the gossip from tonight?"

Susan chuckles lightly. "That would be great."

They hug one more time and then Fanny watches Susan as she walks out the door of the dance hall.

It's a beautiful day full of sunshine. Susan has a bounce in her step as she hums a tune and walks with a brown paper bag full of groceries. As she approaches her house, she notices the new flowers that have bloomed on the bushes near the picket fence. She stops to touch one as she opens the gate and looks up. Her cheery demeanor changes to a frozen look of dread.

A man stands on her doorstep. He has a yellow telegram in his hand and turns to face her as she opens the gate. "Mrs. Thomas Johnson?" he asks seriously. Susan's eyes well up with tears. She knows why the man is here.

"No, not Tom. " She drops the bag as she stares at the man, unable to speak. "Ma'am?" Susan falls to the ground and weeps at the man's feet.

Fanny looks up from her side window and watches Susan fall to the ground. She rushes from the window, out of her house and dashes through the gate to Susan's side. Fanny kneels down and pulls her into her arms. Susan weeps loudly.

The messenger looks down on the two girls with sympathy. Fanny throws her hand out and the man hands her the telegram. She tucks it away and holds onto Susan tightly.

Neighbors come out of their houses to watch the scene unfold. All of them know what that telegram means to a soldier's wife. They watch as Fanny rocks Susan in her lap like a child, smoothing her hair with her fingers. Fanny's eyes, too, well up as the man leaves.

Six months later. Susan sits on the sofa. The curtains are drawn and the house is dimly lit. She holds a pillow tightly to her and looks at the telegram on the coffee table. It's worn and crumbled from the many readings; tape covers a large tear through the center.

The doorbell rings and she gets up to answer it. She opens the front door and the postman hands her a small package. She looks down at it as she closes the door and then returns to the sofa. She makes herself comfortable and then opens the box.

The first thing she pulls out is a folded letter. As she opens it, the penny falls into her hand. She looks at the dented penny for a moment and weakly smiles with recognition. She reads the letter.

> *I never understood why, but I am sure you could shed some light on this for me. Every night Tom kissed this penny and put it in his pocket before we went to sleep. It didn't matter if there was a cot to sleep on or if we were in a fox hole. He held this special ritual night after night. I want you to know how special he was to us, too. He was a hero and a shining light in the wake of despair and death that surrounded us. He is the reason why half of our unit is still alive. I hope this message brings you some peace. His last words were of you. He made me promise to tell you how much he loved you and gave me this penny to give to you. If there is ever anything that I can do, or anything that you might need, I consider Tom a part of my family and I extend that invitation to you for as long as I live.*
>
> *Sincerely, Justin Jocane, or as Tom knew me, Joker.*

Susan stands at a fountain staring into the water as it splashes wildly. She looks up into the sky then back to the fountain again and then smoothes her pregnant belly with her hand. She lifts her closed fist in front of her and opens her fingers to reveal the penny. She stares at the dirty coin for a moment, kisses it and then throws it into the fountain. She closes her eyes tightly, makes a silent wish and walks away.

CHAPTER FIVE
Joshua's Kindness

"She just threw it away!" Harry gasps. He explodes from his sitting position to his knees and demands an answer from Grampa. "How could she just throw it away if it was so special?"

"Sometimes, my boy, you have to know when to let go. It's hard and sometimes painful, but letting go is a part of life." Grampa holds on to his words in his head as if he were saying them to himself. His face reflects a disturbing memory from a time ago that he hasn't let go of.

Young Cecilia walks down the stairs, suitcase in hand. She pauses at the bottom of the staircase and turns to look at her father who sits in his chair in the living room. He stares out the window, lost in a daze.

"Well, I guess I have everything," Cecilia says solemnly.

Her father, startled by her words, snaps out of his daze and looks at her.

"Right, well, I guess it's time to go then."

Cecilia's eyes well up with tears as she looks at her father. She waits for him to say something to make her stay but he just stands and nods his head at her.

A horn honks outside and they both look out the window.

"That's John."

Her dad looks at her and nods again. "You take care of yourself, Celia."

Cecilia swallows hard as she watches her father turn to leave the room. She says nothing. What else is there to say?

Her father stops as tears well up in his eyes. "You know, Celia, you don't have to leave." He turns to see the screen door slam shut. He rushes to the window and watches as Cecilia pulls herself into John's pick-up truck and leans to kiss him deeply.

The truck speeds away down the drive, throwing up rocks and dust as it travels toward the main road. Her father stands behind the closed screen door and watches it disappear. He tries to hold back tears but one manages to slowly slide down his cheek.

Harry lightly touches Grampa's arm as he continues staring out the window, a million miles away. "Grampa? Grampa, are you all right?"

"What? Yes, yes. Fine." Grampa shakes his hand in the air. "Now where were we?"

"The fountain," Harry says enthusiastically.

"Ah, yes. It was time for the penny to move on and it did. The year was 1958."

The park is filled with people. Some sit on benches, some sit on picnic blankets while their children play nearby. Many sit around the fountain, which sparkles with metallic tones from the coins that cover the bottom of the pool.

"Once again, the penny will find itself with someone who will soon know its true value. Next in line, waiting to tell his story, was the last person someone would think would have such an important voice in this world–a child."

A young black boy in a striped red and yellow T-shirt and jeans interrupts the fountain's reflection as his body hits the water. Laughter sounds loudly from nearby.

Joshua gasps and sputters as he comes up from the water. He has a bloody nose which runs quickly down his lips and his chin and discolors the water. He looks around and sees the white kids who threw him in.

"Nobody touch the water anymore, it's contaminated," one of the boys cries loudly.

"Yeah, and I think I heard all the wishes screaming for help," another one yells as he laughs.

The white kids continue to laugh as Joshua looks around defeated, scared and angry. He knows he can't defend himself without getting into trouble with the other white people that fill the park.

"There's a kid at my school that always picks on me," Harry says as he hears the sad beginning to the story.

"Yes, but they are picking on him because of the color of his skin," Grampa informs Harry. "Why is this boy from your school so mean to you?"

"Because I don't have a dad," Harry says solemnly.

"Ahh, so you and this boy may have something in common. You are both faulted for things that are out of your control, things that do not define who you are."

The white boys get on their bikes and pedal away, their laughter leaving with them. Joshua looks around and sees a few of the older white women staring rudely at him. No one dares to help him. No one even looks as if they care.

As he gets out of the fountain, he looks down and sees the money at the bottom. He scoops up some change quickly, puts it in his drenched jean pockets, and scurries quickly out of the fountain. He turns the corner of the park gate and takes off running.

Joshua busts through the front door of a very plain apartment. His mama sits up on the sofa with her legs covered in a blanket. She looks extremely ill. Joshua slams the door behind him.

"I hate white people!" he bursts out loudly.

"Joshua! That is no way to enter a house and greet someone."

"Sorry, Mama." Joshua walks over, his head hung and stands in front of his mother.

"Thank you. Now what is it child?" She sees his face, the rusty color smeared across his cheek. "And what happened to you?"

"I said I hate white people."

Mama's face turns sympathetic but stern. "No, Joshua, you must never say that. Hate is a very strong word. It's an evil word. Not every white person is bad, baby. Look at Ms. Sylvia, she has been so good to us all these years."

"Ms. Sylvia is different. She don't count," Joshua says. But his mother looks at him with disappointment.

"Joshua, you don't sound like the young man who I raised right."

"But, Mama. I was doing nothing wrong. I was just minding my own business. Just walking down the street from school."

"I know, son. But even so, even when you think all the world is bad, you'll still find some good. There is always a little bit of good in everyone's heart. You just gotta look a little harder at some people. But you always find it in the end."

Joshua sits on the floor beside the sofa and looks down at his hands for a moment. A small smirk appears on his face.

"There's one good thing that came out of it."

He reaches in his pocket and pulls out a handful of change. Mama gives him the eye. "Now where did you get that?"

"In the wishing fountain. Those whities, I mean boys, pushed me in. That's how come I got all wet."

"I figured as much."

"When are we not gonna be poor anymore, Mama?"

His mama smiles affectionately at him. The love in her eyes mixes with the regret she feels for the life she has given him. "That's why you are in school, so when you grow up you won't be, honey."

Joshua's back straightens and his eyes grow wide with excitement. "When I'm rich, I'm gonna buy you the nicest house and the fanciest car. And I'll have all the best doctors so you won't be sick no more."

"Well, that's very nice of you." She smoothes his wet hair. "Why don't you get out of those wet clothes before you catch your death. And then," She gives him her listen-to-mama-or-else look.

"Do I have to put it back in the fountain?"

"Well ... they sure seem like pennies from heaven to me." They both giggle. Mama stops suddenly and says very sternly, "But don't you do it again, you hear? Stealing don't make your heart any richer."

"Yes, ma'am."

"Now, go on and get out of those wet clothes, baby, then go run to the store. We need some milk and bread." Mama's face goes pale and she seems short of breath. "I just need to lie down for a few more minutes. And when you get back, I'll fix us a wonderful supper."

Joshua jumps up and kisses his mama on the cheek. "OK, Mama." He walks out of the room and then sticks his head back in. "I love you."

Mama smiles wearily but she's filled with love for her little boy. "I love you, too, baby."

Joshua counts the change while the cashier stares down at him with impatience. He gives her all the change except for the dented penny which he slips back into his pocket. He grabs his paper sack and exits the store.

As he walks along the sidewalk, Joshua passes a variety of stores and looks in. He stops at one window to take a closer look at something he knew he couldn't have when a blond-haired little girl, no more then six, peeks around the store window.

Her clothes are tattered and she is filthy, but her eyes sparkle with innocence. The little girl looks up and notices Joshua watching her which sends her running, barefoot, back into the alley.

Joshua curiously follows her as she runs behind a dumpster, out of sight. He slows down, looks behind the dumpster and sees her squatting on top of several crushed boxes.

A homeless man with a long, full beard lies on top of the boxes next to her. He does not look well, in fact, Joshua thought, he could be dead. Joshua twitches his nose and backs up from the unbearable smell coming from the man.

The little girl eyes up the loaf of bread that sticks out of the bag and licks her lips. Joshua is now more curious than frightened. "Do you want some of this bread?"

Without hesitation, the little girl savagely runs up to the boy. As he puts the bag down, she grabs the bread and runs back to her boxes and begins to rip and pull at the loaf like a wild animal.

She eats quickly, not even taking the smallest breaks to swallow. Joshua cautiously walks over to her and opens the milk. She instantly grabs it, too. She nudges the man hard in the side. He grunts and comes to. As he sits up, he sees Joshua, then the food that the little girl has in her hand. She takes a huge chug of milk and hands it to the man, then breaks off some bread. She forces him to take it.

Joshua steps back, his hands shoved deep into his pockets, and stares at the strange couple. He feels something and looks down as he pulls the penny out of his pocket. He stares at it for a moment and sighs just as the little girl walks up and looks at what is in his hand.

"This is all I have left," Joshua says sadly.

His hand is flat, the penny in the center of his palm. Joshua puts his hand on top of the little girl's dirty palm.

"I don't have much, but Mama says I'll have more if I don't give up and finish school. Mama says God will take care of his children and I guess that means you, too."

They both stare at each other. The girl scrunches her dirty, little nose and squints her eyes. "Are you God?"

Joshua notices the sincerity and innocence of this little child. He shakes his head and smiles at her. He looks down the alley and points to a church steeple in the distance. "No, God lives there," Joshua says with a big smile upon his bruised face. He knows he's done something very good. His face glows proudly as he walks away with his hands in his pocket.

"Boy!" the little girl cries out.

He stops and turns around but the little girl just stares at him in wonderment. He smiles again and walks out of the alley, his head held high.

Joshua enters his apartment empty handed, but yet with a pride filled smile across his face.

"Well, there you are," his mama says looking at his empty arms. "Where's the groceries, baby?"

"They in better hands now, Mama." He beams brighter than he has in a long time and his mother notices it.

"Well, look at that smile. It's been a while since I seen that beautiful smile across you're face! What happened?"

Joshua sits down next to her and starts the story from the beginning, the whole time mama's eyes grow with affection for her sweet boy.

Outside the complex, the little girl unknowingly walks past Joshua's apartment building and turns the corner. She walks up many steps and stops outside two large wooden doors. She looks intimidated by their size, but determination pushes her forward. She grabs the handle, opens the huge door, and timidly peeks inside. She is mesmerized by the beauty of this house of God. She scurries in and walks hesitantly down the aisle, her head turning in every direction to take in everything.

As she approaches the altar, a priest, preparing for mass, notices her. She doesn't see him.

"May I help you child?"

The little girl jumps in surprise and stares at him. He places the chalice down and walks a step or two toward her. "Are you lost?"

"Are you God?" she whispers innocently.

The priest laughs lightly. "I must say, no one has ever given me such a compliment in all my years. No, my child, but I'm one of his messengers."

An elderly woman walks near them and catches the little girl's attention. The woman stops before the votive candles and drops a coin into a metal box. The clank of the coin reverberates throughout the church.

The little girl looks at this new happening with a questioning look. The priest understands, and he kneels in front of her.

"What's she doing?"

"She's praying."

The little girl scrunches her nose and tilts her head to the side in confusion. "What's praying?"

"That's how you send messages to God." The priest motions to the elderly woman. "See, she put her money in that box, and she's telling God what's going on in her life."

She looks even more confused. "You have to pay money to talk to God?"

"No, my child. That's just her way of thanking the church for being here for her. And to make sure it's here for other people who may need it."

The little girl's face brightens as she pulls the dingy penny from her tattered pocket and holds it out to him. "I have this. Is it enough?"

"That's more than enough." The priest looks down at the girl, his face softens as he takes her hand and they walk over to the candles. She puts her penny into the metal box and looks over at the woman who lights another candle.

The little girl mimics the older lady and picks up the wooden matchstick. She looks at it for a moment then hesitates. She looks up at the priest. "Daddy says I'm not supposed to play with fire. Playing with fire burns houses down. Daddy says that's what happened to mine."

The priest is in awe of this special gift that has been sent to him. "Here, let me help you," he says as he takes the wooden matchstick from her tiny hand and lights it from another candle. She points to a candle and the priest puts the flame to the wick and lights it for her.

Observing the old lady's actions, she matches her kneeling position and solemnly bows her head.

The priest places his hand gently on her shoulder, "Just tell God what's in your heart, child. He's listening."

The little girl's eyes close tightly as she prays.

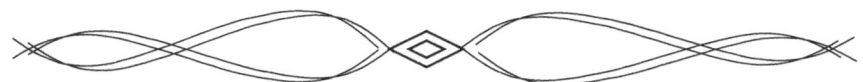

CHAPTER SIX
Zach and Billy

Grampa and Harry sit closely together in the darkness of the attic. Lightning flashes but neither one seems to notice.

"What did she pray for?" Harry quickly asks, interested in the little girl. "What happened to her? Did she find a home? Did the priest help her find a new family? What about the man by the dumpster? Was that her father?"

"Whoa, whoa, Harry. I don't know what happened to her, but I have this feeling she turned out just fine."

"A feeling? You mean you really don't know?" Harry looks disappointed as Grampa continues.

"Seems you've got a fondness for this little girl. She remind you of someone?"

"Well, kinda." Harry's cheeks flush quickly. "A girl at school."

"Oh, I see, and who's that?" Grampa questions him.

Harry turns uncharacteristically shy as he tries to answer. "Um, this girl, Sarah. She's older than that little girl. Sarah's in my grade."

"You like her?"

"Well, yeah, she's my friend."

Grampa smirks. "No, I mean like her, like her," he says as he raises an eyebrow.

Harry looks around uncomfortably. "I dunno. How do you know if you do?" His eyes meet Grampa's as he looks for the answer.

"Oh, you'll know. You'll feel it. Sometimes you might get sweaty hands or you can't stay still when you are trying to talk to her."

"Or you forget what to say and start acting all stupid? Like that?"

The old man laughs loudly. "Yeah, like that."

"Yeah, well, I guess I might."

"Oh, you like her all right." Grampa's matter-of-fact tone and laughter make Harry uneasy and he tries to hide his smile at the thought of Sarah, the prettiest girl in school.

"Stop laughing."

"Sorry." Grampa tries to wipe the smile from his face. Harry's face turns serious as he stares fondly at his grandfather.

"Grampa?"

"Yes, Harry?"

"What happened to Grandma?"

Grampa's face turns solemn and Harry sees the longing and hurt in his eyes. Grampa looks into the chest and pulls out a photograph of himself and his wife when they were younger.

She was a beautiful woman with a very kind face and bright smile. She had a very gentle nature to her and reminded Harry of his mother, Cecilia. "She looks really nice," Harry whispers to Grampa.

"She sure was." Grampa nods as he looks down at the photograph. "Just as nice as she could be. I'm sorry you never got the chance to meet her. She died when your mother was about your age. A heart attack. It was never the same around here after she was gone." Grampa's eyes fixate on something far away, a memory from a long time ago and Harry knows he's about to tell him another story. "The eternal flame of happiness and joy flickered out when she passed away. She was like an angel," Grampa continued in a voice Harry hadn't heard before. "I can still remember how we met. It was1959, but it seems like yesterday."

The cathedral is empty. It glows brightly from the chandeliers hanging from the ceiling and the sweet scent of burning candles fills the air. Ten-year-old Zachary pokes his head out from behind the back of a pew at the rear of the church. He looks from side to side and sees no one.

Zachary scurries quickly over to the metal money box near the candles in the foyer of the church. He looks around once more to see if anyone is watching, then pulls a screwdriver from his back pocket. He clumsily tries to undo the bottom of the metal box from the stand.

He finally manages to fit the screwdriver into the screw and quickly removes it. But he accidentally drops the screwdriver, making a loud reverberated noise. He ducks back into a dark corner and looks around in panic as he hears footsteps. He sinks even closer to the corner and holds his breath, trying to make himself invisible.

The footsteps come closer and closer till he sees a pair of high-heeled shoes. He looks over at the screwdriver only three feet away. The shoes come closer until they stop right next to the tool. A hand reaches down for it and Zachary leaps from the corner while eighteen-year-old Rosemary bends down.

He grabs the money box and runs past her to the big wooden front doors of the church. Startled, she yells after him. "Hey! Hey, you! Come back here."

Zachary looks back nervously as he runs down the steps. He runs into an older woman, almost knocking her down. She catches her balance as the boy continues down the street with the money box in his arms.

Zachary rushes into his bedroom, breathing heavy, and sits down on the floor with the box. He begins to pry it open with a butter knife and after a few minutes the lid pops open. He smiles and then digs inside. His smile grows wider as he pulls out a heaping handful of change and begins to shove it into his pockets.

"What the hell are you doing?" Zachary jumps and looks up to find his older brother, Billy, standing in the doorway of his bedroom. "Where did you get that?" Billy enters the room and crouches on the floor. He lifts the metal lid to the box the word *Missions* clearly embossed above the money slot. "You stole this from the church? That was the last place we could actually be welcomed around here. Empty your pockets, we're bringing it back."

"But I need it," Zachary pleads.

"What do you need to steal money for? Haven't I always provided what you need?"

"But this is different. I really need it."

"What do you need so badly that you have to steal from the church?" Billy asks as he looks at his younger brother.

"Well, it is money for the poor."

"I don't care, we don't steal in this family."

Zachary's faces twists in anger. "Family? What family?"

"As long as I'm around, you and I are a family. You got that? Now get that money together. We are taking it back. Now!"

Zachary gives in, but not happily. He pulls handfuls of change out of his pocket and puts it back into the box. The dented penny drops onto the carpet unnoticed as Zachary continues to empty his pockets until the box is full again. Billy puts the lid back on and stands up.

"C'mon. Let's go."

Zachary sighs loudly, notices the penny and hurriedly sticks it in his pocket with a smile as he follows his brother out the door.

Their father sits at a small kitchen table in the dingy house. He smokes a cigarette and has a small glass of scotch in his hand. He is drunk and in a bad mood. "Where are you two delinquents going?"

Billy puts his arm around Zachary's shoulder, ignoring his father's remark as he heads to the front door.

"Hey boy, I'm talking to you!" their father slurs loudly.

Billy looks at his father with disdain. "I'm going to take care of something. We'll be back in a little while."

"That little son-of-a-bitch in trouble again?"

Billy's face turns red with anger and he turns to look at his father. "Well, maybe if you'd be a father every once in a while he wouldn't get into trouble."

His father grunts with humor. "Oh, you think you are a man?"

"I've been a man longer than you," Billy retorts and slams the door behind him.

The two boys hear something hit the door and the sound of glass breaking from inside the house. Billy urges Zachary to continue along the driveway into the street. They get to the corner and wait for traffic to pass.

"Was Dad always a drunk?" Zachary asks.

The question catches Billy off-guard. "Nah, not always. When I was little and Mom was around it wasn't so bad. He didn't drink everyday. But he was still a mad drunk when he did though."

"I think I'm forgetting Mom," Zachary says with a sigh.

"What do you mean?"

"Just what Mom used to be like and look like, ya know?"

Billy looks down at his brother and places his arm around his shoulder again. "That's because she died when you were real young."

"I do remember some things though," Zachary says with some satisfaction. "I remember that she always smelled like roses. And I remember that she used to laugh all the time."

"Yeah, well I'm glad you remember all the good stuff." Billy changes the subject quickly. "What'd I tell you about wearing my jacket?"

Zachary looks down at Billy's jacket. It's way too big on him. "I couldn't find mine."

"Yeah, well next time ask, lame brain." Billy playfully pushes Zachary, causing him to stumble. Zachary returns the shove. The two laugh and play as they walk down the street. They turn the corner and stop. They stand side by side at the street corner and look at the large architectural wonder of the church.

They cross the street and head up the front steps. Billy holds the box. Zachary swallows hard and looks at Billy. He motions for Zachary to open the door and they enter.

Upon entry, Billy and Zachary spot a police officer, the young woman, Rosemary, and her mother, Betty, in the middle of the aisle. Betty turns her head to Zachary and Billy and her eyes fly open as she points.

"It's him! That's the boy who stole the mission money. That's the little heathen!"

The police officer yells sternly and rushes in their direction as if they were trying to flee. "Hold it right there, boys!" But the boys are already frozen in position. The police officer immediately takes the mission money from Billy and handcuffs him.

Zachary watches the police officer put Billy in the back seat of the police car. He stares out the window at Zachary with a look that implies that all will be OK.

As the police car drives away, Rosemary watches the little boy run after it.

She had also noticed the two brothers' loving behavior. Betty rants and raves as she stands next to her watching the scene. Rosemary only half listens.

"Well, I just hope we don't have another incident like this again. Imagine having hooligans like that in this beautiful neighborhood. I just won't have it!"

Rosemary watches the police car disappear down the street. "He didn't do it," she whispers to herself as she watches Zachary trailing far behind the car, running alone in the street. "He did."

"Rosemary? Are you listening to a word I say?"

Realizing what has happened, she takes off down the street in Zachary's direction leaving her mother on the steps. "Rosemary? Rosemary! Where are you going?" She watches her daughter hurry down the street.

The police station is small and not much is going on. A phone rings occasionally as Billy sits behind a table, a cup of water in front of him. The police officer who brought him in enters the room and stands in front of him.

"Well, you are free to go. I suggest you thank the Lord above that that nice lady at the church decided not to press charges since the money was returned."

Billy's face turns to confusion and relief as he stares at the officer.

"Did ya hear me, boy? You can go 'head now."

Billy stands up and shakes the officer's hand. "Thank you very much, sir."

"Keep yourself outta trouble now," he offers the boy.

"Will do." Billy nods as he exits the room.

Zachary sits near the front doors, his elbows rest on his knees to prop his heavy head. When Billy walks out, Zachary jumps up excited. "Billy!" he cries as his arms squeeze his brother around his waist. "I thought for sure they were gonna lock you up and it would have been all my fault. I'm so glad they let you go."

"Whoa, little buddy, it's not over yet."

Zachary looks at Billy, confusion paints his face as they walk down the steps. "What do you mean?"

"The nice lady at the church decided not to press charges 'cause we returned the money. It's only right that we go and thank her for being so generous."

Zachary makes a face. "We gotta go back?"

Billy looks sternly over at his little brother. "That's right. We have to finish what YOU started. I bet next time you'll think twice about doing something like this."

Zachary is deep in thought as he reaches into his pocket. He bites his lip as he pulls something from his pocket. "Look at what I still have." He holds the dingy penny in the palm of his dirty little hand.

"With all the trouble you put me through? That's mine." Billy grabs the penny out of Zachary's hand and playfully ruffles his hair.

They enter the church through the large doors. Billy looks around for a moment with Zachary standing close. He sees Betty arranging the candles on the altar. Billy walks a step forward, his brother lags behind.

"C'mon, Zach."

They slowly walk toward the altar. Betty turns when she hears them and her righteous church smile is replaced by an aggravated frown at the sight of the boys. "What are you two doing back here? There is no more money to steal."

Rosemary pops up from behind one of the flower arrangements and steps out onto the altar. "Now, Mother, that's not the Christian way. We welcome everyone here." She smiles genuinely at Billy and Zachary.

"Well, ma'am, my little brother has something he'd like to say to you." Billy looks down at Zachary who looks very ashamed and scared. He puts his hand on the smaller boy's back and lightly shoves him forward. "Well, go on. Tell 'em."

Zachary looks down at his shoes and twists his hands together. His words seem memorized and robotic. "I'm sorry I stole the money. I know it is money for people who are less fortunate then we are and they deserve a hot meal and a bed to sleep in just like me." Zachary looks up at Billy.

"And?" Billy raises an eyebrow.

"Thank you for being so kind and not sending me to jail."

Rosemary smiles at Zachary's innocence. She walks over to him and crouches down in front of him. Her smile is so warm. "And you are officially forgiven."

"Just like that?" Zachary asks, surprised.

"Just like that," she says and ruffles his already unruly hair then looks up at Billy and smiles at him. Zachary takes a step back and stands next to his brother.

"Yes, thank you again for being so kind, ma'am."

"You can call me Rosemary."

"Rosemary. That's a beautiful name, ma'am," Billy replies. He and Rosemary stare at each other for a moment, an obvious attraction between the two. Betty interrupts the moment with a loud clearing of her throat.

"Rosemary, I believe the linens still need to be done before the next service."

"OK, mother," she says with a roll of her eyes and then to Billy she adds, "Hopefully, we'll see you at service."

Billy nods his head as Rosemary smiles and goes back to the altar. Betty gives another nasty look in the boys' direction as they turn to leave. Rosemary glances around the large flower arrangement one more time to watch them leave, then concentrates on her church duties.

"Rosemary, what a beautiful name," Zachary mocks as he pokes his brother's side.

"Shut it, twerp." Billy laughs as he gives him a lighthearted shove.

The sun slowly disappears below the horizon as Billy rushes down the sidewalk from another busy day at work. His clothes are filthy. Rosemary spots him from across the street and tries to get his attention.

"Billy! Billy!" she cries out.

Billy finally notices her and stops. She crosses the street to meet him. Billy fidgets and looks around, worried as she draws closer.

"Well, are you deaf or just ignoring me?" Rosemary smiles playfully as she steps up onto the sidewalk. Billy, at a loss for words, just makes an unintelligible sound. Rosemary notices his low comfort level.

"I was hoping to see you and your brother at church this weekend."

"Oh, uh, I had to work," Billy stammers.

Rosemary changes the subject quickly. "I saw Zachary take the money. Why did you say that you took it?"

"Well, I didn't actually say I took it," Billy says defensively. "It was just kinda assumed. You think I'd rat out my ten-year-old brother?"

"I should think not and you're welcome for me stepping in. My mother was ready to send you to the guillotine."

Billy looks at her pursed lips and begins to laugh. Rosemary can't hold her tight face and begins to laugh as well.

"Well, ma'am, if there is anything I can do to repay your kindness."

"Two things. First, call me Rosemary, not ma'am. And second, next time you have to work why not let me come and get Zachary and take him to church with me?"

Billy is confused as to why this nice, pretty girl would want to befriend him and his brother. "Zachary's never been to church before. I don't think you could handle him."

"Oh, a challenge! My favorite," Rosemary says with a smirk. "So, Billy, do you work this weekend?"

"Well, actually, no," he confesses.

"Great! Not only would I love the pleasure of you both accompanying me at church but ... " she begins to slowly walk away, "we're going to have fun and enjoy ourselves at the church fair afterwards." Before Billy can decline or find an excuse, Rosemary waves and flashes Billy her biggest smile. "Tell Zach hello and I'll see you on Sunday."

Billy watches her as she walks, more like floats, down the sidewalk. Billy breathes deeply and continues his walk back home. His step a little lighter and unknowingly smiling the whole way.

The church parking lot is colorfully decorated with Japanese lanterns strung across the trees and the red and white tents. Balloons and crepe paper streamers add to the decorations as children run through a mass of people, balloons flying wildly behind them. Some of the fair-goers play games while others talk over a plate of home cooked food.

Festive carnival music fills the air as Rosemary, Billy and Zachary walk through the crowd of people. Rosemary looks down at a wide-eyed Zachary and asks, "So, Zach, what would you like to do first?"

"Everything!" he exclaims as he takes in all the wonder of the fair.

"Well, then, everything it is!" Rosemary laughs with delight.

Billy breathes deep and uncomfortably looks over at Rosemary. "We can't even afford to be here much less do everything."

"And who said anything about money? I work at this church. I have connections." Rosemary winks at Billy and grabs Zachary's hand. "How about we eat first?" Zachary nods in agreement.

"Do they have hot dogs?"

"All the hot dogs you can eat."

Zachary's eyes get even wider and he smiles big as Rosemary leads him to the food tent. Billy follows, feeling very out of place. Several people wave and say hello to Rosemary but Billy sees their faces turn to polite smiles as they question these two, poor boys. Billy stands taller and his face grows more defensive as he gets in the food line.

A young man named Benjamin stands behind the table serving the food.

"Now, Benjamin, you take very good care of my friend, Zach, here." Rosemary has her hands on Zachary's shoulders and squeezes them lovingly. Billy doesn't miss a thing Rosemary does. "He is a fond lover of hot dogs," she adds.

"Well, my little man, you have come to the right place." Benjamin leans over and whispers with a wink, "I make the best hot dogs this side of 42nd street. How would you like it?"

Zachary thinks for a moment and then says with his best manners, "On a bun, please."

Benjamin smiles as he puts three buns on a plate. He takes the lid off the hot dog warmer and places three hot dogs inside the buns as he talks. "I'm gonna dress up three different hot dogs and you can try them all. You tell me which one you think is the best, OK, Zach?"

Zachary nods and licks his lips as if he can already taste them. Rosemary turns to Billy who watches his brother with a silent happiness.

"Penny for your thoughts," Rosemary interrupts, snapping Billy out of his daydream.

"I'm sorry, just taking in all the, uh, stuff."

"Stuff, huh?" She knows that Billy feels out of place. She takes his hand firmly in hers, catching Billy off-guard. He looks down in surprise. "Benjamin, watch Zach for a second?"

The man nods happily. "Sure thing, Rosey."

Rosemary turns to face Billy and looks deep into his eyes. "I know what a man like you wants." At first, Billy turns flush at Rosemary's suggestive comment. But when she pulls him to a large barbecue grill, he laughs to himself and relaxes. Platters everywhere piled high with steaks, sausages, hamburgers, ribs–the works.

Billy looks at the enormous amount of meat. Rosemary smirks at his overwhelming look.

"So, what shall we try first? The hamburgers are huge. But, then the steaks are so juicy, oh and the ribs, well, you just have to try the ribs."

"What was it that Zach said? I'll try everything."

"Everything it is!" Rosemary motions to the barbecue man behind the table. He piles two plates high with all kinds of meats from the platters. They thank him and walk over to meet up with Zachary who carries a plate with two hot dogs on it.

"Benjamin gave me two more hot dogs! This is great!" Zachary exclaims as they hunt for a place to sit. They find a table, Zachary hurries to sit next to Rosemary, and they begin to eat.

"You might want to slow it down before those hot dogs get the best of you."

Zachary looks at his brother like he's crazy, his cheeks bulging as he shakes his head. "No way." Zachary motions toward Billy's piled high plate. "Besides," he says through his half-chewed hot dog, "I'll be doing a lot better than you will after you finish that."

Zachary bites into his hot dog again. Rosemary smoothes his hair and looks up to find Billy staring at her. This time she feels his eyes and becomes very self conscious.

"Thank you, Rosemary."

"For what?"

"For restoring my faith in humanity."

"Well, in that case, it was my pleasure, Mr. ... I don't even know your last name!"

"Crawford and somehow I believe you really mean that."

Zachary chews happily on his hot dog and notices the looks between Billy and Rosemary. His eyes go back and forth looking at the two, his mouth is so stuffed full of food, he looks like a chipmunk. He rolls his eyes and gets back to his chewing.

The days go by and the three find themselves spending more and more time together. Billy has never seen Zachary in such high spirits and he himself has never felt so excited to see one person as he is when it is time to meet Rosemary. He hates when their time together is over and his stomach turns with anticipation for the next time he can see her.

The three often walk near the lake where Zachary throws rocks into the water and Rosemary and Billy talk along the water's edge. They frequently go to the park as well and watch Zachary play with the other kids, laughing at his awkwardness but noticing how much happier he is. Zachary now has a new glow and perpetually wears a smile.

On a particularly beautiful day, Billy and Rosemary have a moment alone. They sit on a blanket, a picnic under a tree, and laugh uncontrollably. Rosemary throws a grape at Billy's head and he taunts her with a small plate of pie. Rosemary throws her hands in the air as she begs him not to do it. She jumps up from her sitting position and Billy follows. They run around the tree in a romantic game of chase.

The sun creeps toward the hills, the sky ablaze with oranges and pinks. Rosemary stands next to Billy on the top of a hill. He spins her around and then dips her, her giggles echoing through the park.

"My, you do have some way about you!"

"Ahhh, the old boy fooled you with his goofy, unkempt exterior." Billy smiles genuinely at Rosemary as he pulls her up from the dip and spins her out and back in close. Their faces are inches apart and there is a tension between them. Their eyes lock.

Rosemary breaks the silence with a whisper. "Billy?"

"Yes," he whispers back.

"I wish you'd stop thinking about it and kiss me."

Billy smiles softly. "Yes, ma'am." He leans in and kisses Rosemary. They embrace tightly as the kiss turns more intimate.

A few weeks later, Rosemary sits on the sofa of her extravagantly furnished home. She flips through the pages of a magazine as she listens to the rain lightly hitting the roof and touches her lips with her fingers. Her mind is on Billy.

The doorbell rings and pulls her back from her memory. She gets up from the sofa and walks to the front door. She opens the door to find Billy standing before her. He is drenched from the rain, his chest heaving as he breathes. She looks at his face which is tight and grief stricken. He seems disoriented as he stands motionless on the porch.

Worried, she walks out onto the porch and closes the door behind her.

"What is it? You're as pale as a ghost." Billy paces the length of the porch. Rosemary tries to follow him. "Billy? What is it? You're worrying me."

Billy stops and looks at Rosemary. His face stained with tears that have now blended with the rain. He tries to speak but nothing comes out. Rosemary puts her hands on his face gently. "Billy, what is wrong?"

"I left Zach this morning; he was playing in his room with this new airplane I got him for his birthday." Billy begins to pace again. "I told him I'd be home by five and that we'd go out for a hot dog to celebrate. You know how much he loves hot dogs." Rosemary nods but Billy just continues. He leans on the railing of the porch, anger mixed with his grief. "I got home a little late and I, uh, I noticed Dad had taken the car and when I couldn't find Zach I thought maybe he was with him. Maybe he's actually done something with him for his birthday." Billy breathes heavy, his nostrils flare. "That's when I heard the sirens. I don't know why, but it's almost as if I knew."

"Knew what?" Rosemary asks him.

Billy wipes his eyes and meets hers. She knows before he tells her his agonizing memory.

Billy runs down the street toward the sound of the sirens. As he turns the corner, he is overwhelmed by the scene. People stand everywhere. Some point. Some look horrified. Others talk with police officers.

"That's when I saw Dad's car. They told me he had lost control and ran up on the sidewalk."

Billy walks to the car. His dad lies lifeless in the driver's seat. Blood covers his face and his head is tilted in an awkward position. A demolished hot dog vendor's cart sits mangled at the front of the car, smashed and crushed against a building. Joe, the hot dog vendor recognizes Billy and runs over.

"I just kept listening to Joe and he kept saying he was sorry. There was nothing he could do, it happened so quick."

Billy spots his jacket sticking out from the side of the hot dog cart. His eyes go wide with realization, they fill with tears.

"And then I saw him," Billy managed to say through his sobs.

Billy tries to push past the officer and Joe to get to his brother, but they hold him back. He pushes and claws at them but they hold him firmly.

Rosemary cries silently and tries to comfort Billy, but he will have no sympathy.

"He just wanted a damn hot dog! If I hadn't been late, he wouldn't have gone by himself. And of all the cruel jokes, the goddamned irony! The man who we called dad killed him in one of his usual drunken outings that I should've been there to stop."

Rosemary shakes her head vigorously. "No, Billy, don't make this your fault. There is no way you could've prevented any of this. You did everything in your power to raise Zachary and be the father he never had."

Billy breaks down in a violent fit of tears and sobs. "He was just a boy! He had so much still to live for, so much more to see and do."

Rosemary touches him. "I know. I know."

"I love him so much," he cries, "and he was the only person who ever loved me."

Rosemary takes his hand and leans in close to him. "That's not true, Billy." She puts her hand on his face. He meets her gaze then lays his head on her shoulder. Rosemary holds him tightly through his violent sobbing, quiet tears stream down her cheeks.

Grampa's eyes well up with tears remembering his brother all those years ago. "That's when I knew I had a love more powerful than anything. Still true to this day, she loved me till the night she passed away." Grampa realizes his emotions are out on the table and tries to suck them back in. He clears his throat and looks down at the boy lying across his lap desperately trying to stay awake. "That's the last story this penny ever told. It's been with me ever since." Grampa smiles sweetly

THE PENNY

down at this wonderful boy who is his grandson. "C'mon, it's time for bed."

Grampa sits on the edge of the bed as he tucks Harry in. He pulls the sheets up to Harry's chin as the boy moves around to get comfortable, he seems deep in thought. Harry squints his eyes and lets out a heavy breath.

"What you got brewing in that head of yours?"

"Grampa, did you know my father?"

"I thought that breath was mighty heavy for a boy your age. Harry, I can't tell you much about your father. But, I can tell you about your mother. She loves you very much. She would do anything for you." Grampa chuckles. "And knowing Celia, she probably has. She sacrifices a lot for your happiness, and she loves every minute of it, as long as it makes you happy. She never thinks anything is good enough for you, Harry. That's why she has you at that school, and that's why she works so hard."

Harry seems satisfied by Grampa's answer and smiles at him. Grampa tousles his hair and gets up from the bed. He turns off the lamp and the room is completely dark but Grampa finds his way with ease and opens the bedroom door. He looks back at Harry for a moment.

"Grampa?"

"Yes, Harry?"

"Ya know, Zach?"

"Yeah?"

"He wasn't the only eleven-year-old who loved you."

A genuine smile spreads warmly across Grampa's face. With his most sincere tone, he wishes Harry only the sweetest dreams. "Good night, Harry."

"Good night, Grampa."

THE PENNY

CHAPTER SEVEN
The New Keeper of The Penny

The next morning, Harry walks down the stairs. He lugs his heavy suitcase behind him. When he reaches the bottom, he looks around the room. He notices something different about the old house.

It doesn't appear dilapidated and dreary anymore. Everything has a special glow to it. The house now appears to Harry as timeless and mystical. Grampa meets Harry at the bottom of the stairs. Grampa, too, has changed. His face that was once harsh and cold now seems gentle and warm. He seems to have lost ten years of age.

"All set?" Grampa asks Harry.

His disappointment that his time with Grampa is over shows clearly on his face. "Yeah," he mumbles.

They hear Cecilia's car pull up to the house.

Cecilia looks out the window in astonishment. The overgrown and weed-infested gardens now flourish with bright greens and flowering buds. The picket fence and porch railings are freshly painted with a pure white paint.

Cecilia gets out of her car and slowly takes another look around. Harry walks out onto the porch, Grampa follows him and the screen door slams behind him drawing Cecilia's attention their way.

She walks toward the porch slowly and notices a glow about Harry. She flashes him a big smile. "Hey, Harry bug!" Cecilia glances at Grampa, uncomfortably, and tries to fill the awkward moment. "Wow, the place looks great!"

Grampa puts his hand on Harry's shoulder proudly. "Yeah, you've got yourself a hard little worker here, Celia." Harry smiles big. Cecilia looks at the two of them in total shock.

"What happened here?"

They both shrug their shoulders and Harry looks up at Grampa. "Just chores," Harry offers with a smirk.

"Well, Harry, go on and get your things. I'm sure your mom wants to get on home." Grampa looks lovingly at his daughter and adds, "Unless of course you'd like to stay for a while, maybe have a glass of iced tea before the long ride home?"

Harry goes inside to get his suitcase and Cecilia stares at her father, confused at this change in him and her son. She seems indecisive and carefully chooses what she thinks is the safer option.

"No, we better get on home if we're going to beat the traffic, but thanks."

Grampa looks hurt with Cecilia's response, but nods his head. "I understand," he replies as Harry comes out of the front door with his suitcase. He puts it down on the porch, thinks for a moment and sighs loudly.

"Well, I guess this is good-bye." Harry looks up at the older man who smiles down on him.

"No such things as good-byes, my boy. In these parts we say until next time."

"What? Next time I get suspended?" Harry laughs at his own joke and Grampa joins in but then turns serious. He kneels down next to the boy.

"You, Harry, are destined to do great things. You have two choices, the right and the wrong. Every time you come to the fork in the road always choose the good over the bad. It may not seem as pleasant when you choose it, but I guarantee the outcome is sweeter. In fact, some of the best decisions I ever made were the hardest ones to make."

Cecilia watches this unexpected show of emotion. Her eyes well up with tears at the sight of this old man she thought she knew, pouring his knowledge into the little boy she tried desperately to understand. The tears begin to fall in a silent stream down her face though she doesn't even realize she is crying.

"Mom? What's wrong?"

Cecilia smiles through her tears. "Nothing." She wipes her wet cheek. "I was just thinking that I could really use that glass of iced tea."

Cecilia looks at Grampa whose face brightens. Grampa opens the screen door and motions for them to enter. As the screen door slams, Harry tells his mother about his stay. "And I pulled up roots the size of cars and, oh, I met Chester, or actually a part of him."

Later, as the sun begins to settle in the sky, the screen door opens and the three step out onto the porch.

"We really need to go. It's getting late."

Harry throws his arms around Grampa as the man scoops him up in a bear hug.

"Thanks for the greatest adventure I've ever had!" the boy exclaims.

"No, thank you, Harry. Those stories have been hidden away for a long time. They needed to get out." Grampa puts Harry back down and pulls something from his pocket. His worn, wrinkled hand gently wraps around Harry's small, smooth hand. "It's your turn to live, to dream, to conquer. Remember, choose the right road, Harry, and make sure you give this a wonderful story to tell."

Harry opens his hand and finds the penny–the dull and dingy coin with a small dent in the center. Cecilia looks at it with confusion but does not want to interrupt this magical moment between the two most important men in her life.

"It's time for me to let go," Grampa whispers.

Harry closes his hand tightly and with a look of pride on his face says, "It's safe with me, Grampa."

"I knew it would be." Grampa smiles and pats his shoulder as he stands. "Now, go on and get your suitcase in the car for your mother."

"Yes, sir." Harry grabs his suitcase and drags it to the car. Cecilia looks at her father and then suddenly throws her arms around his neck and squeezes tightly.

"I still don't know what happened here, but thank you."

Grampa wraps his arms around Cecilia and squeezes his eyes shut. A look of peace and happiness comes over his face. Tears well up in his eyes as they let go of each other and Cecilia turns to find Harry next to the car watching. She gives another heart felt smile to Grampa. "Until next time, Dad."

"Until next time … Celia bug."

Grampa watches Cecilia walk to the car. Harry opens his car door and gets in.

"Bye, Grampa. See you real soon!"

"You can count on it, boy."

The engine roars to life and Harry waves out the open window as his mother pulls away. Grampa waves back. His hand lingers in the air, almost reaching out to them, not wanting to let go.

As Harry continues to wave he notices something and stares harder at the house. Out of the second floor window, he sees Susan, then Tom with their baby, illuminating with love and happiness. Vito walks into view holding his smiling, little boy Leo. A proud Joshua appears with his arm around the little girl who now has a ribbon in her hair and healthy, rosy cheeks. Zachary with his favorite jacket on. Rosemary stands beside him, beautiful and caring. They smile at him. Harry returns the regards with an awe struck grin and one final wave, then sits back in his seat, satisfied.

Early morning, students shuffle around in the hall between classes. Harry stands in front of his locker putting his books away. Sarah leans against the next locker listening to Harry's animated story.

"And he was not at all what I expected," Harry says as he shoves a large textbook into his locker.

"So, he wasn't burying bodies in the backyard like your cousin said?"

Harry smiles playfully. "Well, yeah—"

Astonished, Sarah gasps. "What?"

"But it wasn't anything human," Harry adds, enjoying her moment of surprise. They laugh for a moment, then Harry slams his locker shut and they turn to walk to class. On the way, Ralph bumps purposefully into Harry and begins to taunt him.

"Awe, look at the lovebirds! Did your mama teach you how to French kiss, too?"

Harry looks at Ralph with a stone face. Sarah gives Harry a pleading don't-give-into-him look.

"What's wrong, Harry? Your little woman said you can't talk?"

Sarah tugs on Harry's arm. "Don't listen to him, Harry. He's just an idiot."

Harry looks at Ralph for a moment and then grabs Sarah's hand calmly in his. "C'mon, we gotta get to class." He walks past Ralph and continues down the hall.

"Hey, Harry!" Ralph calls to him.

Harry stops, looks at Sarah for a moment, who shakes her head vigorously, and then turns to face Ralph. The boy's hands wrap around a straw. He blows a spit ball in Harry's direction. Just as the spit ball comes close to Harry, he moves to the side. The headmaster walks out of a classroom and into the hall. Ralph's mouth falls open with a look of horror as the spit ball hits the headmaster in the face.

The headmaster slowly wipes the spit ball from his cheek and looks directly at Ralph. Harry and Sarah watch in excited anticipation as the headmaster walks over to Ralph and grabs his arm.

"But it wasn't my fault. I swear!"

"Well, you'll have plenty of time to tell your mother the whole story during your suspension." The headmaster drags Ralph down the hall while the other students look on. They pass Harry and Sarah.

"Hey, Ralph?" Harry calls out. Ralph looks at him over his shoulder. "Karma's a bitch, ain't it?" Harry says with a smirk. Ralph gives Harry a look as he disappears into the headmaster's office. Sarah looks at Harry as he pulls the penny from his pocket and flips it in the air. He catches it and puts it back into his pocket.

"What was that all about?" Sarah crinkles her nose.

"It's a long story." Harry smiles at Sarah as they walk down the hallway, hand in hand, and get lost in the crowd of school children.

The End

SHERIFFS INCORPORATED
Screenplay by J.L.Chaka
Story conversion by Jill Pomerantz

BACK STORY

Sheriffs Incorporated grew out of my love for the Three Stooges and Westerns. I wrote the part of Louis with Chris Farley in mind, but with his passing, we'll never ever be able to see him bring that role to life. You'll also notice the influence of Mel Brooks on my writings as well. I hope you enjoy the adventures of the brothers in the old West.

CHAPTER ONE
The Will

Mr. Jonathan Billings, a stylishly dressed lawyer in his fifties approaches the Matheson Estate in an elegant horse drawn coach. He views a row of majestic oak trees lining the drive to a soaring, magnificent Victorian estate just beyond the Chicago River. The mansard roof, reminiscent of Albert Matheson's stay in Paris, and the dormer windows protruding like eyebrows from the four-story façade, bring to mind images of his old friend and client.

Mr. Billings steps down from the coach greeted by the butler. He is directed to the familiar study where he and Albert had shared many conversations, whether legal advise or otherwise. He sits with the prospect of business at hand at the antique oak table of a dark, deep hue that age and generations of polishing gave to the woodwork. Much of the other furniture is monumental in effect, and abundantly decorated with carving in high relief: flowers, fruit, animals, fabulous creatures and human figures, strangely assembled yet skillfully executed. The curtains trimmed with ball fringes and tassels are made from an overpowering massive velvet. The deep red wallpaper, covered with exaggerated damask patterns is almost hidden by the large realistic paintings in wide gilded frames. All the expense and abundance suggest that Mr. Albert Louis Matheson had impeccable taste. I say "had" for the simple reason that our distinguished man of fifty-eight has recently passed. And, it is consequently why, today, a hot summer afternoon in 1888, that Mr. Jonathan Billings has made his final appearance at the Matheson Estate.

Mr. Matheson's three grown sons, Bert, Louis and Alby enter the study as anticipated by Mr. Billings. Bert enters first. Although deemed odd looking due to his large nose, he remains the best looking of the three. Louis enters second, portly and shy, he has always been considered to be deficient in looks and common sense. Despite the fact that neither Bert nor Louis has shown any real promise in aptitude, curly-haired Alby seems to have inherited something of his father's intelligence.

Across the table, Jonathan Billings looks up from his papers. He quickly glances over his bifocals at the contrasting images of the beautifully decorated room to the ungentlemanly appearances of the Matheson brothers. He puckers his brow as he notes Alby's uncombed hair and dirty shoes, Louis's unlaced boots and unbuttoned morning jacket, and Bert's missing suspenders, which causes him to incessantly pull up on his pants.

Mr. Billings gathers himself and greets the brothers. "Good afternoon, boys. Have a seat and we will get down to business as soon as all parties are present."

They sit down, side by side, at the large table in front of Mr. Billings. As they do so, they look up at the portrait of their father, distinguished yet stern, peering down at them from his pedestal above the fireplace. The three young men shift in their seats, shuffling their feet, obviously uncomfortable in the room.

Breaking the awkward moment, Beatrice Matheson, their father's stepsister and her illegitimate son, twenty-year-old Alfredo enter the study.

Mr. Billings raises his head once again and stands upon seeing a woman enter the room. "Ah, Ms. Matheson. How do you do?" He nods to her son. "Alfredo."

"Good to see you again, Mr. Billings," Beatrice politely responds. She then chooses a seat furthest from the brothers. Alfredo follows suit.

A German clock strikes ten. Mr. Billings looks across the room at it, then takes out his pocket watch and opens it. He compares the time and sees that they match.

Squeak, squeak.

"It is ten O'clock," states Mr. Billings. "We shall begin the reading of the will of the late Master Albert Matheson.

Squeak, squeak.

Mr. Billings looks up from his papers. "What in God's name. . . " He first looks over at Beatrice and Alfredo who are staring with repulsion at Bert.

Squeak, squeak.

Mr. Billings turns his head toward Bert. He grimaces as the young man of twenty-five stares blankly in the air while digging his small finger in his ear. Alby adjusts his wire-rim glasses, leans around Louis and smacks Bert on the arm to get him to take his finger out of his ear. The squeaking noise stops. Beatrice looks away in disgust from the three and brushes back her son's black hair from his eyes. She smiles at him then focuses upon Mr. Billings.

Mr. Billings clears his throat, gives the brothers a last disapproving look over his bifocals then begins to read. "'Having sound mind, I leave my paintings given to me by my dear friend Vincent, whom I met in Paris, to my devoted friend and attorney, Jonathan Billings, to whom I also leave a sum of ten thousand in cash.'"

Billings looks to the painting above the fireplace and glances at the signature of Vincent Van Gogh. "Thank you, sir." He smiles with satisfaction then resumes the reading, "'To my stepsister, who did nothing but complain and whine consistently about her inequities, I leave the guest cottage, which she has so conveniently inhabited her entire adulthood and the sum of one thousand dollars to share with her so-called son, Alfredo.'"

Beatrice sobs into a handkerchief then blows her nose. The three brothers look at her. Alfredo stares them down with an evil look, his eyes seemingly glowing red for an instant. They look away.

Mr. Billings continues, "'And to my three sons, Bertrand, Louis, and Albert, who have shown no competency in any field of endeavor, who have failed at everything I have ever asked them to achieve, who have been totally unproductive since the day of their conceptions, I leave my entire estate.'" The brothers look at each other and smile. "'Based on one contingent. They must prove themselves to me.'" Their smiles disappear. "'They will have six months from the reading of this will to purchase or establish a business and to show a profit.'"

Jonathan stops reading and takes out four envelopes. He gives one to Beatrice, who snatches it from his hand, and one to each of the sons. The brothers look at their envelopes.

Mr. Billings goes on with the reading. "'Billings has been instructed to give to each son an amount of two hundred fifty dollars. This is your capital for your business. If you fail to make a profit, the entire estate will be forfeited to my stepsister and her son.'"

The three brothers look at the envelopes and then to Beatrice. She and Alfredo smile then begin to laugh. The laughing becomes hysterical. The three look at each other helplessly as Billings puts away the paperwork.

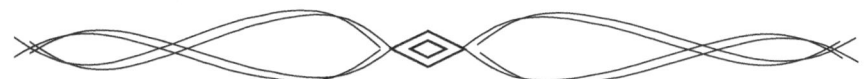

CHAPTER TWO
Getting Down to Business

Realizing what is at stake, the brothers resolve to get to work immediately. Although unsure how to go about starting a business, or even finding a job for that matter, they make the decision to walk the streets of Chicago. With a newspaper in hand they set out to find the one opportunity that will earn them their due share of the will.

"'Wong's Cleaners. For Sale by Owner,'" Alby reads the ad from the Daily News. "Well, let's go try our luck with the cleaning business," he states with enthusiasm. The three approach the building. A "For Sale" sign hangs in the window. They stop, look at the store and enter.

They approach the counter, but Mr. Wong, a proper china-man, takes one look at them and shakes his head no. The brothers leave.

Not to be discouraged at the rejection the three move on to the next opportunity circled in the ads section, Joe Enron's Fuel Company. They enter a small room packed with accountant types working feverishly on books. Mr. Enron greets the boys and shows them a huge record book. Behind them, several accountants slyly exchange papers.

They talk over the details with Mr. Enron, a big, burly, bald man. Unanimously, the brothers shake their heads no and leave.

With a little less enthusiasm the brothers enter Harrison's Bike Shop. The brothers inquire within and are directed to a skinny, near-sighted Mr. Harrison. He proudly shows them his newly invented motorbike. Alby climbs on and Mr. Harrison starts it. He takes off, but not knowing how to control it he runs into the wall knocking down all the display bikes.

The brothers shake their heads at the proposal to take over the shop as they back slowly out the door.

Nevertheless, the young men don't give up. They trod on to Muntzy's Entertainment where strange gadgets are presented to them. Mr. Muntzy leads them to the latest gizmo, a vision box. As he cranks the handle, black and white images move rapidly past the opening. Words written below the scenes tell the story. The brothers look at each other puzzled. Laughing, they shake their heads as if nobody would be interested in something so dumb.

Ready to give up, the brothers try for one more prospect. They enter Joe's Bakery indifferently. But then, a beautiful woman known as Elizabeth Hanlin, brushes up against them as she exits with a basket of goods. She smiles. All three brothers feel lightheaded and weak at the sight, falling madly in love with the vision of beauty. The brothers watch her as she steps up to a carriage. The brothers turn as Joe appears behind the counter. In the meantime, Elizabeth's ugly sister, Penelope, steps from the carriage to allow her sister to enter with the baked goods.

Alby looks at Joe behind the counter and inquires about the woman at the carriage. "Who is that?"

Joe looks out toward the carriage and sees Penelope climbing in. He looks at the brothers strangely. "That's Penelope Hanlin. She lives up the street. Why?"

Without realizing that Elizabeth has disappeared into the carriage, Louis states, "She's the most beautiful woman I've ever seen." The others nod in agreement. Joe looks strangely at them again.

"What can I get you boys?" the bakery owner asks.

"We're looking for a business?" Alby replies.

Joe perks up at the news. "You're in luck. My wife has been sick and I need to sell."

"How much?" Alby asks.

"Two thousand, but I'd take fifteen."

"Fifteen dollars?" Bert says surprised. The other two brothers look at Bert, oddly.

"We only have seven hundred fifty," states Louis.

Joe thinks about it. "Sorry boys, I can't take less than thirteen."

Disappointed, disillusioned, and exhausted the brothers exit the bakery. As they look down the street, they spot the Hanlin's carriage parked in front of a large house just down the street from the bakery. Elizabeth steps down from the carriage carrying the basket of baked goods. She instinctively looks back at them, but the three, not wanting to be noticed turn their heads up in the air and start to whistle a tune. Elizabeth shrugs her shoulders and enters the house.

At the dinner table that night the brothers seem distracted. At first glance you might think they were simply pensive, going over the days distressing events, but look harder at their faces and you might see the telltale sign of love sickness in each and every one of them.

It is at this moment that Mr. Billings enters and sits at the head of the table. He looks each of the boys over and noticing something awry, warns, "Sirs, I will stay around the estate until the provision of the will has been carried out, then I shall make arrangements to leave." He stands and walks toward the door, then turns back around. "One hundred seventy nine days, sirs," he gently reminds them.

Solemnly, the brothers look at each other, their appetites dissipated. Each one excuses himself with the pretext of attending other important business.

Bert enters his room, pulls out a pen and his best stationery then begins to write a letter addressed to 'the most dearest Penelope Hanlin'. After a short time, Bert, satisfied with the content of the letter, seals the envelope. Upon hearing the maid, Mrs. Agatha Walters, turns off lights as she walks down the hall he gives the envelope a kiss. He opens his door and pops out his head. He looks around then hands over the letter as she passes, asking, "Could you post this, please?"

"Sure, Mr. Matheson," she replies. As she approaches Alby's door, he too pokes his head out with envelope in hand.

"Agatha, could you post this?" Alby asks in a whisper.

"First thing tomorrow, Mr. Matheson," she responds.

Her curiosity piqued at this point, she approaches Louis' door with some anticipation. She can't help but look at the door as she passes it. The door opens, Agatha stops, backs up and takes the envelope. "Yes, sir," she states without waiting for instructions from Louis. Louis looks puzzled as he watches her put the envelope in her apron pocket. He slowly closes his door.

Agatha walks down the hall and unable to control herself, compares the envelopes. All are addressed to a Penelope Hanlin. She looks back down the hall and laughs at the closed doors behind her.

The brothers in all their love sickness have allowed five weeks to pass without having done more to secure their estate. Mr. Billings has been watching them and is increasingly concerned. He decides to approach them that evening at dinner.

As Bert, Alby and Louis finish their meal, Mr. Billings enters the dining room and sits once again at the head of the table. He looks over at the brothers, unaware that Alfredo stands in the shadows just around the corner, watching and listening.

Billings decides to get straight to the point. "Sirs, you only have four months and six days before the feat is to be accomplished. What are your prospects?" Jonathan sees that the brothers are puzzled by the question. "What I mean to say is, what are your business opportunities?"

Finally getting it, Alby responds, "We haven't found the right one yet. The money father left us isn't enough, Jonathan." Louis and Bert nod in agreement.

"When I first met your father, he was penniless and he built an empire. It's not the money, sirs. It's what YOU have to offer." Jonathan waits for a response but just gets blank faces. Agitated by their ignorance Jonathan reiterates, "Need I remind the young masters, that if you fail, everything that your father worked for will fall into the hands of Ms. Beatrice and her son."

"You're smart, Billings. What do you suggest?" Louis asks.

"I'm not allowed to intervene in the affair. But if I were in your position, I'd look for a hardship case. Someone who must sell their business under dire circumstances."

Alby, the brightest of the three, ponders what Mr. Billings has been saying. All the while Bert and Louis are just as clueless as when it all began. Jonathan stands and walks toward the door. He turns before exiting.

"I will, however, avail myself for recommendations on enterprises that you may present to me. I'm free tomorrow night," he proposes.

Louis looks at his brothers and with a guilty conscience utters, "I'd like that Billings, but I'm busy"

"So am I," Alby interrupts.

Bert looks at his brothers with the same guilty expression. "Me too."

"Very well sirs." He leaves through the door and looks up toward the heavens. "A little help at any time would be greatly appreciated, Albert."

Alfredo, steps from the shadows of the unlit hallway. Having taken in the whole conversation, he smiles and walks away.

Bert goes to his room and dons his best suit and tie. He puts on his derby and looks at himself in the mirror. Satisfied, he picks up the flowers and the letter from Penelope. He smells it and sighs. He can't help but read it one more time.

> *Bert,*
>
> *I have considered your proposal of marriage and although you have swept me off my feet, I have also had other offers. Please come to my house and meet my father. He is very interested in meeting you, and I will decide if I should entertain your offer of courtship.*
>
> *All my love, Penelope*

Bert puts the letter into his jacket and walks to his door. He sticks his head out and looks both ways. He exits.

Louis and Alby go to their rooms as well, then, one at a time, dressed in a suit and derby they leave surreptitiously through the front door. Like Bert, they both carry flowers and a love letter from Penelope.

Bert, Louis, and Alby turn up at the same address. They look each other up and down and deduce that they are all dressed for the same date. Wanting to be the first at the door, they bump into one another trying to get through the gate. Penelope's father watches them from the open front door.

"Good evening, gentlemen. I'm Mr. Hanlin, Penelope's father."

The three brothers put out their hands to Mr. Hanlin at the same time. He looks at the three hands extended and then shakes each one. "I must admit, that I was taken by surprise when not one, but three gentlemen callers wrote letters to Penelope. I'm afraid Penelope is not used to this much attention and it has made her quite excited. My only concern is that the intentions are honest and not another prank. If it were, be assured that I'm a dead shot with my hunting rifle." Perplexed, the brothers look at each other. "I'm afraid, because of her looks, it has created problems."

The brothers suddenly think they understand that such beauty creates difficulties.

"Oh, I think we understand, Mr. Hanlin. I bet she gets looks wherever she goes. It must be hard not to," Louis remarks.

Mr. Hanlin not sure whether to respond to the odd statement, chooses not to, then turns toward the house and yells, "Penelope! Your gentlemen callers are here." He invites the brothers into the hall. They adjust their ties and hats and ready their flowers as Penelope walks down the stairs dressed in her Sunday best. She looks at each one, fluttering her eyelashes and smiling shyly.

The brothers do a double take, their mouths gaped open. They start moving back toward the door. Penelope's smile fades as she detects their reaction to her ugliness. Her father sees the disappointment and turns to the brothers. Bert hands his flowers to Louis, as does Alby. They get behind Louis who's trying to hand all three bouquets back to his other brothers.

"It's another prank, isn't it, father?" Tears begin to flow as Penelope turns and races back up the stairs, distraught.

Mr. Hanlin's brows turn down in anger. "Wait right there, boys. He marches into his study as Alby and Bert look over Louis' shoulders.

"What do you suppose he's doing?" Louis asks with some anticipation.

"Maybe he's getting the pretty one," Bert says half-heartedly.

As they look at each other, puzzled, the study door flies open.

The boys back up toward the front door unsure of Mr. Hanlin's plans. Penelope's enraged father loads his rifle as he exits the study. The brothers see the gun and, holding their derbies, turn to run toward the gate where they collide and get stuck. Mr. Hanlin takes aim and just as he fires, they squeeze through successfully. The bullet explodes pieces of the gate. He runs toward them as the brothers scramble down the street. Mr. Hanlin stops at the gate and looks at the fleeing brothers, realizing they are out of range.

"I'm not done with you boys! Run! But I'll catch up with you! You'll pay for humiliating my daughter!" he shouts angrily to them.

After running for some distance, the brothers are out of breath and sit on a park bench to rest. A bum lies on the ground using a newspaper as a blanket.

"Well, this is just great! Not only do we not have a business nor much time to find one, but we now have some crazy father with a gun after us and no girl. Things just keep getting worse," states Bert.

Alby looks over at the bum. "Things could be worse. Look at that guy."

The other two brothers look at Alby, the remark not consoling them. Alby adjusts his wire rim glasses to get a better look at the newspaper covering the bum's face. In large letter print the headline reads: CHEAP INVESTMENT-HIGH PROFIT.

Alby stands and moves toward the bum. He grabs the newspaper off him, revealing his unshaven face. "Hey, get your own!" the bum yells. He rolls over and pulls the other papers up for cover as Alby walks back to the bench and sits. He reads the article.

"'General store for sale in booming cattle town.' This is the deal we've been looking for. It's only five hundred dollars. It says to wire replies to Mayor Dunhill, Red Rock, Texas." He looks at his two brothers. They look at each other.

The following afternoon, the brothers decide to show Mr. Billings the ad.

Alby recounts, "It was fate that we had to run for safety into that park last night, Jonathan. We just happened to stop where that bum was lying, and right there on his face was this ad." Alby shows the ad to him.

Billings reads the article and then lays the paper down. The three brothers sit across the table impatiently waiting for his response. "A general store? Are you sure?"

"We've already wired the money. We're going to take it." Alby responds.

"Sirs, this is in Texas. They still ride on the back of smelly animals and bathe yearly. I'm not sure if the young masters are making a good decision."

"We've made up our minds, Jonathan," Louis rebukes.

"Very well sirs." Jonathan stands and walks toward the door. Then, he stops and turns, remembering this morning's visitor. "While the young masters were sleeping, a very irate man paid a visit. I told him that you weren't at home. He seemed distressed and was carrying a firearm. He discussed briefly removing your appendages from their current locations and placing them into an unmentionable area. I figured it best if he didn't know the young masters were home." Panic sets in on the faces of the brothers. Jonathan starts to leave, but turns around adding, "He was accompanied by a female companion whose face was quite displeasing to the eye."

The brothers look at each other in alarm, then get up and run. One of Jonathan's eyebrows rises slightly as he tries to decipher their connection to the man.

In a hurry to leave town, the three young men quickly load their bags into the carriage. Jonathan looks on with Beatrice and Alfredo. The lawyer approaches the brothers. He takes out a case and opens it, revealing a small Derringer pistol. Removing the gun, he holds it out to the brothers.

"It only fires two shots, but it's quite accurate at short distances. I would take some amount of comfort if you were armed," Jonathan explains.

Louis and Bert look to Alby who reluctantly takes the gun and puts it in his coat pocket.

"Considering the situation with the father whose daughter you misled and his accuracy at firing weapons, perhaps it is wise that you leave Chicago for a while. Remember that you only have four months left. Time is of the essence, lest you lose your inheritance. I believe that your father would be very supportive of you fleeing for your lives."

The three brothers momentarily think about his last words then climb into the carriage. They look back at the mansion. Jonathan waves at them. The driver pulls away puffing on a cigar. The smoke rolls back toward them in a cloud.

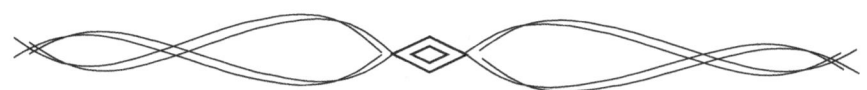

CHAPTER THREE
On the Way to Texas ...

Smoke rolls from the H & ST J. RR as it pulls into Chicago's Union Station. The Matheson brothers board the train as the conductor bellows, "All aboard for Hannibal, Saint Joe, Kansas City."

After finding their assigned compartment, the exhausted trio instantly falls into a deep sleep. Unaware that night has come and gone the brothers awaken as the train pulls into Newton, Kansas with a jolt. Alby awakes and adjusts his crooked glasses. He notes the uncomfortable positions his brothers are in; Louis is wedged into the corner with Bert's foot up on his chest. Bert is sprawled out with his neck twisted in a frightening posture. Alby is about to wake them when he is interrupted by the conductor opening the compartment door. He nods at Alby then shows in a young couple with their son. A groggy-eyed Alby gets up to join Louis and Bert allowing the newcomers to sit on his side of the compartment. He looks out the window and sees the house from the "Wizard Of Oz" twirling down into a field.

"Where are we?" Alby asks.

"Newton, Kansas, sir," the conductor replies.

Alby jumps up. "Newton! What happened to Kansas City?" The conductor takes the ticket from Alby and examines it.

"Sir, you should've gotten off in Kansas City. That stop was last night," he explains apologetically.

Alby shakes Louis and Bert awake. "Louis? Bert? Wake up. We gotta get off." They wake up groaning from the pain of being in the awkward postures and slowly join Alby in gathering the luggage.

The brothers follow Alby through the station and up to a ticket window. There doesn't appear to be a teller. They look around.

"Can I help you?" a voice speaks out from behind the counter.

They look around but still can't find him. "Down here." They lean in and look down to see a very short man trying to look up over the counter.

Alby puts the ticket down in front of the teller, who tries to get it but can't reach. Louis pushes the ticket toward him a little more, closer to his reach, but the short teller continues to struggle only to miss by a fraction. Louis pushes it just a little more toward him. The teller tries again, but still can't quite get it. He finally jumps up and grabs it. Louis and Bert give him an expression of displeasure as he has just spoiled their fun. The annoyed teller reads the ticket and hands it back.

"You'll have to buy a new t . . . t . . . ttick . . . ti . . . ti . . . the tic . . . tick . . .," the teller tries to inform his customers the proper form of action, but unfortunately, not only is he too short for his job, but of all the words in the English language, ticket is the only one he has difficulty pronouncing.

Impatient to hear the rest, Louis helps the teller along. "Ticket."

"Yeah thanks. Sorry, I have trouble with that word," the teller replies embarrassed. They stand looking at each other for an awkward minute, and then he continues, "You have to buy a new one for the train back to Kansas City."

"We already have tickets," Bert tells him.

"You missed your train. It'll cost more money for another ti . . . ti . . . tic . . . tick . . . "

Observing the oddity before them the brothers forget to help out with the word. Finally Louis remembers and impatiently offers, "Ticket?"

"Yeah," the teller replies.

"Isn't there any other way to get there? Another train?" Alby asks. The teller looks at his schedule.

"Nope. Not 'less you join up with the wagon train heading back down the Chisholm Trail. They stop in here on the way back from Abilene. They might take you in."

"Who do we see?" Bert questions.

"Ben Taylor's in town. He's the trail boss. He'd be over at the Silver Spur Saloon," the teller offers. He pulls himself up so he can see them as they turn to walk away. "You're not planning to go in there with those duds on, are you?"

The brothers examine each other's clothes. Not seeing any problem with their wardrobe, they shrug it off. As they walk toward the exit, another customer enters. The customer searches for the teller.

"Hello? Is anyone here?" the customer inquires.

"Down here."

The brothers smile then step out into the street. They are faced with horses, wagons, stray dogs, and men and woman walking briskly to their destinations in the bustling town. Louis takes a deep breath then realizes that he's inhaled a ghastly smell.

Coughing, Louis manages to ask, "What is that dreadful smell?" They all look down slowly and see that they are standing in fresh horse manure.

"Oh my God, people do it right in the middle of the street!" Bert exclaims. Louis and Alby look at him strangely.

"It's the horses, Bert." Alby explains as he shakes his head at his brother's naiveté.

Bert looks down again. "Oh, that's why there's so much."

The boys spot the Silver Spur Saloon across the street. As they head in that direction they shake the manure from their boots.

They enter the establishment and scan the crowd. Behind the bar are a mirror, a hanging gas lamp, shelves, and a cabinet with a spur painted in silver on the front. Two bartenders wearing a vest, tie and white apron serve drinks to some wranglers in short sleeves and suspenders leaning against the bar. Other westerners are engaged in conversation at the bar. In the back of the room, a group of ranchers wear trousers made of a material the brothers are unfamiliar with and kerchiefs hung around their necks. They stand behind a few well-dressed card sharks who wear no necktie deeming them uncomfortable due to the prospect of something tied around their necks. Some dance hall girls make their way around the room generating laughter and wolf calls. The boy's mouths fall open unused to seeing such liberal ladies.

As the brothers gather themselves, they approach the bar. One of the dance girls whistles at them and then comments on their city duds. The brothers look at each other's sack coat, vest, and hat and realize how out of place they really are. Louis shrugs then steps up to the bar, squeezing between two tough looking cowpokes, Dan and Pete.

"Excuse me, gentlemen," Louis politely utters. The two men look at Louis and then at his brothers waiting behind him. Dan and Pete both sniff.

Irritated, Dan asks, "What'd you call me, slicker?"

Pete laughs and takes a shot of whiskey. "I believe he called you a gentleman."

Dan gets in Louis' face and gives him a mean look. "You callin' me a girly, mister?"

Alby steps up. "What I believe my brother was trying to say—"

Pete puts his hand on Alby's chest and pushes him back. "This is between Dan and the slicker here."

Alby's eyes look to Bert. Louis looks to his brothers, wondering what he did wrong and where to go from here. They shrug their shoulders.

"Well, slicker?" Dan presses on.

"I ah . . . well I . . . ah . . . " Louis stammers, unsure of what to say.

Dan looks Louis over. "Give him a gun, Pete. Let's see what this slicker's made of." Pete slides his gun down the bar. It stops next to Louis. He eyes the gun and then Dan. Dan places his hand on his gun. A click is heard. Dan freezes and turns his eyes to the right.

"I believe one of the slickers has a peashooter in your ear, Dan," Pete warns.

Dan rolls his eyes to the right to get a glimpse of his attacker. "I kin see that, Pete."

Alby has the Derringer shoved into Dan's ear. The patrons at the bar move back as they see the gun.

"Alby, you have a gun in his ear. Is it loaded?" Bert questions nervously.

"I think so," Alby replies.

"What?" Dan asks unable to believe what he has just heard.

"I'm sure it is," Alby reassures everyone, including himself.

"Are you sure? I didn't—" Bert continues.

"Yes, BERT, I'm sure," Alby retorts between clenched teeth.

"So you're SURE?" Dan asks impatiently.

Bert moves around to see if he can see the bullets. "Bert, what are you doing?" Alby asks. Bert moves his head near Dan and tries to see inside the barrel. The bar patrons begin moving closer, curious as to whether the gun is loaded.

Dan turns his eyes to Bert. "How many bullets are in it . . . exactly?"

"One?" Louis now wants to know.

"One?" Dan asks.

"Two. There are two bullets in it," Alby reassures. Dan looks at the brothers, asking himself whether there are actually any bullets at all in the gun. Meanwhile Bert has maneuvered onto the bar and is leaning on Dan, bending his hat down over his eyes, irritating him even more.

"Bert." Alby says behind clenched teeth.

"I think I can see the bullets," Bert finally affirms. Everyone in the bar begins murmuring, discussing Dan's peculiar situation. Bert climbs down and repositions himself next to Alby.

"Why don't YOU just look?" Louis asks Alby. Alby looks at him momentarily as if he'd lost his mind, then back to Dan.

Dan smirks at the suggestion. "Yeah, why don't YOU look?"

Looking at Louis, Alby states, "I can't look I've got the gun on him."

Louis figures it out. He points to Dan and says, "Have him look." Dan's eyes dart to Louis. Alby looks at the gun, then Dan. Alby grabs the small gun with both hands. The patrons move in closer to get a look.

"Look in the gun and see," Alby says to Dan.

"Me?"

"Yeah." Alby pulls the gun back and moves it towards Dan's eyes. Dan pulls back slowly; beads of sweat forming on his brow. The crowd moves in closer.

"What's the problem, boys?" A large man in his forties, dressed in dirty trail gear stands behind them. Smelling the horse manure, he sniffs for its source.

"We were just looking for Ben Taylor," Alby remarks.

"I'm Ben Taylor. What can I do for you?" Without waiting for a response he looks at Dan and Pete wondering why they're still standing around. "Dan, Pete, get over to dry goods and get those supplies that you were supposed to be getting." Dan rolls his eyes to the gun, waiting. Ben notices and turns to Alby. "Mister, you can put that popgun away now."

Alby lowers the gun and the two cowpokes walk away toward the door. Dan rubs his ear and looks back at Alby. "City slickers," he says under his breath.

Ben walks over to his table where two other cowhands, Luke and Dutch, are already seated. The brothers follow. Ben eyes them and then says, "Look, uhh—"

"Name is Alby Matheson, these are my brothers, Louis and Bert. We need to get to Red Rock." Alby states.

"I'd like to take you to Red Rock, but I've already got three full wagons. Sorry, boys." The three brothers lean in together and discuss the situation. They break up and Alby makes an offer.

"We'll pay twenty dollars each." Alby offers.

Dutch jumps in, "For that kind of money, I'd carry you to San Antonio on my back." Ben gives Dutch a hard look. "Sorry, boss."

Ben re-evaluates the brothers. "Okay. I'll take you, boys. Twenty-five each. We head out in the morning. Join up at the west end of town." The brothers nod in agreement and start to walk away when Ben adds, "And boys . . . ," they turn around, "get rid of those slicker clothes. There's some rough riding ahead and Indians in the territory. If they see those clothes they might get some strange notion we're carrying something more than just folks."

"Indians?" Ably, Louis, and Bert ask in unison.

Later that morning, the boys head over to the Newton Hotel. Before entering they scrape the horse manure from their shoes with some sticks. The brothers approach the desk and drop their bags. The desk clerk looks up at them. He sniffs. He then lifts his arm and sniffs. Not satisfied that he's discovered the origin of the aroma, he sniffs his hands. He then leans forward toward the brothers and sniffs. He leans back and looks them over, shaking his head.

"Three rooms for tonight." Alby states.

The clerk turns the registrar around. "Sign here. Six bits each room." Alby signs the registrar.

"What's that in American?" Bert asks, confused.

The clerk looks at them oddly. "That is American - dollar and a half a piece." Alby pays with five ones. The clerk gives him change.

The brothers turn to go upstairs, but Alby stops and turns. "Is there a place that we can buy some clothes?" he asks the clerk.

He points with his fountain pen toward the street. The brothers look out the window and see a dry goods store.

Before going upstairs the brothers decide to take Ben's advice and buy some western gear as quickly as possible so as not to raise any suspicions from the Indians.

After a small delay, the dry goods store door swings open revealing a cowboy in a double-breasted red shirt, a bandanna expertly tied around his neck, denim trousers, pointed boots, and a wide brimmed hat. He walks out, followed by two other cowboys, also with double-breasted red shirts, bandannas expertly tied around their necks, denim trousers, pointed boots, and wide brimmed hats. The newly converted cowboys beam from ear to ear, satisfied with their choices in the latest western fashion.

They stroll around town, with bags in hand, to show off their duds before heading back to the hotel. People stop and stare at the odd looking cowboys in red.

CHAPTER FOUR
Trail ride

The following morning the brothers march down Newton Street toward the end of town. There they meet with three covered wagons sitting in a row. On one of the wagons, *Mrs. Twinky's Buns* is written on the side. A group is gathered around Ben. Perched on their horses, Luke, Dutch, Dan, and Pete watch the brothers approach. The people step apart to get a look at the newcomers. Ben moves forward to introduce everyone.

"These are the Matheson brothers. They'll be riding along with us." Ben motions to a short bald man and a large lady. "This is John and Mary Twinky. They're also going to Red Rock." Pointing to a family of five, Ben continues with the introductions. "And this is the Turner family. They're going to San Antonio." Nodding to a black couple he states, "And this is Mr. and Mrs. Wilson. They're going to Dallas. You boys will be riding with the Twinkys."

A grimy old man with whiskers steps up and spits. The brothers look down at the brown gob of spittle on the ground, then back at him.

The man introduces himself to the brothers. "And I'm Buck. Everyone calls me Cookie. I do the grub. Ain't fancy, but it'll keep your gut from yackin'."

Cookie blows his nose with his fingers and wipes his hand on his pants. He then offers his hand to the brothers. They look at his hand in disgust. Buck suddenly bursts out laughing and walks away. The people break away and climb into the wagons. Ben mounts his horse, while laughing, and trots to the head of the train. He waves forward and trots off. The Twinky's wagon starts to pull away and the brothers scramble to jump into the back as it moves off.

Bert, Alby, and Louis, sit behind Mr. and Mrs. Twinky in the covered wagon as it bounces along the Chisholm Trail. The late afternoon sun radiates down on the group while dust rolls up behind the wagons making it a slow grueling journey to their destinations. To make matters worse, Mrs. Twinky, who has a very large behind, farts with every bounce of the wagon. The brothers' faces grimace at each puff of smelly air. Finally, with no other protection, they pull up their bandannas to cover their noses. Mrs. Twinky turns and sees that they have their bandannas on.

"Gets dusty, don't it?" she confirms. The brothers nod in enthusiastic agreement.

As the sun settles in the horizon, the brothers finally find some reprieve. The wagons are circled and everyone dismounts. Cookie folds outs his chuck wagon and prepares to fix up a pot of beans over an open fire. The brothers sit near the fire and watch the other travelers. Mrs. Twinky approaches the beans and leans over to smell them. She smiles and looks at the boys. "Mmmmm, beans, my favorite." She walks over to the kitchen wagon to get a plate. The brothers look at each other, cringing at the thought of her eating beans.

With the sun completely down, Ben and his men ride in and tie up the horses. They approach the campsite. Ben carries over three rifles and throws them down in front of the brothers. Several boxes of shells follow. They look at the firearms and shells lying in front of them.

"You won't get close enough to an Indian to put that peashooter in his ear. Better if you were carrying one of these," Ben firmly suggests.

"Indians? Where?" Louis asks as he frantically turns his head in all directions.

"We're inside Indian territory. Usually they ain't no problem, just come in for food or money for being on their land. That's usually. Lately, it's been a lot more," Ben explains then walks toward the cook's wagon and gets a plate. The brothers look at each other with apprehension.

"Maybe this wasn't such a good idea. We didn't count on Indians. Maybe we should go back," Bert suggests.

"Yeah, Alby, maybe Bert's right," Louis agrees.

"We couldn't go back even if we wanted. Our money is almost gone. After we pay Ben, that's about it," Alby declares. Bert and Louis stare at him with desperate eyes. Alby feels uncomfortable and gets up to walk around. Louis and Bert pick up the rifles and look them over then carefully lay them back down. Alby walks to the outside of the camp. He turns and bumps into Dan. Dan grabs him by his jacket and pulls him up toward him.

"Shouldn't be out here. Things unfamiliar to a man have a way of gittin to him," Dan threatens. Alby starts to pull away, but Dan takes out his gun and puts it to Alby's ear. "How do YOU like it city slicker?" Dan slides the gun down at an angle, pulls the hammer back, and with his free hand tightens his grip on Alby. As he pulls him tighter, Alby's gun pops through the hole in his jacket and is now pointing at Dan's crotch. Dan feels an unexpected sensation and looks at Alby strangely, as if he were doing something unmanly. Alby has no idea that the gun is up against Dan's crotch. Unsure of what's going on, Dan slowly looks down. He eyes the little gun barrel resting on his crotch. His eyes widen as it dawns on him the position that he's in. He slowly looks back up at Alby. In a high pitched, shaky voice he states, "Yur pea shooter is aimed at my privates." Dan then drops his gun and pretends as if he had been playing around the whole time. "Aw heck, just kiddin' ya."

Dan straightens Alby's jacket and shirt and smiles a semi-toothless smile. Alby turns and slowly walks back to the camp, looking back at Dan over his shoulder on the way. He sees Dan spit then disappears from sight. Dan breathes a sigh of relief as he looks down at his crotch.

As Alby enters back into the campsite, he sees that the others are sitting around the fire eating. Moving closer he notices small oblong cakes on some trays. He steps up to Louis and Bert, who are devouring them. Bert looks up with his mouth full of cake and white icing on his lips.

"You've got to try these, Alby. They're delicious," Bert earnestly recommends. Alby looks around at everyone who seems to be equally enjoying the cakes.

"What are they?" he asks.

"Mrs. Twinky makes them. They're Mrs. Twinky's Buns," Louis tells him.

Mrs. Twinky approaches with another tray of the cakes, offering one to Alby. He takes one, bites into it, and smiles.

At that moment, Ben, Luke and Dutch gallop into the camp and spring off their horses. "A small party of Indians has spotted our fire. They're coming in," Ben warns. Everyone jumps up. Ben and Luke run to the wagons and climb in. They position themselves with their rifles. "I want everyone to remain calm. They probably just want some food and supplies." The party waits patiently and silently as the impending gallop of horses is heard. Ben puts his gun away and faces the approaching party.

Five Indians ride in slowly, looking around at the wagons and the travelers. They silently wait as Ben approaches them. Ben waves his hand offering the food and hospitality of the camp.

The leader, Chief Long Nose, slowly climbs down and walks to the cooking pot of beans. He dips his fingers into the pot and tastes the beans. He makes an unpleasant face and spits it out. The platter of cakes catches his eyes. He looks to Ben for approval. Ben nods. The chief picks one up, examines it and then looks suspiciously at the group of travelers. They all smile stiffly. He sniffs it then pokes it with his finger, causing the icing to cover the tip of it. He smells the icing then tastes it. His eyes light up with delight. He bites into the cake and slowly chews it as if it were food from the gods. He smiles at the travelers and holds up the twinky in triumph. The other Indians dismount to join the chief.

After some time of sampling the chief and his warriors mount their horses. A cloth wrapped around a bunch of the cakes is offered to Chief Long Nose. He accepts it with much gratitude. One of his warriors leans over to take one but the chief, refusing to share, turns his horse and gallops away.

Cookie walks to his pot of beans and sticks his finger in and tastes them. He looks around to see if anyone is looking and spits it out.

Out on the trail the next day, Alby and Bert drive the wagon while Louis and the Twinkys play cards in the back, unaware that Chief Long Nose and his warriors have followed them. It isn't until nightfall, when the wagons are circled, that it becomes known. Chief Long Nose and his warriors enter the camp. Obvious they are looking for something

Ben invites them to dismount. The chief obliges. They talk privately and an apparent agreement is made as more of Mrs. Twinky's cakes are bundled in a cloth and handed to the chief. Satisfied, the Indians wave and ride off.

A persistent rain aggravates the third day of the journey. The first wagon gets stuck. Following the trail riding code of etiquette, everyone gets out to push. The brothers, unused to such grueling work, reluctantly follow suit. To make matters worse, Bert, due to his inexperience, falls face down in the mud. The others laugh. Mrs. Twinky, who feels sorry for Bert, offers to make him a few extra cakes.

As night falls, Mrs. Twinky has a large stove going and is making more cakes. Bert is excited to receive his extra share, but once again, Chief Long Nose and his warriors appear requesting more. Pitifully, Bert has to renege his to keep the peace. Later, however, the Indians are seen playing cards with the brothers and all ends well with them.

The last day of the trail ride for the three brothers and the Twinkys is uneventful. By mid-afternoon the wagon train crests a hill. Ben gallops to the top and looks down at the town of Red Rock, Texas. The wagon train pulls up behind him and stops. Two of the covered wagons pull up for camp while the Twinky's wagon drives toward town. Ben gives a quick wave and turns his horse to rejoin the remaining party.

Alby, Bert, and Louis look out from the covered wagon and wave goodbye to Ben and the others. They roll to the edge of town where they pull up and stop at a large tent with a sign. The brothers climb out to say their goodbyes to the Twinkys.

"Thanks for everything," Alby, Louis, and Bert say in unison.

"We'll see you boys around town," Mrs. Twinky reassures. The wagon moves away, leaving the brothers standing in the middle of the street.

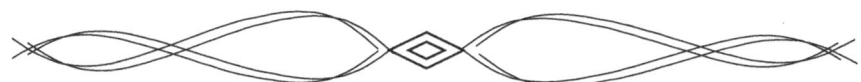

CHAPTER FIVE
A Crooked Business Deal

The brothers scan the town for the general store as described in the ad. Louis spots one across the street and starts walking toward the building. As he approaches, he excitedly picks up his pace. The other brothers follow. A sign above the door reads *Foster's General Store.* They gawk in the window and are delighted with all the merchandise they see. Stepping back to admire it, they look at each other and smile.

"Nice place, huh?" a man says from behind. They turn to find a short, well-dressed man chewing on a cigar. "I'm Mayor Dunhill. You must be the Matheson brothers. I've been expecting you." The mayor holds out a contract and a fountain pen to Alby. "First, lets get a small detail out of the way . . . the contract."

Alby takes it, still in awe of the store. He signs the contract and hands it to his brothers. They sign it and hand it back. The mayor puts the contract in his suit coat.

Looking at the store, Louis states, "It's more than we expected."

The mayor looks the building over. "It should be. It's not the one you bought."

"What?" Alby asks surprised.

The mayor turns and begins walking. "If you'll follow me, I'll take you to your store."

They walk to the other end of town to a store that is dirty and rundown. The door creaks open and several rats scurry as the brothers and the mayor enter. The shelves are nearly bare. The brothers look around in dismay.

"This is our store?" Alby asks with disgust. He exits the general store with his brothers trailing. The mayor pursues them.

"Whoa, fellas, where ya going?" Mayor Dunhill asks. The brothers stop and turn to the mayor.

"Deal's off, Mayor. We want our money back."

"Sorry, the town's already spent the money you sent us. Besides, people around here don't take too well to folks backing out of deals. They might take justice in their own hands. Folks out here have strange notions about protecting their town." He walks past the brothers and slaps Louis on the shoulder. "Ah, hell! A little paint and a few signs, and I'm sure things will work out just fine." He walks away pleased, humming to himself. "Let me know if you need anything. See you boys around."

The brothers look at each other then back at the rundown store. Not knowing what else to do they decide to get down to business and begin cleaning the store. Louis paints the badly repaired counter, Bert makes a new sign, and Alby takes inventory. While examining a desk, he discovers a drawer full of guns and gun parts. A white sheriff's hat and several badges are found lying under some debris as well. Louis quits painting and wanders over to Alby. Bert stops and joins them. Louis picks up the badge.

"Hey, look at this kid's stuff. We could sell this for a quarter," Louis says. Bert grabs the badge and bites it. He looks at it.

"Are you crazy? This is worth at least fifty cents," Bert retorts. Alby grabs the badge away from Bert.

"This stuff is real. Somebody left it here," Alby surmises.

"Well we own the store, so it's ours now," Louis replies as he grabs the badge back. "And if we want to sell it, we can." He picks up the sheriff's hat and puts it on.

Alby sits down behind the desk and opens the top drawer finding wanted posters. He opens another filled with gun parts and tools.

Suddenly the door swings open and a rancher rushes in. Eyeing the three and their matching outfits, he steps up to Louis, who has just put on the sheriff's hat. As the rancher moves toward him, Louis backs away.

"Are you the new sheriff?" the rancher asks.

"What?" Louis asks, unsure if he heard it right.

"It's that cheatin' Casey Putnam. He sold me a calf and now he's got it back at his ranch. It's toting my brand. I just want my calf back," the rancher complains. Louis turns his eyes to Bert and Alby.

"I'm afraid there's been a mistake. He's not the sheriff." Alby informs him.

The rancher takes off his hat and scratches his head. He walks to the side door and exits. He can be seen looking up above the door at a sign. He motions for the brothers to come out. The brothers exit and stand next to the rancher.

Pointing to the sign the rancher asks, "Well then, what does that sign say?" The brothers look up.

"Sheriff's Office," they all say in unison. After apologizing to the rancher the brothers decide to nail the side door of the general store closed so as not to allow in any more sheriff seeking visitors.

"I can't believe we bought the sheriff's office!" Louis exclaims.

"Nailing that door won't change things." The brothers turn to see the mayor standing behind them in the store. He hands the contract to Alby.

"When you bought the store ...you also bought the sheriff's office. Buy the sheriff's office, you become the sheriff. Should have read the fine print," the mayor informs them. He walks back toward the door, then turns to face the brothers. "Remember the townsfolk and their ways of justice. Good day . . . Sheriffs." He exits.

Bewildered and worried, Bert and Louis turn to Alby.

"What are we gonna do, Alby?" Louis asks nervously.

Alby stares at the contract. His trance is disrupted by the sound of tapping on the front door. In the doorway, holding an apple pie is a beautiful redhead, dressed in the latest fashions. The brothers stare at her. She cocks her head.

"Greetings. May I come in?" she asks already making her way in the door.

"Sure." Alby replies shyly.

She walks over and places the pie on the sheriff's desk. "Allow me to introduce myself. My name is Annie Marie. I'm the owner and manager of the Longhorn Saloon next door." She holds out her hand to Alby. Trying to assess their confusion and gloomy expressions, she asks, "Someone die?"

"It seems we've been swindled by the mayor," Alby tells her.

"The mayor?" She laughs as she walks around the store, occasionally picking up discarded remnants of the last proprietor.

"What's so funny?" Alby wonders.

Annie picks up a dust-covered badge from the floor and polishes it with the edge of her dress. "Oh, he's the mayor all right, but not for the people of Red Rock. He's McMartin's mayor. The real mayor and sheriff both met with mishaps . . . fatal mishaps."

"Who's McMartin?" Louis inquires.

"He owns this town. Well just about all of it. You can bet that McMartin is behind this. He's usually behind anything that stinks to high heaven." Annie replies as she walks back to the desk to prop up the newly shined badge. "And what they've done to you with this store sure stinks."

The brothers sniff, look down at their boots and check for horse manure. They shrug their shoulders. Alby looks back up at Annie.

"We put everything we had into this place," Alby informs her.

"There goes our inheritance. Maybe Dad was right about us," Louis says. The statement perks Annie's curiosity. She raises her eyebrows and turns to Alby.

"We can't get our inheritance back in Chicago, if we don't make a profit," Alby clarifies.

Annie walks to the empty shelves and rakes her hand across it. Dust flies. "I hate to break the news to you, but you'd have better chances of making a profit as sheriffs than running this broken down store." Annie's attention is diverted as she hears crashing noises and gunshots coming from her saloon. "Sorry, boys. I have to go before they tear the saloon down. Good luck . . . looks like you'll need it." She lifts her skirt and runs out of the store.

Alby sits slowly, his eyes glazed over. Bert and Louis get in his face to look at his eyes.

"He's got that look again," Bert alerts Louis.

Louis waves his hand slowly in front of Alby's glazed over eyes. Louis notes a smile slowly creeping over his brother's face.

Later that evening in the mayor's office, John McMartin, a large man, with graying hair meets with Mayor Dunhill to discuss his future plans for the city.

As McMartin stands at the window, he stares at the rundown general store across the street. Without looking at the mayor he states,

"Now the town's got their sheriff." Laughing at the thought he adds, "If you can call them that." The mayor walks over with a shot of whisky and hands it to his boss, who gulps it with pleasure. "While they're chasing their citified tails, I'll be running out every homesteader for fifty miles. Soon, we'll be one of the largest suppliers of beef in Texas . . . and you and I will be very wealthy men.

The Mayor pours more liquor into McMartin's glass. They toast.

CHAPTER SIX
Sheriffs Incorporated

Early in the morning, Alby stands in the street, pointing and waiving his arms. "Right there. That's it," Alby says as he directs Louis and Bert on the perfect positioning of the new sign.

Louis hammers in the last nail as Bert holds it in place. Satisfied, they climb down from the ladders and join Alby on the street. They stand back and look at the sign that reads: SHERIFFS INCORPORATED. Other townsfolk stop to look as well. The brothers turn to them, tipping their hats in a gesture of greeting, then walk back into the office.

Inside, appearances have improved as well. The grime has been cleaned up and the clutter organized. A large sign hangs on the wall displaying their services and fees: Cattle Rustling $1.00, Bank Robberies $20.00, Fights $2.50, Horse Thieving $3.00, all other requests are negotiable.

As the boys make themselves comfortable in their new work place, an old woman in her seventies, Betsy Whitaker, wanders into the office and moseys up to the counter. Louis steps up to help her.

"Hello, ma'am. Welcome to Sheriffs Incorporated. What can we do for you?" Louis offers.

She looks at him oddly and then looks around the office. "I'm sorry. I was looking for the sheriff's office."

"You've come to the right place," Louis reassures her.

"Fine! My neighbor, Lyle Branagan, is putting up his fences on my property. I told him to stop and he said that an old hag like me couldn't do nothing about it."

Louis thinks for a minute. He then walks over to talk with Alby. Alby looks over at the woman. They talk and Louis walks back.

"One dollar, ma'am."

"One dollar and you'll make him move those posts back?"

"Yes, ma'am."

"Can I watch?" Betsy asks.

Louis thinks about it, then looks to Alby for approval. Alby nods. "Yes, ma'am, you can."

Betsy takes out a wrinkled dollar, hands it to him then asks, "When?"

Louis puts the money in a drawer and answers, "As soon as we get some horses, we'll follow you out, ma'am."

Later that day at the livery stable, Alby, Louis, and Bert examine an old nag. They immediately notice the poor horse's swayback with its bowed back and pendulous belly. Bert bends over to look more closely at the drooping abdomen. He pushes it in with his finger. Louis steps to the front of the horse and looks at its face. The horse is asleep. He snaps his fingers, trying to get it to wake up. They look at the blacksmith.

"This is the sheriff's horse?" Alby asks unenthused. The blacksmith nods. Bert and Louis look at Alby.

"What are we suppose to ride?" Bert asks.

Without discussion, Alby gets on the unfortunate nag. The other two shrug their shoulders and follow suit. After tracking down Betsy's wagon, the forlorn swayback trails reluctantly behind, carrying the trio to the old woman's ranch. The townsfolk step out onto the street to see the sight. They laugh and point at the new sheriffs.

Betsy pulls up near the fence where some rough looking cowboys are hard at work pounding posts into her land. Lyle Branagan sits on his horse, overseeing the progress. The swayback nag with the three brothers arrives shortly after the wagon. When the nag stops, the brothers fall off into a pile. Branagan looks down at the brothers and then the old horse, which wheezes then slowly falls over dead.

Looking at the horse in dismay, the brothers brush themselves off and stumble over to Branagan. Betsy stands with her hands on her hips, motioning at Branagan with her head. They look up at the man on the horse.

"As sheriffs of Red Rock, we order you to move the posts back off this lady's property," Alby demands.

Louis and Bert pat Alby on the back as if that was easily accomplished. Branagan and his men gather, and then laugh at the brother's simplicity. Branagan stops laughing to look the sheriffs over more carefully. He notices that they aren't packing guns.

"You fellas ain't carrying guns. Don't believe I've ever heard of lawmen that didn't carry guns."

One of Branagan's men, comments, "Hey boss, I heard that in England lawmen don't carry firearms." In a failed British accent he continues, "Hey mate, ah, ah, I'm a lawman without a gun. Stop there. Hey were going to jail, mate . . . " Everyone stares at him, unimpressed.

Studying the brothers, Branagan asks, "You fellas from England? Maybe you're in the wrong country." Branagan and his men laugh again as Branagan climbs down from his horse. He stands in front of the three brothers, draws his gun, and puts it to Louis' nose.

"Is that it? You three in the wrong country?"

"No. We're in the right country," Louis responds.

"That's right. We're not in England. We know that." Bert says smiling. Everyone looks at him irritated for giving his brainless input.

"This here is a Mr. Colt .45. He can put a hole in a man the size of a silver dollar," Branagan tells them. He then puts his gun up to his ear as if he were listening to it. "What's that Mr. Colt?" He listens again. "You say you want to put some holes in these fellas?" He pulls the hammer back and puts the gun to Louis' nose. "Should I let him?"

Alby steps forward to intervene just as Branagan shoves the gun into the air and fires. Startled, the brothers step back.

"Now git! Before Mr. Colt gets mad . . . Sheriffs."

As the brothers slowly back away, Branagan becomes impatient and starts firing at their feet. Trying to evade the bullets, the brothers turn and run in the direction of town. The crooks laugh.

Betsy shouts at the fleeing sheriffs. "I want my dollar back!"

One of the men steps up alongside Branagan, who has his gun dangling next to his side. He bends over and puts his ear to the gun to see if he can hear it talking. Branagan thumps him with the gun. The hired hand straightens and rubs his head where he got tapped.

It is not until night has fallen that the brothers return to their new office. Worn out from the long walk back to town, they collapse into chairs, and look at each other with defeat in their eyes.

"He's right. Lawmen are supposed to carry guns," Louis says.

"We don't know anything about guns. If we were carrying guns, he'd have shot us," Alby retorts.

"We'd be dead right now," Bert adds.

"We can't be sheriffs if we can't protect ourselves," Louis exclaims.

Alby doesn't respond. He stares into space, lost in thought again. Bert and Louis stand and look at him. "Goodnight, Alby." Louis drags himself toward the back room. Bert follows.

"Goodnight, Alby." Alby continues in his pensive state and doesn't respond.

Alone in the room, Alby snaps out of his meditative state and quickly stands. "I got it!" He looks around, but his brothers are long gone.

Alby has an idea he thinks could work. He starts immediately on his creation. Fighting sleep, he works feverishly all night. Gun parts, springs, pins, and other pieces are spread all over the desk. He cuts and measures parts, fits portions together, eyes his work, and continues to assemble. Alby pops open a mold and dumps some metal balls on the table. He pours some black goo from a pot and inspects round black rubber covered balls. Before long morning arrives.

Bert and Louis enter the room. They notice Alby has fallen asleep at the desk Three strange looking gun belts lay on the desk. Louis picks one of the contraptions up to examine it, but has no idea what it is. As he puts it back on the desk Alby awakes and looks around. He tries to straighten his neck. It cracks. Looking up at his brothers he says elatedly, "They're done."

Bert and Louis ask in unison, "What's done?"

Alby, excited to show them his invention, takes the boys outside behind the office. The brothers don Alby's new 'automatic firing guns', as Alby finishes putting up a man-sized target. He walks back and adjusts the apparatus strapped around his own waist. His brothers casually observe him.

"Here goes," Alby states. He aligns his hips with the target then hits the palm-sized red paddles on both of the holsters. The guns flip up at amazing speed, automatically firing. The target is riddled in a matter of seconds. Alby hits a small blue paddle and the guns automatically flip back into their holster-like clips.

Bert and Louis, with their mouths drooped open, look at the target and then to Alby.

"Try it," Alby proposes.

Bert and Louis snap out of their amazed stupor. They align their hips and hit their paddles as instructed. The guns automatically flip out and finish shooting the target to pieces. They hit the blue paddles and the weapons holster. Alby walks up to his brothers and points out other features.

"Now we need to test it on someone," Alby states. He and Louis look at Bert.

"Wait a minute . . . " Bert hesitates.

Within minutes, Bert has large pieces of mattress tied around his chest. A bucket with two cutout holes sits on his head. He stands against the exterior office wall. Louis and Alby stand in front of him, positioning themselves to fire.

In a muffled voice, Bert tries to get his brothers attention. "Guys? Guys? I changed my mind."

"It's okay, I've removed the bullets. We're just firing metal balls," Alby reassures him. "Ok . . . now!"

Panicking, Bert yells in a muffled voice, "Metal balls?"

Alby and Louis hit the paddles as Bert turns trying to escape. Bert is hit with a barrage of little missiles. They bounce off of his bucket helmet and hit the padding. One hits him in the groin and he doubles over. The firing stops.

Alby and Louis bend over the collapsed Bert. Louis removes the bucket. Bert opens his eyes and looks up at them. With serious pain in his voice, Bert says, "That hurt." Louis stands and smiles at Alby.

CHAPTER SEVEN
Making a Profit

Later that night, at the Longhorn Saloon, Jack Barkley, a rough and tough cowpoke, is drunk and in the midst of a barroom brawl. He throws another cowpoke over the bar, causing Annie and her bartender, Sam, to duck for cover. Waiting a few seconds, they slowly peek up from behind the bar to check for flying debris.

Seeing that its safe she turns to Sam. "Get the sheriffs," she orders. The bartender observes the fight, surmising the situation and wondering if he can make it to the door without injury. A table crashes against the wall. Annie sees his hesitation. "Well, go!" she yells ignoring his fear.

Jack spots the bartender running out of the saloon. "Yeah, go get the sheriff. Bring him on. Sheriffs don't scare me." He throws a chair at the bartender who just makes it out the door.

As he exits he sees the three brothers saunter confidently up to the saloon. The sheriffs know there's trouble, without having been told, when a cowpoke flies out the door and rolls on the ground. The brothers enter and stand at the swinging doors.

Jack stops punching the cowpoke mid-swing. He lets the limp man drop as he turns to them. He eyes the brothers and the weird looking contraptions they're wearing. "Who in the hell are you?" he asks heatedly.

"The sheriffs," Alby proudly responds.

"See the badge, " Louis states as he points innocently to his hat, unaware that his badge as well as those of his brothers are on the back of their cowboy hats.

Bert looks at Louis' hat and sees the blunder. He reaches over and nonchalantly turns it around. Then Alby sees Bert has also donned his hat the same way. Shaking his head, he reaches over and carefully places Bert's hat in its proper place. Then Bert looks at Alby and sees that he has made the same mistake. He reaches over and clumsily turns his brother's hat around as well.

Jack looks at Annie and then back at the sheriffs. He laughs and steps forward. "Who wants to die first?"

Alby confidently steps forward. "You're going to jail."

As Jack reaches for his gun, Alby hits the red paddles. His guns flip out and fires. Ball bearings hit Jack all over his body before his gun can even clear the holster. One coated ball bearing bounces off a wall and continues to bounce around the room, until finally striking Jack in the forehead. His eyes roll and he falls forward, his hand still clutching his holstered weapon. Everyone in the saloon eyes Alby as they hear the clicking and springing of Alby's guns snapping back into his holster clips. The bar patrons are in awe.

Louis walks to Annie and hands her a bill. She reads it then hands it to the bartender. She looks at Louis, crosses her arms, and smiles. "Pay 'em," she says to Sam.

Bert and Louis drag a limp Jack through the swinging doors out onto the street toward the sheriff's office. The mayor steps out of the darkness and watches them. He throws his cigar down and walks away.

Alby enters the sheriff's office, followed by his brothers who are helping a wobbly Jack back on his feet. They stop and look at Alby.

"What do we do with him? We don't have a jail," Bert comments.

Alby walks to the desk and opens a drawer. He takes out a pair of handcuffs and holds them up. "I guess we'll have to make one. Right now, just handcuff him to that post." He tosses the handcuffs to Bert.

Bert looks at them and then the post, not sure how it's done. He wraps the handcuffs around the pole. Then holds the ends out and looks at Jack. Jack rubs the bump on his head while staring at Bert, wondering what the hell he's doing. Bert looks at the handcuffs, and then at his prisoner, trying to figure it out.

Not able to take it any longer Jack says, "You ain't the fastest horse in the corral, are ya?"

Bert leans against the pole, his feelings hurt. He moves the handcuffs around and looks up at Jack, his eyes pleading for help. Jack gives in. "Ah, hell." He moves closer to the pole to allow Bert to finish cuffing his hands around the pole. Jack inspects the work and groggily nods his approval. Bert pats Jack on the shoulder and walks away. The prisoner looks up, just now figuring out what he has done to himself.

Late that night, in the back room, the brothers, trying to sleep on two cots, have pillows over their heads to shield them from the clamor Jack is making.

"Hey, you can't leave me here like this. It ain't right," Jack persists.

Louis gives up and sits up on the cot. As he scans the room, he spots a pair of socks next to Bert's boots. He does a double take because the socks appear to be standing on their own. He picks them up and starts to smell them. Grimacing, he pulls away quickly. As he rolls up the socks, they make crunching noises. He exits the back room.

Jack, who is up against the post in the middle of the room with his hands cuffed behind his back, gets the rolled up pair of socks stuffed into his mouth. He makes horrible faces as he moans and tries to scream.

The next morning, the brothers stagger into the outer office and look at Jack. He's still as they left him against the post, but his eyes are now bulged out and he appears to be unconscious. Bert recognizes the socks.

"Hey, those are mine." Bert yanks the socks out of Jack's mouth. Then the brothers realize something is really wrong with their prisoner.

"Is he dead?" Louis asks.

Bert puts his head against Jack's chest then pulls back. "There's a heartbeat."

Alby steps up and spreads his eye open. Jack doesn't move. Alby slaps him. Jack jumps and then snaps back to reality.

"I'm sorry. Really, I am. Please, let me go. I'll be a good boy. I promise."

The brothers look at him, then each other. They shrug their shoulders. Alby unlocks the handcuffs. Jack runs for the door and exits. The brothers move to the window to watch.

Jack runs to the horse-trough to splash water into his mouth. He scrapes on his tongue with his fingers. Then he splashes more water into his mouth. A woman walks by with her six-year-old son. The little boy points at Jack.

"Look Mommy. That man thinks he's a horse."

Jack snaps his head toward them, a crazed look on his face. The woman quickly pulls her son away. Jack looks back at the water in the trough and sees a chunk of horse manure floating. He screams and runs away.

Alby, perplexed by the cowboy's actions, asks his brothers, "What's wrong with him?"

Before they can answer, Betsy Whitaker stomps into the office. She stops and looks them over.

"I'm here to git my dollar back." Alby reaches without hesitation into his pocket and holds out a dollar. She snaps it away.

"You still having trouble with your neighbor, Mrs. Whitaker?" Louis asks.

"Hell yes! You three just made things worse," Betsy shouts.

"Bert and Louis can go out with you to take care of that," he says to Betsy. "Right Bert? Louis?"

She looks at Bert and Louis with an evil eye.

"Yes, ma'am." Bert hesitates due to what happened last time they helped Betsy.

"Yes, ma'am," Louis utters as well.

"How much this time?" she asks suspiciously.

"On the house," Alby states.

With a curt nod, she walks toward the door then stops to look at Bert and Louis. "Well, don't just stand there. Let's go. And this time it'd better work. You boys owe me one." She looks at Alby and asks, "Who do ya think buried that nag of yours anyway?" She exits. With eyebrows raised, Bert and Louis grab their gun belts and run after her.

Meanwhile, Alby goes to the back room of Sheriff's Incorporated to look through a pile of old equipment and supplies. He finds a large roll of wire, wrapped in brown paper. A note is attached. He pulls it off and reads it.

Dear Ben,

You asked me to make something to keep the varmints out of the garden. Well, try this. I call it barbed wire. Folks around here love it.

Your Friend,
Joe Glidden

Alby mouths the words "barbed wire." He lays the note down and strips away some of the paper to reveal a wire with razor like edges. He touches it and jerks his hand back. A smile lights up his face.

In the meantime, Louis and Bert arrive at Betsy's ranch. As she climbs down from her buckboard she states, "This time I'm bringin' my gun." She goes to fetch it when she unexpectedly discovers eight horses tied up at the back of her house.

Some time passes before Louis becomes worried. "What's taking her so long?"

Bert climbs down from his horse. "I'll check," he tells Louis. Bert enters the house. Moments later, he exits with his arms in the air followed by Betsy and seven of Branagan's men, guns drawn. Branagan steps out last and lights a cigar. Louis quickly scrambles to the buckboard at the sight.

"Looks like we have a little problem here . . . Sheriffs." Louis climbs down and is immediately surrounded by seven of Branagan's men. "Should've never came back. Now Betsy is gonna have to bury you fellas next to that nag," Branagan threatens.

He and his villainous friends laugh. Louis looks at the circle of men, moving his hands near his paddles. Branagan's men slowly reach toward their guns. He hits the paddles and turns in a circle, his eyes clinched close. When Louis opens his eyes he sees his targets lying unconscious around him in a circle. He looks at Bert, who smiles and turns to Branagan. Branagan's cigar falls from his mouth. He draws his gun and aims it at Louis.

Acting quickly, Bert rushes Branagan and forces the gun into the air as it discharges. Louis dashes to the fighting men as they struggle over the pistol. Branagan breaks Bert's hold on the gun and hits him, knocking him down.

119

Branagan turns his attention to Louis and finds him standing over his brother who lies on the ground unconscious. He turns to his enemy, enraged and wide-eyed. He swings, knocking the outlaw out cold on his feet.

Later that afternoon, Betsy's buckboard enters town and slowly moves down the street with a full load of Branagan's men. Townsfolk stop to gape and gossip. McMartin and Mayor Dunhill watch through the window as the wagon passes by.

"I thought you said these fellas would be easy," McMartin says to the mayor without taking his eyes off the brothers. The mayor is silent. McMartin turns from the window and eyes the mayor, "Branagan was supposed to run out the homesteaders around his ranch and sell to me." McMartin turns, grabs the mayor's collar and pulls the mayor toward him. "You think his property is worth anything to me now? You're starting to get on my bad side . . . Mayor." McMartin lets go and walks toward the door. He opens it and looks back. "Take care of it. If you don't, I will. When I do, I just might find a new mayor and you'll be joining the old one." He exits.

The mayor walks to the window and looks out, pulling a handkerchief from his pocket. He dabs his forehead.

As soon as the buckboard stops in front of Sheriff's Incorporated, Alby steps out from the office and looks at the pile of men. Louis and Bert climb down.

"You did it," Alby says relieved.

"Damn straight, they did it. Better than Wild Bill's Wild West show," Betsy proudly reports.

Louis holds up five dollars. Alby looks at it and smiles.

"Let's get them inside," Alby states.

Once inside, Branagan and his men begin to awaken and find themselves inside a makeshift cell made entirely of barbed wire. One of Branagan's men approaches the wire and grabs it. He quickly jerks his hand back and puts his mouth on the cut. Never having seen anything like it Louis and Bert go to inspect the strange coils.

"Where'd you get this Alby?" Louis asks as he pricks his finger. He sticks it in his mouth to comfort the small wound.

"Found it in the back room. They call it barbed wire," Alby tells him.

"They could've at least filed off the sharp things on it. Nobody's gonna want to get near this stuff when it's sharp like this," Bert comments. Alby and Louis slowly turn their heads to look at Bert, amazed at his ignorance.

Their attention is suddenly diverted when several popping noises are heard just outside their door. They run outside to investigate. They spot three young boys running off, throwing firecrackers behind them.

Relieved to find nothing serious, the brothers turn to go back inside when they see Mrs. Twinky walking toward them carrying a basket of small flags. "I see you boys have settled in. Stop by my bakeshop sometime. I might have some free samples for you." She starts away, then stops. "You ARE comin' to the Fourth of July celebration tonight, aren't you? I'm making buns and pies," she says teasingly.

"Yes, ma'am," the pleased brothers say in unison.

Mrs. Twinky moseys off as the mayor approaches. He looks in the door at the men in the makeshift jail cell. "What are you boys planning on doing with those men?" The brothers look at each other.

"What do you suggest, Mayor?" Alby asks.

"Well, the judge only comes around about every four months or so. For serious crimes, like murder, we run them over to Abilene. They have their own judge. However, we usually just fine 'em and let 'em go."

The brothers agree to fine each of the prisoners a fair price for their crimes and to set them free. Branagan's men file out in a row and pay Alby as they pass. Alby looks at the wad of money and then at the last prisoner. As Mr. Branagan steps out, Alby looks at his brothers and then back at Branagan.

"What's the charges?" Alby asks his brothers.

Louis looks the prisoner over and says, "He aimed his gun at me—"

"Besides obstructing justice, that's threatening an officer of the law," Alby says to Branagan.

"He hit me," Bert reports.

"Striking an officer of the law. That's fifty dollars in all," Alby decides.

"Fifty dollars!" Branagan can't believe his ears.

"Or we can take you to Abilene to see the judge," Alby warns.

Branagan quickly digs into his pockets. Alby looks at his brothers and smiles. The last prisoner slaps the money into Alby's hands and walks toward the door. He stops and turns.

"You don't know what you've gotten yourself into," Branagan threatens.

"Yeah, and what would that be?" Louis asks.

"Early graves." Branagan exits and slams the door. The Matheson brothers' smiles disappear.

Nevertheless, it doesn't take long for the brothers to forget the seriousness of the situation as the Fourth of July celebration gets underway.

The citizens of Red Rock gather enthusiastically at the town square while the children run down Main Street waving their sparklers energetically. Flickering oil lamps adorn the buildings and American flags hang at every available post in town. The savory aromas of barbecued meats and homemade pies and breads penetrate every nose in the vicinity. Game tables stand at equal intervals as the hosts yell out to those passing by to try their luck. Several kissing booths are in full operation and the music and singing from the saloon fill the night air.

"Come on boys," Annie says as she sneaks up behind them and pushes them into the saloon entrance.

She rushes up to the small stage where she waves her arms to quiet the chattering and carousing crowd. Not getting the response she wanted, Annie steps down and pulls a man's gun from his holster and fires it into the ceiling. The crowd stops instantly. She gives the gun back to the man, nodding her appreciation for the spare bullet.

"You all have known me for years and know I'm a pretty good judge of character," Annie states as she walks among her clients. "I know who the honest gamblers are . . . " she says as she looks at a gambler known for playing fairly. "And the ones who carry those EXTRA cards," she continues as she looks at a seedy gambler. He pulls his hat down over his eyes as several other patrons give him the evil eye. "And I know who's married—even though they say they're not," she comments to a fat bald man sitting with dance hall girls at his table. The girls stand upon hearing the remark and move to another table. Everyone in the saloon laughs. "And I know a good sheriff, when I see one . . . or three." She walks over to the brothers and continues. "And believe me, 'cause I know, these are the best darn sheriffs we've had here in Red Rock in a LONG time." The crowd hoots and hollers. Annie smiles at them, then walks back to the stage. "But what good are sheriffs without horses?" The crowd exchanges nods, agreeing. "Well, I did a little trading."

Harold, a rancher and patron, yells, "What kinda trade, Annie?" Everyone laughs.

"You'll never know, Harold," Annie says smiling. Everyone laughs again. "I got our sheriffs a little something," she adds. She steps down, shoves the sheriffs in front of her toward the door. The patrons follow.

Sam holds the reins of three horses with saddles. He ties the reins to the horse post. The three brothers are stunned.

"They're ours?" Louis asks.

"They're yours," Annie confirms. The crowd cheers. Annie approaches the brothers. "Been a long time since we've had any lawman that was worth spit in this town. You boys deserve it. Hell, since you took over, my business has doubled. People are getting their faith back." Annie looks around at the crowd. She waves them back in. "Lets do some celebrating!"

The crowd moves back inside the saloon.

Annie climbs up on the small stage where Mary, an attractive dance hall girl in her early thirties, stands beside the piano player, and says, "Everyone knows Mary. If she isn't teaching your children at the school, she's singing the prettiest songs you've ever heard right here at the Longhorn. So, Mary, give us a song." Mary smiles, adjusts her school marm glasses then moves center stage. Annie steps down and goes to the bar to help Sam serve drinks.

The brothers sit at a table near the stage and watch as the singer begins. She sings a song slowly and gracefully. She steps down to move among the patrons. Suddenly, the pace jumps and Mary whips off her glasses. She sings suggestively, poignantly to the crowd and then puts her foot up on a patron's table, revealing her leg. The crowd whistles and shouts. The patron at the table reaches to touch her leg. She whips out a ruler from the back of her dress and smacks him on the hand. He quickly pulls his hand back and rubs it while the crowd breaks out in laughter.

Mary approaches the brothers. She takes off Louis' hat and puts it on, then struts around imitating a sheriff as she sings. She arrives back at the table, returns Louis' hat, and sits on his lap. She caresses Louis's hair and face while singing. Annie glances over while serving a customer in time to see it. A tint of jealousy shows on her face. She quickly turns back to her job.

Mary finishes her song and returns to the stage to bow.

Everyone, especially Louis, applauds and whistles.

In the meantime, while the town of Red Rock enjoys the food and festivities, a party of Indians sitting atop their horses watch from a hill outside of town. The chief sniffs the air with his long nose then smiles broadly, rubbing his stomach.

The party, having moved from the saloon to a long table in the square, relishes all the delicious foods the holiday has to offer. Annie puts a forkful of pie into her mouth and then drops her fork upon seeing a group of Indians slowly riding up.

"Don't look now, boys, but we have company." On by one, the townsfolk stop what they are doing and begin chattering among themselves.

The three brothers, now on familiar terms with Chief Long Nose and his tribe stand and walk toward them. The chief, trailed by his men, approaches and puts his fingers to his lips, suggesting that they'd like to partake. Alby looks back over his shoulders at the food table loaded with plates of Twinky cakes. He waves the chief on and then walks back to the gathering crowd.

"These Indians are friendly. We met them on the Chisholm Trail. They just want food. Everyone go back to having a good time," Alby tells the crowd

The chief climbs down from his horse and approaches the table with the cakes and pies. His eyes widen at the abundance of the Twinkys. He waves the other Indians over. Mrs. Twinky brings a fresh tray of her oblong cakes and sets them down in front of the chief. She nods to him. The Indians nod greetings and start grabbing for the delicious desserts.

Over by the saloon, the mayor and several of McMartin's men watch the Indians eating at the tables.

"Ain't this a picture. Redskins eating the food like they belong here, and the sheriffs doing nothing about it," the mayor comments to Howard and John, two of McMartin's men. They shake their heads in disgust.

"Want me to stir things up a little, Mayor?" Howard asks. The mayor smiles. Howard motions to his partner to follow.

Back at the dessert table, Bert and Louis are eyeing the delectables. They pick up a tin plate containing the last piece of chocolate pie. Louis pulls the pie plate toward himself as Bert pulls it back in his direction. The plate moves back and forth as the two struggle over the pie.

McMartin's men approach the chief, who's stuffing another twinky cake into his mouth. Howard picks up a blueberry pie from the table and looks at his accomplice. He smiles.

Meanwhile, Louis jerks the pie away from Bert. It flies from his hand. They look around to see where it went when they notice an unfriendly cowboy wearing the chocolate pie.

John bursts out laughing, doubling over and unable to catch his breath. Howard gives John the evil eye, lifts up the blueberry pie, and waits for John to stand upright so that he can hit him in the face. Rising up, John spots the pie's release and ducks. It's Sam, the bartender, who gets the pie in the face. He wipes away the blueberries as everyone breaks out into laughter. The chief and the Indians look at Sam and join in the laughter.

Sam calmly walks to the table, picks up a cream pie, and throws it at Howard, who ducks. The pie hits the chief square in the face. The chief turns with a serious expression. Everyone stops laughing, waiting to see his response. The chief looks at the other Indians and starts laughing. Everyone joins in, including Mrs. Twinky who laughs so hard she farts. The chief then walks over and picks up a pie. Everyone looks around, wondering who's going to be hit. He slams the pie into his own face and laughs harder. Everyone, even the Indians, stops and looks at the chief. The chief's laughing dies off, as he realizes no one's laughing. He looks around confused. He wipes away the pie from his face and shakes his hand. The excess pie from his hand hits Alby in the face, covering his glasses. Everyone, including the chief and the Indians, starts laughing again.

Breaking the joyous mood, McMartin and the rest of his men intentionally ride their horses into the midst of the party. McMartin climbs down and approaches the chief. The brothers quickly get up to intervene. The chief sees the hate in McMartin's eyes and stands up cautiously.

"What the hell are these dirty redskins doing in my town?" McMartin asks the sheriffs as he scours the town's citizens with a disapproving gaze. "Have you all lost your minds? These savages would just as soon cut out your liver and eat it." The citizens cringe at the thought.

Louis steps up between the chief and McMartin. "Now, wait. They just came into town for some of Mrs. Twinky's cakes. That's all."

Eyeing the cakes, McMartin, disdainfully says, "No GOOD sheriff in his right mind would risk the lives of everyone in town to entertain their likes." Confused, uncertain townsfolk look at the sheriffs and begin chattering among themselves. He continues, "Here's what I think of giving cakes to Indians." He lifts the pan of cakes and dumps them on the ground. He steps on them, grinding them with his boot, all the while giving Chief Long Nose a scouring look.

Realizing things have taken a turn, the chief walks to his horse and climbs on. The other Indians follow. The Indian leader quickly turns his horse and yells a war cry. The other Indians echo it as they race out of town.

The brothers look at the squashed Twinky cakes, then at McMartin.

"Word is that you boys need to make a profit to collect on your inheritance. Well, I understand your situation. I'm prepared to offer you a thousand dollars for that property of ours." The brothers are dumbfounded. Its the answer to their problems.

"Why would you do that?" Alby asks suspiciously.

"The way I see it, you've turned this town around and I can take that property you bought and put it to use." McMartin reaches into his jacket pocket and pulls out a large stack of bills. He holds it out to the brothers. "I won't make this offer again, " he warns.

Alby takes the money and fans it. His brothers move in to take a closer look at the money. McMartin walks back to his horse and mounts.

"I'll have the mayor draw up the contract tomorrow," McMartin states. He tips his hat to Annie and kicks the horse. He and his men gallop out of town. Alby and his brothers are still looking at the money.

"We've done it! We made a profit!" Bert says to Alby as he slaps him on the shoulder. Alby tries to smile. Louis scratches his head. Annie approaches and stops in front of them. She looks at the money in Alby's hand.

"Looks like you got your profit. That's what you wanted, right?" she says slightly disgusted. She shakes her head and walks toward the saloon. The deflated townsfolk follow her, talking and looking at the brothers while shaking their heads in disgust.

Further up the street, fireworks are set off and light the sky as children scurry down the street with sparklers and firecrackers, dogs nipping their heels. Louis stops and stands outside the saloon against a post, watching. Alby and Bert lead the three horses to the livery stable.

The piano music and Mary's sweet voice float out of the saloon's swinging doors as Annie exits and stands next to Louis.

Without looking at him she says, "Folks risk everything they own to come out here and start a new life. They brave the west with its hard life and ways to raise kids and cattle. Then people like John McMartin come along and want it all. People get hurt, run off their own land, and even killed unless there's somebody there to stop it." She looks at Louis. "I . . . everyone thought you and your brothers were different. We thought you cared, but . . . McMartin got to you, too." Annie turns and walks back into the saloon. Louis watches her go in, wanting to say something comforting.

The following afternoon, the brothers, back in their city clothes, exit their office with luggage in hand. They turn to look at the Sheriffs Incorporated sign on the building. They tie the luggage onto their three horses and walk toward the mayor's office. They try the door, but find it locked. They look in the windows then walk away. Across the street, they approach a string of horses tied in front of the Longhorn Saloon and enter.

The three brothers settle in at a table. Sam walks over and puts down three cups of coffee and a plate of Twinkys. The brothers scan the saloon for the mayor and wait. Two of McMartin's men enter and head for the bar. They rudely push two patrons out of the way. Louis starts to stand but Alby puts his hand on him.

"It's not our job anymore, Louis," Alby reminds him. Louis refrains himself.

A tall, evil looking man, Garth Black, enters and moves his shifty eyes around the saloon. He steps up to the bar and waits. Several patrons notice him and quickly move away from the bar figuring he's bad news. Garth repositions himself and throws back his dirty knee-length trail coat, revealing a well used forty-five pistol and a shiny new sheriff's badge.

The brothers spot the badge and are taken aback. At that moment, the mayor enters and eyes them. He moves toward their table, pulling out a contract from his jacket pocket. He sits down, lays the contract on the table, and whips out a pen. He lays it on the contract and pushes them toward the brothers.

Alby picks up the contract and reads it. Suddenly, an argument starts at the table across from them. Two of the men, one a member of the McMartin clan and the other a regular patron of the saloon, suddenly stand in defensive position knocking their chairs over as they do. Everyone's attention is diverted to the impending barroom brawl.

"I say you're cheatin'," says the regular patron.

"And I don't like being called a cheater," replies McMartin's hired hand.

Garth turns from the bar and walks toward the disturbance. The mayor notices the brothers concern.

"Let the new sheriff handle it," the mayor tells them. The brothers look at each other and Alby tries to concentrate on the contract.

"What's the problem, boys?" Garth asks the card players.

"Who are you?" the patron questions.

Garth moves back the jacket, revealing the badge. "I'm the sheriff of Red Rock."

"This man was cheatin'. I saw him dealin' from the bottom," he reports to the new lawman.

Garth eyes the McMartin clan member and the pot of money. He leans over and takes several bills from the pile of money and stuffs it into the patron's shirt. "Now get out," he orders him.

The patron looks down at his shirt and then Garth. "Say, what kinda law is this?"

Garth grabs him by the shirt, shuffles him toward the door and tosses him out. "My kinda law," he grumbles. He walks back to the table, lifts several dollars from the pot and shoves it into his own pocket, then walks back to the bar. The mayor sees that the brothers are disturbed by the new brand of law.

"Well, let's get this deal done. Just sign and you can be on your way back to Chicago," the mayor nervously tells the brothers.

Alby lifts the pen to sign and looks at his brothers. Louis looks at Annie behind the bar. She dries a glass as she watches them closely. He then looks at McMartin's men and Garth, then back at Bert and Alby. As Alby puts the pen to the paper, Louis stops him.

"Wait, Alby," Louis says. Alby stops and looks up. The mayor starts to sweat. He takes off his hat and dabs his forehead. "This is wrong. The people need us."

Bert looks at Alby and nods affirming Louis' statement. Alby drops the pen and pushes the contract back at the mayor, whose eyes widen at the unexpected turn.

"Louis is right. We can't do it this way. Sorry, Mayor. Tell McMartin there's no deal," Alby says. The brothers stand as Alby tosses McMartin's money onto the table. "And take that phony sheriff with you."

"I can't do that. I made him sheriff," the mayor responds with a shaky voice.

Alby reaches into his pocket and pulls out the contract. "We have a contract that says otherwise." As he unfolds the contract he continues, "Says here we bought the general store."

"If you buy the store, you buy the sheriff's office..." Bert joins in.

"If you buy the sheriff's office..." Louis adds.

"You are the sheriff," the brothers recite in unison.

Alby puts the contract away. The brothers get up and walk toward the door. Before exiting, Louis turns to the mayor and says, "Should read the fine print, Mayor."

After the brothers exit the saloon, Annie runs over to their table where the mayor still sits, stunned. She looks at the unsigned contract and the money on the table. She smiles and runs out after the brothers. They stride across the street toward their office, when Annie yells, "Hey, sheriffs! Hey, Sheriff's Incorporated!" The brothers stop and turn to face the approaching saloon owner. Laughing, she jumps up wrapping her arms around them. The brothers respond in the like putting their arms around her waist as they all walk into the office of Sheriff's Incorporated.

Back at the saloon, Garth and the mayor get up to leave. They discuss their dilemma as they exit. "Be a lot easier if I just walked over there and killed 'em right now." Garth says, looking down at the mayor.

The mayor looks around to see if anybody heard the comment. "You want to get us both hanged?"

"Hanging might be better than what McMartin will do to you when he finds out they're still here," Garth reminds him as he walks up to his black steed. He unties it and looks at the mayor who is dabbing his forehead again. "I'll tell McMartin the news." He climbs up on his horse, pulls the badge off his shirt and throws it to the mayor. "If I were you, I'd consider a new job. One a long way from here." He kicks the horse and gallops out of town.

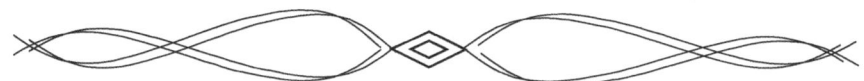

CHAPTER EIGHT
Trouble Brewing

Several fully loaded buckboards pass by the sheriff's office. Alby notices and walks to the window. Annie joins him and watches.

"Those are the Carters, the Johnsons, and the Allens. What are they doing?" Alby questions.

"Looks like they're pulling out." Annie responds before running out the door to investigate. Attentive to her mission at hand, she neglects to hear the gunshots ringing out from her saloon.

Bert and Louis look at each other then toss their derbies off their heads. They grab their sheriff's hats and automatic weapons from the desk, and head for the bar. Alby watches as Annie walks beside the wagons, gesticulating ardently to the farmers.

"Come on, Alby," Louis calls to him as he buckles the paddle belt to his waist. Alby walks away from the window.

As they enter the bar, the swinging noise of the doors suspends the action. Two of McMartin's hired hands stand ready to shoot a bottle off Sam's head. The bartender's eyes roll toward the door, pleading for help. Alby, Louis, and Bert respond by placing their hands next to the paddles of their weapons.

"Anyone who wants to get hurt should leave now," Louis says. The patrons start to run, then stop, frozen in place. Alby approaches Louis and whispers in his ear. Louis shakes his head and laughs. "I mean, anyone who DOESN'T want to get hurt should leave now." Some of the bar goers scatter past the brothers, exiting hastily out the swinging doors.

The clicking and springing of the sheriffs' guns is heard. Those who stayed in the bar, familiar with the sound, run for cover. The two troublemakers, unsure of what is about to take place, stand their ground.

Moments later, Bert and Louis carry the two unconscious McMartin men to the improvised barbed wire cell. Annie enters in a disconcerted state. "McMartin's running off the ranchers around his property. He's pushing his cattle onto their land and branding their stock with his brand. They've had enough."

"Maybe if we helped them put up fences," Louis suggests.

"These ranchers don't have the money to fence in their ranges. But if they don't do something, McMartin will run his cattle wherever he wants."

"We could raise money somehow, to help them," Bert suggests.

Annie walks over to the now occupied cell and examines the barbed wire. "What is this?"

"Alby says it's called barbed wire." Louis tells her.

Annie looks at them and smiles. "Can you get more?"

"Why?" Bert questions, wondering why she would be interested.

"I've got an idea."

Later that afternoon, the townsfolk, under the sheriffs' instructions, gather to discuss Annie's plans. She leads the crowd to the livery stable. She flings the main doors open and the crowd is stunned by what's revealed.

The blacksmith, dressed only in skimpy black leather chaps, flings a whip over his head. Lying over a saddle, dressed, or rather undressed in similar gear, Garth sucks his thumb. "I've been bad, Mommy," he whines.

Feeling the presence of unwelcome witnesses, he and the blacksmith both stop mid-action and slowly look back to see the shocked faces of the unexpected crowd.

Annie, not yet having noticed, continues, "And I'm sure you ALL recognize this." The crowd snaps their heads toward Annie in shock. Annie, confused, looks inside to see what caused the reaction and catches sight of the two men. "No. The cow!" she exclaims in embarrassment. The crowd sighs from relief when they see the lone cow standing in the barn.

Garth and the blacksmith take the opportunity to grab their clothes and run past them.

Now free from the uncomfortable display, Annie gets the cow and leads it toward the livery stable's back doors. She pushes them open to reveal a corral made of barbwire. She walks the cow out into the corral and stands. The crowd delights at the sight.

"This fence is made of barbed wire. There's a man in Illinois that makes it at pennies a foot. His name is Mr. Glidden. I've telegraphed the gentleman and received a response this afternoon." She unfolds a telegraph and reads. "'I'm getting calls from all over the country for my fencing wire. Stop. I can ship you whatever you need. Stop. The more you buy, the less it'll cost you per foot. Stop.'" As everyone begins chattering, Annie raises her voice so as to be heard above the crowd. "The days when men like McMartin can bully other ranchers are over."

A cowhand in the back of the crowd slowly steps away from the crowd. He climbs on his horse and gallops away.

At sundown, the cowhand and Garth report to McMartin. Their boss throws his whiskey glass against the stone wall of the main room as he hears the news. "Damn that town and that Sheriffs Incorporated, too!" McMartin walks over and pours another glass of whiskey. He pulls a twinky out of his pocket and dips it in his drink. He chews while trying to talk. "I wl bum da ho damh tahnwn doaaahnbafa ah lahd cham whuam maiphlamns."

The cowhand and Garth listen intently, wanting to get irate, excited, or show some support, but they can't figure out a word he's muttering. McMartin looks at them as he finishes chewing. Garth and the cowhand shrug their shoulders, clueless as to what their boss has just said. McMartin takes a swig of whiskey and repeats, "I said, I'll burn the whole damn town down before I let them ruin my plans." He turns to Garth and adds, "Take some men into town. Burn down the schoolhouse. Remind them who runs this place."

"When do I get to kill the sheriffs?" Garth asks anxiously.

"There'll be plenty of time for killing later," McMartin responds.

"Good. I need at least half an hour."

"That's a figure of speech."

"Oh." Garth pauses and then asks, "What's that?"

"Do what I told you," McMartin orders.

Garth and the cowboy turn and exit. They immediately start to work on their devious plan. Gathering up five lawless cowboys they head for town. Watching them from a hilltop above, Chief Long Nose and his men sit atop their stallions, dressed in war paint. They ride toward the town.

Meanwhile, Louis and Annie stand outside the saloon under the full moon.

"That was impressive today. The idea with the wire was brilliant," Louis tells Annie.

"You're not one of those men who thinks women shouldn't have brains are you, Louis?" Annie asks as she plays with one of Louis' shirt buttons.

"Who me? No. I . . . kind of like it . . . ," Louis utters, groping awkwardly for words, "almost as much as I like women with breasts."

Annie moves toward Louis to kiss him, then stops as Louis' comment registers. She starts to ask about it when they are interrupted by a familiar voice.

"Indians!" Louis jumps back away from Annie. He looks back to see Mr. Twinky running toward them.

"Sheriff!" he cries. "Indians! They've kidnapped Mary!"

Louis runs to get his brothers, while Annie comforts Mr. Twinky.

The three brothers immediately pack gear onto their horses as Annie and Mr. Twinky stand by. "Don't worry, Mr. Twinky, we'll find her," Alby promises. He swings his leg over his steed ready for departure.

Dong, dong, dong.

"What's that?" he asks.

"Those are the church bells," Annie tells him with some alarm. "The church bells are only rung like that when there's a fire." They look around and spot smoke at the end of town.

Alby dismounts. "One of us should go rescue Mrs. Twinky, and the other two should stay to help out here." Alby looks at his brothers.

"I'll go," Louis bravely volunteers as he climbs clumsily up on his horse. Annie approaches him.

"Be careful, Louis." He tips his hat at her then unskillfully turns the horse and rides out of town. Mr. Twinky watches and waits. After a minute passes he shyly leans over and whispers into Annie's ear. Annie perks up and runs after Louis. "Louis!" she yells, "They went the other way!" Louis pulls the reigns, trying to stop as he gracelessly turns his mount, but still managing to gallop out of town in the right direction.

Alby and Bert tie their horses. The townsfolk run toward the billowing smoke with buckets in hand, yelling, "The schoolhouse is ablaze. "

When they arrive a bucket brigade is formed. Bucket of water after bucket of water is poured on the irrepressible fire. Hours of fighting the inferno the townspeople realize, one-by-one, that saving the school is futile. They stop moving the buckets. Alby and Bert put theirs down and sit on them. They watch the schoolhouse fall, completely destroyed by the fire. They look up at Annie.

"Why would anyone want to burn down the schoolhouse?" Bert asks.

"Can't you boys smell it?" Annie says. Alby and Bert both sniff. "I smell McMartin."

Annie throws her bucket down and walks away. Alby and Bert sniff again, trying to smell the evil odor.

Meanwhile, the chief and his Indians escape down the trail. Mrs. Twinky rides bareback behind one of the Indians, squeezing him around his waist as they gallop out of town. With every bounce Mrs. Twinky's butt hits the horse, creating a gaseous explosion. The Indian riding with her takes notice of the flatulence and sniffs around for the source of the smell. He looks with disgust back at Mrs. Twinky. She smiles.

Not far behind them, Louis trots along on his horse. After noticing yellow spongy material strewn on the path, he leans over watching the trail more closely. He decides to stop the horse and climb down to investigate. He bends down to pick up a whitish yellow piece of bread. He holds it up to the moonlight, sniffs it then tastes it. He smiles and awkwardly remounts.

At sunrise, Alby and Bert stand in front of the smoldering remains of the school house. Alby kicks a piece of the burnt wood. Annie sees his frustration and approaches him. She puts her hand around his shoulder to comfort him.

"What kind of man would do this?" Alby asks.

"McMartin's a ruthless man," Annie responds.

"Poor kids. What'll they do now?" Bert asks.

"Oh, we've taken care of that. Follow me." Anne then leads

them to the saloon. She points to a makeshift placard hanging below the weathered sign of the saloon.

Curious, Alby and Bert stick their heads into the saloon door.

The school marm, Mary, has a makeshift blackboard on the stage and is teaching math to the students who are seated at the tables on one side of the saloon. Business goes on as usual at the bar, where several beer-drinking patrons watch. Mary occasionally looks over at them, checking for good behavior.

As Alby, Bert, and Annie enter to observe more closely, Mary stops and steps down to talk with Annie. "If I taught class and sang to the customers at the same time, would you pay me?"

Annie is slightly put off by the question. "I guess, but you don't have to—"

"I figured I could use the extra money to help rebuild the school house," Mary interrupts.

"If you think you can . . . " Annie replies as Mary walks away. Then she turns to Alby and Bert and whispers, "This should be interesting."

Mary signals her piano player at the table to come up to the stage. She walks over and whispers in his ear. He shrugs his shoulders and begins playing. Mary raises the pointer to the math problem on the board. "Billy, what's the answer to this problem?" she asks her ten-year-old student.

Billy stands and answers, "One hundred twenty four."

Mary nods and smiles, then steps over to the other side of the stage and begins singing and showing a little leg. The patrons perk up, paying closer attention. After a chorus, she steps back and points to another problem.

"Jenny, what's the capital of our country?" she asks her eleven-year-old student.

Jenny stands and answers, "Washington DC." She sits back down as Mary dances back over to the other side of the stage, shows a little leg, and begins the next chorus. The patrons liven up again. Mary steps down while singing and mingles with the customers. She calls out another student's name for the next problem while singing. In this manner, the schoolwork and saloon song are merged into one act; the kids and patrons all enjoying themselves.

Alby, Bert, and Annie smile at one another. Mary finishes her number and lesson at the same time. Everyone applauds.

CHAPTER NINE
TO THE RESCUE

The afternoon sun beams down hard on Louis as he continues following the trail of twinky bits. His tracking, however, is suddenly stopped when two horses block the path in front of him. He looks up to find two Cherokee Indians sitting atop their horses with guns pointed at him. Louis slowly raises his hands.

The Indians lead him into a camp where others immediately surround him. He looks past them for Mrs. Twinky. One of the Indians, seemingly in charge, leads him to a teepee. Inside, Chief Long Nose is sitting cross-legged eating a twinky cake. Large sacks of flour and sugar marked *US ARMY*, sit in the corner. Mrs. Twinky is on the other side of the teepee making up yet another batch for the chief and his tribe. She turns to see Louis. Despite her plight, she waves and gives him a smile.

"Mrs. Twinky, are you okay?" Louis asks.

"Oh yes, they can't get enough of my buns," she tells him.

Louis looks around and leans toward her. "Might want to call them cakes instead," he suggests.

"Why?"

"Sounds better. Trust me."

"Okay," she says smiling.

"Right now, we have to get you back home."

Mrs. Twinky looks at the chief and the others. "I don't think they're going to let me leave, Louis."

Louis looks around at the Indians and notices a woman in the corner with her arms crossed. She seems to be pouting. "Who's that?"

"That's Crying Rain. She's the chief's wife," Mrs. Twinky tells him.

"Can you teach someone else to make those?" Louis wonders.

Mrs. Twinky thinks about it. "It's a family recipe. I really shouldn't." Louis gives her a pleading look. "Well, maybe just this time." Louis smiles.

The kidnapped bakery chef works well into the night with Crying Rain, teaching her the family recipe for Twinky cakes. After several failed batches, Crying Rain finally achieves the perfect result. By morning she is ready to present the cakes to her husband.

At sunrise, Chief Long Nose waits impatiently in his teepee. When Crying Rain finally enters with the prized desserts she smiles at him. He examines the cakes sternly then looks to Mrs. Twinky for her approval. She nods him on. The chief bites into one. He chews and thinks about it. Then he smiles. Crying Rain smiles back. Louis takes advantage of the moment and pulls Mrs. Twinky toward the horse.

"Remember sweetie, don't share that recipe with anyone. It's a family secret. Follow it and everyone will love your buns," Mrs. Twinky tells Crying Rain. The other Indians beam a big smile at Crying Rain. Louis pushes Mrs. Twinky up on the horse as the chief waves goodbye.

Back at Red Rock, an excited Annie runs out of the telegraph office and toward the office of Sheriffs Incorporated. Once inside, she sees Alby oiling the automatic firing devices, but doesn't see Louis anywhere in sight. "He isn't back yet?" she asks. Alby and Bert shake their heads. Hiding her disappointment, Annie hands the telegram to Alby. "Should be here on tomorrow's train."

Alby reads it. "You bought all of this wire?" he asks.

"Oh, they'll pay me back eventually. We're gonna need at least three wagons to haul it though."

Alby puts his supplies away and stands. "We'd better start finding some help then."

It is late in the afternoon when Alby, Bert, Annie and several of the townspeople meet at the Abilene train station. They load bundles of barbed wire onto three wagons, which will be delivered to the

Johnson's, Carter's, and Allen's ranches first as they are in most need of immediate protection from McMartin.

By the time Louis and Mrs. Twinky finally ride into town after a long, malodorous journey, poles have been planted and barbed wire has been strung at all three ranches.

Louis stops the horse in front of Mrs. Twinky's Buns Shop, but notices the streets are unusually deserted. He climbs down from the horse, helping Mrs. Twinky dismount as well. Sensing something is awry, Louis heads straight for Sheriffs Incorporated.

Meanwhile, McMartin and several of his cowpokes sit atop the hill on their horses watching the final fence installation. McMartin agitatedly turns his horse and gallops off to his ranch house. Once there, he gathers fifteen men on horseback and loads his Winchester rifle. He climbs back onto his horse and rides away toward Sheriffs Incorporated.

Later that night, the empty wagons roll into town with the exhausted fencing crew aboard. Alby and Bert enter the dark office. As soon as the oil lamp is lit a gun click is heard. They turn to see McMartin, Garth, and several of McMartin's men surrounding them with guns pointed.

"Hello, boys. I'm very disappointed with you," McMartin says glibly. He directs the brothers to the door with the loaded Winchester

Outside, as Louis walks toward Sheriffs Incorporated, he spots Alby and Bert stepping out the door with their hands above their heads. He stops in his tracks when he sees McMartin and his men walk out behind them armed with guns. He notices that Alby and Bert do not have their weapons. He looks toward the Longhorn Saloon and sees Annie being led out of the saloon by Garth at gunpoint. Then, to make matters worse, McMartin's men appear from behind buildings all over town, guns and rifles loaded and ready.

"You couldn't leave things alone, could you?" McMartin says after spotting Louis in the street. Pointing his gun at him, he continues, "Now, we'll do things my way. Drop the gun belt." Louis hesitates. McMartin puts his gun to Bert's head and cocks the hammer. Convinced, Louis quickly unbuckles the automatic weapon. It drops to the ground with a thud.

Garth takes the opportunity to shove Annie, causing her to fall to the ground. She snaps around and gives the ruffian a piercing look. Louis sees her on the ground and starts to go to her. McMartin moves his gun from Bert to aim it at Louis. Garth steps past Annie and out into the middle of the street, challenging Louis to a deadly duel.

"Give him your gun belt," McMartin orders one of his cowhands. The cowhand unbuckles his gun belt and throws it at Louis' feet. Louis looks down at it.

"Louis, no!" Annie yells.

Louis bends down and picks it up. He slowly straps it on.

"Let's see how you handle a real gun," McMartin challenges him.

Louis slowly turns to face Garth then takes several steps toward his opponent. McMartin and his men ready their weapons. Garth draws before Louis is able to go for his gun. A shot is heard and Louis flies backward, landing motionless on the ground. As he hits, his gun fires into the air.

Garth steps forward and stops. He looks down and feels his chest. He smiles and falls over dead. Before McMartin's men can react, they are suddenly ambushed by Indians. The brothers new allies point their rifles and bows at McMartin and his men, ordering them to disarm. Chief Long Nose steps out of the darkness to face his archenemy and crosses his arms. He looks to the brothers and nods in salutation.

Annie springs up and runs frantically to Louis. She turns him over carefully to see that he's been hit in the shoulder. She rips off a piece of her blouse and places it on the wound.

Suddenly, to the brother's surprise, Penelope and her father step out from behind a building. Smoke is still pouring from Penelope's rifle. She walks toward Louis and yells, "I saved him, Father. Now he's mine."

Everyone, even the Indians, recoil at Penelope's ugliness. Even the horse she passes reacts to her ugliness. Penelope looks down at Louis and Annie, who is bent over him. "Where's your brothers?" Penelope asks Louis.

Alby and Bert duck down in the crowd.

In a disguised voice, Alby replies, "Dead! They're dead."

Bert follows suit and disguises his voice as well. "Injuns killed 'em both!"

Not acknowledging the responses from Bert and Alby, Penelope turns to Annie. "He's mine. Get away from him." She lays her foot on Annie then pushes her over. She then grabs Louis by his arm and pulls. He moans and tries to resist. Annie springs up angrily. But Penelope persists with her retribution and swings the rifle at her. Annie is able to block it before she pulls back her fist, knocking Penelope in the face and onto the ground.

Annie returns to help Louis stand. He leans onto her shoulder as Penelope makes another run at them. Annie kicks her in the stomach and doubles her over. Penelope's dad approaches her to help.

"Don't just stand there, you idiot, stop them. She's stealing my man!"

"What did you say?" her father asks stunned at his daughters lack of respect.

"Daddy, she's taking my man!"

Without responding, her father grabs her by the ear and drags her away. "Idiot, am I? I spend money and time to satisfy your every whim. That's being an idiot! All this way for you to make a fool of me. THAT'S an idiot!"

"Daddy, my ear!" Penelope complains.

"You know what you're problem is?" he asks as he walks toward their carriage. "You're spoiled rotten. Maybe an all girl school can teach you some manners."

"Daddy, no. Please!"

As Penelope is dragged away by her dad, the town becomes animated once again. The citizen's of Red Rock pat the Indians on their backs and shake their hands in gratitude. The Indians happily push McMartin's men toward the sheriffs' office. The chief drops the confiscated weapons in front of Louis and his brothers. He nods and disappears with his tribe into the darkness. The town's citizens then crowd around McMartin and his men to ensure no escapes. The mayor appears and moves through the crowd.

"What's going on here?" the mayor enquires.

"Don't just stand there you idiot. Do something!" McMartin orders the mayor.

Louis steps up on the porch and looks around at the citizens. "I think this town needs a new mayor. One that McMartin doesn't own. What do you people think?" The citizens yell their approval in unison. "Just to be fair, how may folks want the old mayor to remain in office?" He looks around, but no response is heard. He steps down, pulls the mayor's hat off and jerks the cigar from his mouth. The mayor is flabbergasted. Louis spots Betsy in the crowd. He steps down and pulls her through the crowd and up beside him. He raises her hand. "You folks all know Betsy. How about Betsy for mayor?" The citizens yell their approval in unison once again. Louis plops the hat on her head and sticks the cigar in her mouth. Betsy turns and smiles at the crowd. "Looks like you're out of a job, Mayor."

Alby and Bert step up to join Louis.

"What's the first order of business, Mayor?" Alby asks Betsy.

Betsy looks around and spots McMartin. "Put that man in jail and throw away the key." Betsy replies, pointing at McMartin. The citizens applaud.

Louis leans over to Betsy. "Are we fining him?"

Betsy leans over and whispers to Louis, "How much you need?" The brothers huddle and quickly discuss it.

"Six hundred fifty."

Betsy whispers, "That much?" The brothers nod.

"Six hundred fifty dollars it is then."

McMartin scoffs at it. "I won't pay it."

The new mayor snaps her head around and stares at McMartin. "That's okay. Someone get my rope from my buckboard." Betsy winks at Alby. McMartin quickly reaches into his jacket and pulls out a wad of cash. She grabs the cash and thumbs through it. She hands a portion to Alby. "There you go, Sheriff. Now, git that man into jail and don't bring him out until the judge arrives from Abilene."

"What judge?" Louis asks.

"The one I'm gonna wire in the morning." Betsy replies.

The crowd laughs. Bert and Alby escort McMartin toward the office. The rest of McMartin's men stand waiting. Louis looks them over. "You fellas want to join your boss?" The men make a mad dash away. "I didn't think so." Annie steps up to Louis and wraps her arms around him.

Betsy looks around and sees the old mayor still waiting. "Boo!" The mayor, finally getting the hint, runs away. Betsy looks around at the remaining citizens. "Well, don't just stand there. Someone give me a light." Everyone immediately starts searching their pockets.

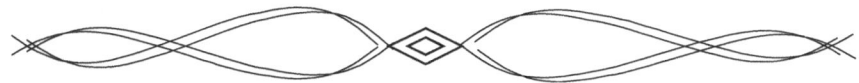

CHAPTER TEN
Father's Lesson

The next morning Alby, Bert, and Louis pack their bags. They re-don their best city clothes and depart for the Abilene Train Station with Betsy and Annie. By early afternoon, the buckboard arrives with its travelers. Passengers are already entering the train.

"Sure you have to leave? We'll miss ya," Betsy tells the brothers with tears in her eyes.

"We've got some business in Chicago, Betsy. We have to go," Alby replies apologetically.

"There'll always be a badge waitin' if ya want it," Betsy promises.

"Thanks, Betsy," Alby says.

Louis walks up to the buckboard and helps Annie down. She gets close to his face as Alby and Bert walk toward the train, waving. Louis looks at them then to Annie.

"Annie," Louis begins, "I . . . "

She puts her fingers to his lips. "You don't have to say anything, Louis." She then kisses him passionately. Betsy smiles and looks in the opposite direction. Annie pulls away and climbs onto the wagon. She blows Louis a final kiss as Betsy slaps the horses with the reins and the buckboard departs. Louis grabs his bags and walks toward the train.

At the Matheson Estate, Jonathan sits in the den behind the dark, ornate desk. According to the telegram from Texas, the brothers should be arriving at any minute, and the family attorney wants to be sure all is in order before their entrance. Beatrice and Alfredo sit patiently waiting, hoping only for the worst.

As the door opens, expectant eyes turn to the three brothers. Polite greetings are exchanged as they enter and take their seat at the familiar table. Alby, without wasting much time, reaches into his pocket and pulls out an envelope. He proudly lays it on the table in front of Billings.

"There's seven hundred sixty dollars, Billings. Ten dollars profit."

Shocked and angered, Beatrice quickly stands and pulls Alfredo from the room. Billings nods his satisfaction to the brothers.

Not long after arriving, Louis determines he misses Annie too much. He makes the decision to take his unpacked bags and head back to Texas on the next train out.

"Please don't try to change my mind," he glumly asks Alby and Bert, "I finally know what I want in life and how to go about doing it. Nothing can stop me." With teary eyes, he walks to them, drops his bags and hugs each in turn. Before walking out the door, Louis makes a final stop to the den. He stands in front of his father's portrait and looks up at him. "I know it's kind of late, Dad, but now I understand all those things you tried to teach us. That a man has to find his destiny and when you find it …well, I just understand." He starts to turn then stops. "I love you, Dad."

Billings enters and puts down a tray of drinks. Alby and Bert follow him in. Billings pours four drinks and hands each of the brothers a glass. He holds his up for a toast. "I thought I'd never hear myself say this, but … I'm very proud of you three." Billings looks back over his shoulder at their father's portrait. "And I know that your father would be too." They drink their toast.

Billings puts his glass down and takes an envelope from his pocket. He hands it to Louis. "I called my connections in construction. This should be sufficient to build a very nice school in Red Rock."

Louis takes the envelope and puts it into his pocket. Alby and Bert look at Louis and smile. They walk outside to say goodbye. Louis hugs Alby and Bert and shakes hands with Billings. "If you ever get down Texas way, look me up," Louis tells them as he climbs into the carriage.

Beatrice watches with Alfredo from the window. Louis looks up and waves. They quickly disappear out of view.

Louis cleans his automatic gun and looks back at the photo on the wall of him and his brothers in their sheriff's outfits and the automatic weapons that Alby designed. He sighs as he thinks how the past six months have not lessened the emptiness he feels without his brothers.

A knock at the door stirs him from his thoughts. The door opens and Mayor Betsy catches Louis turning away from the photo. She looks at it and then to Louis. "You know, Red Rock has been really growing, and I'm afraid it's created a problem," she hints to Louis.

Louis sits up to listen. "What's that, Betsy?"

Betsy walks over and sits on the edge of the desk. "It's kinda hard for a sheriff to be everywhere all the time. I just think ya might need a little help." Louis becomes a little uncomfortable. "I know it's your job to pick the help. I figured good help was tough to find around here, so I went outside the state to get—"

"Betsy, you shouldn't—" Louis begins to interrupt but the door swings open and Alby and Bert walk in. Louis jumps from his chair and runs to them. He hugs Bert and then Alby so hard he lifts them off the floor. He looks back at Betsy and smiles.

"Then you approve?" Betsy asks smiling. She steps up to them and pats them on the back. Louis stops her and kisses her on the cheek. She blushes and looks around. "Now stop that. We can't have people seein' the sheriff kissin' on the mayor." She steps outside and tries to gain her composure. She pulls a cigar stump out of her pocket and shoves it in her mouth as she walks away. The brothers laugh.

That same afternoon, its back to business as usual. Alby and Bert are back in their sheriff's suits and inspecting their automatic weapons.

"So if you two are rich, why work as sheriffs?" Louis asks them.

Alby and Bert look at each other then Louis. "Oh, we're not rich. We gave the money to Aunt Beatrice and Alfredo," Alby informs him.

"What?"

"That was dad's money, not ours." Bert nods his head in agreement. "We'll make our own," Alby adds.

Louis stands and opens the door. He invites them to exit with him. "Come on, I want you to see something." Louis leads them in front of the schoolhouse and stops. Alby and Bert are stunned when they see the name of the school: ALBERT MATHESON SCHOOL

"Dad paid for it so … " Louis begins before being interrupted by an excited young boy.

"There's a cowboy shootin' up the saloon. Miss Annie said to come get you," the child reports as he looks up and down at Alby and Bert, noticing the outfit is the same as Louis'.

"Tell Annie, we'll be right there," Louis tells him. The boy runs off half confused.

The brothers turn and start to follow, when they are again hit by a familiar smell.

"What's that smell?" Bert asks. The three look down. They're again standing in fresh horse manure. "We need to have a serious talk with these horses." Louis and Alby laugh and throw their arms around Bert. They walk away laughing. "What? I'm serious."

A wagon rolls by the Longhorn Saloon causing a cloud of dust to blow in through the swinging doors. A drunken cowboy stops twisting the arm of a dance hall girl when he hears the swinging of the doors. Releasing her, he tries to look through the cloud of dust to see who entered. Out of the cloud of dust, the three sheriffs emerge.

"Who in the Sam hill is that?" the drunk cowboy asks

Annie steps forward from the bar and leans against it, looking very confident about the outcome. "That there my friend, is Sheriffs Incorporated."

Patrons in the bar scramble for the doors. The cowboy looks around, watching everyone escape, until he's standing alone. Patrons run out the door as three clicking and springing noises are heard, followed by the sound of ball bearings bouncing off of the cowboy. A thump is heard as he hits the floor, followed by the clinging of their spurs as they walk across the floor.

"Here's your bill, Annie," Louis announces.

"Are you still gonna charge me after we're married?" she asks to the surprise of Alby and Bert.

"Yep," Louis replies.

"You're a hard man, Louis," Annie quips.

"Louis! You're getting married?" Alby asks stunned at the news.

"That's great, Louis!" Bert exclaims.

"Congratulations!" the two brothers shout in unison as they affectionately slap him on the back.

"How about we take this out in trade?" Annie asks Louis in a sexy, bedroom voice.

"I don't know. What do you have to trade?" Louis plays along. "Well, let's go upstairs and see what we can find." They run up the stairs leaving Alby and Bert to take care of the unfinished business.

As Bert and Alby pull the unconscious cowboy from the saloon, Penelope and her father are exiting the hotel with their luggage. They walk past a buckwagon with an arriving load of barbed wire. Penelope snags her dress on the edge and fights furiously, trying to get her dress free. She loses her balance and falls back, ripping her dress away and revealing her curvaceous figure.

Alby and Bert stop. Bert releases the cowboy's legs, dropping them and staring in awe. Other men in the town stop and stare at Penelope's beautiful body.

Bert starts to walk toward her.

"Bert, where are you going?" Alby asks.

Bert turns to Alby, half dazed, infatuated."Well, ah, she needs help."

"Bert? I thought—"

Bert continues toward her. "Well, looks aren't everything." Bert crosses the street. Alby laughs and drags the cowboy away.

Back in Chicago, Elizabeth Hanlin reads a paper touting the accomplishments of Sheriffs Incorporated in Red Rock. "Brothers Tame Cattle Town." She scans the paper want ads and eyes an ad. "School Marm Wanted in Red Rock, Texas. To teach in schoolhouse of booming cattle town. Singing skills helpful. Contact Mayor Betsy in Red Rock, Texas." Elizabeth draws a heart around Alby's face and smiles.

The End

SAM'S SHADOW
By Karen Hicks

BACKSTORY

A member of my family who suffers from Alzheimer's disease inspired this story and although fictional, it includes many incidents that actually happened. I think Robert Duvall or John Mahoney would be great in the role of the grandfather and possibly Ethan Embry as the grandson. I workshopped the script from beginning to end with veteran television writer, Larry Brody, who said he was moved to tears over the touching scenes but also liked the fact that I interjected moments of comedic relief. It won first place in the "Present-A-Thon" contest, and as a result, a production company requested a copy of it. I've also been able to get the script to other producers through contacts I've made at TV Writer.Com, a website run by Larry. It's a tough business though, and I have to keep making those contacts. That's why I'm happy to have this opportunity to share Sam's Shadow with you in short-story format. I hope you enjoy it and it touches your heart!

CHAPTER ONE
A Harsh Winter

In the heart of Illinois, a mail truck putters up to a forlorn farmhouse and its metal barn situated on a desolate road, breaking the silence of the hibernating countryside. All around are frozen, barren fields, some of which once belonged to the owner of the dilapidated farm who retired and sold off his beloved acreage. The mail truck pulls over to the farmhouse and stops next to an icy mailbox at the entrance to the driveway. Judy, the driver, quickly shoves a stack of mail in the box and glances at the house as if paranoid someone might see her. Unfortunately, though, she's been spotted and there's no way to avoid him.

The front door of the house flies open and out comes Delbert Prichard, a 72-year-old curmudgeon on a mission. Donning a pair of overalls and big, sloppy boots, he braves the cold and trudges steadfastly down the driveway. "About time you got here!" he bellows.

Judy quickly puts the truck in gear and zooms off down the road and waves her arm out the window as if to say, "Yeah, yeah." Delbert scowls. "Someday I'm going to report that woman," he mutters to himself. With a trembling hand that's adorned with a diabetic ID bracelet, he opens the mailbox and takes out the contents. He shuffles through the bills and junk mail and finds a treasure in the midst–a small yellow envelope. His face lights up with delight as he opens it and slides out a homemade Happy New Year card with a beautiful hand-painted butterfly. He runs his fingers over it gently and allows his thoughts to drift back to twenty-two years earlier.

It's a warm, spring day in the meadow, and blades of long grass ripple in the breeze. Above, the sun blazes against a perfectly serene blue sky where a magnificent butterfly dances and shows off its vibrant colors.

Nearby, the sound of a little boy's giggles is heard. "Come on, Grandpa, hurry up!" Sam Prichard demands gleefully.

The butterfly abruptly takes off, and its shadow skims across the meadow.

Sam's shadow pursues it as another one belonging to Delbert follows. "I'm right behind you, Sammy." Delbert catches up and his shadow merges with Sam's and forms one silhouette. A few more steps and . . . whoosh! The butterfly gets bagged with the net. "I got him! I got him!" shouts Sam, the sweet-faced five-year-old who beams with pride.

"You sure do," Delbert says with less enthusiasm. "He doesn't seem very happy, though."

Sam looks up, squints into the sun and strains to see Delbert's face through the incandescent rays. "Please, Grandpa. I'll take good care of him," he pleads.

Delbert leans down, bringing himself into focus. His face of fifty years is kind and gentle, yet his eyes reveal a hint of mischief. He holds a jar with holes punched in the lid. "OK, Sammy. Let's put him in."

Trapped, the butterfly flutters frantically in the jar.

"Let's go show Grandma," says Sam who slips his tiny hand in Delbert's as they meander back to the farmhouse.

"Delbert! What are you doing outside without your coat?"

Startled out of his daydream, Delbert glances up from the card. He sees his loving wife, Emily, shivering on the front porch while clutching a sweater around her frail shoulders.

"I forgot," Delbert replies as he returns to the house and clumps up the porch steps.

"You also forgot to take your diabetes pill," she scolds.

Delbert frowns and hands the card and stack of mail to her as they step inside.

The living room is cozy and decorated with old-fashioned country furniture, and a small Christmas tree stands in the corner. Emily admires the card. "Sam never forgets a holiday or birthday, does he?" She sets the card on a table and exits into the kitchen with the mail.

Delbert scans the living room as if searching for something. Emily returns with a glass of water and a pill and hands them to him. With a snarl, he pops the tiny white pill in his mouth and swallows it down while Emily watches intently.

"I want you to stop being so rude to the mail lady," she says.

Delbert snaps back. "Is it too much to ask to have the mail delivered on time? Charlie used to deliver it at—"

Agitated, Emily interrupts and finishes his sentence while tapping her watch. "At three o'clock everyday. I know, I know. You could set your watch by him." Her expression softens. "Charlie retired. Judy delivers the mail now."

Delbert narrows his eyes at her and hands back the glass. "Out with the old, in with the new, eh?" He glances around the room again and pats his pants pockets. "Have you seen the car keys? I need to go to the hardware store."

"Why? You never fix anything anyway." Emily picks up a pair of broken eyeglasses from an end table next to her chair and shakes them at him. The left temple is missing. "Not even my reading glasses, which I keep asking you to."

"You never asked me to do that. And yes, I do fix things."

"No. You just tinker around," she says and sets them back.

"I've never tinkered around." He kisses her gently on the lips. "Except with you. Now, will you help me find the car keys?"

Emily laughs and helps him with his search. She finds the keys inside a potted plant and takes them out, jingling them in the air.

Delbert looks puzzled. "How did those get in there?"

"Maybe it's God's way of telling you it's time to give up driving," she teases, although her expression grows serious.

Delbert balks and snatches the keys from her hand. He grabs his hat and coat off a nearby rack and puts them on and heads for the door. He hesitates and goes back and kisses her again. "If I'm not back in an hour, you can send out a search party."

As Delbert heads back to the front door, Emily makes her way toward the kitchen holding the water glass. She staggers, and the glass plummets to the floor and shatters as she collapses lifelessly on top of the broken pieces. Delbert reels around, horrified.

"Emily!"

That evening on the sixteenth floor of a plush Chicago office building, a New Year's Eve party is underway. Sam, now a handsome and successful twenty-seven-year-old architect, is in the middle of giving a toast. "This has been a banner year for me. It was beyond my wildest dreams making junior partner at one of the most prestigious architectural firms in Chicago." A teetotaler, he raises a can of soda in response to a few hear, hears and continues. "I'm learning to be an optimist, and that's why I can stand boldly before you and ask our illustrious leader, Mr. Benjamin Mason, if he would also consider me for the position of . . . son-in-law." But Sam doesn't look at Mr. Mason, the distinguished-looking gentleman standing across the room nodding his head in approval. Instead, he looks directly at Victoria Mason, the boss's stunningly beautiful daughter who suddenly realizes she's just been proposed to.

Ecstatic, she darts over to Sam and kisses him feverishly as everyone applauds. Except, that is, two of Sam's colleagues and closest friends, Tran Nguyen and Brad Jenkins, who seem less than enthused over Sam's sudden proposal to the 26-year-old socialite. After all, there's something annoying about a spoiled little rich girl who gets everything she wants. Now she has Sam to add to her list, and she's latching onto him with those perfectly manicured claws. "Marking your territory before I take off on my two-week ski trip next week?" she whispers in his ear.

Saved by his ringing cell phone, Sam retrieves it from his belt clip. "Hello?"

On the other end is Delbert with the bad news. "She's gone, Sammy," he sobs. "My Emily's gone."

On a bitterly cold day at the Holy Cross Cemetery, mourners filter out as a burial service for Emily ends. A grief-stricken Delbert remains standing beside the casket, oblivious to the stinging wind.

A few feet away, Sam kneels down and brushes the snow away from a two-person headstone engraved, "Tom Prichard, Loving Father" and "Rachel Prichard, Loving Mother." Grief overwhelms him, and memories of his parents' funeral come flooding back.

Visibly shaken and standing next to two caskets, fifteen-year-old Sam stares at the ground with tears streaming down his face. Delbert and Emily fare no better having just buried their only child and his wife. Delbert reaches over and takes Sam's hand.

Sam is so deep in thought he doesn't immediately notice that Delbert is now kneeling down next to him. When he finally does, he reaches over for Delbert's hand and squeezes it gently.

At the farmhouse a few days later, Delbert rummages through his toolbox in the garage, muttering to himself. He seems disoriented and confused. Sam enters from the kitchen sipping a cup of coffee.

Delbert glances up. "Sammy, go back in and get me one of my pills, will you? Your grandmother gets so upset when I forget to take them." Concerned, Sam looks at Delbert curiously for a moment and then goes back inside. Delbert continues rummaging, growing more agitated by the minute. "Darn kids."

Sam returns with an empty pill bottle, and Delbert looks sharply at him. "I want you to tell your friends they aren't allowed to come in my garage after school anymore. I know they're stealing my things!"

Baffled, Sam looks at the empty pill bottle and back at Delbert again. There's something very wrong here.

Outside the Community Medical Center, Sam clutches a pharmacy bag as he heads toward the parking lot where his red Dodge Viper is parked. It's an older model but still a beauty. Delbert shuffles behind, arguing. "I don't need a pill machine to remind me when to take my pills!"

"Obviously you do," Sam disagrees. "The doctor said you were over-medicating yourself."

"That's because your grandmother always kept track of my pills. But I'll get in the habit of doing it for myself," Delbert reasons. He opens the passenger door of the Viper and bangs it against another vehicle. Sam scolds him with a harsh glance.

The following morning in the kitchen, the pill machine rotates and buzzes loudly on the counter. Hovering over it, Delbert flinches while Sam smiles proudly. "Ha! It works! Now all you have to do is take the pill out of the compartment, and you can't get another one until it automatically dispenses it to you at the same time tomorrow."

Delbert scrunches up his face. "I still think it's a waste of money." He swallows the pill down with a glass of water and then sits down at the table and reads the newspaper.

Sam grabs his car keys and kisses Delbert on the cheek. "I've gotta go, Grandpa. I promised Victoria I'd take her to the airport. I'll see you in about a week."

Without looking up, Delbert responds flatly, "Don't screech out of the driveway with that hotrod of yours. It leaves marks." Sam nods and heads out of the kitchen. The front door slams, and Delbert puts the paper down. No one in the world could look sadder than him.

At O'Hare's passenger drop-off area, Sam unloads a designer suitcase from the luggage rack of his Viper and hands it to a skycap who checks it in. Sam turns to Victoria. "Not much luggage for two weeks."

Victoria nuzzles up to him. "Everything I need is at the cabin. Except you."

Sam kisses her gently. "Tell your friends no wild parties. You're engaged now."

"Oh, really?" Victoria holds up her left hand and wiggles her bare ring finger. "I don't see a diamond." And with that, she sashays into the terminal leaving Sam with a worried look on his face.

That night at the farmhouse, Delbert sleeps in his recliner while clutching tightly to a picture of Emily.

The sun rises and peeks through the kitchen window. The pill dispenser rotates and buzzes loudly. Delbert enters from the living room, flustered. He can't figure out how to turn it off and becomes agitated and yanks the cord out of the socket.

A few days later, Judy pulls up in the mail truck and opens the mailbox. There's still mail left inside from the previous days, and she slides everything out and takes it up to the house.

She knocks on the door. No answer. She knocks again. "Mr. Prichard?" Slowly she opens the door and peeks inside to discover Delbert sitting in his chair, listless.

At the hospital, Delbert is hooked up to an I.V. and watches TV from his bed. Just outside the doorway, a doctor talks to Sam. "He'll be fine, but his diabetes has to be controlled or there could be serious consequences. Once he's back on track with his medicine, his confusion should decrease." He pauses for a moment. "But in order for that to happen, he'll need full-time care."

Sam stiffens. "I won't put him in a nursing home if that's what you're getting at."

The doctor shrugs. "What other choice is there?"

Sam stares long and hard at Delbert.

The next day, the Viper zooms along the expressway heading toward Chicago. An old suitcase is strapped to the luggage rack–obviously not Victoria's. Inside the Viper, Sam is at the wheel with Delbert sitting shotgun. Apprehensively, the two men glance at each other, and it's difficult to tell who is more panic-stricken as they set off on their new adventure as roommates.

CHAPTER TWO
The Farmer and the City Boy

Walking into Sam's townhouse, Delbert seems out of place amidst the smooth, contemporary furnishings. "I've been here before, haven't I?"

Sam is surprised by his grandfather's lack of memory. "A few times," he replies. "But you never seemed very comfortable."

Delbert picks up a small, modern sculpture from the shiny marble fireplace mantle and studies it with a frown. "I can't imagine why," he says sarcastically.

That night, Delbert settles into the spare bedroom and falls asleep, tossing and turning. Sam watches him from the doorway and remembers the night he went to live with his grandparents.

Sam, fifteen, has a restless first night's sleep in the farmhouse. A nightmare forces him to relive the horrible car crash that took his parents' life and spared his own. Deeper and deeper he drifts back to that evening.

On a long stretch of highway, Tom drives his family home from an art exhibition. Not an event he or Sam cared about, but Rachel loved it and is grateful to them for making her thirty-fifth birthday a special one. As Sam nods off to sleep in the back seat, rain suddenly comes down in torrents. There is zero visibility, and out of nowhere, a truck veers into their

*lane. With a loud screeching of tires, the dream is over and
Sam jolts up in bed.*

*Delbert, who watches from the doorway, goes to him
and gently lays him back down and slides the covers up around
his shoulders.*

Now it's Sam's turn to comfort Delbert, and he sits on the edge
of the bed and gently rubs his arm. "It's OK, Grandpa. It's OK." The
trembling Delbert calms down and drifts into a peaceful sleep.

The morning sun streams through Sam's bedroom window. Sam
is fast asleep until the sound of the TV blaring wakes him up. Groggy,
he slides out of bed and follows the sound into the living room where
Delbert sits on the couch eating crackers out of a box.

Sam frowns. "Don't you ever sleep in past six o'clock?"

Delbert stays fixated on the TV. "I just get up whenever I wake
up. Whatever time that happens to be. I didn't know where I was at
first."

"Did you take your pill?" Sam asks in a fatherly tone.

Delbert fiddles with the remote control. "Oh. I forgot. I've been
trying to figure out this blasted thing."

Sam takes the remote and turns down the volume. He snatches
the box of crackers out of Delbert's hands. "Is this your idea of
breakfast?"

Delbert gives him the old stink eye, but Sam pays no attention
and flips through the channels with the clicker. "There's *Gunsmoke.* You
like that don't you, Grandpa?"

He grins from ear to ear. "Hey, I haven't seen this in years!"

Sam goes into the kitchen, which is visible from the living room,
and returns with a glass of water and a pill. He hands them to Delbert
who protests.

"I wish you'd quit fussing over me. I can take care of myself."
Reluctantly, Delbert takes the pill.

Sam goes back to the kitchen and makes a pot of oatmeal on the
stove. While he stirs the bubbling porridge, he senses that Delbert is
staring at him. He glances up, startling Delbert.

"Why are you looking at me like that?" Delbert asks
suspiciously.

"Like what?"

"Like you're mad at me."

Sam is perplexed. "Mad at you? Why would I be mad at you? I just looked up at you because you were looking at me."

"I wasn't looking at you."

Sam takes a deep breath. "Let's just drop it, OK?" He takes an orange from a bowl on the counter and peels it. He tries not to look up at Delbert who is still staring at him.

Delbert persists. "I want to know why you're mad at me."

Sam grits his teeth. "For the last time, I'm not mad!"

Sam shoves an orange peel in his mouth and smiles a big orange grin at Delbert. "See?" Sam says with garbled words. "I'm smiling!"

But this seems to disturb Delbert who, in his Alzheimer's state of mind, sees something quite different. To him, Sam's expression is cold and heartless as he stares back at Delbert with a sinister smile.

Sam is taken aback by Delbert's obvious look of fear. Sadly, he takes the orange peel out of his mouth. "You used to crack me up with that, Grandpa."

The oatmeal bubbles and sputters on the stove. Sam turns off the burner. Delbert turns his attention back to the TV and calms down.

The next day, Delbert is up early and dressed in his Sunday best. He stands in front of the mirror going through the frustrating process of tying his tie. The once simple routine has become a chore and takes three attempts to get it right. The tie ends up being too long, but he simply tucks it in his waistband. Satisfied with the results, he slips on his jacket.

Sam is still in his sweats working intensely at his drafting table. He takes a sip of coffee as Delbert enters wearing his spiffy suit and carrying his bible tucked under his arm. Sam peers over his coffee cup.

"Going somewhere?"

"It's Sunday, isn't it?" asks Delbert rhetorically.

"*That* you remember?" Sam asks in amazement.

A couple of hours later, the two cruise through town in the Viper looking for a church that appears to meet Delbert's standards.

Sam grows weary. "Why couldn't we have just found one in the Yellow Pages instead of driving all over town?"

Delbert stares out the window. "Can't tell what a church is like from the Yellow Pages."

"Can't tell from the inside of a car either," Sam snaps back. "We could've driven out to your own church in this amount of time," he continues.

Finally, they come across one that pleases Delbert. "That one!" he shouts as he points to a quaint little church with stained-glass windows. The sign reads, "Full Gospel Church."

Inside, an entirely African-American, charismatic worship service is underway. A seemingly spirit-filled choir claps and dances in time to lively gospel music.

Sam and Delbert stand quietly amidst the hallelujahs and praise-the-Lords. Sheepishly, they glance at each other.

Later in the parking lot, Sam and Delbert sit in the car without saying a word. Finally, Sam admits, "I liked it."

Delbert agrees. "Me too. We'll put it on our 'maybe' list." And with that, Sam starts the engine.

That afternoon in the townhouse, Delbert sits on his bed and counts the money in his wallet.

Sam peeks in the doorway. "Will you be OK if I run out for a few minutes? I need to get some groceries."

"Sure, go ahead."

Sam seems relieved at the thought of having some time alone. He retrieves his car keys from the kitchen counter, turns, and nearly plows into Delbert.

Agitated, Sam asks sharply, "What are you doing?"

"I'm going with you."

Sam stiffens. "I'm kind of in a hurry. I need to get back to finish some work for my meeting tomorrow."

"So don't waste time yapping." Delbert follows him through the kitchen to the door that leads into the garage. He suddenly stops in his tracks. "Oops. Forgot my coat."

Sam waits impatiently as Delbert shuffles back to his bedroom.

Later, Sam and Delbert drive through town. Delbert squirms in the passenger seat. "I don't like this car. How much did you pay for this thing anyway?"

"Not as much as you might think," Sam replies. "It's an old model that needed a lot of work." He nudges Delbert with a smile. "And thanks to everything you taught me about cars, I managed to fix it up and save quite a bit of money."

Proudly, Delbert returns the smile as they stop at a red light. "Where are we going again?"

"Just a little market I like," Sam says. "I like it because you can get in and out quickly."

The light turns green and Sam continues down the road, passing a huge bulk food store. Delbert sees it and practically jumps out of his seat. "Food Monster! Let's go there!"

"I'm not going to Food Monster."

Delbert crosses his arms and pouts.

Exasperated, Sam let's out a heavy sigh. "Oh, all right."

Delbert smiles triumphantly as Sam makes a U-turn in front of a sign that posts "No U-Turn" . Suddenly, red lights flash behind the Viper, and a police siren blares. Sam checks his rearview mirror. "Oh, great." He pulls over and the cop tucks in behind him. Nervously, Sam digs in the glove compartment for his registration.

Delbert seem indignant. "I've never had a traffic ticket in all my years of driving."

Sam shoots him an icy glance as the cop approaches his window.

Inside the Food Monster, Sam tugs on a grocery cart and tries to free it from a long line of other carts. It doesn't budge. He shakes it violently until it breaks loose. He stares in amazement at its huge size!

Sam pushes the cart as quickly as he can through the endless aisles. He has to keep slowing down to allow Delbert to catch up. Delbert spots a monstrous pack of toilet paper and drags it off the shelf and plops it in the cart.

Turning down the condiments aisle, Sam glances back at Delbert who's approaching him with a gallon jar of mayonnaise. "Come on, Grandpa, how much mayonnaise can two guys eat?"

Undeterred, Delbert puts the jar in the cart.

In another aisle, Sam notices a big bottle of aspirin and grabs it off the shelf. "Ah. Something I can use." He looks over his shoulder at Delbert who lags behind. Sam taps his fingers impatiently on the cart and glances at a clock on the wall that shows it's five thirty.

Later at the checkout stand, the clock now reads six thirty. Delbert and a very tired-looking Sam are next in line to be checked out. Their cart is overflowing.

"Finally," says Sam with a sigh as Rita, the grocery checker, pulls their cart up.

"Can I see your club card?" she asks.

Sam's face goes blank. "My what?"

Outside the store, Sam strains to push the loaded-down cart out the door and into the parking lot. Delbert follows with a sheepish look on his face as Sam grumbles to himself. "A forty-dollar membership fee on top of a one hundred and seventy-three-dollar and . . . ." he pauses to check the receipt, "twenty-four-cent grocery bill."

They approach the Viper, and Sam pops the trunk and shoves in the monster pack of toilet paper. It takes up half the space. Sam and Delbert look at the overloaded cart and back at the tiny trunk again.

That night at the townhouse, the moon spills through Delbert's window and washes over the bed where Delbert is curled up under the covers. He stares out the window with sad eyes.

Meanwhile in the living room, Sam stands at the window talking on his cell phone to Victoria. "I miss you," he whispers.

"I miss you too," Victoria coos as she steps out of the hot tub on the patio of a luxurious Aspen cabin. Her rich, snobby friends, Roxanne and Brittany, remain submerged in the bubbly water. "Even though you didn't call me yesterday," she scolds while slipping into a terry-cloth robe.

"I was . . . busy," Sam says nervously. "Look, Victoria, I have something to tell you."

Victoria walks inside the cabin and closes the patio door behind her. She unleashes her pinned up hair and sits on the arm of a chair in the tastefully decorated den. "Busy working on the Patterson account I hope," she interrupts. "Daddy's counting on you."

"I know. I think landing that account is a requirement if I want to keep my position."

"So nail it then," Victoria commands. "Our future depends on it. And speaking of our future, Roxanne and Brittany told me that Tiffany's has *the* engagement ring to die for."

Sam's voice cracks. "Tiffany's?"

"Yes. To die for they said. So we have to check it out." She gets up and saunters over to an easel set up in the corner. There's a really bad painting of the Aspen snow-capped mountains propped up on it. She smiles with pride. "And then there are the preparations for my art exhibit. I'm almost as excited about that as our engagement. In fact, I have a surprise for you when I get back."

"That makes both of us," Sam says.

"What?"

"Oh, nothing. By the way, Grandpa was released from the hospital. In case you might be wondering."

Victoria notices a spec of lint or something on her painting. She gently blows it off. "Oh . . . that's great, honey."

Brittany and Roxanne come inside, giggling and dripping wet. Victoria narrows her eyes at them and quickly wraps up her conversation with Sam. "I hate to cut this short, but I should go. I need my sleep if I'm going to tackle that black-diamond run in the morning. Good luck with the meeting tomorrow. Just stay focused, and you'll be fine."

Back at the townhouse, Sam snaps his cell phone shut. "What could possibly derail my train of thought?" He rubs his head as the beginnings of a headache surface.

Morning arrives all too soon. Sam is in the kitchen dressed for work and quickly chugs down the last few drops of coffee.

Delbert sits on the couch staring at him. "If I knew you were just going to take off and leave me by myself all day, I wouldn't have come out to visit you."

Sam quickly snatches up a large portfolio from his drafting table. "I'm late for work, Grandpa. I have to run."

"And what am I supposed to do?"

"What do you normally do?" Sam picks up the remote control and turns on the TV. He hands the clicker to Delbert who seems perturbed at the insinuation.

Sam hurries into the kitchen for a few seconds and returns with the cordless phone. "Here. You can call me . . . if it's something really important. I taped my number to it." He points. "This button turns it on."

Delbert grabs it out of his hands. "I think I know how to work a telephone!" he says sharply. He studies the buttons for a moment, and then with embarrassment asks, "This one, you said?"

"Yep," Sam replies.

"When will you be back?"

"Between five-thirty and six. I'll see you later, OK?"

Delbert ignores him.

"Come on, Grandpa, don't be that way. This is my job. I can't just *not* go to work. Especially today. I have a very important meeting, and people are depending on me."

Delbert's expression turns sad, his voice soft. "There was a time when people depended on me too."

Filled with guilt, Sam pats him on the shoulder and exits through the kitchen. The door slams shut, and Delbert suddenly looks very nervous. He sits and stares blankly at the television.

At the farmhouse, Sam, fifteen, reclines on his bed and sketches some architectural designs in a sketchpad. Heavy metal music blares from an old boom box. There's a knock on the door, but he doesn't hear it.

The bedroom door opens, and Delbert pokes his head in. "Sammy? Sammy!"

Startled, Sam turns the music down. "I told you not to call me that anymore."

"Sorry. Sam," Delbert corrects himself. "I was just wondering if you would be interested in earning some money."

Traveling alongside a cornfield, Delbert gives a sullen-looking Sam a lift in the bed of his pickup truck. The window between them is open so they can talk to each other. Delbert glances at Sam in his rearview mirror. "A little corn detasseling never hurt anybody."

Sam scowls. "Sounds boring."

Delbert pulls up next to a group of teenagers waiting at a four-way stop. "Something tells me you're not going to be bored for long."

There are two girls in the group. Both are very pretty, and one is very voluptuous. The voluptuous one is Shawna

Evans who is fifteen. The skinny one is her 13-year-old sister,
Cassie. The teenagers pile into the pickup truck, and Sam
quickly sits up straight as he takes notice of Shawna.
Delbert smiles and shakes his head, sensing trouble.

Delbert's eyes grow heavy, and he falls asleep.

Meanwhile, Sam races up the front steps to his office building clutching his portfolio.

Inside, he darts over to the elevator and squeezes between the doors just as they slide shut. He steps out onto the sixteenth floor and scurries over to a door that has a sign that reads, *Mason Architects*. He opens it and breezes by Cheryl, the receptionist, who promises to bring in a pot of coffee for the meeting.

Sam slithers inside the conference room and closes the door. Mr. Mason sits at the head of a long table. In the seat next to him is Mr. Patterson, a rich but humble man in his sixties. Mr. Mason remarks, "Nice of you to join us, Sam."

Sam steps up to the table and extends his hand across it to offer Mr. Patterson a handshake. "Good morning, Mr. Patterson. Very sorry I'm late."

He accepts the handshake. "Promptness is essential in the business world, son. But I'll allow it . . . this time."

Sam is grateful. "Thank you, sir." He sets his portfolio on the floor and takes a seat next to Tran who teases him.

"So how was your weekend? I heard you got yourself a Del."

Sam narrows his eyes at him and responds curtly. "Yes. Yes, I did. Thanks for asking."

Brad joins in on Tran's fun and smiles mischievously at Sam. "How's that working out?"

Sam gives him a hard look as well. "Fine. Just fine. Didn't come with quite as much memory as I had expected, but I'm sure it can be fixed." Sam shoots one last warning glance at each of them.

Mr. Mason is incensed. "Can we cut the idle chit chat and get down to business?"

"Sorry," Sam apologizes.

Mr. Mason gets the ball rolling. "As everyone knows, Mr. Patterson is consulting with three architectural firms, ours being one of them, to discern which one can best capture the specific vision he has for the design of a new retail shopping plaza. He has discussed certain elements in detail with Sam who has drawn up some preliminary sketches." He turns to Sam. "The floor is yours."

Sam takes a deep breath and stands up. "Mr. Patterson, you expressed a desire to bring back the charm and uniqueness that is lacking in today's cookie-cutter architecture. A desire to bring back the days before shopping malls and superstores." He takes his design from the portfolio and places it on a metal ledge on the wall. He points to the vividly colored drawing that is reminiscent of retail designs of the fifties but with a contemporary flair. Mr. Patterson leans in, giving Sam his full attention. Sam continues with more self-assuredness. "Back when people strolled leisurely downtown and peered into storefront windows that had captivating displays. This is Mr. Patterson's dream–affordable shopping in a quaint, homey environment with good old-fashioned architecture and charm."

Mr. Patterson smiles warmly. "Very nice, son. Very nice indeed. You have set the bar quite high for your competitors."

"Thank you, sir," Sam smiles sincerely. Suddenly, the magic of the moment is broken with the ringing of Sam's cell phone.

Mr. Mason and Mr. Patterson both become irritated at the interruption as they watch Sam nervously take the phone off his belt clip. "I'm sorry. Excuse me a moment." He answers it. "Hello? What? This is not a good time. Can I call you back?" Embarrassed, he turns sideways and tries to whisper, but his growing frustration causes him to speak louder. "Did you press the off button? It's the big red one in the middle. At the top. No, at the top. Just push it. Just aim and push. No, that's the volume. Turn it down. No, down . . . the arrow that points down!"

All eyes are on Sam who shrinks with humiliation. He continues talking to Delbert. "Did you get it? Oh. Well, that works, I guess. OK, I have to go now."

 Sam hangs up the phone and turns to them. "That was my grandfather. He was doing battle with the TV remote, and the remote was winning. So he just decided to unplug the TV." Everyone continues staring at him. "But he's got the phone figured out," he laughs nervously.

Mr. Mason rubs his chin as he looks at Sam suspiciously. Cheryl breaks the tension by bringing in coffee for everyone.

After the meeting, Mr. Mason walks in Sam's office and leans against the door with his arms folded. "I think Mr. Patterson was quite impressed for the most part. Just a few minor changes and I believe the account is ours. Good job, Sam."

Sam looks up from his computer. "Thank you, sir."

"Your grandfather must not have realized you were in the middle of a very important meeting."

Sam gets the hint. "Ok. I'll talk to him."

Mr. Mason pats him fatherly on the back. He picks up a framed photo of Victoria from Sam's desk and looks at it adoringly. "By the way, isn't your grandfather's name Delbert?"

Sam squirms in his chair. "Yep."

"He wouldn't happen to be the 'Del' Tran was referring to by any chance?"

Sam confesses. "My grandfather hasn't been doing well since my grandmother died. So he's staying with me right now."

"Oh? For how long?"

Tran walks by the door. "Yes, Sam, just how long will he be staying with you?" Tran continues down the hall, but Mr. Mason waits for Sam's answer.

"I'm not sure," Sam sighs.

Disapproval washes over Mr. Mason's face. "This comes at a very inopportune time."

"Death usually does."

He bristles at Sam's sarcasm and sets the photo down. "What does Victoria think about it?"

"You did *what*?" Victoria screams at Sam as he drives her home from the airport. Her face is distorted with horror.

Inside Victoria's white-on-white shabby chic apartment, she flings her coat on the couch and marches into the kitchen.

Sam sets the suitcase down in the living room and sinks into a puffy taffeta-covered chair. "I don't know what you're so upset about," he calls out to her. "This is just a temporary situation until he gets better."

Victoria returns with a glass of wine in one hand and a can of soda in the other. Softening, she hands the soda to Sam and slides down on the floor and curls up at his feet. "I just wish you had discussed it with me first. After all, we're engaged now and what you do affects me. Affects us."

Sam reaches down and strokes her luxurious locks. "You're right. I'm sorry."

She wraps her arms around his leg and leans her head adoringly against it. "I'm sorry too. I just don't want anything to jeopardize everything you've accomplished. You deserve the Patterson account, and nothing should stand in your way."

Sam puts his soda down and pulls her up onto his lap. "Let's not fight. I promise you, he won't get in the way of our plans." He lifts her chin and kisses her softly.

A BMW with license plates that reads, "MS VCKY" is parked in front of Tiffany's jewelry store. Inside, Victoria and Sam sit at a glass display case filled with diamond rings. Victoria practically squeals with delight as she holds up her left hand and admires a platinum ring with a huge diamond encircled by several smaller ones.

Delbert stands behind them, and he leans down to get a good look at the rock. He positions his head right in between Sam's and Victoria's, and he scrunches up his face in disapproval of the ring. "Kind of gaudy, isn't it?"

Victoria casts him a frosty glance.

Later outside Sam's townhouse, Victoria pulls up in the BMW. Sam is in the passenger seat and Delbert is in the back. Inside, Victoria keeps her left hand on the steering wheel as if showing off her flashy diamond ring. She glances back at Delbert in the rearview mirror and then turns to Sam. "Well, that was romantic." Her words drip with sarcasm. "Just the way I always dreamed."

Somberly, Sam opens his car door. "He insisted on going."

"No, I didn't," Delbert protests.

Sam ignores him and keeps his eyes on Victoria. "Besides, it's your fault for talking me into buying a two-seater sports car. Which I'll have to sell to pay for that ring."

Delbert leans forward. "I told you to get the other ring, the one with the small, single diamond. It's simple, but elegant."

Victoria rolls her eyes. "Come on, Sam, you're a junior partner. Live like one!"

"If only my position with the company was as solid as that rock you're wearing." Sam starts to get out of the car but realizes he forgot to kiss Victoria. He leans over and gives her an unenthusiastic peck and then glances back at Delbert. "Come on, Grandpa."

The two men slide out of the car and watch as Victoria screeches off down the street. "I don't know what you see in that woman," Delbert confesses.

A couple of weeks later, the morning starts out in the usual way at the townhouse. Perhaps too routine for Sam who seems agitated as he works at his drafting table.

Delbert stands at the front window gazing out. Suddenly, the sound of guns blazing from the TV distracts him, and he turns to look. "Hey, isn't this that show . . . oh, I can't think of the name . . . ."

Without looking up from his work, Sam replies flatly, *"Gunsmoke."*

"Yeah, that's the one . . . with that marshal . . . uh . . . . "

"Matt Dillon."

"Yeah. And Chester. Or it Festus?"

Sam grits his teeth. "Both. They're two different people."

"Oh, well," Delbert says lightly, "I can't remember. It's been too long since I've seen this show."

Sam buries his head in his hands, at his wits end with the constant questions about a TV show that Delbert watches daily and then forgets about.

Turning back to the window, Delbert watches a florist truck pull up the street. The driver delivers flowers to an elderly lady, and Delbert suddenly seems sad. "What day is this?" he asks softly.

"It's Saturday. Valentine's Day," Sam replies.

"Valentine's Day?" The first one without Emily tugs at his heart. "Why don't we take a drive out to the farm?"

"I can't, Grandpa. I told you I have a business luncheon."

"A business luncheon on a Saturday?"

"Trying to get a jump on the competition. I think Mr. Patterson's going to like the changes, and with a little wining and dining, I think we've got this in the bag." Sam stands and stretches. "Then tonight I'm taking Victoria out for what I hope will be a victory celebration. You can go with us if you want." His tone is more obligatory than genuine.

"I don't want to go out for dinner," Delbert pouts. "I want to go to the farm. You haven't taken me there since I came out here to visit you."

"Yes, I have, Grandpa. Last week when we took down the Christmas decorations, remember?"

"No. I don't. Why are you saying these things?"

Sam stares at him for a moment. "Uh-oh." He jumps up and heads to the kitchen. "I forgot all about your pill. You haven't eaten anything either, have you?"

"I'm not hungry."

Sam grabs a diabetic testing kit off the counter and leads Delbert to the couch. "Have a seat and we'll test your blood."

Delbert sits. "I'm tired of having my finger poked."

"This is a new tester. You use it on your arm." Sam takes a blood sample and applies it to the test strip. The meter beeps, and he reads the number. "One-eleven. Steady numbers for over a week now." He sighs and scratches his head in bewilderment.

"That's good, isn't it?" asks Delbert noticing Sam's frown.

"Yeah, Grandpa," Sam smiles weakly, "It's good." He pats him on the knee and takes the test kit into the kitchen. He returns with a pill and a glass of water and holds them out in front of Delbert who stiffens.

"You wouldn't try to poison me, would you?" Delbert asks suspiciously.

"Poison you?" Sam asks in disbelief. "Geez, Grandpa, don't you appreciate anything I'm doing for you?"

"If I'm such a burden, take me home."

"Please take your pill so I can fix you something to eat. I need to start getting ready for my meeting."

Delbert pretends to pop the pill in his mouth. He drinks the water and hands the glass back to Sam. Casually, he slides his clutched hand with the pill in it under his leg.

"You fooled me with that once before, Grandpa, but I'm on to you now. Let me see your hand."

Delbert pulls his hand out, palm side up. It's empty.

Sam slides his hand under Delbert's leg and retrieves the pill. He holds it in front of Delbert and says sternly, "Take it." Defeated, Delbert obeys.

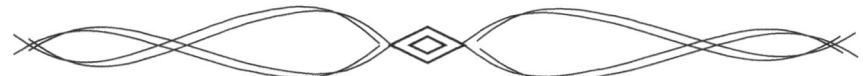

CHAPTER THREE
Grandpa Escapes from the City

Delbert searches for something in his room. He looks under the bed, in the pocket of a pair of pants and in the dresser drawers. Worried, he hurries out of the room and down the hall to the bathroom and knocks on the door. "Sammy! I can't find my wallet!"

Sam opens the door. He's in his boxer shorts, and he has shaving cream on his face. "I'll find it for you in a minute, OK?" He steps back to the sink and picks up his razor and continues shaving. He's obviously not too concerned about what seems to be a common occurrence with the wallet.

But Delbert is almost hysterical. "I've looked everywhere, and it's nowhere to be found. I've got all my money and credit cards in there. You didn't take it, did you?"

Sam puts down the razor and squeezes past Delbert and goes down the hall into Delbert's room. He slides his hand between the mattresses and retrieves the wallet, holding it up to Delbert. "It's where you always put it."

Delbert grabs it. "How did you know it was there?" he asks accusingly.

Sam gets up. "Lucky guess." He heads back to the bathroom to finish shaving.

Delbert slides the wallet in his pocket and follows Sam. "So are you taking me to the farm today or not?"

"Not. I have things to do."

"Well, I have things to do too, you know." Sam ignores him, trying to prevent an argument, but Delbert persists. "Why don't we go pick up my car and bring it back here so you don't have to cart me all over the place anymore? Then I can drive myself back there whenever I want."

"You're not used to driving the expressways." Sam leans into the mirror above the sink and glides the razor up his neck.

"Then just take me home, period." Delbert waits for a response but gets none. "I don't want to be here anymore!"

This hurts Sam's feelings, but he continues to ignore him. Enraged, Delbert lunges at Sam, knocking the razor out of his hand and causes him to stumble backwards. He latches onto the shower curtain to keep from completely falling into the bathtub. Delbert leans over him, his eyes wild. "Did you hear what I said? I want to go home!" Delbert storms out.

Blood trickles down Sam's neck where the razor sliced him. Trembling, he stands up and wipes the blood and shaving cream off his face with a towel as he looks at himself in the mirror.

Moments later, a car engine revs. "No . . . don't tell me!" Sam throws down the towel and bolts out of the bathroom.

Outside, the automatic garage door opens and the Viper shoots out in reverse with Delbert at the wheel. He backs into the street and slams on the brakes.

Sam races out still barefoot and clad only in his boxers. He approaches the car, and Delbert quickly locks the doors.

Sam taps furiously on Delbert's window with one hand and clutches the door handle with the other. "Grandpa, turn off the engine and get out of the car. Now!"

Smugly, Delbert revs the engine.

Sam tries a new, relaxed approach with a forced smile. "Come on, pardner. Get out of Dodge." He taps on the window. "*This* Dodge."

Delbert lowers the window just an inch or so. "Are you going to take me to the farm?"

"I can't today, but maybe tomorrow."

"Wrong answer." Delbert shifts into drive and puts his foot on the accelerator, creeping forward.

Sam holds his grasp on the handle and pounds on the window as the Viper picks up pace. "What are you doing? Stop the car!"

Delbert keeps going, looking straight ahead.

"I swear, Grandpa, if you don't get out of this car right now I'll . . ."

Delbert stops the car. Sam breathes a sigh of relief, but then Delbert turns and gives him a sinister look. Suddenly, Delbert floors the accelerator in pure defiance, and the Viper shoots ahead. Sam stumbles forward and watches in horror as the Viper disappears down the street.

In the townhouse a short time later, Officer Daniels takes a report. "Don't worry, Mr. Prichard. Vipers are fairly easy to spot. We'll find him. Just sit tight."

Sam sits tight all right, but in the passenger seat of Tran's Lexus, which is stuck in traffic on the expressway. Tran, who's driving, tries to calm his worries. "Don't panic, buddy. It's only ten forty-five, and the meeting doesn't start until one. You might make it."

Sam looks at him as if he's nuts. "Sure, if Grandpa's not laid out in a ditch somewhere, *and* if he's headed straight for the farm. Even with that, can he remember how to get there?" Sam seems to have aged ten years as he stares anxiously at the endless traffic that looms before them.

About a half a mile ahead is the Viper, also stuck in traffic. Inside, Delbert clutches the wheel, overwhelmed by the vast number of vehicles that surround him.

The traffic begins to move, and Delbert excels slowly. Soon he's clipping along at a decent rate. He approaches an array of freeway signs. He glances from one sign to another, unsure which way to go. He veers off in the direction of the business district. He changes his mind and swerves back, darting across lanes of traffic and cutting off someone behind him who lays on the horn. Flustered, Delbert forges on.

Around noon on a country road, the Viper emerges over a hill. The farmhouse is straight ahead. Delbert squints from the glare of the sun, and he shades his eyes with his hand. He trails off into the other lane where a limousine is directly in his path. The horn blares, causing Delbert to turn sharply and lose control of the car. He plows into his own mailbox at the farmhouse. He's unhurt but dazed as he stares at the mailbox and remembers a similar incident fifty years earlier.

Delbert and Emily, young newlyweds, drive up the road in their Chevy Coupe with a sign in the rear window that reads, "Just Married." They stop in front of the farmhouse, bumping the mailbox slightly. Delbert gets out of the car and walks around to Emily's door and opens it. She steps out, and they walk up to the house kissing and giggling. At the porch, Delbert whisks her up in his arms. "Welcome home, Mrs. Prichard." He kisses her tenderly and carries her up the steps and into the house.

Delbert snaps out of his daze by a tap on his side window. He looks up, and shadowed by the sun is the silhouette of a young woman.

"Emily?" he asks.

"It's Cassie, Mr. Prichard. Remember me?" She leans in closer, revealing her beautiful face. Her long, ruby-red bridesmaid's dress billows in the breeze. She clutches a coat around her shoulders.

Delbert studies her for a moment, his face brightening. "Cassie? Oh, of course, I remember you. You're a friend of Sam's."

She smiles and nods as Delbert shuts off the ignition and gets out of the car, taking the keys with him.

The limo driver, Joe, walks up to Delbert. "Are you all right?"

"I'll live." Delbert cringes at the sight of the damaged car. His focus wanders to the mailbox, and he leans over the slanting pole and opens the box and peeks inside. Empty.

Cassie admires the car. "Is this *your* car?"

"No," Delbert sighs. "It's Sam's."

"Sam owns a Viper?"

"Yeah. Fancy hotrod. It has too much power for street driving."

Cassie suppresses a smile as Kevin, the best man in the wedding party, emerges from the limo and joins them. "We need to speed this up. We've got a reception to go to." He notices Delbert's shaking. "Is he OK?"

"I'm fine!" Delbert snaps.

Inside the limousine, Rick, the groom, looks out the window at Delbert. He turns to his gorgeous and shapely bride, Shawna, now twenty-seven. "Hey, didn't you say you dated a guy who lived here?"

"Yeah," she says. "What a nightmare that was. His grandfather– that old guy out there–always barged in on us at the most inopportune moments. If you know what I mean." She giggles, but Rick's jealous expression causes her to stop. She nuzzles up next to him lovingly.

Meanwhile, Delbert sees a local police car emerging over the hill. "Uh-oh. The marshal's here."

Cassie whirls around to see the squad car driving toward them. In the opposite direction, Tran's car comes up the road.

Delbert looks over his shoulder and strains to see who's in the Lexus. "And here comes Festus . . . and that other guy."

"You mean Chester?" Cassie asks as Delbert smiles at her curiously.

"Yeah. How'd you know?"

"I watch a lot of *Gunsmoke* reruns," she explains.

"They have reruns of that show?"

The squad car pulls into the driveway, and Officer Adams steps out. Cassie nudges Joe and they walk over to the cop and explain the situation.

Meanwhile, Tran's car stops alongside the Viper. Sam jumps out frantically and glances at Delbert just long enough to make sure he's OK. He dashes to the front of the Viper and examines the damage. His hands fly up to his head in disbelief. "My car!"

Tears well up in Delbert's eyes. "I'm sorry, Sammy. I'm sorry."

Sam paces for a few moments, trying to calm himself down. "Are you OK?"

Delbert nods.

Sam turns sympathetic. "Well, you must be because you actually drove this baby on the expressway and found your way here. If I weren't so angry, I'd be impressed!"

Delbert puffs up with pride.

Cassie walks over with Officer Adams and gazes fondly at her first love. "Happy Valentine's Day, Sam."

He spins around at the sound of the familiar voice. "Cassie?"

She smiles shyly.

He can't believe his eyes. "I haven't seen you since—"

"Since your high school graduation," she says.

Sam continues to stare at her as if she were the most beautiful woman in the world. To him, she is.

Officer Adams interrupts their reunion. "Is that your car, sir?"

Sam doesn't take his eyes off Cassie. "Huh? Oh, yeah."

"And this is your grandfather?"

"Yes," he replies, still staring at Cassie. He remembers what a skinny, awkward little thing she used to be.

Deep in the field with the hot sun blazing overhead, sultry Shawna detassels corn. Just a few rows over, Sam detassles too, but he puts much more effort into catching glimpses of Shawna between the cornstalks. He licks his lips and wipes the sweat from his face with a red and white kerchief he takes from his back pocket.

Suddenly, Cassie sneaks up behind him. "Don't pollinate yourself."

Sam practically jumps out of his skin. "What?"

"Corn detasseling is a strange thing. The process of plucking off the tassels so the plant can't pollinate itself. Since you're spoiling all the corn's fun, I thought I'd come over and spoil yours."

"Why don't you go back to your own rows and stay out of mine?" Sam responds rudely.

"I've got my quota for the day. Thought you could use some help." She lifts her ponytail and wipes the perspiration from her neck with her hand. Sam offers her his handkerchief, and she mops up her moist neck and face. When she's done, she ties the kerchief around her neck.

Sam shrugs and lets her keep it. He continues down the row, picking off tassels. "Soooo . . . does your sister have a boyfriend?"

"Yeah, about ten of them."

Sam doesn't think it's a big deal. "Think she'd like to have one more?"

Her face drops with disappointment. "I figured you for the type who would prefer a challenge."

"I'm fifteen," he says matter-of-factly. "I don't think so."

Cassie rolls her eyes.

Tran notices the obvious chemistry between Sam and Cassie and seems to approve. He nudges him out of his stupor. "If you leave now, you can still make it."

Sam explains to Cassie. "I have a very important business meeting I can't miss." She nods as Sam takes Delbert by the arm. "Come on, Grandpa, let's see if the old hotrod still runs."

Delbert jerks away. "I'm not going back!"

Cassie senses that something's not quite right with Delbert, and she walks over to him. "Maybe he can come with me. Shawna just got married, and we're on our way to the wedding reception at the Elk's Lodge."

The idea agrees with Delbert. "Oh, I like the Elk's Lodge."

"Shawna's settling down, huh?" Sam asks indifferently.

"Well," says Cassie with a wink. "I don't know about that." She notices Tran checking his watch impatiently. "So how about it? Can he come with me? I'll take good care of him."

"I think it's a great idea," Tran says.

Hesitantly, Sam agrees. "OK you win, Grandpa. Give me the keys."

Delbert checks his pants pockets. "Now what did I do with them?" A Cheshire grin crosses his face as he slides the keys out of his coat and jingles them in the air.

Sam exhales a sigh of relief.

That afternoon, Mr. Mason and Mr. Patterson arrive at Giacinto's Italian restaurant in Chicago.

Meanwhile, Sam speeds to get there, traveling along the expressway in the dented Viper. A large truck moves in front of him, and he flinches. Regaining his composure, he defiantly whips around the truck, forging ahead. He picks up his cell phone and punches in a phone number.

Mr. Mason and Mr. Patterson are seated at a table inside the restaurant. Checking his watch, Mr. Patterson grows more impatient by the moment.

Mr. Mason's cell phone rings. He answers it. "Yes?" He glances nervously at Mr. Patterson. "Would you excuse me a moment?"

In the lobby, Mr. Mason whispers loudly into the phone. "Where are you? You should've been here ten minutes ago!"

"I'll explain later," says Sam. "I just picked up the drawings, and I'll be there in fifteen minutes–tops."

Mr. Mason angrily snaps his phone shut and returns to the dining room.

Sam has beads of sweat on his upper lip. He taps on the steering wheel. "Come on . . . almost there." Suddenly, there's a loud pop as Sam's front tire blows. He swerves and pulls off the expressway.

He exits the Viper and walks to the front and inspects the tire. It's not a pretty sight. Sam is near hysteria–no, make that borderline nervous breakdown. "What is *this*?" he shrieks at the shredded tire. He frantically paces back and forth and then lunges at it, kicking it violently. "You stupid . . . ahhh!" He gives it another kick and then makes a call on his cell phone. "Hello? Triple A?"

Sporting a brand new tire, the Viper careens around the corner and screeches to a stop in front of the restaurant. Sam hops out clutching his rolled up set of plans.

Mr. Patterson emerges from the front door of the restaurant with Mr. Mason following behind. Sam sprints over to them. "I'm sorry, Mr. Patterson, I had a flat tire and—"

Mr. Patterson puts up a hand to shush him and marches down the sidewalk with Sam and Mr. Mason pursuing him. "Save it, son. I've made up my mind to go with Brighton Architects. I can't do business with such irresponsible people no matter how good their work is." He hesitates to make a point and looks back at Sam. "And yours is superb."

Back at the Elk's Lodge, Shawna's wedding reception is in full swing with people dancing and drinking.

Cassie sits with Delbert at a table. Tran, feeling good from too much champagne, brings over two plates with wedding cake. "This is a great reception! Thanks for inviting me."

"The more the merrier," Cassie replies. "And you seem very merry."

Tran holds out a plate in front of Delbert but then pulls it back just as Delbert is about to take it. "Oh, wait. You can't have this." Delbert's face drops.

Cassie notices Delbert's diabetic bracelet and his disappointment. She glances over at Kevin who is in deep conversation with a pretty girl on the other side of the room. "Actually, I'm not in the mood for cake right now. Why don't you take both pieces over to Kevin and his friend?"

Tran obliges and half walks, half dances his way through the crowd.

I don't like this music," Delbert moans. "Where's Sammy?"

He's at a meeting, remember?" Cassie asks gently.

"He won't forget to pick me up, will he?"

Cassie pats his hand. "No, of course not."

The upbeat music switches to a ballad, and Delbert watches Shawna slow dance with Rick. Other couples join in.

Cassie feels sympathetic toward Delbert. "I heard about Emily. I'm so sorry. I was out of town and didn't even know about the funeral until I got back, or I would've been there."

"They said she had an aneurysm," he says softly.

"That must've been devastating for you. I know how much you loved her."

His eyes fill with tears. "Still do. Did I ever tell you how we met?"

Cassie shakes her head.

"Remember that old barn I had?" A lit candle on the table mesmerizes Delbert.

Fifteen-year-old Sam holds a ladder steady for Delbert who hammers a new board onto a small wooden barn behind the farmhouse. "I don't know why I keep repairing this relic. Don't get much use out of it anymore."

Niblet, his pet pig, runs into the barn. Sam laughs. "Niblet likes it."

Delbert laughs and climbs down. They take the ladder inside the barn and prop it against the wall. Sam goes to Niblet and rubs his belly. "There are a lot of memories in this old barn. Did you know my dad held dances here? He played the banjo, and my Uncle Carl played the fiddle. Well, he tried."

"Sounds exciting," says Sam unenthusiastically.

They walk back out of the barn, and Delbert nods. "It was. This is where I first met your grandmother. She was quite the hottie back then."

Sam chuckles as Delbert closes the door.

Cassie pats Delbert's arm affectionately. "Would you like to dance?" She stands and extends her hand. "Please."

Delbert takes her hand, and they make their way to the dance floor. Cassie leads the dance as they take stiff steps in a circle. Delbert is apprehensive at first but becomes more relaxed.

Meanwhile, at Victoria's apartment, the doorbell rings. She opens the door to find Sam standing there with a bouquet of red roses.

"Sam, what are you doing here so early?"

He hands her the flowers and walks in. "I can't take you to dinner tonight. And . . . I blew the meeting."

"What? What happened?" She closes the door and sets the flowers down on the coffee table. "Did your grandfather do something to get in the way?"

Sam bristles. "Life happened today, Victoria, and the *meeting* got in the way."

"That's an odd thing to say."

Sam notices the Aspen painting propped up against the wall. "Speaking of odd."

Victoria pouts. "That was supposed to be your surprise. I was going to wrap it and give it to you tonight. Don't you like it?"

Sam walks over to the painting and struggles for the right words. "No, I do. What I meant by odd is that it's unique. Interesting."

"Oh. Actually, I was going to ask if you'd mind my keeping it until after the art exhibit. I'd like to display it."

"Mind? Would I mind?" he thinks to himself. "No, no. Keep it as long as you like," he says out loud, relieved. He goes to her and puts his hands on her shoulders. "I'm sorry to do this to you, but I have to go. I left Grandpa at a wedding reception, and I have to pick him up."

"A wedding reception? Sam, what's going on?"

"It's a long story."

He walks to the door, and Victoria slides in front of him. "Do you realize we've hardly talked about our own wedding? And every time I go to your place and we start getting romantic, your grandfather comes waltzing out of his room and interrupts us?"

Sam stifles a laugh. "He doesn't realize what he's doing."

"Oh, I think he knows exactly what he's doing. He doesn't like me, I can tell. You're letting that man get in the way of everything you've worked so hard for. Why?"

Sam hesitates and then kisses her lightly on the lips. "I really need to get back."

He walks out leaving Victoria fuming.

Later at the Lodge, Sam walks in with a defeated look on his face as he stands with his hands shoved in his pockets, scanning the room. He spots Delbert and Cassie and enjoys watching them dance.

From the bar, a tanked Tran zeroes in on Sam. With a drink in his hand, he swaggers across the room and puts his arm around his shoulder. "Hey, buddy! How'd it go?"

"It didn't," says Sam flatly.

Tran slides his arm off Sam's shoulder. "Oh." He takes a sip of his drink. "It's a good night to get drunk then." He drags Sam over to the bar and addresses the bartender. "A drink for my friend here." Tran turns to Sam. "What'll you have, partner? Make that junior partner." He pokes his finger on Sam's chest. "No, wait. *Former* junior partner."

Sam grabs Tran's hand. "OK. I get the point." With a sigh, Sam sidles up to the bar. "I'll have a whiskey."

Tran is shocked. The bartender pours whiskey into a shot glass and plops it in front of Sam who merely stares at it for several moments. Finally, he picks it up and turns to watch Delbert and Cassie. He brings the shot glass up to his nose and breathes in the aroma. He flinches and abruptly pulls the glass away. His mind reels with memories of a bad experience.

It's late in the evening, and Niblet stands in the middle of the barn making grunting sounds up at the loft. He seems to be scolding Sam, who sits up there with his legs dangling over the edge while drinking whiskey from a bottle and smoking a cigarette. Tired of being ignored, Niblet waddles over to the corner and plops down.

Sam decides to get comfy as well and leans against the wall. He sets the whiskey bottle down, and it tips over, spilling the contents over the edge and onto a stack of hay below. But he's too intoxicated to notice. He drifts off to sleep and the cigarette slides from his fingers and lands in the whiskey-soaked hay that instantly catches fire.

Later, outside the barn, two fire trucks are parked nearby as what's left of the barn smolders in the background. Niblet lies on the grass with an oxygen mask over his face as a fire fighter, Bob, assists him. "He'll be all right," he says to Delbert. "Just a little smoke inhalation."

Emily clutches onto Delbert who is in a trance, looking at the remains of his beloved barn.

Sam stands next to him, sobbing. "I'm sorry, Grandpa."

Delbert doesn't seem to hear him but remains fixated on the barn. He's lost in a memory of long ago:

The faint sound of music and laughter drifts from the barn. Through the opened doors, people can be seen dancing to a lively tune played by Emmett Prichard on the banjo and Carl Prichard on the fiddle. They begin a new song, a slow rendition of "You are my Sunshine."

Delbert, fifteen, and Emily, fourteen, smile flirtatiously at each other from opposite sides of the room. Delbert saunters over to her and whispers something in her ear and she giggles bashfully. He takes her hand and they begin to dance, completely absorbed in each other.

Delbert is pulled out of his daydream by a tugging on his arm. "I didn't mean to do it," Sam cries with despair.

"People are what matter," says Delbert as he turns away from the smoldering remains of his barn and hugs his grandson.

"Don't you realize you could've been killed? I couldn't stand to lose you too." He hugs Sam even tighter.

Sam clutches his glass of whiskey as if it's poison. Tran nudges him with a can of soda. "Maybe you should stick with your safe and sane soda."

Sam sets his glass down and takes the soda. "Maybe you should switch to coffee."

That evening, Sam, Delbert, Cassie and Tran enjoy a piece of pie at the Perk Up café.

Sam smiles at Cassie. "This was a good idea."

"Yep," says Delbert. "This sugar-free pie is almost as good as Emily's."

Tran chugs down some coffee. "Time to visit the restroom again."

Delbert follows him down the corridor. "Me too."

Sam turns to Cassie. "Thanks for driving Tran. I think he's sobering up now. And thanks for keeping an eye on Grandpa back at the reception."

"I didn't mind at all." She takes a sip of coffee. "Tran tells me you're engaged."

This takes Sam off guard. "Uh . . . yeah. At least I think I still am. She's not thrilled about my shadow, there." He points in the direction of the restrooms where Delbert is.

"How do you plan to take care of him when his Alzheimer's progresses?"

Sam is taken aback.

"He does have Alzheimer's, right? I assumed that's why he's living with you."

"No," says Sam, feeling as if he's been punched in the stomach. "He was over-medicating himself, and I'm just trying to get him back on track." He pauses, concerned. "But he's been back on track for awhile, at least as far as his diabetes. It's his memory that keeps getting worse. Not to mention his temper and paranoia. He follows me around constantly, and he hides things."

Cassie looks sympathetic. "Well, he certainly has the symptoms of someone with Alzheimer's. I know because I work at a nursing home in the adult daycare center."

"Adult daycare?"

"There is such a thing, you know. You should check one out in your area because he really shouldn't be left alone while you go to work. But the first thing I'd do is have him evaluated."

Delbert storms out of a Chicago medical clinic clutching a small pharmacy bag and heads to the parking lot. Sam trails behind, sullen and quiet.

At the Viper, Sam starts to open the passenger door, but Delbert pushes his hand away and opens it for himself.

"That doctor doesn't know what he's talking about," Delbert blurts out. "He's a quack who just wants my money! Charging me for all these expensive tests and office visits, making me buy pills I don't even need! Well, I'm not going to take them. I don't have Alzheimer's disease!" He shoves the pharmacy bag into Sam's chest and gets in the car, slamming the door.

Sam gets in on the driver's side and looks at Delbert with compassion. He reaches over to help him with his seatbelt, but Delbert grabs the strap and fastens it himself.

That night at the townhouse, Sam and Delbert sit somberly in the dark of their respective bedrooms, deep in thought.

A few days later, Sam is dressed for work and sporting a haggard look with dark circles under his eyes as he drives Delbert to adult daycare.

Delbert fidgets in his seat. "I forgot my sunglasses."

"You don't wear sunglasses," says Sam matter-of-factly.

"I do too when it's glary out like it is now. It hurts my eyes!"

Sam looks as if he's about to pop a vein and turns the car around.

Back at the townhouse, Sam parks in front and jumps out of the car. "I'll be right back."

As he races inside the house, Delbert stares out the windshield. He notices the dent in the hood from where he hit the mailbox. "Hmm . . . I wonder how that happened."

Sam returns with a pair of sunglasses and gets in the car. He hands them to Delbert. "Here. You can wear a pair of mine."

Delbert tries them on. He looks cool in the sporty Oakley's. He admires himself in the visor mirror and smiles.

Suppressing a laugh, Sam starts the engine.

But no sooner than he does, Delbert's eyes widen. "You're not going to believe this."

Sam's smile fades. "Don't tell me."

Delbert slides the sunglasses down his nose and looks pokerfaced at Sam. "I gotta pee."

"No, you don't. You're just stalling."

Delbert strokes the side of his seat. "I'd hate to see this fine upholstery get soaked," he says obnoxiously.

Sam narrows his eyes at him and shuts off the engine.

Later at the Senior Center, the Viper careens into the parking lot. Sam hops out and goes to Delbert's door and opens it. Delbert doesn't budge but crosses his arms defiantly and stares straight ahead.

"Come on, Grandpa," says Sam firmly.

"No. I'm not going to let you stick me in that daycare for old people. I don't need babysitting."

Sam tugs on Delbert's arm.

He pulls back. "I can take care of myself. Just because I forget things once in awhile doesn't mean I'm an invalid."

Exasperation sets in. "Do you like making me late all the time? Do you realize how much trouble I'm in at work?" He gently tries to pry Delbert out of the car.

"Let go of my arm! You're hurting me!"

Sam loosens his grip as people stop and stare. "Knock it off, Grandpa. People think I'm abusing you."

"You are abusing me. Mental abuse!"

"*I'm* abusing *you*?" Sam releases his arm. "Fine. I'll go in and get you signed up. When you get cold, come inside."

Sam proceeds to the front door of the center.

Delbert looks startled, then frightened. The bluff worked. He gets out of the car and hurries after Sam. "Oh, all right. Have it your way."

Sam breathes a sigh of relief and escorts Delbert to the front door.

Inside the adult daycare room, Delbert scrunches up his face at the sight of several elderly people involved in various low-energy activities. "I see dead people," he moans.

Later, Sam scurries down the corridor of Mason Architects and is cut off at the path by Tran, Brad and Mr. Mason as they come out of the conference room.

Mr. Mason's scowl stops Sam in his tracks. "I'd like to see you in my office."

The office is richly decorated with an expensive, mahogany desk, fine leather chairs, and custom-made drapes. All carefully chosen to display his success and grandiosity. Mr. Mason looks out the window as Sam sits quietly waiting for the bomb to drop.

"I don't want to appear cold-hearted. I admire all that you're doing for your grandfather. But the truth is your work has suffered since he moved in with you." He turns to face Sam. "I made you junior partner because you're talented, dedicated and focused. Now I find myself making excuses for you and handing your assignments off to interns who earn far less than you. That isn't fair."

"No, it isn't," Sam admits.

"What would you do in my position?"

"I don't know."

"I think you do. Why don't you mull that over today, and I'll see you at Victoria's art exhibit tonight." From the look on Sam's face, it's obvious he's forgotten all about it. "Well, I see your work isn't the only thing you're neglecting."

That night at the North Shore Art Gallery, high-society types filter in. Soothing classical music plays as guests sip champagne and observe paintings hanging on the stark white walls.

The Aspen painting is prominently displayed on an easel, and Victoria stands proudly next to it and chats with Roxanne, Brittany and Mr. Mason.

Sam enters with Delbert, and Victoria's face turns sour when she sees him.

Delbert shuffles over to the painting and studies it. "Not bad. But it's no Norman Rockwell."

Sam tries not to crack a smile, but Victoria seethes. "Norman Rockwell? He was safe and predictable," she says flippantly.

"Yeah. I like that."

Victoria's had enough of Delbert's impudence, and she pulls Sam aside. "Do you plan to bring him along on our honeymoon too?"

"What's the matter, doesn't he fit in with the ambience around here?" He softens at her wounded expression. "I'm sorry. Do you want us to leave?"

Victoria takes his arm. "No. This night is important to me, and I want to share it with you."

They stroll through the gallery and look at Victoria's other hideous oil paintings, mostly landscapes with no heart or soul. There's even an ugly butterfly with thick orange paint. Not nearly the caliber of Sam's delicate, almost transparent, water-colored butterflies.

"What do you think?" Victoria finally asks.

"Nice." Sam's voice cracks. "Very nice."

She crosses her arms, offended. "Please, don't gush or anything."

Suddenly, something crashes behind them. They turn to see Delbert on the floor along with the Aspen painting and easel.

Victoria is mortified.

Sam races to Delbert's side, shooting a sharp glance at Roxanne and Brittany who just stand there doing nothing. "Wouldn't want you two to break a nail or anything." He pulls Delbert up gently.

"I . . . I tripped. I don't know how but . . . ."

Victoria picks up the canvas and sees that it's damaged. Like a snarling wolf, she grits her teeth at him. "You idiot. Look what you've done!"

Instantly she knows it was the wrong thing to say.

Outraged, Sam grabs her by the arm. "Don't ever call him that again. Do you understand?"

"I . . . I'm sorry. I shouldn't have said that."

Someone's hand pulls Sam away. It belongs to Mr. Mason. "I think it's time for you to leave."

Sam doesn't bat an eye. "I think you're right." And with that, he releases Victoria and escorts Delbert out.

Victoria chokes back the tears.

Outside in the parking lot, Sam guides a trembling Delbert to the Viper. "Are you OK? Did you hurt yourself?"

Delbert jerks away. "Why did you bring me here? Who cares about all that artsy-fartsy nonsense anyway!"

"Obviously not you."

"I've never seen such crap. That back there was just a spoiled little girl playing make believe."

Sam's jaw tightens. "And what constitutes good art to you, Grandpa? The painting above the saloon bar on *Gunsmoke*?"

Delbert stops to contemplate this. "I don't think there was a painting, was there? I think there was a mirror . . . or some shelves maybe."

Delbert takes off again, leaving Sam gaping after him. He throws his hands up in disbelief at the things Delbert remembers. "I don't care what they had! *That's* make-believe! The reality is my life is suddenly down the crapper, a word you so eloquently use, and all you seem to care about is getting back to TV Land!"

Sam catches up, his anger growing with every step. At the Viper, Sam opens the passenger door for Delbert who studies Sam's face.

"You're mad at me, aren't you? I can tell because there's a vein popping out right there." Delbert pokes his finger at a protruding vein on Sam's forehead.

Sam pulls his hand away, the stress of the past several weeks coming to a boiling point. "Stop it! Why can't you just act normal?"

Fear sweeps across Delbert's face, startling Sam into releasing his grip. Delbert slides down into the car, his chin quivering.

Sam closes his eyes in anguish, realizing what he's done. He opens them and looks down remorsefully at Delbert who has a tear traveling down the crevice of his cheek. Gently, Sam shuts the door and walks around and gets in on the driver's side.

Delbert stares blankly out the window, his hands shaking as they rest in his lap. "I like *your* artwork," he says softly.

"What?" Sam asks.

Delbert turns and looks at him through watery eyes. "You asked me what kind of artwork I like. I like yours." Turning his head to look out the window again, he asks weakly, "Can we go home now?"

Sam's heart breaks for him, and he leans over and fastens Delbert's seatbelt. Sitting up, he grasps the steering wheel and thinks for a moment. He draws in a deep breath, slides the key into the ignition and starts the engine.

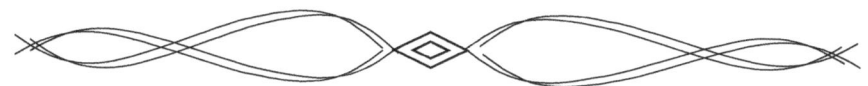

CHAPTER FOUR
Country Roads, Take Us Home

It's a beautiful spring day as a Dodge Ram pickup truck loaded with boxes and Sam's drafting table travels down a country road. Sam is at the wheel with Delbert in the passenger seat. They glance at each other and exchange smiles.

Later, the truck pulls into the driveway of the farmhouse. Sam jumps out and runs around to Delbert's door and opens it. Delbert steps out excitedly.

As they walk up to the front door, Delbert glances over at the garage. "I can't wait to drive my car again."

"Uh-oh," Sam's expression seems to say. "It probably has a flat tire from sitting for so long," he hopes out loud.

Sam unlocks the door, and they walk into the house. Delbert breathes in the familiar surroundings and closes his eyes as if receiving a warm hug. When he opens them, they're filled with tears. He turns to Sam and hugs him. "Thank you."

With a firm pat on the back, Delbert releases Sam and heads to the staircase. "Time to reacquaint myself with the old commode." He takes five steps up and stops. "I don't remember these steps being so steep."

Sam looks concerned. "You're not used to climbing them, so be careful."

As Delbert makes his way up and out of sight, a car horn blares outside. Sam goes out to investigate. It's Cassie walking up the driveway wearing old, comfortable clothes and holding an apple pie. She tilts it for Sam to see while flashing him a radiant smile.

Thrilled to see her, he nods and smiles back.

Later in the kitchen, Sam fixes a pipe underneath the sink.

Cassie, who is busy wiping down the stove, can't seem to keep herself from taking quick glimpses of Sam's outstretched body. "You guys could use a new stove."

"We could use a whole new kitchen." Sam rummages for a wrench in the toolbox.

"This is quite a sacrifice you're making for your grandfather." She kneels down and hands him the wrench, allowing her hand to linger in his for a moment.

"Not really," he says. "I'm just stumbling through this caregiving stuff one day at a time."

"Still, it's a sacrifice. You always hated living in the country."

Sam lifts his head to get a good look at her. He smiles. "Well, at least the scenery is beautiful."

Cassie blushes as Delbert walks in holding a pair of eyeglasses and smiling proudly.

"I fixed Emily's glasses." His expression turns sad. "Kind of silly, I guess."

"I think it's sweet," says Cassie while getting up. She pats him on the arm and goes back to cleaning the stove.

Delbert bends down, straining to see Sam. "Need some help?"

"That's all right, Grandpa. I've got it."

"Two heads are better than one."

"I can handle it."

Feeling useless, Delbert walks out.

Suddenly, the pipe breaks and water gushes out from underneath the sink. Sam quickly slides out from the cabinet, drenched.

His horrified expression causes Cassie to burst out laughing. "I'm sorry, but that's what you get for dismissing your grandfather like that."

Sam scampers to his feet and takes one step on the wet floor, and down he goes.

Giggling, Cassie comes to his aid. "Oh my gosh, are you OK?"

"See? Just stumbling through," he chuckles.

Delbert walks by, looks at the mess and shakes his head. He opens the back door and walks outside and shuts off the main water valve.

Inside, the water that's flowing out from under the sink slows to a trickle and then stops. Cassie pulls Sam up, and he rubs his hip, laughing.

Delbert walks in, and the sight of them together seems to make him happy as he smiles approvingly. "I took care of it."

"Thanks, Grandpa. I guess I could use your help after all."

Sam's cell phone rings from the kitchen table.

Cassie sloshes across the floor. "Ooh, let me. You're wounded." She picks up the phone and stifles a giggle, "Sam's Plumbing and Repair."

Sam chuckles.

"Hello? Helll-ooo?" Cassie puts the phone down. "I guess they don't need a plumber."

From the bedroom of her apartment, Victoria sets the phone back into its cradle on the nightstand. She fumes with jealousy.

While Sam unloads his drafting table from the truck, Cassie comes out of the farmhouse carrying a wall calendar. "Emily was a very organized person. She made entries into this calendar for upcoming events. Doctor appointments, church meetings,… " she hands the calendar to Sam, "birthdays."

He takes a look at it. "Uh-oh. I've never forgotten before. But he doesn't even realize it's his birthday."

"It doesn't matter. We really should do something to celebrate. What do you think he'd like to do?"

He ponders this for a moment. A smile sweeps across his face as he gets an idea.

Later that afternoon, at Go-Kart Land, Delbert speeds along the racetrack trying fiercely to catch up with Sam who is in the lead. He passes Cassie around the curve and puts the pedal to the metal as he moves in on Sam. Closer . . . closer. He laughs fiendishly and pulls ahead, crossing the finish line.

Later at a restaurant, Delbert sits stoically in a booth with Sam and Cassie as three waitresses clap and sing, "Happy happy birthday, we are glad you're here. Happy happy birthday, we wish you all good cheer."

As the waitresses applaud and walk away, Delbert frowns. "I really hate that kind of crap."

This annoys Sam, but Cassie laughs. She gestures to a cupcake that's on the table in front of Delbert. It has a lit birthday candle in the center of it. "Why don't you make a wish and blow out the candle?"

Delbert dips his finger in the frosting. "OK. I wish I could eat this cupcake." He blows out the candle and licks his finger.

Sam slides the plate away. "Too much sugar. Cassie has a sugar-free pie at home for you." He hands Delbert a small envelope. "Here, Grandpa, a twenty-two-year tradition. It's not one of my better ones because I made it in a hurry."

Delbert takes the card out of the envelope and grins from ear to ear as he admires the butterfly design. "I can still remember the first one you ever made for me. You were only five years old, and you used crayons. You gave it to me the day we caught that butterfly."

"I remember," says Sam fondly.

Delbert's smile withers. "I can't remember what I did five minutes ago, but I remember that day. Life was good then, wasn't it, Sammy?"

Sam nods and squeezes Delbert's hand.

Delbert stares down at the table sadly. "I think maybe that doctor might have been right." He looks up. "And that scares me."

Sam's expression mirrors Delbert's. Then, with a deep breath, Sam tries to be brave for Delbert's sake. "We'll get through this, Grandpa. Together."

This seems to reassure Delbert who gets a little of that old twinkle back in his eyes. "But I do remember you mentioning something about taking me to Sears for some new clothes."

Inside the men's department at Sears, Sam carries a store bag filled with purchases as Delbert follows him through the aisles. Sam's cell phone rings, and he pulls it off his belt clip. "Hello? Hey, Tran, how's it going? Yeah, sure, come on over. I'll be home in about an hour."

Sam and Delbert head toward an escalator that goes down to the appliance department. Sam continues talking on the phone. "Hang on a second, Tran." He turns to Delbert and gestures to the escalator. "Let's go down and check out the stoves before we go home. Be sure to hang onto the rail."

Sam turns back around and steps onto the escalator and finishes his phone conversation. "Sorry about that. Anyway, if I'm not there in an hour, Cassie will let you in. Yeah, she is nice. I know. OK, man. I'll see you later." He clips the phone back to his belt and steps off the escalator. He turns back to assist Delbert but discovers that he never got on the escalator at all and is still standing on the main level.

With fear, Delbert stares down at the intimidating moving steps.

Sam shouts up to him. "Grandpa, what are you doing?"

While holding onto the rail, Delbert slowly extends one foot over the top step but then quickly retreats it back. "I don't think I can."

Worried, Sam darts over to a nearby elevator. "OK, Grandpa. Don't try to come down. I'll take the elevator up."

Inside the elevator, Sam presses the number "2" button. The doors close, but the elevator doesn't move. He presses the button again, but still nothing. "Great!" Sam presses the "open" button, and the doors slide apart.

He steps out and glances up at the top of the escalator—but no Delbert in sight. Not wanting to waste any more time by going across the floor to the "Up" escalator, Sam panics and bolts up the "Down" escalator. He skips every other step until he reaches the main level.

Sam searches frantically through the aisles for Delbert. Finally, he stops and stands in one spot, looking in all directions trying to catch a glimpse of him.

Mike, a sales clerk, escorts Delbert from across the room. He points to Sam. "Is that him, sir?"

"Yes, that's him," says Delbert with a vacant look in his eyes. But his mind plays tricks on him, and it's Sam as a little boy he sees.

Twenty-two years earlier in the exact location inside this Sears store, Sam stands in the middle of the aisle sobbing and clutching a teddy bear. He looks up at Delbert and sniffles. "Grandpa, where were you?"

"I was just right over there by the elevator."

Sam rubs his swollen red eyes and walks over to him. "I couldn't find you. I was scared."

Delbert smiles reassuringly at Sam. "No need to worry. I'm right here." Sam takes his arm and escorts him out of the store.

That evening at the farmhouse, Delbert sits by himself in the living room. He stares out the window at the orange sky as the sun goes down. A tree casts long, eerie shadows across the wall.

From the kitchen, Cassie can be heard talking to Sam, Brad and Tran. "Is Delbert OK out there?"

"Yeah. I think he's asleep in his chair. Too much of that great, sugar-free pie," Sam replies.

"Sugar-free? I could've sworn it was the real deal," Brad says.

Delbert watches the shadows that, in his mind, seem to come to life and take on demonic form. They drip down the wall and creep across the floor, slithering up his chair. They close in on him, and he trembles with fear.

Meanwhile in the kitchen, Sam sits at the table with Brad and Tran while Cassie clears the table. "That was great." Sam rubs his full belly.

"Thanks," Cassie replies.

Tran pats Sam on the back. "So how does it feel to be a freelance architect?"

Sam gets up and takes his plate to the sink. "Thanks for not saying unemployed. But to answer your question, it feels scary."

"Brad's jealous. He'd love to have his own business."

Brad shrugs. "Someday, someday."

A light bulb goes off in Sam's head. "Hmmm . . . my own business. I never thought of it like that. I should hire myself an electrical guy. I hate doing load calculations. So, Brad, whenever you've had enough of Mason, I'll put you on my payroll."

"That would be now. He's been a pain ever since you left."

Tran chimes in. "I don't know if it's because he misses you or because Victoria is miserable without you. When she ain't happy, ain't nobody happy."

Cassie tries to pretend this talk of Victoria doesn't bother her as Brad nudges Tran disapprovingly.

Delbert walks in. His eyes are glassy, and he seems agitated. "Is this a private conversation or can anyone partake?"

Cassie smiles warmly at him. "Hey, birthday boy, come on in. Would you like another piece of pie?"

Sam slides a chair out for Delbert who ignores it. "Did you leave me out there so you could come in here and talk about me?"

"We weren't talking about you, Grandpa."

"Yeah. Sure," Delbert says stiffly. "Well, I have to get up early for work tomorrow, so I'm going to bed. Enjoy your conversation."

There's an awkward silence as Delbert retreats up the stairs. Finally, Tran turns to Sam. "He has a job?"

Brad looks at Tran as if to say, "you moron" and throws a wadded up napkin at him.

Inside the lobby of the Chicago Building Department, Delbert waits for Sam who signs out a set of plans at the counter.

Sam turns and bumps into someone. "Oh. Mr. Patterson!"

"Well, hello, son. How are you?"

Sam shakes his hand. "Doing OK, I guess. Just picking up some electrical revisions. How's the retail center coming?"

"The framing is up. Starting to take shape."

Sam fidgets nervously with the blueprints. "Well, it was nice to see you again, sir."

As Sam starts to walk away, Mr. Patterson touches him on the arm. "Sometimes I think I was too hasty in my decision to part ways with Mason Architects."

"It's OK. I understand. I had to part ways with them myself."

This takes Mr. Patterson by surprise. "I'm sorry to hear that. I hope it wasn't because of this grumpy old goat," he says while pointing a thumb at himself. "I used to be a fairly nice guy. Until my wife passed away." Sam glances at Delbert, understanding completely. Mr. Patterson continues. "I want you to know I was happier with your design. I should've stayed with you."

Whatever tension was between them seems to have instantly vanished. Sam smiles. "No hard feelings. Business is business. You did what you thought was right at the time."

Sam walks over to Delbert. "Ready?"

The two head out the door and Mr. Patterson observes them curiously.

That night at his drafting table, Sam studies the National Electrical Code book while trying to make sense of his revisions.

Delbert walks up behind him holding a plate with a peanut butter sandwich and taps him on the shoulder.

Sam nearly flies out of his seat. "I'm going to hang a bell around your neck."

Delbert holds the plate out to him. "I made dinner."

A smile creeps across Sam's face as he looks at this wonderful old man who never ceases to amaze him. "Thanks, Grandpa."

Delbert shuffles back to the kitchen. "I would've made soup too, but someone put locks on the stove knobs. You'd think a toddler lived in the house."

After Delbert is fast asleep in bed, Sam drowns his troubles in the shower. The hot, steamy spray flows down his back, soothing him. He turns off the water and tries to slide the shower door open, but it sticks. The more he tries to move it, the more it gets stuck in the track. Frustrated, he jiggles it violently. It doesn't budge. He jiggles it some more without success. Finally, he manages to slide it open several inches, and he steps one foot out and tries squeezing his body through. With a grimace, he forces himself out. He grabs a towel and rubs a clear spot on the foggy mirror and looks at himself. "What are you doing here?"

Cassie stands on the front porch holding up a DVD. "I thought you could use a good laugh, so I rented *The Money Pit*!"

Sam, dressed in sweat pants while holding open the front door, chuckles and gestures for her to come in as he towels off his wet hair. "Great! I love horror movies."

With a fire crackling in the fireplace, Sam and Cassie sit on the couch sharing a bowl of popcorn. They're fixated on the movie, and Sam suddenly grabs her and shields her eyes with his hand and screams, "Close your eyes! Here comes another scary part where the bathtub falls through the floor. Aaahhh!"

Their laughter subsides as Sam slowly pulls his hand away and stares into her eyes, searching for approval. He seems to find it, and he kisses her softly. "Cassie . . . ."

She slides her arms around his neck and pulls him close for a long, tender kiss. Blushing, she turns back to the movie, and soon they're laughing again at the antics of Tom Hanks.

Their giggles travel upstairs to Delbert's room where he's in bed, wide awake, with a huge grin stretched across his face.

The sun rises gloriously over the farmhouse, and birds chirp happily. Daylight peeks through the living room window and wakes Sam who is curled up on the couch with Cassie who is still fast asleep. He smiles lovingly at her and gently brushes the hair from her face and kisses her tenderly several times. First on the cheek, then her eyes . . . nose . . . lips.

Cassie stirs, and with her eyes still closed, she speaks dreamily. "I don't want to wake up. I'm having the most awesome dream."

"Am I in it?" Sam asks.

Slowly, she opens her eyes and gazes into Sam's. She runs her fingers lightly over his face as if verifying that he's real. "You're in all my dreams."

The clock on the wall chimes six times, and she glances at it. She sits up with a start. "Oh, my gosh! I've gotta go." She slides on one of her shoes.

Sam stands up and scratches his head. "Don't worry. It's way past midnight and you haven't turned into a pumpkin or anything. And I was a perfect gentleman, wasn't I?"

Hesitating, she slips on the other shoe. "Of course. You always were a gentleman–with me."

It was meant as a jab for giving Shawna all the attention when they were teenagers. Sam suddenly looks remorseful.

Cassie stands and grabs her purse and car keys from the coffee table. "I have to run home and get ready for work, but maybe we can do this again. Only next time, bring on a little of that bad boy image for me, will you?" She kisses him lightly on the cheek, and with a flirtatious wink she's out the door.

For an early May in Chicago, the afternoon warms up considerably. Victoria and Mr. Mason take a not-so-casual stroll through Lincoln Park. Crying, Victoria dabs her nose with a tissue as her father tries to console her. "Why don't you come over to the house this weekend? You and your mother can go shopping at Bloomingdale's on Michigan Ave. That always cheers you up."

"I don't really feel like it, Daddy."

He puts his arm around her shoulders. "What to do, what to do? My little girl's heart is broken, and I haven't the power to fix it."

She turns to him and sniffles. "Haven't you?"

Back at the farmhouse, Sam is in high spirits as he washes his truck to the beat of "Born to be Wild" blaring from a boom box on the porch.

Delbert comes out and watches Sam. He likes the music and dances a little jig right there on the porch. He mostly stands in place and moves his hips, but he really gets into it and twirls his arms in the air.

It cracks Sam up. As the song ends, Sam's cell phone rings. He tosses the sponge into the bucket and dries his hands off on a towel and pulls the phone out of his pants pocket. "Hello?" A look of shock comes across his face. "Mr. Mason? How are you?"

Sam motions for Delbert to turn the radio down. Delbert tries to oblige but inadvertently hits the channel button and goes through a series of stations—heavy metal, punk, opera and, Lord have mercy, rap. That does it. Delbert yanks the radio plug from the extension cord, and his expression turns blissful. "There's nothing better than good old peace and quiet."

In the meantime, Sam strays down the driveway, deeply involved in his phone conversation. Grinning, he puts the phone back in his pocket and heads back up the driveway. "That was Mr. Mason, my old boss."

Delbert gives him a stony look.

Sam recoils from it by retrieving the sponge from the bucket and finishing up the truck. "He wants to see me next week in his office. He said you can come along if you want."

Sam smiles up at Delbert but sees he's disappeared back into the house. For a moment, Sam's smile disappears as well. But it soon returns as he contemplates his future while making happy swirls on the side of the truck. The sudsy water splashes onto his bare feet.

CHAPTER FIVE
Letting Go

Dressed in business attire, Sam sprints up the steps of the Chicago office building.

Meanwhile, Delbert is at the adult daycare center in the Faircrest Nursing Home. It's a beautiful facility where the residents seem happy and well cared for. He sits at a table with other elderly people. Cassie, who wears a name badge with the title "Activities Coordinator," is assisting them with making picture frames out of decorated Popsicle sticks and colorful buttons. She pays particular attention to Delbert who actually seems to be enjoying himself.

Mr. Lloyd, the director of the nursing home, is seated at his desk in his office conferring with Mr. Patterson. "This is wonderful news, Mr. Patterson. Faircrest desperately needs an Alzheimer's unit, but we've never been able to raise the funds."

Mr. Patterson shrugs and smiles. "What better way for a rich land developer to invest his money? The returns would be very rewarding."

"Your wife would be pleased."

"She loved the people here and volunteering her time. Until that wretched disease got a hold of her. I felt so helpless watching her deteriorate day after day." Getting choked up, Mr. Patterson pauses to regain his composure. He looks up at Mr. Lloyd, misty eyed. "Hopefully, someday there won't be a need for Alzheimer's facilities."

Back in Chicago, Sam pushes the office door open and peeks in at Mr. Mason who sits at his desk reading over some documents. He peers over his glasses and smiles broadly at Sam. "Come in, son, come in. Take a seat."

Sam obliges and squirms nervously in his chair.

"Where's your grandfather?" asks Mr. Mason, pretending to be disappointed.

"He's in adult daycare. A friend of mine works there, and he feels comfortable with her." Sam says the word *her* quietly as if trying to hide the fact that his friend is female.

Mr. Mason picks up on it. "I see. Well. I'm glad he's doing better."

Such concern all of a sudden. Sam didn't like it. "I didn't say he's doing better. But, yes, in general he's feeling more comfortable in his own surroundings."

Mr. Mason raises an eyebrow at Sam's tone, but dismisses it. "Sam, let me get right to the point. I believe we can work something out that will allow you to return here to your former position and yet provide adequate care for your grandfather. If you're interested."

"I'm listening."

Mr. Mason stands up and goes to the window and looks out. "The best scenario would be if you moved back to the city where you belong. We'll pay for daycare or an in-home nurse to stay with your grandfather while you're at work."

Sam bristles. "The best scenario? For who?"

Undeterred, Mr. Mason continues. "Another scenario would be that you stay out in the country, and we'll still pay for your grandfather's daycare services. We'll even throw in a company car."

"That's very generous, but—"

"That's the best I can do. If you want to work from home, even on a part-time basis, I'm afraid I can't go along with that. Not for a junior partner position. You'd be hard pressed to find any employer who would make such an accommodation."

Back at the Faircrest Nursing Home, Mr. Patterson walks down the corridor past the adult daycare room and notices Delbert. He summons Cassie over to him.

"Hi, Mr. Patterson, how are you?" she asks.

"Oh, fine, fine. I was wondering, that man over there—what is his situation? If you don't mind my asking."

"Delbert? Well, I've known him and his family for years. His wife died not too long ago. He has Alzheimer's, and his grandson takes care of him. His name is Sam. He lost his job recently, so things have been kind of tough."

Mr. Patterson looks guilty.

"Sam's an architect. A very cute architect." Cassie smiles.

"And a talented one at that," Mr. Patterson adds.

"Oh, do you know Sam?"

"I think I'm beginning to."

Mr. Mason continues to try and lure Sam back into the fold as he stands with his back to the window. "I can kick up your executive leave so that you'll have plenty of time to take your grandfather to appointments or whatever you might need it for."

Sam's mind seems to be reeling. "I have to admit it's tempting."

A familiar, sensual, voice comes from the doorway. "Knock, knoooock!" Sam twists around in his chair to see Victoria walking in holding a tray with three cups of coffee.

Mr. Mason gives her a peck on the cheek. "Hi, sweetheart."

"Hi, Daddy." She sets the tray on the desk and looks at Sam seductively as she hands him a cup of coffee. "Welcome back, Sam."

Annoyed at her presumption, he snaps back. "I haven't made a decision yet. We're still in the discussion phase."

Victoria hands a cup to her father. "Oh. But you *are* going to accept, right?"

Sam blows on the steaming coffee and takes a sip.

After a long silence, an impatient Mr. Mason extends his hand to Sam for a handshake. "Why, of course he is. Right, partner?"

Sam shakes his hand, but notices that Mr. Mason isn't even making eye contact with him. "What kind of handshake is that? The guy's so distracted he's even checking his watch for the time," Sam says to himself.

Sam's thoughts drift back to a warm, lazy night at the farm.

A brooding fifteen-year-old Sam sits on the porch swing. Delbert sits on the railing in front of him with his hand outstretched. "The handshake–the smallest of gestures but very significant. Go ahead. Shake my hand. Let's see what you've got."

"I'm not in the mood."

"Come on. Humor your old grandpa. It's one of the most important things I'll ever teach you."

Sam obliges half-heartedly.

"Now," says Delbert, "act like you mean it. Firm, but not too tight. There you go. Look me in the eyes. Good. That's very good. People will judge you based on your handshake, as you will judge others. It reveals character. Major decisions in your life will result from a simple handshake."

Sam releases Mr. Mason's hand and stands up. "I appreciate your offer, but I can't accept."

From the look on Mr. Mason's face, he's not used to being turned down. "I won't ask you back again. This is your last chance."

Victoria tightens her jaw. "That goes for me too," she says with a firm cross of her arms.

"I'm sorry." Although it's sincere it is all Sam can muster as he walks out on Victoria and her father and all that could've been a very lucrative future.

With the eyes of every employee upon him, Sam, self-assured and optimistic, marches boldly toward the lobby.

Brad turns to Tran and whispers, "If ever there was a time for a mutiny, it would be now." Tran nods as they watch their former colleague exit the building for the last time.

Later that day at the Faircrest Nursing Home, a stressed out and sickly-looking Sam inches his way down the corridor toward the adult daycare room. He veers off to a nearby restroom.

He leans over the sink and splashes water on his face.

The knob on the restroom door turns, and Delbert walks in. "Sammy?"

Sam looks up, his face pale. "I blew it, Grandpa. My job. My future." He shuts the water off. "And you. I can't even take care of you the way I should. I'm trying, honest to God I am." Sam grabs some paper towels and blots his face.

It's evident that Delbert doesn't completely understand what he's talking about. Still, his heart breaks at the sight of his grandson on the verge of what seems to be an emotional breakdown. At first Delbert says nothing. And then, with gentleness and sincerity, he says something that releases Sam of the enormous responsibility he's placed on himself. "That's all anyone can do, Sammy."

It's what he needed to hear, and he turns to Delbert and buries his face in his chest, sobbing.

In the parking lot of the nursing home, Sam and Delbert sit in the truck as Cassie leans into the driver's window. "Are you sure you're feeling well enough to drive?"

"I'm sure," says Sam as he starts the engine. "Some impression I must be making on you. A struggling architect with a mental problem."

Cassie smiles and shrugs. "It was just a panic attack. Nothing to be ashamed of. I have those on a daily basis." She steps back and allows Sam to back up the truck.

Crunch! He hits a Cadillac that's driving through the parking lot. Sam steps out of his truck, practically numb with despair.

At the same time, the driver's door swings open on the Cadillac, and out steps Mr. Patterson who greets them. "Sam. Cassie."

Sam's mouth drops open as he turns to Cassie. "You know him?"

She nods. "He volunteers here."

Mr. Patterson assesses the damage. "I was hoping I would run into you, Sam. Not like this of course."

Sam corrects him. "I think *I* was the one who ran into *you*. I'm sorry. I feel like I have some strange voodoo curse thing going on in my life."

"I doubt that," he shrugs. "Besides, there's no real harm done; just a minor scratch. But maybe it will even the score between you and me, and we can start over with a clean slate."

"What do you mean?"

Mr. Patterson rubs his rumbling tummy. "I never discuss business on an empty stomach. Are you guys free for lunch?"

The Lakeside Steak House overlooks a sparkling Lake Michigan where a few colorful sailboats drift by. Delbert, Sam, Cassie and Mr. Patterson dine at an outdoor table.

"You want me to design an Alzheimer's unit?" asks Sam with delighted surprise.

Mr. Patterson saws off a piece of steak. "I can't think of anyone more qualified." He glances at Delbert who's entranced by the sailboats. "For many reasons. The job's yours if you want it."

"If I want it? Are you kidding? I'd be honored. It's a big job, but yes!"

This pleases Mr. Patterson. "Don't worry about the electrical or mechanical plans. I can contract those out. I just want you to come up with a brilliant design. Something that looks good and the residents will be happy and comfortable in. So do we have a deal?"

Sam shakes his hand firmly. It feels right, and he smiles broadly. "Absolutely."

Cassie kisses Sam on the cheek and gives him a big hug. "Congratulations."

"Let's seal the deal with something sweet." Mr. Patterson summons over Stacey, a waitress carrying a dessert tray filled with goodies.

Delbert's eyes bug out. "Got anything that's sugar-free?"

Mr. Patterson pulls up the cuff of his shirtsleeve and slides his arm over next to Delbert's, comparing diabetic bracelets. "Have they got anything sugar-free? Why do you think I picked this place?"

Delbert grins happily.

Under a white gazebo decorated with flowers where the wooden barn once stood in the back yard of the farmhouse, Sam and Cassie cut into a scrumptious-looking wedding cake as it sits on a banquet table. A string quartet plays a mesmerizing ballad as the newlyweds dance together. They both look radiant and very much in love. On Cassie's left hand is a simple, yet elegant, wedding ring. It's the same one Delbert liked so much at Tiffany's jewelry store.

The guests look on, including Mr. Patterson, Brad, Tran, Judy the mail lady, Shawna, and, of course, Delbert. Looking sharp in his tuxedo, he gazes fondly at Sam and Cassie.

While couples begin dancing, Delbert makes his way over to Sam and cuts in. Obliging, Sam happily steps aside. As Delbert dances with Cassie, it's Emily's face he sees.

Fifty years earlier at a simple outdoor wedding reception, Carl and Emmett play "You are my Sunshine," on the banjo and fiddle. Delbert dances with his new bride, Emily, as he looks lovingly into her eyes and sings the words to their favorite song.

Delbert kisses Cassie fatherly on the cheek as the dance ends. "You're just as beautiful as my Emily was."

Sam walks over and puts his arm around Delbert's shoulders. "Thanks for being my best man, Grandpa."

His smile indicates he couldn't be more honored.

Weeks later, huddled around a desk inside their office in a small commercial center, Sam, along with his new business partners, Tran and Brad, put the finishing touches on the design for the Alzheimer's unit. "Prichard, Nguyen and Jenkins Architects" is displayed on the front window.

Upon completion of construction, an outdoor grand-opening ceremony is under way next to the beautiful new wing. A very pregnant and glowing Cassie sits next to Delbert who is in a wheelchair. It's obvious from his glassy stare that his Alzheimer's has progressed.

Mr. Patterson stands at a podium welcoming the guests. Seated behind him are Mr. Lloyd, several city officials as well as Sam, Tran and Brad. Teary-eyed, Mr. Patterson leans into the microphone. "It gives me great pleasure to announce the grand opening of the Harriet Patterson Alzheimer's Wing!"

Everyone applauds as the city manager presents a plaque to Mr. Patterson.

Cassie exchanges smiles with Sam and rubs her tummy affectionately.

A few weeks later, inside the farmhouse, Delbert sits in his wheelchair in front of the TV. *Gunsmoke* is on, but he doesn't seem to realize it. He has a bib around his neck as a nurse, Gail, feeds him. She scoops up some food from his plate and brings the spoon to his mouth.

He clutches onto the handle with a shaky hand, and they both guide the spoon to his mouth.

The front door swings open, and Sam and Cassie come in with their newborn baby girl. Gail blots Delbert's mouth with a napkin and steps aside as they bring the baby to him and set her in his lap.

Cassie kneels down next to Delbert. "This is your great-granddaughter, Emily Rachel Prichard."

A tear of joy spills down Delbert's cheek as the baby grasps his finger with her tiny hand.

On a beautiful, warm and sunny day, a butterfly sits on the branch of a tree outside the farmhouse. Sam screeches into the driveway in his truck. With a devastated look on his face, he gets out and races up to the house.

Meanwhile upstairs, a pale and gaunt-looking Delbert lies in bed staring at the ceiling, breathing slightly laboriously. Cassie and Gail are at his side in the cheerfully decorated room adorned with family photos, a *Gunsmoke* poster and Sam's many butterfly cards.

Sam rushes in and takes Gail's place at Delbert's side. He scoops up his frail hand and squeezes it gently. "Grandpa?"

No response.

Sam turns to Cassie. "Did you call the doctor?"

She nods sadly. "Yes, but . . . he's tired, Sam. You've got to let him go."

His eyes brim with tears as he turns back to Delbert.

In the meadow, five-year-old Sam sobs as Delbert holds the jar containing the butterfly. "No! I don't wanna let him go!"

Delbert kneels down next to him and puts his arm around him. "He'll be happier."

Sammy rubs his nose and sniffles.

"You love him, don't you?" Delbert asks.

Sam nods, taking short little gasps as his sobs taper off. Delbert hands him the jar and Sam wipes away a tear and unscrews the lid.

The butterfly flutters and flies out, soaring into the sky and disappearing into the warmth of the sun as Sammy and Delbert romp through the tall grass, giggling.

"I love you too, Sammy."

The End

MR CHR🎄STMAS

Screenplay by J.L. Chaka
Story conversion by Jill Pomerantz

BACK STORY

Mr Chrismas was developed upon the innovative concept of a Christmas decoration service that I once saw reported in a news article. I wanted to do a different kind of Christmas story with a different type of lead character. Enter Alvin, a young handicapped man with a heart of gold. I hope this story touches your heart and puts you in the holiday spirit.

CHAPTER ONE
Pops' Hardware

The Cane house in Midville, Illinois sits on Oak Street in a quaint residential neighborhood. The trees are turning the last color of fall and their leaves are beginning to cover the ground of the sizeable backyard. Big brother Joey, pretty little Carol, pudgy Denise, and the mentally challenged Alvin play in the leaves. Their forty-year-old mother, Arlene, furiously rakes the leaves while occasionally shooting a cutting glance to her husband, Joe, who sits in his lawn chair reading the paper. "Pops", as he's known by his children, is oblivious to everything.

The year is 1985 and the kids are too busy playing to notice the tension between their parents. Seven year old Denise and eight year old Carol creep up to the side of the house looking for the boys in a game of hide and seek. As they near the corner an alien figurine's head is shoved into their face. The girls scream and run. Ten-year-old Joey and his "slow" brother, Alvin, who just turned six, step around the corner beaming smiles.

On Thanksgiving Day, through the dining room window of their house, the Canes can be observed celebrating in their usual chaotic way. The table is decked out for the Thanksgiving dinner with a smorgasbord of side dishes. The turkey sits on a white platter at the head of the table, awaiting Pops' annual carving ritual. Joey dances a couple of action figures from the movie "Alien" on Denise's plate trying to irritate her. It works.

"Mom . . . Joey is playing with his toys at the table," she whines.

Arlene enters the room with a bowl of mashed potatoes and places it on the table. "Joey, don't play with your toys at the dinner table."

Joey moves the toys onto his lap and continues the re-enacted fight scene. Meanwhile, Alvin has climbed out of his chair and into Pops', headed straight for the turkey. Carol eyes his moves as he stands in the chair and picks up the carving knife. She's quick to tattletale. "Mom, Alvin is trying to carve the turkey."

Suddenly, Pops enters the room. Grabbing Alvin by the back of his shirt collar with one hand and taking the knife with the other, he lifts him from the chair and plops him back into his own. And so the chaos continues, a scene typical of any house in America.

As the seasons move on, the once colorful autumn scenery is replaced with snow covered trees and a house decorated with lights for Christmas. In the Cane house, the cheerful noises of children and the sounds of packages being opened replace the chaos of the Thanksgiving dinner. Christmas wrapping paper is strewn about the living room floor, as the children work on a pile of presents under a nicely decorated tree. Pops, however, is not present. Arlene helps Alvin remove a toy from a package as she occasionally glances at Pop's favorite chair. Empty again. She finally pulls the toy from its package as the phone rings. Handing the toy to the six year old Alvin, she answers the phone. "Hello. Cane residence."

On the other end, Pops tries to talk above the noises in a bar. "I'm stuck in Des Moines. They've had one heck-of-a snowstorm here."

Arlene tries to hide her anger from the kids and turns away as she talks. "What about Christmas dinner?"

"Well, obviously I'm not gonna make it. I'll try to get out tomorrow."

"You do that. Have another drink. I'll ask the mailman to cut the turkey." Slamming down the phone, she wipes her tears then turns back around to face the kids. She puts on her best "everything is fine" smile. "So who wants hot chocolate?" she asks.

In the spring of the following year, the Canes find themselves in court, finalizing the divorce proceedings. Pops bursts out of the courthouse doors dragging his two sons along with him. Arlene follows, dragging her young daughters with her. They all collide on the sidewalk as Pops gets one last quip in. "Fine. Take the house. At least I won't have to spend my weekends fixing everything all of the time."

"That would be kind of difficult since you are never home!" Arlene snaps back.

"That's because I'm on the road selling hardware to put food on the table."

Teary-eyed, Denise looks up at her mother. "Mommy, is Pops leaving?"

Arlene pulls her to her side to comfort her. "Yes, dear."

Denise and Carol begin crying as Pops struggles to pull the boys along with him. "Mom! Denise! Carol!" the boys cry out.

Eighteen years later, customers dressed in festive holiday season attire are busy entering and leaving Cane Hardware, located in an insignificant strip mall. A large banner in the window advertises last minute specials on Christmas decorations. Although, a light evening snow falls against the landscape of the small town, the lack of cheerful Christmas lights in the surrounding residential district make what would be a picturesque scene a bleak one.

In the plumbing aisle of the store, twenty-three-year-old Alvin fumbles to put pieces of pipes into bins. The lengths are the same, but the diameters of the pipes are different. He stops, confused, and scratches his head. Two shiny black wing-tip shoes step into his view. Alvin looks down at them and then follows the legs up past the "Manager" name tag to see Pops looking down at him. "What are you doing, Alvin?"

Alvin tries to keep his composure and slurs out his answer. "I'm shtocking partsh."

Pops shakes his head in disgust. "I can see that. You're doing it wrong." He kneels down and takes two of the mismatched pieces from the bin. "These are different diameters."

"But dey are the shame length," Alvin defends himself.

Pops holds the two pieces side by side so Alvin can see the ends. "But they also have to be the same diameter." Pops tosses them back into the bin and stands. "Just reorganize them right." Shaking his head at Alvin's ineptness, he steps away. As Pops leaves, he passes Joey who is standing at the end of the aisle watching. He's wearing an assistant manager nametag.

"Get your stupid brother straightened out, will you."

Joey nods, looks down, then starts to go after his dad for the insult but stops and approaches the befuddled Alvin. "I'll fix that, Alvin. Go take down the Thanksgiving decorations. Then put up the Christmas decorations."

Alvin stands, beaming a smile. "Chwistmash decorashuns! Wow. Tanksh, Joey!" As he sprints off, Joey can't help to chuckle.

Later, Pops works the checkout counter as an attractive twenty-six-year-old Carol and her slightly heavy sister, Denise, enter the store. While checking a customer out, Pops spots them but they look away, avoiding his eye contact. He continues his work as the girls spot Joey in the plumbing department. He is finishing straightening out the pipe bins. Denise watches him briefly, admiring his attention to detail. "Hi, Joey."

Joey stops and wipes his hands on his red smock. "Hey, Sis. You too, Carol."

Carol rolls her eyes. "Ha, ha. Funny, Joey."

Denise brandishes a large baggie of turkey. " Since you couldn't make it to Thanksgiving dinner . . . again, we brought Alvin some of Mom's turkey. You know how he loves Mom's turkey."

Joey is puzzled by her comment about not making it to dinner. "Yeah. Look, we didn't come because Pops said we weren't invited."

"That's a lie. I heard Mom on the phone with Pops inviting you," Carol snidely remarks.

"That's not what Pops said," Joey explains calmly.

Carol crosses her arms. "Yeah, right. Come on Denise." Carol spins around with Denise trailing. Denise tries to smile at Joey while leaving. Joey sighs and turns to go back to work.

In the holiday aisle, Alvin has put away the Thanksgiving decorations and is unboxing the Christmas ones when Denise removes the baggie of turkey from her purse. She takes out a small piece and dangles it by the side of Alvin's head, teasing him. Unsuspecting, Alvin places ribbons and garlands on the shelf. Carol shakes her head and rolls her eyes. Suddenly, Alvin stops and sniffs. He spins around and beams a goofy smile. "Denish!" he exclaims joyfully, then grabs for the turkey. But Denise playfully pulls it from his reach.

Carol has reached her limit with her sister. "Quit teasing him and just give it to him so we can leave. I have shopping to do."

The moment is spoiled by Carol, so Denise gives in and hands the turkey over. Denise gives her sister a disapproving glance. "Happy?"

Alvin quickly opens the baggie, digs out a piece, and chokes it down. He takes out another and begins to stuff it in his mouth when he realizes that he's forgotten his manners. He stops and swallows his last bite then wipes his mouth on his sleeve. He slowly approaches Denise and shyly kisses her on the cheek. "Tank you, Denish."

Denise smiles a loving smile. "You're welcome, Alvin."

Alvin turns his attention to Carol, who has never really gotten along with him since day one. Carol realizes what's coming. "You're not gonna give me a kiss too?"

He smiles a big smile. "Yesh."

Denise gives Carol the evil eye, coaxing her into her rightful duty. Carol unwillingly leans toward him. Alvin instantly kisses her on the cheek, and then pulls back. "Dat wash my Thanksgiving kish. For Chwistmash you git anothver."

Carol mumbles beneath her breath. "I can't wait."

Denise hears her snide comment, elbows her, then turns back to Alvin with a gentle smile. "Thank you, Alvin. From both of us."

Carol grows impatient and scans her watch. "We need to go."

Alvin suddenly remembers something. "Ooh, ohh. I fordot." He kisses the inside of his hand, cups it, and holds it out to Denise like something precious. "Datsh a kish for Mom."

Denise takes it gently from him and studies her closed hand. She's always lost for words every time Alvin gives her a kiss for Mom. Carol takes her by the arm to break the trance and pulls her away. "We have to go. Bye, Alvin."

Alvin waves with his fingers as they disappear from sight. He quickly sneaks another piece of turkey from the bag before shoving it into his smock pocket. Merrily, he goes back to work. Joey, who has been watching from the end of the aisle, looks down, turns, and walks away.

Later in the week, the holiday shopping season has kicked into high gear and the hardware store is busy with a flurry of customers doing last minute Christmas shopping. Joey and Alvin are busy helping customers with their Christmas decoration needs as Pops mans the checkout register along with a young part-time girl named Pam.

As Alvin assists Mrs. Johnson, an elderly woman, select an artificial tree, she discusses her dilemma with him. "I'll take it, Alvin. But I have a problem. My daughter is out of town and I'd need some help putting it up."

Alvin considers her problem for a minute. "I tan put it up fa you." He leans toward her. "But I have ta do it on luncsh bwake. Otay?"

She smiles. "That's fine, dearie."

Joey has his feet up while eating his lunch in the backroom when Alvin enters and shyly moves around the room, trying to get his courage up. "Ish it otay if I bowow your car?" Alvin asks shyly.

Joey nearly chokes on his sandwich. "Yeah it'd be OK, if you had a driver's license."

"I don't haf one, dough. Maybe you tan give me a wide."

Joey finally gives in and puts down his sandwich. "Where to?"

After Alvin and Joey finish decorating the Christmas tree, Mrs. Johnson steps up admiring the tree. "It's beautiful boys. But I didn't pay for the ornaments or lights."

"Dat's otay. Der mine. I fixed dem," Alvin admits.

"It's OK, Mrs. Johnson. Alvin likes to fix decorations that arrive broken," Joey explains.

She digs into her purse and pulls out a fifty-dollar bill. She hands it to Alvin. His eyes enlarge. "Wow! Fifty bucksh." He thinks about it and then starts to hand it back.

She puts her hand up to stop him. "No. I won't take no for an answer."

Alvin looks at Joey and smiles. At that moment, Mrs. Johnson's daughter, Cleo, enters through the front door. She is unaware of Alvin and Joey's presence as she shouts out to her mother. "I'm back in town, Mother. You here?"

"I'm here, dear."

As Cleo enters the room, she's awestruck by the beautifully decorated Christmas tree. "Wow. That's beautiful. But I told you that I'd help you when I got back into town, Mother."

"I couldn't wait. Didn't these boys do a wonderful job?"

Cleo smiles at them and then nods her approval. "I didn't know anyone did this sort of thing. It's a very creative idea . . . a Christmas decoration service. Mmm. It's about time someone thought of that. I'm sure lots of people need it. I'll tell all my friends."

Joey and Alvin climb into the truck to go back to the hardware store. Alvin examines a one hundred-dollar bill as Joey watches him. "It was shure nice of Mish Cleo to give ush a hundred. I made a hundred fifty bucksh for lunsch."

Joey starts the truck as he considers the possible business opportunities as suggested by Cleo. "Yeah. You sure did."

"I'm bywing lunsch tomowow," Alvin declares.

"OK," Joey mechanically says as he ponders the Christmas decoration idea.

A few days later in the hardware store, Pops furiously works the counter with two checkout girls trying to keep up with the long line of customers, who are rolling up carts of Christmas decorations. But Pops has had enough. He steps aside to let the other check out girl takeover. "Cover my register. I'll be right back."

He steps through the store and rounds the aisle corner. He runs into a flood of customers who are raiding the shelves for Christmas decorations. Wading through the crowd, he finds Joey re-stocking the shelves. Another line of customers leads around the corner. He follows it around to find Alvin seated at a table writing down each person's name and address. A sign above him reads "Mr. Christmas Decoration Service." Pops scratches his head, then turns to fight his way back through the crowd. Passing Joey, he motions him to follow. They enter the back room and close the door. "OK, what's going on? Why we having a run on Christmas decorations? And who's Mr. Christmas?"

"We're Mr. Christmas. Alvin picked out the name."

"And the purpose is what?"

"Pops, it's a decorating service."

"Why do we need that?"

"People want it. We're getting twenty five dollars for inside and twenty five for outside."

"And who's going to do this and when?"

"We are . . . Alvin and me . . . during lunch, after work. Who cares?"

Pops thinks about it and it begins to sink in. "Does anybody else do—"

"Nope. We're the only one," Joey interrupts.

"OK. But you still have to get the other work done."

"OK." Joey turns around and starts to leave.

"Joey," Pops calls after him. Joey stops and turns. "Maybe think about some part time help."

"Already placed the ad Pops." Joey smiles and walks out.

The wheels are beginning to turn. Pops finds himself even more intrigued by the idea. "Mr. Christmas?"

The Mr. Christmas Decoration Service picks up over the next week. Alvin and Joey find themselves busier than ever. They even decorate the Christmas tree for big Mr. Lampton, who just happens to run the competing hardware store in town. As they finish decorating the tree, Mr. Lampton nods his approval.

While hanging some outside lights at another customer's house, Joey discovers that he is afraid of heights. Ashamed to admit it, he gives Alvin the task of setting up any decorations beyond the height of a ladder. Alvin has no problem with that and immediately takes charge. When Alvin instructs two young boys on how to unload the Christmas decorations from Joey's truck at the hardware store, Joey begins to notice that there is something more to Alvin than anyone had previously imagined.

During a break in the Christmas action, Joey approaches Pops who's standing near the front counter with his arms crossed. He is watching Alvin, who's set up a chair near the front entrance. While eating a turkey sandwich in a Santa stocking, he works on broken Christmas decorations and greets customers entering the store. One customer enters and says hi to Alvin by name. It doesn't go unnoticed.

Pops shakes his head in disgust. "Does he have to do that every day? Why can't he eat lunch in the storage room like everybody else?"

Joey can't believe what he's hearing. "Yeah, the storage room has great atmosphere. Especially when you're trying to eat. I know, personally, I like the smell of paint thinner while I'm eating."

Pops gives him a side glance. "Don't get smart."

"What's the harm? He likes the customers . . . and they like him."

"It's embarrassing."

"Alvin's not embarrassed. I'm not embarrassed. It must be you who's embarrassed." Pops doesn't respond so Joey continues. "Why do you have to be embarrassed of your own son? Why can't you just accept him?"

"There are some things a man just can't accept. When you get older you'll understand."

Joey looks at him odd as he walks away. "I'm twenty-seven, Pops. How old I gotta be?" He quickly trails after him into the stock room to continue the conversation with his father. "I'm getting tired of you and Mom treating Alvin like he's some kind of leper. He's got a lot to offer."

Pops removes the inventory chart and thumbs through the pages. "Leave it alone, son. It doesn't concern you." He switches subjects to avoid the debate. "We'll need to up these orders on Christmas lights."

"Screw the lights. I'm tired of your off color comments about how he is. Of how he's a retard and will never be capable of anything. It's not his fault he's the way he is."

Pops stops thumbing through the pages. "I know . . . it's my fault."

Joey is silent for a second, thinking about his father's comment. "What do you mean, it's your fault? That doesn't make any sense." Pops doesn't respond, so he reaches up and turns his dad around, waiting for an answer.

He hangs the inventory chart up. "Your mother tried to convince me to put him in a home for special kids. I thought he'd get better in time."

"Better? He's not sick, Pops."

"I should've listened. I'm tired of dealing with it. He'll never be good for anything but cleaning up and mopping floors."

"That's not true."

"It's time for both us to face reality. He's never gonna be normal. He'll never be like you and me."

As Joey turns, he sees Alvin standing in the doorway. He is accompanied by an attractive blond by the name of Christine. They both had been listening. Alvin turns and runs away, while Christine holds up a box of ornaments and tries to explain. "Sorry. I just wanted to exchange these ornaments. The girl at the front desk said the manager was back here…. Is he gonna be OK?"

Joey gives Pops a hard look. "I don't know. I need to go after my brother."

"Go ahead. I'll come back later."

Joey races out after Alvin. He bursts through the main doors and stops in the middle of the parking lot. He spins around searching for his brother but finds him nowhere in sight.

After an hour of driving around town and calling out Alvin's name, Joey turns up nothing. Then, as he drives down a residential street, a car going the other way slows down and stops next to him. It's Pops. He too, is out searching for Alvin. Joey would like to ignore him, not liking what his father has put Alvin through, but he reluctantly rolls down his window to talk with him anyway.

"No luck, huh?" Pops asks.

"Nope," Joey responds coldly.

Pops gives an accepting nod, looks down, puts the car in drive and pulls away. Joey turns to say something, but he's already gone. He puts the truck in gear and drives away.

That night, after driving from one part of town to the other, Joey returns home in hopes that Alvin is there. Upon entering the house, Joey finds Pops lying on the couch asleep. He throws his car keys on the coffee table then heads for Alvin's room. When he finds only emptiness he sits on Alvin's unmade bed with his head in his hands. He can't help thinking how terrible Alvin must feel. Hoping that he may have gone to visit his mother, Joey takes out his cell phone and dials.

Denise answers. "Hello."

"This is Joey."

"Hi guy. What's up?"

"Alvin's not there is he?"

"No. Why?" she asks, concerned.

"He got upset at the store today and took off."

"Oh no. Should I wake Mom?"

"No. He'll probably come home after he cools off. I'm sorry I called so late."

"If he shows up, I'll call you."

"Thanks."

Joey drops the phone and looks around the room. On the nightstand is a picture of him and Alvin in their younger days. Joey picks it up and stares at it. He gently places it back and stands. As he looks around the room, it becomes obvious how much Alvin loves his family. Adorning the shelves and dresser top are numerous pictures of all the family members. Joey slowly walks around looking at Alvin's possessions. A pant-leg hangs out of one of the dresser drawers. Joey opens the drawer to tuck in the leg when he notices a stack of cutout newspaper articles. Curious, Joey lifts the handful of articles and reads the top one. It's an old high school article about the star running back, Joey Cane, and their latest football game. As Joey thumbs through them, he notices that his brother had collected all the school newspaper articles about him. Joey puts them back, closes the drawer and exits the room.

Briskly moving through the house, he grabs his keys. Pops looks over as he passes. Joey notices that Pops is now awake. "I'm going back out to look for him."

"Maybe it's nothing, but Alvin had that part time job at the Y over the summer. I can check it out," his dad offers.

"No Pops. I'll do it. I don't think he wants to see you right now."

Pops looks down. "Yeah. I suppose you're right."

Joey slams the door behind him as he leaves. Pops sits up looking concerned.

At the YMCA, Joey approaches a lone figure mopping a hallway. As he gets closer, he recognizes the figure as Alvin. Stopping, he leans against the wall and watches Alvin mop. Alvin is deep in thought and doesn't see Joey until the mop slaps against his brother's tennis shoe. Alvin, stops and looks up apologetically. "Oh, Joey? I'm shorry." He then takes a shop rag from his back pocket and bends over to clean off his shoe.

Joey reaches out and stops him. "That's OK, Alvin." Alvin puts the mop into the bucket. Joey continues. "Did you come back to work for the Y?"

Alvin shakes his head. "No. It helpsh me tink."

"I'm sorry you had to hear that."

"Maybe Popsh is wight. I'm shtupid. Maybe all I can do is mop floorsh."

"That's not true." Joey grabs the mop and bucket and pushes it against the wall. "And I'm gonna prove it. Come on."

Alvin has his hands over his eyes as Joey drives through the residential neighborhood of the small town. Alvin grows impatient. "Wheah we going Joey?"

"Hang on, just a little further." Joey's truck turns into a residential neighborhood, beautifully decorated with Christmas lights. He slows the car down. "OK. Now, Alvin."

Alvin uncovers his eyes and is in awe at the sight. "Wow! dese are budiful wights!"

"They should be. Mr. Christmas did them. Alvin, YOU did these lights."

Alvin's mouth drops open. "I did?" Alvin studies one of the houses passing by, then remembers. "Oh dat house. I memba. She had dat big dog dat liked me sho much."

"That's right."

Alvin spots another with a high roof. "And dat one. I memba. I had to cwimb way up on da ladda. Memba, Joey?"

"Yep. You had to do it because I'm scared of heights."

As the car slowly travels through the neighborhood, Alvin hangs out the window and shouts, "IT'SH ME, MISHTA CWISTMISH!"

The neighborhood dogs start barking as Joey's truck disappears down the beautifully lit street. "I'm pwetty good. Huh, Joey."

"Yeah, you are Alvin. And don't ever forget it."

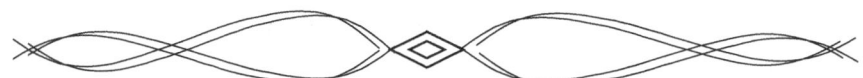

CHAPTER TWO
The Retirement Home & the Witch

Joey had invigorated Alvin's zest for life and has allowed him to man the Christmas department exclusively since the customers' demand for the brothers' service seems neverending. Alvin also manages a couple of younger employees and seems to have everything under control. They are so busy, that Pops has allowed the work to spill over into regular work hours. No more decorating just during lunch breaks and after work.

While heading off to a morning job, Joey notices Pops standing off to the side watching Alvin. He knows Pops feels bad for what Alvin had overheard and, worse still, Alvin hasn't said a word to him since the incident. "What's going on Pops?" Joey asks on his way out the door.

"Maybe I should have a talk with him."

"He needs some time, Pops. Let him enjoy this." Then he pats Pops on the shoulder. Outside, he helps Alvin load tie down several Christmas trees in the back of his truck. Pops watches for a minute then walks away. Joey puts the truck into gear as Alvin goes over his customer list.

"OK, who is first on the list for delivery?" Joey asks.

"It jusht saysh Elmwood Weetiament Home."

Alvin hands the list to Joey who reads it as he drives. "Someone paid cash for the tree and decorations. No name." He then hands the list back to Alvin.

Alvin thinks about it for a minute. "Maybe it belongsh to all of dem."

Joey smiles. "Maybe."

Joey and Alvin enter the lobby at Elmwood Retirement Home with the tree. The administrator, Ethel Cratchet, a scraggly and unfriendly looking woman in her fifties, rounds the reception desk to intercept them. "Can I help you?"

Joey and Alvin prop the tree up on its trunk. A branch snaps up and swipes her nose. "Well!" she snips.

Joey notices her rubbing the end of her nose. "Oh, sorry."

Alvin looks at the list and then at Mrs. Cratchet, who seems to Alvin to be very much like a witch. She glares at him with a disapproving scowl while she awaits her answer. Alvin quickly hands the list to Joey, afraid to talk with the mean old woman. Joey takes it and unfolds it for Mrs. Cratchet. "We're from the Mr. Christmas Decoration Service. We have a tree for delivery."

She snatches the list away. Alvin jumps back behind Joey.

She carefully reads it then hands it back. "Well, you have the correct address. But we didn't order a tree. You'll have to take it back."

Joey and Alvin look at each other not sure what to do. The residents of the home have begun to gather to see what the commotion is all about. "Look. It's already paid for, along with decorations. We may as well put it up," Joey offers. The curious onlookers await Mrs. Cratchet's response.

"I'm afraid that's out of the question. Besides, we already have a tree," she snidely replies. Then she steps aside to reveal a tiny unattractive ceramic Christmas tree resting on a small table in the corner. Alvin laughs at the sight of the tree. Mrs. Cratchet gives him the evil eye, causing him to move further behind Joey. He dares only to peek over his brother's shoulder.

By now, the congregation of elderly, some of which are on walkers and others in wheel chairs, has grown to quite a mass. Joey looks around at the sad wrinkled faces, and then back to Mrs. Cratchet. "Well, ma'am, someone here paid for it and it wouldn't be right to take it back."

Mrs. Cratchet taps her foot as she looks around at the aged faces. They all look away as if she might turn them to stone. "I see," she responds as she steps out to the crowd. She points at the tree. "Would whoever ordered this tree step forward." They all look at each other, but no one speaks a word. She turns back to the two brothers. "See. It must be a mistake. You'll have to take it back."

Joey gazes around at the sad miserable crowd. He sees something in their faces, a glimmer of hope or desire. So he decides to pursue the issue. "Who would prefer this beautiful tree over . . . " he points at the tiny tree on the table, "that one?"

The elderly look at the tree that Joey and Alvin are holding, then they look at the little ceramic tree, and then finally, they look at Mrs. Cratchet. Again, no one speaks.

Alvin leans toward Joey and whispers, "I tink if dey shay shomething they'll be in twuble."

Joey whispers back. "You're right. Here, hold the tree, Alvin." He steps forward, takes out a small notebook and flips it open. He starts tearing out the small pages, handing one to each of the residents. "Let's have an anonymous vote."

Mrs. Cratchet is alarmed by the suggestion. "Excuse me, young man. What are you doing?"

Joey stops to look back at Mrs. Cratchet just as he's handing an old man a piece of paper. "They don't have the right to vote?"

The residents all look to Mrs. Cratchet, waiting for her reply. She scans their faces and senses some hostility in their eyes. "Sure they can. I'm not running a prison." she says unconvincingly through an awkward smile.

The old man immediately snaps the piece of paper from Joey's hand. Suddenly, all the residents are putting out their hands and swarming in on Joey. He is soon immersed in a crowd of elderly residents.

Later, Mrs. Cratchet hovers over Joey as he goes through the votes. He looks up and smiles. "It's unanimous. They want our tree." Then he holds up a single piece of paper and cringes. "Except one. It says they need their Depends changed." Everyone laughs. A few of the elderly look at each other wondering if the one next to them is the culprit. Alvin looks at an elderly woman standing next to him. He leans toward her and sniffs. Not smelling anything, he smiles. Joey hands the note to Mrs. Cratchet. She tosses it and then stomps away.

Alvin and Joey proceed to put the tree up while the elderly residents anxiously look on. Then Alvin brings in boxes of decorations and the crowd continues to watch with anticipation. As Joey starts to reach into a box of decorations, he stops and looks at Alvin. "It's their tree. Maybe they should decorate it. What do you think, Alvin?"

"Yeah! Tum on! Help ush!" Alvin shouts to the residents. The residents eagerly move in, each grabbing an ornament from the box. Alvin beams a smile.

With everyone's cooperation, the Christmas tree is becoming a work of joy; quickly adorned with ornaments and lights. To ensure everyone's involvement, Alvin and Joey help some of the more disabled to hang ornaments. As Alvin helps an older woman, Wilma, hang an ornament, an old man bends over in front of him. Alvin cringes at the smell and pinches his nose. He then points his finger at the old man's butt suggesting he had found the one with the dirty Depends. Wilma snickers.

Once finished with the decorating, they all stand back and admire the tree. "Wait," Joey says. "There's one more thing." He plugs in the lights and everyone breaks into applause over its beauty. Caught up in the emotion, Wilma leans over and kisses Alvin on the cheek, causing him to blush.

Out of the crowd, Dorothy, a small frail woman of eighty five, steps up. She holds out a list to Joey. "What's this?" he asks.

"Since you're Mr. Christmas, we thought maybe you could help us with our Christmas list. We don't get out much."

Joey reads it as Alvin looks on. He looks up at her from the list, puzzled. "It's just a list of names and addresses."

"They're our grown children," she explains. Joey pages through the list, not sure what to make of it as Dorothy continues. "Since we have a tree now, we'd like to have a Christmas party." The other elderly residents chime in their agreement.

"Why don't you just call them and invite them?" Joey asks.

"The wicked witch listens in on our phone calls and would never allow it. Besides, all of our kids have those fancy answering machines. We can't ever reach them."

Alvin takes the list from Joey's hand. "We tan do it. Wa Mishta Cwistmish."

Joey is startled by Alvin's claim and starts to rebut but is deterred by the cheers of the elderly residents.

While Joey drives back to the hardware store, Alvin studies the long list of relatives. "Why'd you tell them we could get their families to come to a Christmas party, Alvin?"

"Caush der nicesh people."

Joey puts his hand on Alvin's shoulder. "One day that big heart of yours is gonna get you in trouble."

Alvin smiles. "I know."

With the decorating service flooding in new customers, keeping the Christmas decorations aisle stocked was turning into a full time job. One afternoon while Alvin and Joey are restocking the Christmas decoration shelves, Christine approaches with her box of ornaments. Joey sees her and is captivated by her beauty. "Hi," she says.

Joey stares at her, motionless. Alvin who is knelt down working on a lower shelf looks up at him, wondering what's wrong with him. He shrugs it off and goes back to work. Joey slowly stands as she moves toward him with the ornament box. She holds it out to him. He takes it without taking his eyes off her. "Hi," he finally manages to say.

She clears her throat. "I wanted to exchange these. Remember? I said I'd come back later."

Joey snaps out of it and looks at the box. "Oh. Yeah."

"Some of the ornaments were broken when I opened it," she explains.

Joey looks over the box. "Right. I'll get a new one." As Joey turns, he falls over Alvin and lands on the floor on top of the ornament box. Alvin scrambles to help him up. Joey stands, and notices the flattened box in his hand. He gently shakes it to hear how the ornaments faired. Hearing rattling from the box, Christine laughs. Alvin dusts off Joey's clothes as he turns to see where the laughter is coming from.

"Wowwww!" Alvin exclaims when he sees the beautiful girl in front of him. Christine looks away, blushing.

Joey tries to recover some of his dignity. "This is my brother, Alvin." She steps forward and puts her hand out. They both look at her hand as if an angel were offering a greeting. Alvin swallows and gently shakes it. Then Joey finally snaps back to reality. "Oh . . . the ornaments." He quickly runs to the shelf and searches for a replacement.

Alvin smiles a big smile and nods. She smiles back. Joey returns with the box and holds it out to her. Taking it, she puts it under her arm and waits for a minute as if expecting Joey to do something.

"Oh, uh, let me walk you to the counter," Joey offers nervously.

As she turns to leave, Alvin looks at him oddly as if what he just said really sounded stupid. Joey shrugs his shoulders and runs to catch up with her.

"I can tell you and your brother are very close. I'm sorry that I overheard the conversation the other day. It was personal."

"Oh, that's OK."

"My sister and me are very close like that. He's very lucky to have a brother like you."

As they reach the counter, Pops, who is manning one checkout counter, looks up and spots Joey, who is standing awkwardly with his hands in his pockets. Pops smiles at Joey's obvious infatuation. He rolls his eyes and continues working.

Christine puts out her hand. Joey shakes it. "Thanks so much for helping me with the ornaments."

Joey fumbles for words and finally gets some out. "That's what we're here for."

She looks down at his hand still clasped in hers. "I guess I'll checkout now."

"OK. Good idea," Joey says mindlessly.

She looks down at their joined hands. He looks down wishing he could keep it that way. Their eyes meet and without having any idea what to say, decides to let go. She smiles, turns and walks away.

Joey is off in another world as he watches her from across the store. Alvin is leaning against the rack watching him. A big grin stretches across his face.

"What did you shay to her, Joey?"

"I don't know. What do you say to an angel?"

"Maybe whatsh your phone numba? Den you tan see hehr adin."

Joey's eyes enlarge at the thought that he may never see her again. "Oh crap!" Joey tears off running through the store to try to catch her, but, finds it difficult to make his way through the customers.

Outside, in the parking lot, Christine steps out with her package and climbs into her Volkswagen. She slowly puts her keys in and starts the car. She looks back at the store, hoping that maybe Joey will exit and stop her. He doesn't, so she drives away. Not a minute after, Joey bursts out the doors just as her Volkswagen drives away. Running his hands through his hair, he spins in a circle, and stumbles back toward the store.

Joey and Alvin sit at the kitchen table with the list of the retirement home resident's children. Joey has just finished calling someone and marks their name from the list. Alvin has just dialed a Mr. Sommers and is waiting.

"Hello, Sommer's residence," Mr Sommers answers, irritated.

Alvin is not dismayed. "My name ish Alvin, I'm Mishta Cwistmish. Your muver ish in da home and she wantsh you—"

Mr. Sommers rudely interrupts. "I'm not interested. And don't call again." He hangs up, leaving Alvin with a dial-tone. Alvin looks at the phone and sticks his tongue out at him. He hangs up and looks at Joey. "Why ish evewybody sho mean?"

Pops enters the room and answers the question. "That's the way people are today. Nobody gives a crap about anybody else." They both turn to see their father standing in the doorway with his arms crossed. "You'll never get them to go. You'd have to put a gun to their head to get them away from their investment portfolios and townhouses." He turns and walks away.

"I'm not gwiving up. He'll shee," Alvin says, picking the phone up again.

Joey nods in agreement, then picks up his cell phone, runs his finger down the list and dials the next name.

The following day after work, Joey and Alvin decide to pay some personal visits to the people on the list. Their first stop is Mr. Sommers' house. Joey pulls up and parks in front of the huge, expensive looking house. Numerous luxury cars are parked in front. They can see through the windows that they are having a party. Joey climbs out and Alvin follows.

At the large double-entry front doors, Joey rings the doorbell and waits. He quickly looks up the name, then puts it away. He tries to check his hair in the door's reflection, but the door opens too soon. A man in his fifties, dressed in a three-piece suit appears at the door. He holds a martini in one hand and is obviously tipsy. "What can I do for you boys?" he asks.

"Mr. Sommers?" Joey enquires.

"Yes, that's me," Mr. Sommers answers suspiciously.

"Your mother is in the Elmwood Retirement Home," Joey begins

"I know. I pay damn good money to keep that old bitty in there. So?"

"Well, they're having a Christmas party and she wanted you to come."

Mr. Sommers takes a drink, then laughs, "Oh, she does?" He turns to the crowd in his beautifully decorated living room. "Hey, the old folks home is having a Christmas party. Anybody want to go?" The crowd bursts into laughter. He continues. "You sure?" Nobody responds. He turns back to Joey and Alvin. "I guess not boys."

"But sheesh your muver," Alvin says, not giving up so easily.

Mr. Sommers looks at Alvin then gets close to smell his breath. Alvin pulls back from him. Mr. Sommers leans toward Joey and says, "You'd better cut him off. He's really slurring. He isn't driving is he?"

Joey grabs Mr. Sommers by his tie and yanks him forward. "Watch your mouth," he says, upset by the remark.

Mr. Sommers yanks his tie away. "I think you'd better take off, boys, before I call the police." He slams the door.

Alvin and Joey have no better luck with any of the others. The attempt to convince family members to visit the elderly residents of the retirement home fails. The next day, while working a decorating job, Joey realizes that he and Alvin have to talk about the futile task they have taken on. He opens another box of lights and hands them up to Alvin who is on a ladder. Joey puts his hand in his pockets and looks down, knowing what he's going to say will break his heart "Alvin, could you come down for a minute?" Alvin finishes his lights and climbs down. "I know you're not going to want to hear this, but we have to tell them that we can't get anyone to come."

"Oh no. We tan't do dat, Joey."

"I'm sorry. Their party is this weekend and we have to tell them. It's not right to get their hopes up." Joey bends over and picks up another string of lights. He hands them to Alvin. "We'll go over there tomorrow after work to tell them. Sorry." Joey turns and walks away. Alvin sadly watches him.

The next day, Joey and a reluctant Alvin, enter the lobby of the retirement home. The residents begin to gather, waiting for word. Dorothy steps up and approaches them. "I told everyone that you called and had some news for us."

Joey is hesitant to respond. "I'm afraid there's a little problem," he announces.

Albert, an elderly man in the back of the crowd, shouts, "Couldn't get no one to come could you? I figured as much." The residents start murmuring.

Joey puts up his hands to settle them down. "No. It's just that—"

Alvin sees that he's in trouble and blurts out, "Dey want to bwing presntsh."

Joey looks at him, shocked, not knowing where he's going but plays along anyway. "Yeah, they don't know what to get you. We just need a . . . list."

They all release a sigh of relief and laugh. An old woman standing next to Albert, elbows him. "See, Albert. Not only are they coming, they're bringing presents." Joey and Alvin look at each other wondering what they have done.

Later, the crowd dissipates and the last resident steps away from writing their desired Christmas present down on the list. Joey picks it up, folds it and puts it in his pocket. The residents are now across the room seated at the card tables and talking "What are they gonna say when we show up with the presents and no one is with us?"

"Will dey be mad at ush, Joey?"

"I don't know."

Mrs. Cratchet stands in the doorway undetected. She overhears the brother's conversation and smiles.

In the truck, Alvin takes out the list and begins to read. "Dish one wants fuzzy wabbit housesh shoes," he says, laughing. Joey slams the steering wheel with his fist. Alvin's smile disappears. "What's whong, Joey?"

"What's wrong? What isn't wrong? We lied to them. Now they expect them to show up with presents." Joey takes the list from Alvin.

He looks it over then hands it back. "Where we gonna get the money to pay for all of that?"

Alvin shrugs his shoulders as Joey starts the truck and puts it in gear. Alvin finds another as they drive away, "What's a whap dancesh?"

"A what? Let me see that."

Alvin hands him the list. "I think some of these people have issues. Here." Joey hands the list back to Alvin. "He's not getting a lap dance. Maybe a swim suit calendar. Not a lap dance."

Alvin thinks about it for a minute and then asks, "But what's a whap dancesh?"

"It's where a girl sits on your lap . . . and dances."

"Soundsh weird. Don't it huwt?"

"We need to have a long talk."

Early the next morning at work, Pops sips on his morning coffee as he goes over the books. Joey is awaiting an answer. Pops finally looks up. "If you and Alvin want your Christmas bonus early that's fine. But what's it for?"

"I'd rather not say."

Pops looks him over. "Fine." He takes out the company checkbook and begins writing the check.

Joey and Alvin grab a couple of carts at the local Wal-Mart and begin their Christmas shopping for the elderly residents of the retirement home. Alvin tries on some bunny house shoes and hops around the room. Joey nods his approval. A young girl watches Alvin while her mother shops. Alvin sees her and puts on a hopping show until he collides with a rack of clothes. He quickly hangs the clothes back up as she giggles.

Alvin coaxes Joey into modeling women's robes as he gives him a thumbs up or down. Joey exits the dressing room in a sexy night gown. Alvin claps frantically, then looks around hoping nobody saw him. Joey feels weird and runs back into the dressing room. Finally, he exits in a conservative one. Alvin gives him a thumbs up.

In the office supply aisle, they look at calendars. They both stare at one that has a girl with very large breasts. Joey looks at Alvin for his approval. Alvin nods excitedly. Joey shakes his head and comes back with one that has a girl with smaller breasts. They walk away with it.

Shortly, Alvin returns and kisses the calendar girl on the lips. Joey steps back and pulls him away.

In the bedding department, Alvin is under a comforter and walking around like a monster. The little girl from before walks by and screams. Alvin quickly takes it off and runs.

In the electronics department, Alvin listens to a radio with headsets on. He turns and wiggles his butt to the beat of rock and roll music. When he turns to see if Joey is laughing, he finds several older women ogling him instead. One winks at him. He freaks and dives for the floor.

Joey and Alvin finish shopping and push two fully loaded carts up to the counter. As the counter clerk rings up the items, she lifts up a large pair of ladies flaming red underwear. She looks at Alvin. He nods toward Joey as if to imply they belong to him.

On the drive home the cab of the truck is filled with bags from their shopping spree, Alvin spots a night club billboard that says "Lap Dances Nightly." He excitedly points. "Joey! wook. Whap dancshes." Joey looks over at the club and then at Alvin. Alvin smiles.

In the club, a big breasted exotic dancer, wearing a black leather outfit and carrying a small whip with tassels, steps up to Joey and Alvin's table. She slaps the whip against her hand and eyes Alvin with sexual desire. Alvin looks at Joey and swallows. He then looks back at the dancer who is moving toward him. He smiles a daffy smile.

As Joey leads Alvin out of the club, Alvin can hardly walk from his experience, but he's smiling from ear-to-ear in a blissful daze. Joey opens the passenger door and starts to put him in. Alvin tries to get out and head back for the club. Joey forces him in and quickly runs to his side of the truck. He manages to get in and they speed away.

When they finally get home, Joey and Alvin immediately start wrapping the gifts from their shopping spree. Pops stands in the doorway looking at the presents that cover the living room floor. He shakes his head and walks away.

Pops is finishing tallying up the day's totals as Joey unlocks the main door and enters. Pops notices Joey carrying the two Santa suits. "Still going through with it?" Pops asks.

Joey stops. "Yep. You know, it may sound silly, but this is important to him."

"I know," Pops solemnly replies.

"Do you?" Pops looks up as Joey steps away with the suits. "We're changing and leaving from here. I'll lock up when we leave."

Later, in the storage room Joey and Alvin finish dressing in their Santa costumes. While adjusting his costume, Joey notices Alvin looking around the room for something. "What's the matter, Alvin?"

"Where's da Shanta bearwd?"

Joey cringes. "I'm sorry. I forgot them."

"Oh shoot, Joey."

"Sorry."

"Dat's otay."

As they finish dressing, the store phone rings. "Finish getting ready, Alvin. I'll get that." Joey steps into the main store and answers the phone. "Cane Hardware."

On the other end is Mrs. Cratchet from the retirement home. "I'm looking for the boys from Mister Christmas."

"I'm one of them. How can I help you?"

"You can forget about coming to the home. I know all about your scam."

"Scam?"

"I overheard you two talking. No one's coming and you've just been leading them on." Joey is speechless. "In fact I've already told them about you two. They don't ever want to see your faces around here again. Goodbye, and merry Christmas."

Joey closes his eyes and shakes his head. As he gently hangs up the phone, Alvin exits the storage room and approaches. "I'm wheady Joey," he announces.

Joey takes off his Santa hat and leans against the counter. "We're not going."

"Why, Joey?"

"That old witch at the home overheard us talking. She told them that nobody is coming."

"No, Joey. She tan't."

"She did. And they never want to see us again."

"Neva? Oh no . . ."Depressed by the news, Alvin wanders toward the back door and exits. Joey follows. As Alvin seats himself on the back stairs, a gentle snow starts to fall. He leans his head back and lets the snow hit his face. Joey steps out and looks down at him. He puts his hand on Alvin's shoulder. Alvin leans forward and drops his head as Joey sits down beside him on the step. "Popsh wassh wight."

"About what?"

"People don't tare."

"Yeah. I'm sorry."

Alvin slowly looks up, smiling. Something just clicked in his mind. He stands up straight. "I haf an idea Joey."

"Yeah. What is it?"

Alvin looks down at him. "I haf ta show you." He heads for the door. "Tum on."

Joey stands and follows. Alvin leads Joey back into the storage room and turns to face him. "Gimme da lisht, Joey." Joey takes the list out of his pocket and hands it to him. "Shtay here," Alvin commands as he exits. As Joey turns to see what he's doing, the door to the storage room closes and locks with a clunk.

Joey runs to the door and tries to open it. "Alvin! What are you doing?" Alvin doesn't answer. Joey presses his head against the door to listen.

In the main store, Alvin takes the keys from the drawer and opens the gun cabinet. He reaches in and lifts a handgun.

"Alvin . . . what are you doing? Answer me."

Finally, Alvin answers from the other side of the door. "I'm shorry, Joey. I haf to."

"What are you gonna do Alvin? Have to what?"

"Mishta Cwistmish can't wet dem down." Joey listens but doesn't understand. "I wuv you, Joey."

Joey listens to his footsteps moving away. He pounds furiously on the door. "ALVIN! Come back!"

CHAPTER THREE
Alvin On a Mission

Alvin walks down the main street in his Santa outfit, dragging two large canvas bags full of gifts. He doesn't even try to hide the gun. Stopping mid-street, he looks around. A city bus is just pulling up to drop off passengers. Alvin calmly walks to it, throws the two bags into the bus, and steps on.

The driver, a black, sixty-year-old man named Charlie, puts his hand on the lever, getting ready to close the door. Alvin looks around at the only two remaining occupants of the bus and then at Charlie.

Charlie grows impatient. "You getting on or what?"

Alvin raises the gun up. With his other hand, he takes out the list, and hands it reluctantly to the driver.

Charlie opens the list, looks at the gun, and then scans the list again. "What's this for?"

"It'sh a wisht."

"I can see that. What do you want me to do with it?"

"I want you should pick dem up."

Charlie looks at the gun. "OK, just take it easy fella." Then he closes the door behind Alvin and puts the bus in gear. As the bus pulls away Alvin explains "My name'sh not fella. It'sh Mishta Cwistmish."

"OK, Mr. Christmas. Whatever you say," Charlie nervously replies as the bus moves down the street.

Back at the store, Joey diligently digs at the lock on the door with a screwdriver. A large splinter of wood gives way as he pries.

Moving to the hinges, Joey starts forcing out the pins. They slowly begin giving way.

On the streets of an affluent residential neighborhood, the bus comes to a stop in front of a large house. Inside the bus, Alvin is finishing the story of why he commandeered the bus to the bus driver and several passengers. "So it wash up to me, Mishta Cwistmish to make dem be nicesh." Everyone on the bus stares blankly at him. "And my name ish not weally Mishta Cwistmish. It'sh Alvin."

A woman in her sixties, Martha, speaks up. "Well, I think you're right Alv . . . I mean Mr. Christmas. It ain't right that those kids won't pay their parents a little respect. I didn't understand the part about you getting the lap dance, but—"

Charlie gives her a raised eyebrow, then jumps in. "Look kid. I understand how you feel. It ain't right that someone's parent is running around with a Depends that needs changing, and it's a nice thing that even old folks get what they want for Christmas . . . even fuzzy shoes and visits by their children." He lifts his left leg, which happens to be a prosthesis. "I lost this leg in the war. People treat you different when you ain't like them. I know how you feel kid, but there's the right way to deal with things and there's the wrong way to—"

Charlie is interrupted by Thelma, the bus dispatcher. "Bus 39 come in."

Charlie picks up the microphone and responds. "Bus 39. Charlie here. What's up Thelma?"

Thelma continues, "Charlie, where are you at? I've gotten a dozen phone calls from Tenth and Main, Jefferson and Second Street and—"

"I know Thelma. I've got a little problem," Charlie announces as he eyes Alvin.

"What is it?" she asks.

Charlie studies Alvin and the other passengers thinking of his options. "I'm broken down. Get a sub to cover my route."

"Give me your location and I'll send out a maintenance—"

Charlie interrupts her. "I can't do that, Thelma. I'll call you back." Charlie turns off the radio before Thelma gets more inquisitive.

Alvin stares at him, surprised by his actions. "Why did you do dat?"

"What am I gonna do? Turn in Mister Christmas? You do know that my wife is going to kill me." He nods toward a bag of ribbons and wrapping paper behind his seat. "I was supposed to help wrap tonight."

Alvin laughs then turns toward the door. Charlie pulls the lever to open the door. Just as Alvin leaves, Bob, a businessman in his thirties, approaches Charlie. "Open the door, bus driver. I'm getting off."

Charlie stands. "Sorry. I can't do that."

"Are you crazy? You can't possibly let him go through with this. He's got some serious mental issues."

"The kid's on a mission. Go sit down . . . business man."

Bob pulls out his cell phone and dials 911. Charlie instantly grabs for the phone. Bob resists and a struggle ensues. As they fight, the phone gets knocked from Bob's grip and lands in the middle of the aisle. Bob jumps for it. Charlie follows, but hits the deck hard. He moans from the pain. Bob finds himself free from the driver's clutches and goes for the phone. When he is just in reach, Martha bends down to pick it up. Then Charlie jumps on his back, pushing him down. Bob and Charlie look up at Martha, who now has the phone. Charlie stands and limps to her. She looks at Bob, then at Charlie. She hands the phone to Charlie. He turns it off and pockets it. Bob leaps toward the door for a quick escape. He slams the handle back and readies to exit, but Charlie wraps his arm around his neck and exerts great effort to pull him back. As the two struggling men look up, they're caught off-guard by the sight of Mr. and Mrs. Sommers staring at them through the bus folding doors, their hands above their heads. They stop struggling.

Later, as the bus moves down the street, Bob is sitting in a seat alone, his mouth gagged and his hands tied with wide green gift ribbon.

Meanwhile, back at the hardware store, the door Joey has been working on falls open as it finally gives way. He steps out onto the fallen door and looks around. He quickly goes to the counter and picks up the phone. As he dials, he notices that the cabinet door is open, the keys still dangling in the lock. He inspects further and notices an empty space once occupied by the gun.

Pops answers on the other end. "Hello."

"Pops, Alvin is gone. I think he has a gun."

"Oh my God."

At the local police station, Joey and Pops stand in front of the night sergeant's desk. Sergeant. Holloway, is looking at an eight by ten picture of Alvin. The picture is one of Alvin's least flattering as he is wearing a baseball cap sideways and is sporting a strange grin.

"HE'S on the loose with a gun?" the sergeant asks sarcastically.

"Yes, Officer. I think so," Joey responds.

"Did you see him take the gun?"

"No. But it's gone and—"

The sergeant interrupts. "Maybe you misplaced it."

Pops doesn't appreciate the insinuation. "We're not in the habit of misplacing guns, Sarge."

"Maybe somebody else took it. Did you think of that?" the sergeant shoots back.

"No. I'm pretty sure he took it," Joey admits.

"OK. Let's say that he did take it. Is he dangerous?" the sergeant inquires.

"He wouldn't hurt anybody, Officer," Joey assures.

At that moment, Alvin may be proving his brother wrong, as he nonchalantly points his gun at a terrified Mr. Henderson, another family member from the list. Alvin fumbles with the list, trying to ensure he has the right guy, then shoves it in Mr. Henderson's face. "Dat's you, wight?"

Mr. Henderson reads it. "Yeah," he reluctantly admits.

Alvin motions him forward with his gun. "Dood. Letsh go . . . pweash."

Back at the police station, Sergeant Holloway takes out a missing persons report form and begins filling it out. "Normally we don't file a report until they've been missing twenty four hours. But considering that he has special needs like you say, we'll make an exception." He looks up at them as he begins. "So what was he wearing when you last saw him?"

"A Santa suit," Joey says nonchalantly.

The sergeant looks up. "A Santa suit?"

"Yeah."

"Anything else? I mean he's not accompanied by elves or reindeer right?" the sergeant teases.

Joey doesn't see the humor. "What?"

"Sorry. A little Christmas humor. We'll send out the report right away. I wouldn't worry too much. He looks harmless."

Downtown, a middle-aged bum named Lenny, pushing a shopping cart full of clothes, approaches a passing business man. "Got some spare change, buddy. Gotta call my mom for Christmas." The businessman scoots away. Lenny sneers at him and resumes pushing his cart. "Yeah, right."

Meanwhile, Alvin prods another couple onto the bus by gunpoint. The bus is now full. As the new couple tries to find seats the murmur grows louder and louder until Charlie stands, raising his hands to settle everyone. "OK, OK. Calm down. First, let's have all the cell phones."

Everyone moans as Charlie has them throw their only means of communication into a grocery bag. He then opens the bus window and throws the bag out. The hostages moan again.

The bag of cell phones lands in Lenny's cart as the bus disappears from sight. Lenny looks around, not quite sure where it came from. He looks inside the bag then up at the sky. "Thank you, Lord."

On the bus, Charlie raises his hands to calm them down again. "Alvin is gonna explain why you are all here." He sits back down as Alvin steps forward.

He adjusts his Santa hat and smiles foolishly. "I'm Mishta Cwistmish. Or you tan call me Alvin. Anyway, it all shtarted when . . . "

Half an hour later, Alvin finishes his story and is looking over a completely quiet bus. Everyone is staring at Alvin . . . speechless.

Charlie stands and asks, "OK. Does anyone have any questions?" Everyone's hand shoots up. Charlie knows where it's going. "That DON'T have anything to do with Mister Christmas getting a lap dance." All the hands drop. Then Mr. Henderson looks around at the others and raises his hand. Charlie acknowledges him. "You. Go ahead."

Alvin leans in toward Charlie. "Dats Mishta Hendershon."

"Mr. Henderson. Go ahead," Charlie rephrases.

He stands. "Yeah. I have a question," he states as he looks at the other hostages. "What gives you the right to tell us how to live? To drag us out of our homes by gunpoint?"

Everyone nods in agreement. Charlie steps aside to let Alvin respond. Alvin steps forward. "I don't know. My Popsh saysh dat I am not shmart. Udder peoples shay dat too. Maybe itsh twue. But I know dat doze people are shad 'cause dey are awone. Den my Popsh shaid dat da only way dat you would go derr is if shomeone put a gun to yur head. Sho I did." Everyone is a little put off by the purity of Alvin's words.

"Well, I don't know about the rest of you, but I've spent a lot of money to keep my father at Elmwood. Believe me it isn't cheap," Mr. Henderson states.

Once again, everyone nods in agreement. Charlie waits for Alvin to respond. Alvin appears to be losing the battle to bring them over. "Peoplesh wanted to put me in da place becaush I wash not like uddersh. I'm gwad dey did not caush I'd be shad 'caush I couldn't shee my famiwy. 'Caush I wuv dem." Alvin approaches Mr. Henderson. "Don't you wuv dur fadda?" he asks sincerely.

Mr. Henderson becomes uncomfortable as the other bus occupants look at him, awaiting his response. "Yes, of course I do. It's just that every time we're together we just end up fighting. I'm trying to reduce my stress levels." Charlie and Alvin don't seem convinced. "That's on my doctor's orders."

Charlie remains unconvinced. "Yeah, right."

Alvin turns and walks to the front of the bus. Mr. Henderson sits as Charlie approaches Alvin and pulls him aside. "You didn't expect this to be easy, did you, kid?"

Alvin removes his hat and scratches his head. "Maybe Popsh was wight. Dey don't tare."

"They care, kid. They just don't realize it. It's been so long for them. You have to help them realize they do."

"How?" Alvin asks.

"Hey, if I knew that you think I'd be driving a bus? I'd be on Oprah or Dr. Phil."

Suddenly, Alvin looks up and puts his cap back on. He turns to Charlie and says, "Maybe dey justsh forghat it."

"Now you got it, kid."

Alvin spins around, a big smile on his face, and approaches the first hostage seated on the bus. "Who did you shleep wid when you got shcared at night?" Alvin asks in anticipation.

The lady thinks about it, "My daddy." Her eyes tear up. "I was daddy's little girl."

Alvin lights up and looks back at Charlie. Charlie grins. Alvin quickly picks another family member. "When you dot an owie, who made it all betta?"

"My mom," the hostage replies and starts to tear up. "I was always climbing trees. Mommy called me her little monkey."

Alvin stares at her a minute. "Montey?"

She nods as she blows her nose into a Kleenex. Alvin is about to ask someone else what they remember of their parents when the well dressed occupants offer an outpouring of guilty feelings, telling each other about their childhood and what their parents did for them.

In a darkened alley in the rundown part of town, Lenny sits in a cardboard box with a pile of cell phones. He picks one up, examines it, then dials. "Mom?"

On the other end, an aged voice replies, "Who is this?"

"It's me Lenny. I just called to wish you a merry Christmas."

At the Henderson house, Mrs. Henderson and her teenage daughter, Melissa, return home from shopping to find the front door wide open. They look around the house cautiously. "Dad, we're home," Melissa announces. There's no answer. They nervously look at each other.

At Bob Moore's house, his attractive girlfriend, Susan, steps up to the open front door and looks in. "Bob? I'm here. I hope you're ready." She enters and looks around, puzzled.

At the police station, the news of missing people is pouring in. A couple of police officers, Ted and Hank, man the phones, which are ringing off the wall. Ted is still filling out a report as he answers yet another call. He covers the receiver and remarks to Hank, "What the heck's going on? Half the town's gone missing."

Hank covers his receiver as well. "Better call the chief in."

Charlie and Alvin are standing at the front of the bus staring at the hostages, who are crying for their moms and dads. Alvin is proud of his accomplishment. "Pwetty dood huh?"

"Yeah. But kind of weird, Alvin. Maybe we should go now. " Charlie climbs into the driver's seat and puts it into gear. As the bus moves into the business district, it stops at a red light. A police car pulls up next to them.

One of the officers can't help overhearing the passengers call out for their moms and dads and the sobbing. As he stares at the bus full of hysterical people, the light turns green and the bus pulls away. As it does, he spots Alvin with the gun in his hand through one of the windows. He quickly pulls out a copy of the photo, then grabs for the radio microphone.

Joey and Pops finally return to the station after a futile attempt to find Alvin on the streets. They make their way through the crowd of concerned citizens and relatives and several reporters. The police chief meets them and leads them behind the night desk away from the crowd.

"You found Alvin?" Joey asks with anticipation. The chief tries to find the words to describe the situation.

Pops grows impatient. "Is he OK?"

"Alvin has . . . How do I say this?… Hijacked a city bus."

Pops falls back against the wall in shock. "Oh my God."

The chief takes a breath. "There's more."

Pops looks at him with exasperation. "More?"

The chief continues, "He's kidnapped a busload of the community."

"What?" Pops asks, shocked.

Joey realizes what's going on. "Oh no. He didn't."

"He didn't what?" he asks.

"I think I know what Alvin is doing."

"What? What is Alvin doing?" the chief asks, realizing that Joey knows something.

"Delivering a Christmas wish."

"To where?"

"Elmwood Retirement Home."

The chief grabs his hat from the rack and stops at the desk. "Get some cars over to the Elmwood Retirement Home. That's where he's taking them." The chief stuffs on his hat and steps past Joey and Pops. "You two with me."

Several reporters nearby in the crowd hear the tip and race out.

On the hijacked bus, Charlie's curiosity gets to him. "So what's in the bags, Mister Christmas?"

"Oh! I almost fordot the pwesents." Alvin picks one up and opens it revealing a pile of gifts. Taking one out, he reads the name on the tag. He walks to one of the hostages. "Dis is for your muver. Itsh a bwankee. Her toesh get cold at night and thish will keep dem warm." Alvin moves to the next passenger and searches. He comes out with another package. He presents it to him. "Your muver wanted shom housh shoes caussh her feet getsh cold when she getsh up evwee night 'caush she don't schleep well der." Alvin leans toward him. "Der bunny shoesh. I twied dem on. Dey feel weel good. I pwomise." Alvin moves on to disperse the other presents.

The city bus full of the Christmas hostages pulls up at the front entrance and parks. Almost immediately, three police cars arrive and block off the street. A couple of TV vans aren't far behind. The chief, Joey, and Pops climb from the chief's car. The chief immediately gets on his walkie-talkie. "I want those exits secured. No one in or out." As he puts his walkie-talkie away, he reaches into his vehicle and removes a bullhorn. The officers at the other vehicles take cover and draw their weapons.

"This is Chief McElroy. I want you to come out with your hands up and no one will be hurt." Suddenly, the doors of the home open and the elderly residents begin piling out with their hands held high. "No! No! No! Not you. Go back in," the chief shouts through the bull horn.

The residents reluctantly file back in as if the chief had just spoiled their fun.

He tries again. "This is for the bad guy in the bus. I repeat . . . the bad guy in the bus. Come out with your hands up." He releases the bullhorn, waiting.

Inside the bus, the hostages are looking at Alvin, waiting. Alvin bends down and looks through the windows, then looks around for the bad guy. Charlie stands and taps Alvin on the shoulder. Alvin looks at him. "Who dey tawking to?"

"You."

Alvin straightens. "Me! Why?"

Charlie reaches over, lifts Alvin's gun-hand and nods.

"Oh."

As spectators begin to congregate, a plumbing truck races up and slides to a halt. Joey and Pops approach the chief as half a dozen men pile out of the plumbing van. The men are dressed in an assortment of uniforms and suits.

"Who's that?" Joey asks, concerned.

It's obvious that the chief would rather not admit he knows them. "That's our volunteer SWAT team."

The six men collect at the rear of the van as the door is swung open. Immediately, there's an argument over equipment.

The chief approaches them. "What's going on?"

Earl, the town's grocery store butcher, wearing an apron and white hat, steps forward with three bullet-proof vests. "There's not enough vests for all of us. There was only enough in the SWAT team budget for three vests."

Bob, of Bob's Plumbing, wearing a white jumpsuit with Joe's Plumbing on the back, makes his argument for the vests. "Well, we're using my truck, so that counts for something. I should get a vest."

Vincent, the town's baker, dressed in his white apron, doesn't like what he's hearing. "Oh, so the rest of us just get shot and bleed to death?" The three farmers nod in agreement.

The chief grabs the vests away from Earl. He turns and walks back to his car "For Pete-sakes . . . " he mumbles to himself. He gets into his car and cuts the vests apart with his knife. He then removes a roll of duct tape from the glove compartment and steps out of the vehicle. He walks back to the men, distributes half a vest to each, and slaps the roll of duct tape into Earl's hand. "There. Now put them on and shut up."

As the others in the group try to fit their half of the vest on and duct tape them into place, Earl removes a small black handbook from his back pocket and hands it to the chief. "Here's the SWAT manual, Chief."

The chief takes it and opens it. He squints as he tries to read the super small print. He can't make anything out, so he moves it closer, then pulls it back away. "Holy crap, Earl! You'd need a space telescope to read this." Earl takes it back and tries to read it. The others crowd around to give it a try as well.

Earl looks up at the chief. "I told them to reduce it to make it fit. It's kind of small."

The chief finishes going over the plan with the SWAT team. They march off with their rifles toward the back of the building. One of the men has his vest taped onto his back. The chief starts to say something but just shakes his head. Joey and Pops approach the chief, concerned. "He's not dangerous. Is all this necessary?" Pops asks, worried for his son.

"In case you haven't noticed, your son has hostages at gunpoint," the chief retorts.

Joey approaches the chief. "Let me go talk to him. He'll listen to me."

The chief studies Joey for a minute. "I can't let you go in there. If you think you can talk some sense into him,… " he hands Joey the bullhorn, "be my guest."

Joey positions the bullhorn in front of his mouth. "Alvin. Alvin. It's me. Joey."

Inside the bus, Alvin perks up upon hearing Joey's voice and starts moving toward the back of the bus to get a look at him. Charlie quickly retrieves him and pulls him back to the front. "What are you doing?"

"Dat's my bwother, Joey. I was jusht donna wave at him."

Charlie pulls Alvin toward a window and points at a couple of the policemen stationed behind a police car with weapons drawn and pointed at the bus. "See that?" Charlie asks.

"Uh-huh."

"If they can see you, they WILL shoot you."

Alvin's eyes enlarge as he straightens up. "What do we do, Chawlee?"

"We have to get off this bus. The problem that you have is how do you keep everyone together?" They both look at Charlie's bag of Christmas supplies.

CHAPTER FOUR
Hostages on Parade & Forgiveness

Shortly, the bus doors open and the hostages parade out. They are all chained together with wide Christmas ribbon. Charlie heads up the back with Alvin, who has the gun pulled up under Charlie's chin. The bus driver acts like a distressed hostage. "Don't shoot! He's got a gun on me."

The policemen scramble behind their vehicles as the parade of hostages moves toward the retirement home's front door. The chief quickly gets on the walkie-talkie. "Hold your fire. We don't want casualties. Hold your fire."

As the parade of hostages enters the retirement home, the deputy, Kyle, approaches the chief. "Chief, we don't have anyone inside you know."

The chief removes his hat and throws it down, then he calmly reaches down, picks it up, and dusts it off.

"I hate to bring this up, but my grandmother's in there," Kyle quietly announces.

The chief gives him a sharp look then motions toward the hostages entering the building. "You think you have problems?" He nods toward the hostages. "That's my wife."

The chief's wife, Wanda, wrapped with large red ribbon, tries to wave to her husband with her hands bound to her sides.

The chief continues, "And my mother-in-law is inside."

The deputy shakes his head in disbelief.

Just then, the chief spots a local reporter, Kelly Mann, and her cameraman, Russ, scurry into the front of the building.

"Dang it!" the chief huffs, then throws his hat down again. He takes out the walkie-talkie and grips it tight. "Now listen! No one, I mean no one goes inside!" Then in a fit of anger, he throws the walkie-talkie down on the ground. It smashes into a hundred pieces.

The deputy looks down at it. "I'll get another radio." He quickly steps away.

Joey and Pops look at each other then at the home.

Meanwhile, inside the retirement home, Charlie and Alvin finish untying the hostages as Mrs. Cratchet verbally attacks them. "And if you think that you can just parade in here like a couple of hoodlums and—" Charlie and Alvin look at each other, then look down at their hands filled with ribbon they had just removed from the hostages, and then back at Mrs. Cratchet, "tie people . . . uh, what? You can't—" she manages to say, realizing she's in trouble. She is gagged and bound with the ribbon to a chair, causing the entire population of the home break into applause.

At Arlene's house, her latest suitor, Carl, a middle-aged man with very thinning hair and a comb-over, checks himself in the hallway mirror, then scans his watch. "Arlene! Girls! We need to get a move on if we're gonna make that dinner reservation." he shouts up the stairs.

"Just about ready, Carl." Arlene shouts back.

Carl whistles as he primps around the living room. Picking up the remote, he turns on the TV. A special news bulletin is on.

Ken Richards, a well dressed local anchorman, is seated at the anchor desk. The picture of Alvin, wearing the cocked hat and stupid grin, is displayed behind him. Ken recaps the latest events for the TV audience. "A local Midville citizen is holding hostages at the Elmwood Retirement Home."

Half grinning, Carl shakes his head at the incredible news story as Arlene, Carol, and Denise come down the stairs dressed for their dinner date. Arlene finishes putting on of her earrings as she approaches Carl, who thoughtlessly blurts out the report. "Check out this dope on TV. He's holding a bunch of old folks hostage. What's he gonna do, steal their Social Security checks? What an idiot."

Arlene drops her earring in shock as she and the girls recognize Alvin on the screen in front of them. Arlene can barely get the words out. "That's my son."

Denise is shocked. "Mom, what's Alvin doing?"

"I don't know, dear."

Carl tries to recover in his own dumb but unconvincing way. "Nice looking kid . . . ah not as smart as the women of the family, huh?"

Arlene finally realizes what an ass Carl is. She steps to the front door and opens it, waiting. "I think we'll skip dinner, Carl."

Carl reluctantly steps to the door and stops. "You know I had to pull strings to get these reservations," he whines.

Denise steps to her mother's side. "Why don't you go pull your strings somewhere else."

Carl sneers at Denise. "Maybe you should have a talk with your daughter about her manners."

Carol joins her mother and sisters at the door. Arlene proudly puts her arms around her daughters. "She's right. Go pull your strings somewhere else, Carl. As a matter of fact don't bother coming back or calling."

Carl steps out the door and turns around. "And I was going to order a VERY expensive bottle of wine."

Denise slams the door in his face.

Racing back to the TV, Arlene and her daughters crowd around it. Ken Richards presses on his ear-piece as additional news is received. "This just in. It would appear that channel seven has one of its own reporters, Kelly Mann, on the inside," he announces.

Kelly Mann, microphone in hand, slowly creeps around the corner with Russ following. Kelly straightens her dress , stands straight with her shoulders back and walks straight toward the crowd of hostages and home residents. Russ hesitates and murmurs to himself, "Oh, boy. I don't get paid enough for this." He quickly follows her as she approaches Charlie and Alvin. Alvin turns and mindlessly points at them with the gun. Alarmed, Kelly throws up her hands, while Russ raises the camera over his head.

Charlie urges them to lower their hands. "It's all right. Alvin's not dangerous."

They lower their hands and then Kelly signals Russ to get in position to film. Russ quickly readies the camera as Kelly prepares for the interview.

Back at the Cane house, Arlene and the girls intensely watch as Ken Richards, the local anchorman, continues his report. "Now we take you live with Kelly." The image from inside the retirement home is displayed on the screen. Ken rotates in his chair to face it. Kelly is standing in front of Alvin and Charlie.

"Ken, I'm here with the lone gunman at the Elmwood Retirement Home. Behind me . . . " she turns as the camera follows, "on one side of the room are the residents and the other side are their grown children who were brought here by gunpoint. Let's ask the one they're calling Mr. Christmas why he's doing this." Kelly approaches Alvin and Charlie. She holds the microphone out to Alvin.

He nervously leans toward the microphone. "Hi evewybody."

In the Cane household, Arlene pulls her girls to her side as they watch the report.

The cameraman zooms in on Alvin's face, which fills the TV screen. Kelly continues her interview. "Why did you bring these good people here by gunpoint?" she asks from off screen.

Alvin looks at her. "Joey and me . . . " he waves to the TV audience, "hi, Joey . . . are Mishta Cwistmish. We help dem put da Cwistmish shtuff up. And dese—" He turns to look at the residents. The camera pans over to show them wave at the camera, then pans back to Alvin as he continues, "nicesh peoplesh wanted to shee der kidsh for Chwistmish. So I got on da bus—" Alvin pulls Charlie into the frame. "Dis is Chawlee. He dwives the bussh." Charlie tries to smile. "And he helped me get dem heawr." Charlie frowns knowing he may be considered an accessory.

In the meantime, at a gala event, Mayor Al Buchanon, overweight and wearing a tux, sips on a drink as he makes his way through his formally dressed guests. A few hands pat him on the back as he passes through. He shakes another hand as he makes his way to a small crowd. As they part, he sees that they're watching the kidnapping event unfold on a small TV. Alvin's goofy face fills the screen as off-screen Kelly pursues her line of questioning, "Are you saying that

Elmwood was abusing the care for the residents by not allowing their children to visit?"

The mayor sprays out his drink.

Alvin continues, "Oh dat's not twue. Dey justsh didn't want the Chwistmish twee dat we bwought here." Then he turns to look at Mrs. Cratchet, who's still tied in a chair. The camera focuses in on her. She tries to call for help, but her words are muffled. Alvin turns back around as the camera follows him. "Evewybody calls her da wicked witch at da home caush she's sho mean."

Russ zooms in on Mrs. Crachet's face. Her eyes widen in anger at Alvin's last comment. The mayor, having seen enough, angrily turns and forces his way through the crowd. The two assistants tag along as he fights to get through. "Get my car!" he demands.

Outside the retirement home, the deputy approaches the chief with a portable TV that's broadcasting the event. "Chief, you gotta see this." He plops the TV on the hood of the police car.

Joey sees Alvin's face on the TV. "Alvin!"

The chief realizes who it is. "Oh my God. What else?"

The deputy's cell phone rings. He answers then hands it to the chief. "It's the mayor?"

The chief takes the phone, listens for a minute then hands it back to the deputy.

"What'd he want?" the deputy asks.

"He's on his way."

"Does the mayor have a relative in there?"

"No . . . he owns it."

Arlene and Alvin's sisters watch the event on the TV as Alvin continues his interview with Kelly. "Can I shay shomething?" Alvin asks her.

Kelly urges him on. "Sure. Go ahead."

Alvin looks directly into the camera. "I wassh tinking about my famwie. Abowt Joey, Popsh, Mom, Denish and . . . Cawol." He looks down. "And how dat I wuv dem so mucsh and shometimes we don't shay dat to dem so dey don't know." He looks at Kelly off-screen. "You know?"

"Yeah," Kelly answers softly.

Alvin looks into the camera again. "Sho I shay it now. I wuv you my famwie. Joey, Popsh. Mom, who I div kissish to Denish for when I shee her. And Denish for being nicesh to me. But Cawol ish shtill mad at me caush I pwayed twicks on her when we gwowed up. I'm shorry Cawol." He kisses his hand and cups it. He holds it out to the camera. "Dis ish for you Cawol caush I wuv you too."

Everyone in the retirement home is silent, speechless.

In the Cane household, Arlene and the girls are deeply touched. Carol steps toward the door, stops, and looks back at her mother and Denise. "Well, what are we standing here for? My brother is in trouble and he needs us." Carol heads out the door. Arlene and her daughter, Denise, smile at each other, then hurriedly run after her.

Just as Alvin finishes his speech, Charlie approaches and whispers in Alvin's ear. "We've got a little problem, Alvin. We need to talk."

Alvin puts up his index finger to Kelly. "Chawlie and me haf to tawk." Kelly drops her microphone, looks at the cameraman, and shrugs her shoulders. Charlie pulls Alvin to the side and turns him so Alvin is facing the two groups gathered in the large room.

"What's wrong with this picture?" Charlie asks.

"I dunno."

"On one side of the room are the nice old people. On the side of the room are their grown children." Alvin still doesn't get it. Charlie continues to explain. "It's been like that since we got here. They're not getting together."

"Why?' Alvin asks.

"People have a lot of baggage. You know . . . problems. You can't just expect them to throw it away because you want them to."

"Why not, Chawlee?"

"Because it's hard to let go of it. There are feelings, bad memories. It's not like you can just toss them in a garbage can and get rid of them."

"How tum?"

Charlie puts his hand over his heart. "Because they're not physical, not real."

Alvin looks down at his hand and makes a fist as he did when he gave the kisses away. He slowly looks up at Charlie. "Da kissish I div are weal. Dey come fwom my haught."

Charlie cups his hand on Alvin's fist. "Yes, they are."

"If I tan take good fwom my haughty, maybe dey tan take bad fwom ders."

Charlie smiles and gives in. "Yeah, maybe they can."

"I haf an idea."

Outside the retirement home, the local citizens are crowding the streets to watch. The crowd parts as the mayor's car pulls up. The chief turns to watch as the mayor struggles to get his big body out of the car and make his way to the chief. The mayor inquires about the situation before reaching him. "Why haven't we taken him?"

The chief repositions the TV so the mayor can see. The camera view shows a scan of the residents and a close-up of Mrs. Cratchet. "There's a lot of innocent people in there and I'm not going to put their lives in jeopardy," the chief explains.

"Meanwhile, they're dragging my reputation through the mud," the mayor retorts.

"I'm sorry about that, Mayor. But we have to let it play out."

The mayor scans the area. "And where's my SWAT team? Are they ready to go? I lobbied for that money for six months."

The chief rolls his eyes. "Yes, sir. They're positioned around the building and are standing by."

The mayor scans the area to try to see them. "Where's a radio?"

Claiming the radio from a nearby officer, he hands it to the mayor. The mayor immediately begins taking charge. "This is the mayor. SWAT team leader, come in."

Behind the retirement home, our small town wannabe SWAT team members are patiently awaiting word, when they hear the mayor on the radio. The butcher picks up the radio and answers. "SWAT team leader."

The static laden voice of the mayor blares from the radio. "I want you boys to be ready when I give the word. You got it?"

"Got it. SWAT team leader out," the butcher over-dramatically responds then lays the radio down on the ledge of a stairway that leads down into the retirement home. The radio slides over the edge and bounces down the concrete stairs. The others in the SWAT team stand from their card game on the ground and approach the railing. They all look down the stairs and at the pieces lying on the landing.

The plumber looks back at the butcher. "Good job SWAT team leader. Now what do we do?"

The butcher shrugs his shoulders. "We move in when the time's right."

"And how do we know when that is?" the plumber inquires sarcastically.

"Don't worry. We'll know."

Out front, Arlene and the girls arrive by car. They quickly exit, and run up to meet Joey and Pops. Pops and Arlene share a cold look.

"What are these people doing up here, Howard? Shouldn't they be behind the police line?" the mayor asks irritated.

Joey hears the mayor's comment and answers. "We're his family." The mayor looks Joey over. "Good. Maybe you can talk some sense into him." He takes out his cell phone, and dials.

Inside, the phone rings. Everyone in the place looks at it. Charlie picks it up and holds it out to Alvin. "It's your show kid."

Alvin takes the phone.

Meanwhile, his family, the chief and the mayor all watch in anticipation as Alvin, who's now on the screen holding the phone, answers. "Hewo."

This is Mayor Buchanon. I can't begin to tell you how much trouble you're causing, son."

"Shorry."

The mayor shakes his head and hands the phone to the Cane family. They all look at it. Arlene reaches out and takes it, then slowly raises it to her ear. "Alvin?"

"Mom!" Alvin excitedly exclaims as he covers the phone and shouts to Charlie, "It'sh my mom, Chawlie!"

Charlie gives him a thumbs up as Alvin returns to his phone call with his mother.

"Listen to me, Alvin," Arlene pleads. "This is very dangerous what you are doing. These men have guns and someone could get hurt . . . I want you to put the gun down and come out. Everything will be OK . . . I promise."

Alvin considers her advice momentarily. "I'm shorry Mom. I tan't wight now. I wuv you." He hangs up the phone.

Arlene is stunned by his answer and slowly hands the phone back to the mayor. He puts it away, considers the situation, then steps to Howard. "Howard, can I speak with you please?" The chief follows the mayor a short distance away. The mayor shakes his finger at Howard as he talks. "This has gotten out of hand. I want him out of there . . . now! I don't care how you do it!"

Joey and the family overhear their conversation. Joey knows that they're becoming desperate and that Alvin could be put in danger. "We have to get in there before it's too late," Joey warns, then nods for them to follow. He silently leads them toward the building.

Inside, Alvin is trying to solve the indifference between the residents and their grown children. Standing alone in the middle of the room, with a trashcan placed before him, he turns to face the two divided groups. "I know dat even dough we aw here togetta you haf bad feewings fa each over. We haf to twow dem away. So der is da twash can. Go head."

No one speaks. Alvin examines the faces of the crowd and comes to rest on Charlie's face. Charlie looks down, knowing how much this means to Alvin.

Meanwhile, unknown to Alvin and Charlie, Mrs. Cratchet is using her time to free her hands from her binding.

Unseen by the local authorities, Joey and the others in his family creep up to the edge of the building and around to the back. They spot the SWAT team trying to get the vest, which had been put on backwards, off a team member. Joey rolls his eyes at their incompetence and leads his family down the basement stairs. Putting his jacket against the basement window, Joey elbows it in and begins helping the others through the opening.

Unfortunately, Alvin is not having any luck bringing the residents and their children together and is now circling the room carrying the trashcan.

Watching from the side, Charlie can't stand it anymore and finally approaches Alvin. He takes the can and faces the crowd, "Don't you people get it? He's asking you to give up all of those things that keep you apart from each other."

Mr. Sommer's speaks up. "We know what he's asking. It's not that easy after years of broken promises, lies, and back stabbing. You can't possibly expect us to do that. You don't know what you're asking."

"Doesn't he?" Charlie asks firmly.

"If it's so easy, then you do it. I'm sure you have as much baggage as the rest of us." Mr. Sommers retorts.

Charlie puts the can down and straightens, realizing the truth in Mr. Sommers words. His expression turns somber, the pain from his past resurfacing. Seeing that Charlie is in trouble, Alvin steps forward and lifts the can. "I tan do it."

Everyone looks to Alvin, waiting, not sure what to expect from the young handicapped man.

Unnoticed, Mrs. Cratchet slides to the floor, the ribbons falling beside her. Hiding in the shadows, she watches Joey and his family exit from the basement door and walk around the corner. She slips through, crawling out on all fours.

As Joey and the family round the corner, they see Alvin standing in the middle of the room looking down at the trashcan. Every eye in the room is locked on him, waiting to see what is inside their kidnapper's heart. Joey sees that Alvin is deep in thought and about to speak. He puts his arm out to stop the family from approaching as Alvin begins. "Peoples tawk about me and shay dat I am retawdwd. I dunno, maybe dey are wight. But it makesh me mad and shad too. So I take dat bad feewing about dem . . . " He puts his hand over his heart and closes it as if grabbing the pain. Slowly, he makes a fist, then moving his hand out over the trash can, he opens it to drop it. "and I twow it away. Caussh it only makesh my hauwt shad."

Alvin's mother wipes a tear away and puts her arms around her daughters.

Alvin looks up as the residents and their children. A tear rolls down his cheek. He again moves his hand to his heart and makes another fist, taking another pain. "And my Popsh, I know he saysh dat I'm dum and dat I neva will be any good fa nothing . . . and it hurts my haught vewee vewee much."

Pops looks down. Tears roll down his cheeks. Joey sees him struggling with his emotions and puts his arm around his shoulder.

Alvin straightens out his arm, his fist over the can. He opens it. "But I fogive him caush I wuv him so mucsh."

Pops wipes his eyes and looks up at his family through the moistness. Arlene smiles through her tears and nods for him to go to Alvin. Pops steps out onto the floor and puts his hand on Alvin's shoulder. Alvin, with tears in his eyes, turns to see Pops, and lunges into his arms.

Pops embraces him as he sobs. "I'm sorry for ever hurting you, Alvin. I love you very, very much."

Everyone applauds. The rest of his family then joins them on the floor and take turns embracing Alvin.

Having escaped her kidnappers, Mrs. Cratchet exits from the basement door and finds herself facing the SWAT team, their weapons pointed at her. Unfazed by the threat, she puts her hands on her hips. "Oh, for crying out loud. Aim those at the ground, you grunts. Now!"

The SWAT team, not sure what to make of her, lower their weapons as she approaches them, "Ten hup, you simpletons."

The SWAT team responds in unison. "Yes, ma'am!"

Inside the retirement home, Alvin has broken their resistance. They now are each pairing up with their family member and are walking up to the trashcan to dump their baggage.

As the TV reporter, Kelly, watches the moving event, she wipes tears from her eyes and motions to her cameraman with her Kleenex. "You getting all this?"

He nods as he repositions the camera to capture the confessions.

At this point, the SWAT team is cornered by Mrs. Cratchet. She has taken control and is putting them into action. Gathered behind her, they are poised to storm the home. "Now is the time to move, boys, before we start racking up a body count. It's time to strike," she commands. The men ready their weapons and follow her into the building.

Mr. Sommers and his mother are the first to cleanse their hearts. They approach the trashcan. Mr. Sommers grabs the imaginary baggage from his heart. "I forgive you, Mother, for burning all my Playboy magazines when I returned home from college and for telling my first wife about my affair," he halfheartedly recites, then opens his hand releasing the baggage.

His mother grabs her baggage and holds it over the can while eyeing him. "And I forgive you for being a crappy son and never inviting me to your house for the holidays and for not calling me on my birthday . . . creep."

They both take a deep breath and smile at each other.

Mr. Sommers is surprised by the result. "Mmm, I feel better." He looks at his mother. They embrace. He starts crying as they hug. "I love you, Mom. I'm sorry." She pats him on the back as she leads him away.

Outside, all the policemen, including the deputy and the chief, watch the events on the TV. They burst out laughing and applauding, then break down crying. The coldhearted mayor crosses his arms and rolls his eyes.

Mrs. Cratchet leads the SWAT team through the dark stairwell, all the time, giving instructions. "And remember to shoot first and ask questions second." She stops at the stairwell landing and quietly pushes open the door to the main floor.

In the lobby, Mr. Henderson and his father are on deck to dump their baggage in the trashcan. His father clasps his hand over his heart then dangles his hand over the can. "I regret sending you to military school so young."

His son interrupts, adding, "And not telling me that you moved."

His father considers it for a second. "And that too. I'm sorry, son."

"Took me six months to find where they moved to," his son comments to the audience.

Everyone laughs as they hug and walk away.

Behind the unsuspecting crowd, Mrs. Cratchet and the SWAT team enter the room.

The policemen, who had initially been called to the scene for a kidnapping, are now gathered around the TV watching the heartfelt moments unfold inside. Some are laughing while others are holding back their tears. It comes to an abrupt halt when the chief notices the SWAT team through the cameraman's view inside. The chief leans toward the TV in shock. "Who ordered the SWAT team in?"

Their expressions turn to one of dread as the chief realizes what's about to happen. "Oh my God. Those idiots! Come on!" The chief and the others race toward the building. As they near the entrance, the immense crowd of spectators who were behind the police lines breaks through and converges toward the building.

As Mrs. Cratchet and the SWAT team break through the crowd, the laughter and talking cease. "Look out! He's armed!" she shouts, pointing at Alvin.

Without hesitation, the SWAT team moves in with their weapons raised.

Alvin, stunned by the event swings around with the gun still in his hand.

Joey sees how his brother and the gun are misconstrued. He dashes toward Alvin. "Alvin! Drop the gun!"

Alvin turns and looks at him, but it's too late. The butcher has already dropped to his knee and taken aim.

At the same time, the chief and his men burst through the doors, their arms thrashing to get the SWAT team's attention. "No! Don't fire!" the chief shouts loudly.

But the butcher has Alvin in his sights and pulls the trigger. Alvin drops the gun just as the butcher's gun clicks. Everyone in the room, shocked and bewildered, freezes. The butcher's gun didn't fire.

After a moment of pause, everyone breathes a sigh of relief as the chief walks over and snaps the rifle away from the butcher. Pulling the lever back, he checks the chamber. He looks up at the butcher, puzzled. "It's empty."

The SWAT team members all look at each other. The plumber unwillingly raises his hand. "Sorry. I was in charge of bullets. I forgot."

The chief hands the rifle back and chuckles. Everyone bursts out laughing.

Joey and Alvin embrace. The rest of the family ensues.

The mayor finally arrives, out of breath. He doesn't get why everyone is laughing. "What?" he asks wryly. His ignorance causes everyone to laugh harder.

Later, as the police and crowd are dispersing, the mayor unpleased with the events, approaches Mrs. Cratchet. She looks disheveled.

"Ethel," he begins, eyeing her unruly hair and disorderly appearance, "you are dishonorably discharged."

She cringes. "Again?"

The mayor shakes his head disgusted with her and walks away into the crowd where everyone is congratulating and hugging each other.

The chief inspects Alvin's gun as Alvin and his family gathers around. He looks in the empty magazine, laughs, and hands it to Pops. "Going to press charges, Chief?" Pops asks.

"No. Consider it my Christmas present to your family."

"Thanks."

As the chief starts to walk away, his mother-in-law, Marge, and his wife, Wanda, intercept him. The chief puts his arm around his wife and kisses her on the cheek. Marge raises an eyebrow to her son-in-law. "So it takes a kidnapping to get to see you?"

The chief tries to make amends. "I've been busy. Sorry. Merry Christmas, Marge."

She frowns and approaches him. "You know, I've been meaning to tell you something for a long time."

Expecting the worst he asks, "What's that Marge?"

She breaks into a forgiving smile, "I'm glad you're my son-in-law. You're a good man." The chief kisses her on the cheek. The three walk away together.

Dorothy steps up to the Cane family. "Well, you boys delivered like you said you would." Then she leans forward and kisses both Joey and Alvin on the cheek. Stepping aside, she reveals Christine, the blond from the store, and a young redheaded girl named Sam, who is wearing leg braces. Joey's mouth drops open upon seeing Christine. Dorothy realizes that Christine and Joey immediately recognize each other. She notices how they locked eyes on each other, but don't know what to say. "I'd like you to meet my granddaughters, Christine and Sam," she announces. Before she can say another word, Joey steps forward to face Christine.

"Hi."

She smiles a teasing smile. "Hi, again."

Pops sees that something serious is happening between them and signals Arlene and his two daughters to give them some privacy. Dorothy smiles and follows them.

Alvin is staring at Sam, his mouth drooped open as well. Sam smiles a shy smile and looks down. Joey looks back at Alvin and lifts his chin to close his mouth. "Aren't you going to say something, Alvin?"

Alvin is spellbound by Sam. "What do you shay to an angel?"

Christine is very impressed with Alvin's line. "That's the most beautiful thing I've ever heard." She looks at Joey. "Why don't you have lines like that? Then I wouldn't have to break my ornaments just to get your attention."

"Yeah, I know. I wish I would have thought of . . . " Then it dawns on him what she just said. He pulls her to him and they kiss.

Later, as the rest of the residents enjoy their time with their visiting children, Charlie steps up to Alvin and his family to say goodbye. Charlie puts out his hand to Alvin. "Well, bucko, you took us for one heck of a ride. It was very interesting, but I have to go now."

Alvin wraps his arms around his neck and hugs him. "Tanksh Chawlie. I toudn't dun it widout you."

Alvin releases him and Charlie pats him on the shoulder. "Sure you could have. Don't ever doubt yourself . . . Mister Christmas."

Joey offers his hand to Charlie. "Thanks for watching out for him, Charlie."

Pops offers his hand and they shake. Charlie wanders off. Alvin remembers something and runs after him. He runs out of the building just as the bus pulls away. Joey steps up behind him and they watch the bus disappear together. "What's wrong?" Joey asks.

"He foghot to get wid of it fwom hish haught."

Joey puts his arm around Alvin and turns him to go back in. "Somehow, I don't think he forgot, little brother." They walk back in together.

In a residential neighborhood, the bus pulls up and parks in front of a nice middle class home. As Charlie steps from the bus, it starts to snow. He looks up, smiles, then steps to the front door and rings the doorbell. Charlie's son, Wilson, opens the door. Freshly fallen snow decorates Charlie's gray hair.

His son is startled by the sudden appearance of his father. They had not spoken since his wedding. "Dad?" he asks, surprised.

"Hi, son," Charlie says, obviously feeling uncomfortable.

"Dad what—" Wilson starts.

Charlie interrupts, "I know that I've done some things that hurt you. I'm really sorry, son."

His son's wife, a thin pregnant blond, steps up next to Wilson. He puts his arm around her shoulder and makes the introduction. "This is my father."

She puts her hand out. He shakes it, then looks down. "Look, I'm sorry for not coming to your wedding. I'm sorry for a lot of things. I—"

Wilson interrupts, "Dad. It's OK."

"It is?"

"Yes, it is. I . . . we forgive you." He swings the door open. "Now, come on in. We can talk."

Charlie wipes his feet. "I'd like that . . . very much."

The front door closes as the snow softly drifts down. After a short time passes, the door reopens and Charlie steps out. He clasps his hand on his heart, then holds it out. He opens his hand letting the past fall away. Looking up at the snow falling, he chuckles to himself. "Thanks Mister Christmas." He turns and goes back into the house.

It's a beautiful Christmas day as snow lightly falls and the delightful sounds of people enjoying each other's company echoes from the Cane house. Through the window, Alvin can be seen with his entire family at the dining room table preparing to dine on a feast.

Alvin sits down next to Joey on one side of the table. Sam is seated next to him. His sisters and Christine are on the other side. Arlene is seated at one end of the table and the turkey is placed at the end where Pops sits awaiting his ritual carving. Pops enters with the carving knife and fork and steps to the head of the table. He starts to carve then stops and looks up. "You know I've been in charge of carving the old bird for what seems like forever. Maybe it's time for someone else to take over."

Pops makes his way around the table and stops between Joey and Alvin. Alvin looks at Joey believing he's the lucky one. Pops lowers the knife and fork down in front of Alvin. Alvin's mouth drops open with delight. He gently takes the knife and fork and like a person who's just been knighted, he stands and walks to the front of the table. He looks around at the faces. "Otay, who wants a weg?" All of their hands go up, including Pops'. Alvin points the fork at them. "Otay tut it out." Alvin smiles as they all burst out laughing.

In the Cane hardware store, a woman reaches down and puts pieces of pipes into a bin. The pipes are mismatched so a guiding hand reaches into the bin, picks up two pieces and reveals the different diameters. Mrs. Cratchet looks down at the pieces of pipes in Alvin's hand. Alvin, now wearing an "Assistant Manager" badge explains. "Dese are diffaent diamtas. Could you wedo dem pwease." He stands and as he walks away his brother meets him. Joey is wearing a "Manager" badge and is carrying a backpack with a baby in it. His wife, Christine, is with him. "I'm taking off for a couple hours, Alvin. Can you cover for me?"

Alvin plays with one of the baby's toes as he talks. "Shur, Joey."

Joey and Christine exit as Alvin rejoins his wife, Sam, who's seated near the door greeting the customers. Alvin plops down, gives her a kiss on the cheek and picks up a string of lights to work on. A regular customer, Mr. Monroe, walks in and smiles as he passes.

"Hi, Mr. Monwoe."

"Oh hi, Alvin. Hi, Sam."

Sam gives a wave and smile. "Hi, Mr. Monroe."

And at night if you look down over the community of Midville, you see that not just about every house, but the whole town is gorgeously decorated with lights. It would appear that the small town takes Christmas very seriously. Or maybe you don't have to if one of your residents is Mr. Christmas himself.

The End

"FOR THE GIRLS"

Screenplay by Jackie L. Young

Story Conversion by Jill Pomerantz

BACK STORY

For years I had wanted to do a screenplay about women in an office environment fighting against a glass ceiling. I had met secretaries who had some really interesting stories while working in offices in the Midwest. It wasn't until my brother, Dan, mentioned that Oprah had suggested on various occasions that she would like to do a movie with some of her favorite stars that I decided to finally write it. After all, who better to come to the rescue of a group of office women who have given up on life than Oprah? As you can guess, my choice for the title role (and written for) is Oprah. Other recommended casting includes; Diane Keaton as Rose, Julia Roberts as Ali, Halle Berry as Chantelle, George Clooney or Jack Nicholson as Barry, Danny Glover as Willie, and of course John Travolta as Henry...or...Henrietta.

CHAPTER ONE
THE GIRLS

A woman's strength comes from being able to adapt and yet still be strong enough to fight back.

-Yuri Kochiyama-

The prominent Harrison & Haney Insurance Company, the tallest building in downtown Omaha, echoes its renowned image in the adjacent Missouri River as the morning summer sun glimmers across the city. Being part of a nationwide company, its employees come from all walks of life. Each of their experiences and problems commences as the city begins to thrive with activity.

Chantelle Smith, a black woman in her late twenties, stands in front of the bathroom mirror of her north Omaha apartment. The morning sun creeping in through the small window illuminates the bruise on the side of her face as she tries to camouflage it. She flinches as she adds makeup, the fresh bruise still sensitive to the touch. Turning to her hair, she tries to force it down, but the more she combs it the more it resembles a tight Afro. She gives up and leaves, turning off the light.

She enters the bedroom and tiptoes to her dresser not wanting to wake Drey. She looks at him stretched out on his stomach, dominating the bed. She stares at the multiple tattoos on his back and arms and shivers with anxiety. She quietly picks up her purse. Just before she swings her purse over her shoulder, she notices the zipper has been pulled back. Her wallet lays open inside. Setting her purse back on the dresser, she opens the wallet to find only two single one dollar bills remaining. She draws her lips together and closes her eyes, trying to contain her anger. She gazes suspiciously at Drey's pants, which lay in a crumpled heap next to the bed. Chantelle eyes him, then the pants. She quietly approaches the bed and kneels down to reclaim her money from his pockets. But his large hand instinctively reaches out and clasps her wrist, stopping her.

"Whatchu doin', girl?" Drey asks accusingly.

Chantelle knows what Drey is capable of and fearfully responds, "My money is missing. I need some back for lunch."

"I told you last night that I had to borrow it."

"I didn't hear you."

"You should listen. There ain't nothin' in there for you, girl." He releases her hand as she stands. She stares at him with contempt, wanting to say something, but knows better. She turns and leaves quietly for work.

Chantelle walks up exhausted to her old beat up car that's parked at the street curb in front of her apartment building. Reaching down, she touches a new dent on the fender. "Damn him!" she curses. She opens the car door. Trash and empty booze bottles fall out unexpectedly. She kicks them angrily and closes the door. Before she starts the car, the loose ceiling cover hits her on the head. She slams it back up into place. She puts the car in gear and squeals away.

The alarm clock in Alice Thompson's bedroom has been going off for the last five minutes. She lies in a clump under her covers undisturbed by the annoying beep. Like the lump under the covers, nothing has progressed to better things since the eighties. Ali still lives in her parent's home, occupying the same bedroom whose walls are still adorned with posters of her high school idols, Van Halen and Motley Crew. The only new addition being the framed Associates Degree in

Business Administration, which crookedly hangs on the wall by the cluttered desk

Her elderly mother, Betty, enters and turns the alarm off. "Dear, you're going to be late for work again. Wake up." Her daughter, underneath the covers, rustles and moans. Betty reaches down and shakes the body. "Time to get up. Come on, dear."

Back in the kitchen, Betty and Edward Thompson watch the local news on a small TV while finishing their breakfast of pancakes and sausages. Ed takes a sip of coffee and nods toward Alice's room.

"That girl needs to wake up," Ed states, fed up with the daily routine of motivating his grown daughter into some semblance of a life.

"I did wake her," Betty replies, exhausted.

"No, I mean REALLY wake up. When's she gonna get with the program? She's already had a failed marriage, which didn't last longer than six months. What's she gonna do? Allow herself to rot in her bedroom every time something goes wrong?"

"Don't blame her for the failed marriage, Ed. Bob just couldn't help her through her depression after the miscarriage. It's all hormonal, you know. She's trying."

"Ten years ain't trying, Betty. If we hadn't pushed her to go to that community college and then coax her through the business administration program, she'd be waiting tables for minimum wage. She doesn't even date or have any life outside of work. It's like she's given up. If you think that's trying then I'm a monkey's uncle."

Alice's staggers into the room just as Ed finishes his sentence. Not seeming to notice, she pulls up her elastic waisted blue leisure pants and adjusts the white blouse that has been worn so many times it's begun to show the wear. Her long dark hair is parted on one side and frizzes out on the ends. Ed eyes her matted hair sticking up in the back as she opens the fridge to get the orange juice. Discouraged with the outcome of his only daughter, he shakes his head and goes back to his breakfast.

Forty-eight-year-old Rose Wilson enters the kitchen of her small south side apartment. She looks at the white square clock on the wall and notes that she is still on schedule. Woody, the poodle she depends on for the least bit of affection, is put outside for his morning bathroom ritual. The coffee finishes perking just as expected and the paper is positioned in front of her morning bowl of maple flavored oatmeal and next to the glass of orange juice placed just so on the table.

Occasionally glancing at her watch, Rose takes a spoonful of oatmeal and delicately eats it as if an etiquette officer were watching her. She scans her watch again. Then she stands and opens the door for Woody, pats him on the head, and closes the door. Before leaving for the office of H&H Insurance, she checks herself in the hall mirror. She scans the unstylish white and blue plaid suit and moans at the lack of luster in her life. She schedules everything just so it appears she has an appearance of a life. Everything has its place and time from breakfast to supper to bedtime to her movie night, where she sits alone and cries over Cary Grant and Gregory Peck films. There's no room for spontaneity or for a meaningful relationship. Rose sighs and takes a last glance at her watch and heads out the door.

It's 7:30 am and the morning rush of employees files through the revolving doors of the Harrison and Haney Insurance building. Will Davis, a black man in his early fifties, dressed in a gray guard's uniform, stations the information and security desk just before the two main elevators. He smiles and greets the employees by name as they pass on their way to the elevators. Willie, as he is affectionately known by all, is a big man with graying hair at the temples. He is always pleasant and seems to remember the names of everyone that passes through the doors of H&H. When he senses a little more than a greeting is needed, he offers words of encouragement. To the surprise of some of them, Willie can also recall any event from the news or the weather conditions in detail. He's a walking information center.

"And how we doing this morning, Miss Smith?" Will asks, noticing another unsuccessful attempt to cover up the bruises. Chantelle is distracted with thoughts of her miserable life and passes without a word. But this doesn't affect Will's positive attitude. "Have a good day, ma'am." He watches her enter the elevator, concerned. It's not the first time he's noticed the bruises.

When Rose enters, he scans his watch and grins. She pretends not to notice that he's checking her arrival time.

"Morning, Will," she offers as she passes by.

He smiles. "Morning, Miss Wilson. That's sixty four."

Rose stops and turns. "Sixty three," she states matter of factly.

Will considers it, but doesn't buy it. "One Monday, at seven forty five. Remember?"

"That was prearranged with my boss. It doesn't count." She smiles a conquering smile and enters the elevator.

"I stand corrected. Sixty three it is." He smiles and turns to greet other incoming employees.

Later, a few minutes to eight, Ali enters the main doors. She finds herself walking across the lobby floor alone. Feeling pressured to reach the twenty-fifth floor on time, she steps hurriedly toward the elevators.

"Morning, Miss Thompson," Will offers.

"Am I late, Will?" she asks looking around at the emptiness.

"No ma'am, you have two minutes. You'll make it just fine."

Up on the twenty-fifth floor, Rose is already at her desk reading her morning e-mails and Chantelle is looking through the accumulated work in the in-basket. Ali makes her way to her desk across from Rose, who scans the clock on the wall as she types. She notices that it's already five after eight and Ali is just now situating herself at her desk and putting her purse away. As supervisor, Rose takes note and gives Ali a disapproving eye. Ali is saved by the ring of the telephone. She picks up immediately and informs Rose that Mr. Castle would like to see her in his office.

Rose steps down the hall passing the office door that bares the name "Allen Kendal, VP of Sales" and enters the door baring the name "Barry Castle, President of Sales." As she enters, Barry, a well dressed, good-looking man in his forties, practices his putting technique with a golf ball and paper cup. He doesn't break his concentration, conversing as he putts.

"Allen is out of pocket this morning. He mentioned last night that last month's sales report should have went out yesterday and didn't."

Rose tries to explain. "I know. I'll talk with—"

Barry looks up at her and interrupts, "I need that out today. I also didn't see next month's sales forecasts."

"I'm working that out with the girls and—"

He interrupts again as he sinks the ball in the cup. He smiles smugly to himself and retrieves his golf ball. "I have a tee time this afternoon and I'd like to think that I can count on you to finish the reports and get them out on time. I'm sure Allen will be there and will be interested to know if all is in order." He turns to face her directly. "Is that a problem?"

Rose is intimidated as usual. "No, sir."

"Good." He stares at her waiting for her to depart. She stares back, not sure why she's waiting. "Is there something else?" he asks perturbed.

Rose tries to laugh it off but it comes off fake. Barry returns a laugh that's anything but genuine and escorts her to the door.

"Happy teeing today," Rose manages to say.

He stares at her for a second, trying to decipher the comment. "What?"

"I mean, have a good golf game."

"Oh. Thanks."

The door closes. Rose lets out an embarrassed breath of air and looks up. "God. Why'd you say that?" She makes her way back to her desk, feeling somewhat humiliated by the latest experience. She stands between Chantelle and Ali's desks, almost lost and disconnected. She takes a breath and looks at them. The girls are busy typing, knowing that the crap from Barry always rolls down hill into their laps. They pretend to be engrossed in their work.

Rose tries to put on her best everything-is-great smile before she begins. "Well, how is it going this morning, girls? Both have a nice weekend?"

Chantelle and Ali exchange looks. They think after all these years of working for her she'd at least know that neither has a life to speak of. But that's always been her icebreaker on Monday mornings. So they play along as usual.

"Fine," Ali and Chantelle say in unison.

"Good, good," Rose uncomfortably responds. The girls wait an awkward minute for her to continue. "Barry would like the monthly status report that was due yesterday, today. The sales projections, too." Chantelle rolls her eyes while Ali fumbles through her files to find the work folder. "OK. There we go." She heads back to her desk feeling as if the subject has been settled.

At that moment, Barry and some of the other executives appear dressed in golf attire. Carrying their expensive clubs, they noisily make their way through the office causing everyone to stop and look. When the men enter the elevator and disappear, Rose stands and steps to the windows. She waits patiently for their appearance on the street below. As she watches, Ali and Chantelle step to her side.

"Executives sure have the life," Ali comments.

"Yeah, at our expense. We're stuck in here while they play golf and drink imported beer," Chantelle adds begrudgingly.

"They say that's where most business deals are made," Rose utters.

"Yeah, right. And who says that? Them? Don't defend them. That's their justification. Listen, sister, I know men. They'll tell you anything to get what they want. Booty or golf. It's the same thing," Chantelle rebukes.

Ali mouths the word booty to herself.

"No, it's true. I read an article on it in Woman's World. Even some woman executives golf and make deals," Rose adds

Chantelle puts her hand on her hip, skeptical. "Oh, yeah? Then why aren't you out there with them?"

"Because I'm not an executive. I'm just a supervisor."

"Right. That's what they say." Chantelle says, nodding her head toward the men as they appear below. "That's Eddie, the supervisor of the mail room with them. It's because you're a woman. That's why you're not with them. Men stink." She heads back to her desk.

Ali follows leaving Rose alone at the window staring down at the executives as they disappear from sight. Then Chantelle's comment finally hits her. "Booty?" she says to herself.

The summer sun beats down on the H&H executives as they approach the tenth hole of the Crestridge Golf Course. Vice President of sales, Allen Kendal, an overweight man in his early sixties steps to his tee and places his ball. He positions himself and swings. The drive sets the ball down on the fairway several hundred yards down and in good position. Barry and the other executives cheer and collect their golf bags. As Barry walks, he turns to talk with Allen, but finds himself alone. He looks back and sees Allen outstretched on the green dead from a heart attack. He quickly rushes to him as the others follow.

A large crowd gathers for Allen Kendal's funeral. Most of them are employees from H&H Insurance Company. Several family members, along with Barry and other top executives, greet guests at the main door of the mortuary. Allen is laid out in the "Fountain of Eternal Life" room, where an open casket lay before a small, plant filled fountain area. Large wreaths and flower arrangements adorn the area. A large framed picture of Allen with his H&H white golf hat is positioned next to the casket. He poses with a dim grin, reminiscent of his constant conversations about his hemorrhoids.

At the door, Rose, Ali, and Chantelle enter together. Rose is dressed in a classic black dress while Ali sports one of her black office leisure suits. Chantelle appears in a short black skirt matched up with a pair of white high-heels. They take their seats just as Barry steps to the podium to deliver his eulogy to Allen.

"Allen was our VP at H&H and I've known him, or I mean knew him, since he's dead now…" Allen's wife cries audibly with the admission. "Anyway, I knew him for over twenty years of his over thirty years of service at H&H. He was a husband, father, brother, friend, and a golfer. He loved golf." His wife nods her agreement as she wipes her tears. "I'd like to think we learned our life lessons on the golf course. If you think about it, life is a lot like golf."

"Life is like golf? What?" Chantelle mumbles in disgust. Ali, seated next to her, elbows her to stop as Barry continues.

"In life, you make choices like on the course. Am I gonna drive this ball, chip it, or putt it? Do I use a nine iron or a wedge? It's about making important decisions." Allen's wife stops sniffling to look up at Barry in puzzlement. "And the holes could be life goals that you set for yourself. Allen had goals like being the VP and he made them. There's eighteen holes on a course and let's say you divide the number of years by how long he was alive …" His wife, bewildered by the strange eulogy, cries out loud again.

Ali, Rose, and Chantelle look at each other perplexed. Their mouths drape open in confusion. Although Barry's audience looks at him with vacant stares, he continues.

"Then you'd get, I don't know, about three or four years a hole. Anyway, maybe it's when we make major decisions in our life. But the point is sometimes in our life we may get a hole-in-one or a birdie, or it's just lousy like a bad day on the greens." Barry turns and salutes the casket. "Now he's playing on the big course up there with the big guy. And I bet he doesn't have a handicap." Barry laughs, expecting one in return from the audience, but they just stare instead.

"Where in the hell is he going with this? Every conversation with the man always led to a discussion of his inflamed hemorrhoids," Chantelle whispers to Ali and Rose. Rose tries to hold in her laugh. Ali elbows her.

"You know, 'cause he's the big guy. So play through, buddy. You deserve it." Barry drops his salute and steps down as the pastor steps up to the podium. Everyone is speechless; no clue what it was all about. The pastor smiles awkwardly at Barry as he watches him find a seat.

"Thank you, Barry. That was a. … uhm ... very interesting analogy. So if there's golf in heaven, you think God has an angel for a caddy or carries his own clubs?" He looks out at the faces to see if it got a laugh, but only Barry, who's smiling and nodding, seemed to have gotten it. "Good food for thought. OK, please bow your heads in prayer to … the big guy."

A few of the funeral attendees lift their bowed heads in response to the sarcasm.

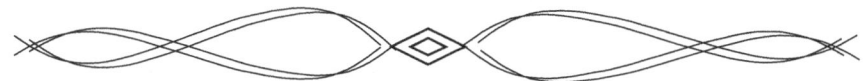

CHAPTER TWO
OPHELIA

As morning makes its full appearance at the H&H Insurance office in New York, Ophelia Jones, a successful and attractive black woman in her forties, steps through the main hall and toward her office. Everyone stops and stands at the sight of her. Pleased to see her back after a long absence, they offer heartfelt welcomes. She blushes as she realizes how well she is liked and respected. When she reaches her large office, she finds it filled with welcome back balloons and flowers. Left speechless by the overwhelming reception, she scans the flowers, and takes a card from one bouquet on her large mahogany desk and opens it. Before she can begin reading, the face of an attractive twenty-five-year-old black woman named Cecil appears from behind the flowers. She extends her hand up over the flowers to Ophelia.

"Hi, I'm Cecil."

Ophelia puts the card down and shakes her hand. "I'm Ophelia Jones and—"

"I've heard all about you. You're a legend around here." Cecil rounds the desk before Ophelia can get out another word. She takes Ophelia by the arm and leads her toward the door. "Ted asked me to make sure I brought you directly to his office the moment that you arrived. He's so excited to have you back. Come on." Cecil pulls her along the hallway to Ted Haney's office and knocks. She enters without waiting, pulling Ophelia through the door.

Ted Haney, a black executive in his early sixties, hangs up the phone and stands. A grin creeps across his face from the sight of an old friend. Cecil nods toward her prize.

"Look what just arrived." Ted rounds the desk and steps in front of Ophelia as Cecil goes to the door. "I'll give you two some privacy. I'll be in my office if you need anything." She closes the door.

"Her office?" Ophelia asks with a raised eyebrow.

Ted puts his arm around her shoulder, guides her to a chair, and seats her. He sits on the edge of his desk and looks her over. "You look great. How do you feel?"

Ophelia leans back in the chair and smiles a knowing smile. "You're evading the question, Ted."

Ted looks down and smiles. "Get right to it. You don't mess around, never did." His smile fades.

"You used to count on that when you first started this company. When it was just you, me, and Lou. Remember?"

She knows he remembers and that it bothers him. He turns somber and moves to sit behind his desk. Ophelia recognizes the move as a way to distance himself from her. She stands, walks to his desk, and sits on the edge to close the gap.

"Don't hide behind your desk on me, Ted. Come on. Out with it."

Grinning, Ted responds, "You're one of a kind, Ophelia."

"Her office, Ted?"

"You were gone three months, Ophelia. We brought her on temporarily, and she—"

Ophelia finishes for him. "She just happened to work out."

"Yeah. You left a big hole in the company, Ophelia," he says apologetically.

"And you filled it, knowing we had an agreement. Knowing I'd be back."

"We weren't sure if you would be back. The prognosis wasn't good and …"

"I see."

"I'm sorry. We were hoping that you would want to retire. You deserve it."

"Retire? And do what, Ted?"

"Everything that you've wanted to do. You don't need the money. Why not?" he asks.

"Because that's all I have. This is my family … or was," she responds.

"I forgot that your mother passed. Well, you still have your cat. People consider their pets family, right?"

"Now you're trying to do a sales job on me, Ted. And not a good one. Besides, I gave Benny to the neighbor when I went in. They grew attached to each other. Kind of like my ex who grew attached to his tailor."

Ted leans back thinking. "Yeah, that was a kicker to find out that Marv was gay. Man, who would have thought?"

Ophelia interrupts, "OK, Ted, enough reminiscing. I need a job and you owe me one." She looks expectantly at Ted, who seems to be running through something in his mind. "What is it, Ted?"

"I have a VP position that might be open," he responds with some hesitation.

Ophelia stands. "And …"

"It's not local. Omaha, Nebraska."

"Omaha? Nebraska?"

"I also have an opening in the mail room if you want to start over."

"Don't get funny. Once is enough."

Ophelia, dressed New York sharp, enters the main lobby of the Harrison and Haney Insurance building in Omaha, Nebraska. She approaches Will at the desk. He acknowledges her before she can say a word.

"Good morning, Miss Jones."

Ophelia is slightly put off. "You know my name. It would only be fair if I knew yours."

"Willie, ma'am. Or you can just call me Will."

"Thank you, Willie. Now if—"

"Twenty fifth floor, ma'am."

"Thank you," she offers.

"Your welcome." As she steps away he adds, "Eighty two."

She stops and turns. "What's eighty two?"

"That's gonna be the high today in New York City. Just thought you'd like to know."

She studies him for second, trying to figure his angle. Then she smiles. "Thank you for that, Willie." The elevator door opens and several businessmen exit. She enters and pushes the button to the twenty-fifth floor.

When she steps off the elevator, she heads to the office marked VP of Sales. Once there, she spots Ali and Chantelle overstuffing boxes with Allen's files and personal belongings. She stands in the doorway with her arms crossed, observing them. Ali and Chantelle each pick up a box to carry to storage when Ophelia interrupts. "Is this the Sales VP office?"

"It was. He died, honey. Can we help you?" Chantelle asks.

"I'm the new VP and don't call me honey, honey."

The girls drop the boxes then quickly bend down to pick up the spilled belongings. Ophelia steps in to help.

"Did Barry hire you?" Chantelle inquires.

"Corporate office."

Chantelle starts laughing.

"What's funny?" Ophelia asks, irritated.

"Nothing," Chantelle shoots back. They hurriedly pack the belongings and head toward the door.

"Oh, girls." They stop and turn. "Could you point me to Mr. Castle's office?" They both point down the hall. Ophelia steps past them and walks confidently toward Barry's office. They watch her disappear.

Ali smiles. "Barry is not going to like this, sister."

"He is gonna shit, man," Chantelle says back. Then she realizes what Ali said. "Did you say sister?" Ali nods. Chantelle turns and walks away with the box. "Don't. That ain't right."

"Can I say booty?" Ali asks as she watches her walk away.

Chantelle raises her hand as if to say, "don't go there" and continues out the door. When she looks toward Barry Castle's office she sees nearly everyone from the sales floor gathered around his door, listening.

Inside the office, Barry is on the phone with Ted, his boss at corporate headquarters. "Your replacement VP just arrived. We were thinking of filling the position with someone in house," Barry says a little distressed.

"She's one of our best, Barry." Ted says on the other end of the phone. "And since she's already there. I think we'll go with it for now. But tell your people there in Omaha to keep up the good work. Bye, Barry."

Barry finds himself listening to a dial tone. He calmly places the phone down, then agitated, picks it back up and slams it down several times. "We'll go with it. Keep up the good work. Nah nah nah," he says mimicking Ted. He then stops his rambling, having heard a giggle from outside. He stands and quietly creeps to the door, he throws it open to reveal nothing. He sticks his head out and looks both ways. He shrugs and closes the door.

The following day, Rose, Chantelle, and Ali assist Ophelia with organizing her new office. Several boxes that were shipped from New York have arrived. As they unpack, Ali seems out of sorts and unusually nervous. It doesn't go unnoticed that she has been keeping an eye on her watch. When nine O'clock comes around she excuses herself from the room.

"I'll be right back," she states. As she departs, Rose and Chantelle can't help but giggle.

Ophelia stops unpacking her things. "OK, what's going on? She's a wreck."

"Today is water bottle delivery day," Rose tells her.

"She has a thing for water?" Ophelia jests.

Rose motions her to follow her and leads her to the doorway. She peeks out. Ophelia and Chantelle follow. All three peek around the doorway. Ali is at her desk with her compact out, touching up her makeup and occasionally checking her watch.

"She has a thing for the bottled water guy," Rose tells her.

"The girl's delirious over the guy. Has been for years. It's pathetic." Chantelle adds.

As the elevator doors open, every female eye in the office looks up. A very attractive, well-built man in his late twenties steps out. Luke

Davidson picks up the two bottles of water and props them up on his shoulders. His gray T-shirt clings to his abs as he maneuvers himself to the first water cooler. Ophelia watches him with raised eyebrows.

"My God. He is a fine specimen," she states.

"The girl is way out of her league," Chantelle says.

The three women look back at Ali to see her plan of execution. They observe her nonchalance as she works at her desk pretending to not notice him.

"What is she doing?" Ophelia questions.

"She always does that," Rose says, rolling her eyes.

"But she's not doing anything," Ophelia notes.

Several of the office girls immediately make their way to the water cooler, but not because they are thirsty.

"It's a strategy," Rose tells Ophelia.

Ophelia looks at her oddly. "What kind of strategy?"

"She's playing hard to get."

"From my experience, if you play hard to get, you don't get got."

"That's what I told her. She thinks she's Doris Day or some shit," Chantelle states. Ophelia shoots her a disapproving look. "Sorry. But it's true."

After replacing the water bottle, Luke lifts the other and heads for the other end of the office where Ali is seated at her desk. Ophelia scans the office and locates the other water cooler. It's only ten feet from Ali's desk. As Luke nears the water cooler, Ali puts away documents into a folder and drops them. They slide to the floor. She stands and bends down. She's disappeared from sight. Ophelia stretches to try and see what she's doing. Luke reaches the cooler and disconnects the old bottle of water.

"What is she doing? He's right there," Ophelia asks, irritated.

"Maybe it's part of her plan," Rose says.

"The girl ain't got no plan," Chantelle states.

Suddenly, Ali stands and seats herself back at her desk. As Luke replaces the bottle, he turns in her direction. Ophelia becomes animated and moves her hands about in frustration. "He's looking at her. Turn and look!" Ophelia demands to no one. Luke steps to her desk and talks. "He's talking to her. What's he saying?"

The three slide around the corner of the doorway and slowly edge toward her desk to get within voice range. Ali stands and walks to the supply cabinet. Taking out a package of small drinking cups, she hands them to him. Ali follows him back as he loads the cups into the dispenser. As he does, he looks up and talks with her. The three girls edge closer and closer until he finally lifts the empty container and leaves.

Ali turns to go back to her desk but stops when she sees Rose, Chantelle and Ophelia huddled at the wall with no apparent motive for being there. The three smile and quickly disperse back to Ophelia's office. Ali shrugs it off and heads back to Ophelia's office.

As the three girls help to finish organizing Ophelia's things, Henry, the mail person, approaches with the mail cart. He stops at the door to meet the new mail stop. Ophelia notes his good-looks and an undeniable feminine quality. As she looks at him a bit closer she notices the subtle shade of lipstick. He extends his hand to Ophelia. She offers hers and receives a delicate handshake.

"I'm Henry. I'll be servicing you, well not servicing, but you know, dropping off and picking up any mail. I stop at nine and two each day." Henry can't help but admire Ophelia's Ralph Lauren charcoal skirt with a black double-belt and jacket. His mouth parts as he steps closer. "That IS a Ralph Lauren piece from his fall collection. I'm right, aren't I?"

"Yes, Henry," Ophelia confirms with a smile.

"It's darling," he adds. Barry steps to the doorway and starts thumbing through the mail on the cart. Henry spots him, rushes to the cart, and lightly smacks Barry on the hand. "No, no, no, no, no. Stop that."

Barry starts to turn, then stops and looks closely at Henry. "Henry, are you wearing lipstick?"

Henry dips one eyebrow. "Noooooo," he says in his best manly voice. He rolls his eyes and turns the cart around. Barry follows trying to get his mail. He flips a feminine wave to the girls and Ophelia. "Nice meeting you Ophelia. Work, work, work."

As he disappears down the hall, Ophelia smiles. "Henry is … different, isn't he?" Rose, Ali, and Chantelle eye each other wondering whether to let her in on the secret. "Is he gay?" she asks.

"He's way past gay," Chantelle says, letting her in on the secret.

"Henry has been saving up to become—" Rose begins to confess.

"A woman?" Ophelia interrupts. They nod. Ophelia reflects back remembering a quote that would apply perfectly to the situation. "'One is not born a woman, one becomes one.'"

"Wow. Who said that?" Ali asks.

"Simone de Beauvoir, a French author."

"That's beautiful," Ali states.

Barry steps over to Ophelia's door, leans in and coldly announces, "Staff meeting in the main conference room in ten minutes."

Ophelia starts to say something but Barry is already gone.

Ten minutes later, Ophelia follows the wave of male executives into the conference room and finds a seat. She looks around, and to her chagrin, notices that she is the only female in the room. Barry, who is already seated at the head of the conference table, waits for everyone to sit. Once everyone finds their place, he stands and clasps his hands.

"I'd like to introduce Ophelia Jones. She will be filling in for Allen as VP of Sales." Everyone nods and shoots her a luke-warm welcome smile. Barry sits back down, looks over his agenda, then unexpectedly stands and walks toward the door. "Excuse us Miss Jones. We'll be right back."

All the men stand and follow Barry out of the conference room, leaving Ophelia alone at the table. The door closes. She looks around, sensing something is wrong. After a few minutes of tapping on her notepad with her pen, she stands, slides her chair back, and exits. In the hallway, she looks both ways, then walks back to the office pool and looks around. Rose, Ali, and Chantelle see her and, knowing what happens in the staff meetings, they act busy to avoid eye contact.

Ophelia approaches Rose, perplexed by the men's disappearance. "Rose, did you see the men exit the conference room?"

Ali and Chantelle shoot Rose glances as she contemplates how to break the news to her. "They're in the men's room," Rose whispers to her.

"What? All of them?" Ophelia asks, stunned. Rose nods, almost embarrassed. "Why?"

Rose considers how to answer when Chantelle stands up from her desk. "It's what they do to women who attend the staff meetings. They meet in the men's room and make their decisions. It usually works. The women never go back. Men stink."

She plops back down and goes back to work. Ophelia turns to Rose, stunned by their audacity.

"Welcome to the Midwest," Rose announces.

"We'll see about that," Ophelia says defiantly. She turns on her heels and marches to the men's room. The girls look at each other and slowly stand. The other women in the office, having overheard the discussion, also stand. Suddenly, everyone races after her to observe. Crowded at the end of the hallway, they watch. Ophelia stops and with one determined push she enters. The girls race down the hall to listen at the door.

Ophelia steps into the men's room. Initially nobody notices her. Then one by one, they turn their heads. Finally, one of the executives taps Barry, who is taking a leak at the urinal, on the shoulder. Barry shakes his hand at him not wanting to be interrupted and continues with his discussion.

"As far as I'm concerned, the commercial account forecasts for this quarter aren't

reflective … " But Barry senses something is wrong and stops talking. As he looks over his shoulder, he sees Ophelia leaning against the sink with her arms crossed. He pees on his shoes, then quickly zips up as he turns. "What the … you can't—" he starts to say.

Ophelia interrupts. "This is a waste of a totally good conference room. But maybe we should rotate. One week in the men's, the next week in the women's." She walks over to Barry and looks down at his wet shoe. "You tinkled on your shoes." Barry shakes his foot. "Let's get something straight, Barry. You may not like me because I'm a woman or because I'm black, or maybe you think I'm the competition, but let me make this clear. I will be   attending the staff meetings whether you hold them in the conference room or in the men's room or on the roof. I will be involved in the decisions at this company.

She turns and opens the door. The sound of women scurrying back to their desks echoes down the hall. Ophelia opens the door, then turns back around to face the men. She shakes her head, disgusted by their antics. She exits, letting the door swing shut behind her.

Ophelia struts down the hall on the way to her office. One by one, the women employees stand and slowly start clapping. By the time she reaches the end of the hall, all the women are standing and applauding. She urgently steps into her office and closes the door.

Inside her office, Ophelia goes to her desk and leans against it in pain. Reaching for the desk, she opens the drawer revealing an arsenal of drugs. She lifts out a bottle of pain pills and quickly opens them. Popping a couple of them, she takes a drink of coffee from her cup and collapses in her chair.

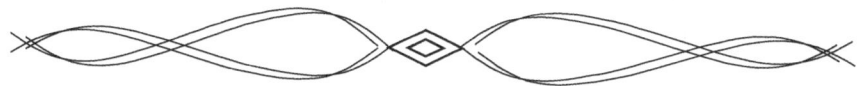

CHAPTER THREE
BOOTIES AND GOOD OLE BOYS

As the week progresses, Ophelia settles in and adjusts to the new job. The daily ins and outs are, by now, routine. That is, until she receives a letter. She steps to Rose's desk with the letter in her hand.

"Rose, Barry's office is locked. Does he have an appointment or is he out today? I don't show anything on the calendar."

"He's golfing with the other execs. They always golf on Tuesdays and Thursdays," Rose informs her.

"Oh. I see," Ophelia says, a little perturbed. She looks out the window at the beautiful sunny world beyond the office windows. An idea comes to mind. "It is a nice day to hit a few."

Ali perks up at her desk. "Oh, do you play golf, Miss Jones?"

"I've been in a tournament or two."

"Golf is like booty," Ali says.

Ophelia's gaze at the beautiful day outside slowly turns to Ali. "What?"

"That's what Chantelle says," Ali informs her. Chantelle drops her head on her desk, so embarrassed that she can't think of anything to say.

A devilish thought comes to Rose. "Why don't you go play?" She says to Ophelia

Ophelia's attention is diverted from Ali's dumb remark. "Yeah. Why don't I?" She then remembers the letter in her hand. "And I want you to take a look at this letter contesting a policy rejection for me."

Rose takes it and looks it over. "Allen always did these. I never—"

Ophelia interrupts, "You'll do fine. And, Rose, I'm leaving you in charge."

"Me?" Rose asks surprised.

Ophelia nods then spins around and struts back to her office. She pokes her head back around the corner. "Oh, Rose, I'll need the address of the course they're playing. Thanks."

Later, Rose, Ali, and Chantelle stand at the window looking down at the street below, watching Ophelia leave the office building.

"That sister has some gonads," Chantelle states. Ali and Rose look at her, disgusted. "What? She does." She looks at Ali, still upset over her remark and says, "Golf is like booty?"

Ophelia arrives at the Crestridge Golf Course dressed in her golfing attire. Barry and the other three executives he's playing with are just teeing off at the second hole. Ophelia sets her clubs down, takes out her driver and tees off at the first hole.

Down the hill, Eddie, the mail room supervisor, notices Ophelia getting ready to drive the ball. "Hey, Barry, ain't that Allen's replacement teeing off?" he says just as Barry gets ready to swing. All the men look. Barry holds his swing and looks over his shoulder. He looks at Ophelia, frowns and turns back to his ball. He swings. The slice sends the ball out into the trees to his left. The men turn around to see the ball bounce down through the tree limbs and land out of sight.

Dale, the fifty year old VP of marketing, chuckles. "Nice hook, Barry. Looks like you're gonna start off with a couple of double bogeys."

Barry turns his attention back to Ophelia as she lines up for the drive. "One was a bogey."

Dale rechecks his score sheet. "Nope. Got you for a double on one." Dale turns and looks at Ophelia. She swings a perfect swing. The ball drives straight and sure and lands a few feet on the green. The men look at each other, impressed. "She's gonna eagle on one."

"She'll get a bogey," Eddie puts in his opinion.

"Lucky shot. Come on," Barry says. He gathers his clubs and heads for the next drive. Dale and Eddie watch her gather her clubs.

"Five-spot says she eagles," Dale bets.

"I'll take that bet," Eddie plays along.

Barry notices them still lingering. "Are we playing or not?"

They turn to follow. As they approach their next shot, Eddie and Dale, now with a bet to monitor, are more interested in Ophelia's outcome on the hole than playing out their shots.

Ophelia steps up and removes the putter from her bag. She checks the alignment, and confidently approaches the ball. Eddie and Dale watch intensely as she puts the ball in for a double eagle. Eddie unwillingly forks over the five dollars to Dale, who is beaming a smile.

"She's good. Too bad she's a woman. We could use her on the team," Dale whispers to Eddie. But Barry overhears the comment, gives Dale the evil eye, then blows his chip shot to the green. He slams the club into the bag and storms away. Dale and Eddie look at each other, not sure what's up with Barry.

Later, on the back nine, while Barry is off in a sand trap trying to chip out, the others have already taken their shot and are waiting on the green for Barry. They can hear him cursing and swearing over the hill and see occasional wisps of sand shooting up, followed by more cursing.

Meanwhile, Ophelia steps to the tee and looks down at them. "Playing through!" she shouts.

Eddie and Dale wave her on and step to the side. She tees off, as they watch. Again, the ball sails true and lands near the hole. They're stunned.

"That was an outstanding drive," Dale states, impressed.

"Excellent form too," Eddie compliments.

Barry's ball finally chips up onto the fairway, but several feet off the green. They look at Barry's ball, unimpressed, then at her ball sitting a foot from the hole.

"I wonder if she gives lessons." Eddie wants to know. They watch as she approaches and readies to putt.

"You're an excellent golfer," Dale says to Ophelia as she studies her shot.

"Thanks," Ophelia replies. She putts and it goes in. She steps to the hole to retrieve her ball.

"Every golfer has a little trade secret that gives them an edge. What's yours?" Eddie asks.

As Ophelia puts her club away, she tries to think of a clever answer and remembers what the office girls had said earlier. "Booty," she says.

As she steps away, Eddie, not sure if he understood, calls after her. "Booty? Did you say booty?"

She turns while moving on ahead. "Yep, booty."

Dale turns to Eddie. "She said booty. What's that mean?"

Eddie looks at her bag as she moves down the hill. He spots the fuzzy booties on her clubs. He looks over at the cloth ones on his. "Her club booties. That's it. I bet they maintain the temperature of the clubs or something like that."

Dale nods in agreement. "I bet you're right. Man, we got a booty problem."

Barry finally arrives on the green, and he's out of breath and exasperated. He hears Dale's last comment about booty and just gives him an odd look as he steps up and prepares to chip the ball to the green. Then he sees that Ophelia is walking down the hill to the next hole. He stops and stands straight up. "Where is she going?

"She played through," Eddie tells him.

Barry spins around, furious. "What!"

"Barry, you should have seen it. She eagled the hole," Dale says.

"You let her play through?" Barry asks, annoyed. He goes berserk and pounds his three iron on the ground until it's bent and mangled. Out of breath, with the mangled club in his hand, he staggers back to them. "OK, onward." He shoves the mangled club into his bag and stumbles away.

Dale looks down Barry's golf ball still on the fairway. "Barry, you still have a ball in-play."

Barry rushes over to the ball and gives it a swift kick. "Now I don't." He stumbles away as Dale shrugs and follows. Eddie looks around to see if anyone saw the ordeal then quickly follows.

Ophelia, looking flush, enters the clubhouse with her clubs falling off her shoulder. She goes to the nearest wall and allows them to slip from her arm. She props them against the wall and rushes into the ladies restroom. She hurries into a stall, closes the door, and throws up.

After splashing water on her face Ophelia makes her way to a small table and sits down alone. She takes the pills from her purse and chases a couple down with a swig from her bottled water.

Barry and the other executives barge through the door alive with conversation about the woman who played through the men's team and, what's more, didn't bogie any hole on the course. Then Eddie notices her at a table.

"Hey, there she is," Eddie says in a hushed voice.

The conversation dies out as the men line up for cold beers. Barry looks frazzled and unhappy with the day's results and occasionally shoots glances of angst over at Ophelia. Finally, unable to contain himself, he approaches her table with a beer in his hand. Ophelia sees him looking down at her but does not return the glance.

"Have a seat," she says to him inexpressively.

Barry sits and immediately starts in. "What was that all about? You played through my whole team. You trying to make me look bad?"

"Seems you were doing a pretty good job of that on your own. You know you could fix that hook by just not twisting—"

Barry interrupts, "Don't tell me how to golf. It so happens our team was in the finals three years in a row."

"That's very impressive, Barry. Really, it is."

"Yeah, I know. So, uh, there you go," Barry says, starting to feel unsure where to take the conversation after her last comment. He stands and hovers, trying to figure the angle. OK, so, uh, see you back at work."

He departs to join the other golfers at the counter, but finds himself alone. As he turns back to Ophelia he see the other golfers have converged on her table. They barrage her with questions and compliments.

The next day, the human resource manager, Jake Sawyer, an overweight man in a cheap green suit, sits in the chair in front of Barry's desk. Barry is reclined in his chair reviewing the employee file on Ophelia.

"If it's a performance issue, I have an excellent brochure from corporate on Miss Jones," Jake states nervously, not pleased that Barry is reading the file.

"No, that's fine Jake." There's a knock at the door. "Come in," Barry says while continuing to read.

The door opens and the company security manager, Paul Sorenson, pokes his head around the edge of the door. "You wanted to see me, Barry?" Paul asks as he adjusts his loud tie.

Barry motions him in while flipping a page. "Thanks, Jake."

Jake stands, uncomfortable with what's going on. He exits as Paul enters and approaches Barry's desk. Barry hands the folder to him.

Paul flips it open and scans the first page. "What's the problem, Barry?" Paul asks.

"That's what I want you to tell me. Corporate sent her here, but there's something going on. Why would a VP in New York take a pay cut to come here? And the other day, she barged into the men's room and started babbling about holding meetings on the roof or something weird. I don't know."

Paul flips through several pages and reads. "I see. Are you thinking that she may be part of an investigation?" he asks.

"I hadn't thought of that. Could be something like that. Who knows?"

"I'll check into it and let you know what I find."

The next day, Rose and Ali enter Ophelia's office with two boxes of documents. They put them on her desk with looks of disbelief. They wait for Ophelia to finish reading a document before saying anything. She finally looks up and removes her reading glasses.

"What's this?" Ophelia asks.

"You asked me to look into the rejected policy application, right?"

"Right. One policy. What are these?"

"When I went to pull the original rejected policy, I found all of these," Rose informs her.

"You know that our company doesn't accept every policy request. No company does."

"Yeah, but these don't have any justifications for the rejections," Rose tells her, surprised.

"That can't be. Our policy requires it."

"Well, they don't. And there's a lot of them. This is just some of them."

Ophelia eases back in her chair and thinks about what to do. "First, let's get a hold of the rep for the one I gave you so I can answer the letter. I'll need the justification from him. Then you and Ali can look at some of the others. I'm sure it's just an oversight by someone."

Ali and Rose leave with the boxes. Ophelia puts her glasses back on and continues reading.

Meanwhile, in lounge somewhere in Georgia, two of the field reps sit at the bar drinking a couple of mixed drinks. One is Alex Carter, a man in his forties, with graying hair. It's apparent that he's well on his way to making a night of it. His buddy, Jack Styles, another rep in his fifties with thinning hair, finishes off his drink and orders another. Jack's cell phone rings. He flips it open to answer.

"Jack Styles."

"Mr. Styles, My name is Rose Wilson. I'm with H&H Insurance," she states on the other end.

"What can I do for you, honey?"

"I was hoping that you could help me."

"Sure," Jack says naively.

"We have an inquiry by a …" she reads from a file, "Leonard Marsh of Raleigh, North Carolina, whose policy request was rejected. It didn't have any justification listed. He was applying for home and life and—"

Jack takes a frustrated breath and sneaks a sip of his new drink. "Yeah, yeah, yeah. I remember." Jack sneaks another gulp.

"I need it for a response letter. It's policy that we—"

Jack interrupts, "Yeah, yeah, I know." He lets the phone drop, rolls his eyes up at his partner and takes another drink. He returns to the phone. "Look, just put something down or have Allen fix it."

"I can't do that. Allen died. Didn't you hear?"

"No. Sorry to hear that," Jack says, unaffected by the news. He covers the phone and leans to his buddy. "Al died."

Alex raises his glass. "Here's to Al!" he says loudly. Jack sneaks a toast to Al and they take a big drink. He returns to the phone. "Like I said, Al or Allen took care of that stuff."

"I don't understand," Rose says.

Alex orders a couple of drinks and urges Jack to hang up.

"You must be new, honey. I've been doing this for twenty years. It's nothing personal. Poor blacks and single mothers don't fit into the economics of it. You don't make money and we don't make money. Allen knew that. Talk to your boss. He'll explain it to you."

Rose slowly hangs up the phone, not believing what she has just heard. Slowly standing from her chair she walks almost mindlessly to Ophelia's office and stands in the doorway. Ophelia looks up. Without a word, Rose steps in and closes the door behind her.

Later, Ophelia storms into Barry's office with Ali, Rose, and Chantelle following. Each is carrying a box of documents. They place the boxes on his desk. Barry stops typing on his keyboard and takes off his reading glasses.

"What's going on here?" he asks.

Ophelia waits for the girls to leave, steps to his desk and leans in toward him. "For God's sake, Barry, this is the twenty first century. And here we are, back where we started." Barry's mouth is parted, lost for words. "These boxes are full of rejected policies from your reps in the field who seem to believe that they are at liberty to decide who should and shouldn't receive insurance from this company. For God's sake, do you realize a black man, a BLACK MAN and a BLACK WOMAN, ME, helped start this company over thirty years ago so that anyone, regardless of sex, race, or sexual preference could buy insurance. My God what have you done?"

"I don't know what you're talking about!" Barry replies, astonished.

"Do you know what your rep said?"

"No."

"He said that poor blacks and single mothers don't fit into the economics of it."

Barry falls back into his chair. "I didn't know."

"If we don't get sued, Ted will fire everyone, I mean EVERYONE ... including you." Ophelia, tries to hide the pain and exhaustion, but it weakens her. She moves to the chair to catch her breath.

"Are you all right? You don't look well," he asks, concerned.

Ophelia regains her composure and stands. "The girls will have to go through every file. Any rep involved will have to be fired."

Barry looks around for an answer. "There's got to be another way. I can't just fire my sales force."

"You're not losing your sales force, Barry. You're just getting a new one. One that won't arbitrarily discriminate against people for the ECONOMICS of it." She goes to the door and looks back before stepping out. "This is your field office. If you want to call Ted and handle this, I'll stay out of the way."

Barry considers it for a moment. "Maybe this does need a woman's finesse."

She stares at him a second, insulted by the feministic remark. "I'm a VP. I do my finessing at home on my own time. There's absolutely no hope for you, is there? You know you are the most self centered, egotistical, male chauvinistic man I have ever met. You are a pig, Barry."

The door softly closes. Barry stares at it. "Only my ex-wife talks to me like that. She likes me," he says to himself, smiling.

Fed up with the prevalent male-chauvinist attitude in the Omaha office, Ophelia gets to work on a plan. Pacing the floor, she says to her assistants, "Rose, you, Ali, and Chantelle go through every single rejection in those boxes." She stops pacing and turns to Rose. "How do you put up with the male chauvinist attitude from that ..." She points toward Barry's office. "That, that ..."

"Pig?" Chantelle offers. The other girls look at her in shock.

"No. I already called him a pig," Ophelia states matter of factly.

Rose's eyes widen. "You called Barry ... I mean Mr. Castle a pig?" Rose says in a higher octave voice.

"Oh yeah, and more."

"Dirtbag?" Ali timidly offers.

"Yes. Dirtbag. Thank you, Ali," Ophelia says politely.

"You're welcome."

Ophelia switches back to the subject. "And send out query letters to all of them to see if we can help with any of their insurance needs. We'll have to reprocess their applications."

Rose quickly takes notes. She looks up with a worried grimace. "All of them?"

"All of them. We have to make this right." Ophelia falls back to her previous conversation as she begins pacing again. "And just when you think that maybe after everything, the equal rights movement, Martin Luther King, burning bras, women's rights, the whole mess, that people would get it."

Rose stands up and throws her fist into the air. "Yeah! "

Everyone looks at her. She sits back down. Ali is wiping her tears because she's so moved by Ophelia's passion. Chantelle is staring at Ali and shaking her head.

"But they don't get it." Ophelia pauses for a moment. "But they are going to get it."

They all look at her. "How?" they say in unison.

"We're going to show them. Thursday the girls are going golfing with the men. We'll do it on their turf."

The idea doesn't appeal to the girls. They look at each other, stunned. Ali raises her hand with a question.

"What is it, Ali?" Ophelia asks.

"Well . . . we don't know how to golf."

"I do. Bring some comfortable clothes on Thursday," Ophelia tells them. She takes a breath, her ranting and raving over and turns to go back to her office. "Now I have to call a friend to see if we're all going to have a job tomorrow."

As she disappears, the girls, concerned by her last comment look around at the others in the office.

Chantelle shakes her head, impressed with Ophelia. "I told you the woman had gonads."

The next couple of days, the office works non-stop to reprocess the applications of the rejected customers and to identify the sales representatives responsible.

On Thursday morning, the work continues before the impending golf invasion. Ophelia finishes reading through a document on her desk. She removes her reading glasses disgusted by what she's just read. She looks up at Rose who is standing in the doorway

"How can anyone in their right mind have signed off on this expense report?" Ophelia questions.

"Allen had the final authority and we'll never know," Rose answers.

Ophelia tosses the report down on her desk. "We're going to have to start pulling expense reports for all of the reps."

"We're already buried with reprocessing the applications."

"You and Ali keep working on that. Put Chantelle on the expense reports. I want to know how many rats we have."

"She's not in yet. I'll let her know when she does."

Ophelia checks the clock. It's already eight thirty. "Send her in when she gets here." Rose starts to leave. "Rose."

"Yes."

"All the rats have to go. Ted wants anyone associated with this scandal fired immediately. That's going to be your job."

"What? My job?" Rose asks, surprised.

"You've just been promoted to executive assistant to the VP. You'll be firing the reps and hiring new ones. Of course, you'll have to work with HR, but I want you to do the interviews."

This is normally where Rose would back paddle to avoid additional responsibilities and express self doubt, but Ophelia has invigorated her and she responds enthusiastically to her own astonishment. "OK. I'll send in Chantelle when she arrives. I'll have a list by the end of the week with the reps involved."

As Rose disappears, Ophelia smiles, knowing that Rose just stretched herself more than she knows. As she starts to return to work, the familiar sound of the mail cart approaches. Henry's smiling face appears in the doorway and Ophelia immediately discerns a darker shade of lipstick and a hint of eye liner. She pretends not to notice.

"How's the golf queen?" Henry chimes.

Ophelia tries to finish reading the document while conversing. "Oh, you heard?"

Henry rolls his eyes. "Are you kidding? You're a celebrity. Can I have your autograph? Just kidding."

Ophelia laughs to herself.

"No seriously. Ali told me what you said about not being born a woman, but becoming one." He feigns wiping his tears. "I was touched."

"I'm glad."

"Oh, I also wanted to ask … I know that you girls were going golfing this afternoon … and I shouldn't ask, but—"

"Yes, Henry. You can go."

Henry's face lights up. Then he becomes emotional, almost in tears, and then lets out a relieved sigh. "Thank you." As he looks up, he spots an employee waving his mail at him. He puts his hand on his hip and snips at him. "Yes, I see you. Just hold your horsy. I'm coming." He trots away. "Jeez."

Ophelia laughs to herself as Chantelle appears in the doorway. Ophelia looks up to see that she's covering up a new bruise. She removes her glasses and stands. "Step in and close the door."

Chantelle, reluctantly steps into the room and slides the door closed. Ophelia moves around the desk and sits on the edge.

"Please sit," Ophelia commands. Chantelle cautiously sits, looking down at the floor. Ophelia moves closer to inspect the bruise, then pulls back. "You know the makeup doesn't hide the abuse, don't you."

Chantelle doesn't say anything.

"Oh honey, life is too short to go through it being abused. You're too smart for this."

"He's just going through—" Chantelle begins.

Ophelia finishes for her. "Rough times. Things will get better when he sorts out his life. He really does love me. That rarely ever happens without counseling. And he's not the first one to abuse you, is he?"

Chantelle looks up, a tear in her eye, and shakes her head gently.

"I smoked cigarettes for a lot of years. It was a hard habit to break. Dating men that you know are going to abuse you is a habit too. It's hard to break the habit … unless you really, really want to." Ophelia brushes Chantelle's curly black hair away from her bruise. "You're pretty and smart and you don't have to do this to yourself. When you want my help, all you have to say is 'I'm ready.' And I'll be there for you. Understand?"

Chantelle nods.

Ophelia moves back to her chair and sits. "Rose has some work for you."

Chantelle rises from her chair and walks to the door, opens it, and turns to face her. "Thanks."

The door closes. Ophelia takes a breath to chase the pain away, then opens the drawer to reveal the drugs. She removes a bottle and unscrews the cap. She grabs her glass but realizes it's empty. She goes to the coffee center where she meets Rose and Ali. As Ophelia fills her glass with water, she scans the office area and its drab 80s décor.

"So I guess we still have our jobs," Rose comments to Ophelia.

"There's concern by corporate, but they're giving us some leeway to fix it. But Mr. Haney is coming out next month to get status personally."

"The president of the company is coming here?" Ali asks nervously.

"Yes. And I don't think this will do," Ophelia responds.

Ali and Rose turn to see what she's looking at.

"Does it look that bad?" Rose asks.

"Honey, it looks like a bad 1980s flashback."

"I liked the eighties," Ali says.

They both look at her and raise an eyebrow.

"I agree. It's bad," Rose states.

"We need a makeover. Does anybody know an interior designer? 'Cause we definitely need one," Ophelia says.

"Russell in the art department did their area. He's very good," Rose offers.

"Give Russell a call. I'd like to see what he did." As Rose leaves to call Russell, Ali has a grin on her face. "And what's that for?"

"Rose kind of has this thing for Russell. He is kind of cute in a weird sort of way. That is, if you like ponytails on men," Ali states.

"Pony tail? I don't care if the man has three arms as long as he can help us escape the eighties."

CHAPTER FOUR
FIRING AND HIRING

The next day, a tall, thirty-nine-year-old Russell Johnson, with his sandy colored hair pulled back into a pony tail, takes Ophelia and Rose on a tour of the art department. The decor is sleek and modern but conservative. Ophelia is blown away as Russell leads them through the cubicle layout. She observes the affectionate glances Rose gives him as he points out the features of the cubicles.

After the tour, Ophelia, Ali, and Rose stand in the elevator as it makes its way back to the twenty-fifth floor.

"Well, what do you think?" Rose asks anxiously.

"I thought he was very attractive, intelligent, very polite, and I especially liked ... the pony tail. A little thin for me, but very sexy."

Rose turns flush. Ali rolls her eyes. "I meant the interior design," Rose corrects her.

"Oh, that? I liked it. Let's do it."

The elevator door opens to the sales floor and they exit. Ophelia walks briskly to her office. Rose and Ali step quickly to keep pace.

"I know that you already have a full workload, Rose, but I'll need you to work CLOSELY with Russell to make sure it gets done before Mr. Haney arrives."

"It's not a problem," Rose says.

Ophelia veers off to her office as the girls return to her desk. Ophelia smiles to herself. "I didn't think so."

As the men finish teeing off and head down the hill at Crestridge Golf Course, Ophelia and her accomplices arrive. Ophelia is wearing her white tournament hat and stylish white golf clothes. Henry arrives on the scene in a white visor, yellow sunglasses, and a matching yellow outfit. It borders between being feminine and masculine.

The others, however, lack taste in there choice of attire. Ali is wearing blue sweat pants, tennis shoes, and a black Van Halen T-shirt. Rose is dressed in oversized white shorts, a yellow Silver Bullet shirt, tennis shoes and white bobby sox. Chantelle is wearing a black T-shirt, black shorts, and a black hat with an "X" on the front.

By the time the women gather at the tee, the men have noticed them and are staring. Barry tilts his sunglasses down to take a better look. Eddie, the supervisor of the mail room, shakes his head. "My god. She brought the girls from the office."

Barry squints to focus better. "What ARE they wearing?" The others burst out laughing at their horrible taste in fashion.

Henry is carrying his clubs to the green and can't help but overhear them laughing. "Hey! Hah, hah. Very funny." He removes a driver and starts running toward them. "Let's see how funny it is when I put this up your—"

Ophelia grabs his arm and swings him back. "Whoa, Henry. Ignore them."

Henry steps back. He hands the driver to Ali who is first to tee off. Then he moves away with his hand on his hip. "Men," he hisses back at them.

Ophelia assists Ali with her stance and from behind, shows her the arch of the swing and how to hold the club. Then she steps back to give Ali room. "The only way to learn is to do it," she advises her from afar.

Ali closes her eyes, pulls the club back, and swings with all her might. The club smashes the ground behind the ball, sending a large chunk of grass and dirt flying ten feet. "Where'd the ball go?" she asks as she looks off in the distance for it.

Everyone looks around. Then Henry looks up and sees the ball coming straight down from above. "Aeeee! Run!" he screams.

They run for cover and dive in all directions as the ball comes back down to earth, landing with a thud. The men's team bursts into laughter as they watch the girls get up and return to the green. Ophelia takes hold of Ali, glides her back to the tee and repositions her.

"This time, don't close your eyes," Ophelia says sternly.

Ali looks over her shoulder at her. "Oh, OK." She slams another. This time it slices toward the men. They all duck.

"That's OK, Ali. We'll try it again at the next hole," Ophelia reassures her. "Chantelle, it's your turn."

Chantelle, turns her hat around backwards and prepares to swing. Not realizing that she is holding the club too high above the tee, Ophelia steps in to push the club down and reposition her. Chantelle concentrates and swings as hard as she can. She completely misses and the club breaks free and flies through the air. She tries again, but the ball bounces off several trees and lands back in front of her. Frustrated, she kicks the ball out onto the fairway.

Rose steps up for her turn, approaches the ball and readies herself as if she knew what she were doing. She starts to swing but Ophelia stops her, whispers in her ear, and steps back. Rose swings and the ball actually lands straight out on the fairway. The girls jump up and down and clap.

When Ophelia takes her position at the tee, the men and Barry decide to play on now that the entertainment has ended.

The men, having finished at the eighteenth hole, stand near the clubhouse looking back at the course. They watch as Chantelle, caught in a sand trap, chips and chips but is unable to hit the ball out. She becomes frustrated, grabs the ball, and throws it as hard as she can. Henry, standing with the other girls on the green, is hit in the groin by her ball. He doubles over.

Eddie and Dale are laughing so hard they fall to the ground. Barry is not amused as he watches the disaster over his sun glasses.

"So much for her playing through today," Barry says sarcastically. The others laugh.

"In their defense, for never having played before, I've seen worse," Dale says laughing.

"Come on, let's get some beers," Barry says.

Later in the clubhouse, the ragtag girls and Ophelia enter looking exhausted and beat. Barry and the others are crowded around the bar, watching them as they land at a table.

"God, we suck at this," Rose complains.

"The ball's too small. It's stupid. Trying to hit a tiny ball with a skinny bent stick. It's stupid," Chantelle adds. The others turn and look at her, then burst out laughing.

"You did fine for the first time," Ophelia tells them.

Barry sneaks up from behind and says, "OK, so you've made your point. I get it. So secretaries can play golf too."

The girls turn to find Barry standing behind them.

"They have as much right to play as the men do," Ophelia says perturbed.

"Have your fun then. When the company tournament starts it'll be a closed course. Then you and your girls can play somewhere else," Barry states then starts to walk away.

"Maybe we'll try out for the tournament," Ophelia replies snidely.

Barry stops, looks down, and slowly turns. He eyes the motley crew at the table. "You're not serious. There's no way these girls can qualify next week."

"That's your opinion," Ophelia retorts.

"I'll make a deal. If the girls qualify, we'll let them in our golf league. If they fail to qualify, you promise that they'll never set foot on the course again."

Ophelia extends her hand. "Deal."

Barry shakes it and returns to the men. Shortly after, the men roar with laughter.

The next morning, Rose knocks on Ophelia's office, enters, and waits for her to finish typing on her PC. When Ophelia looks up, Rose lays a folder on her desk. Ophelia picks it up, and studies it.

"It wasn't as bad as we first thought. We only found that half a dozen of the eighteen reps were involved," Rose informs her.

Ophelia closes the folder and hands it back. "Have them come in and then fire them. Use the conference room. Then get with HR to find replacements."

Rose hesitates, unsure if she should say what's on her mind.

"Is there something else?" Ophelia asks.

"Well … this golf thing. I really don't want to join the men's golf league."

Ophelia smiles. "You don't have to."

"I don't?"

"Nope." Ophelia goes back to her typing.

Rose studies her for a moment. "It's not about golf … is it?"

Ophelia returns to her typing and says, "Now, you're getting it."

Rose smiles and briskly steps out of the office to get busy on some phone calls.

When Rose returns the next day, she finds Russell waiting for her to go over the remodeling plans. They take a walk around the area as he explains the decorating scheme with a couple of contractors. Suddenly, Rose spots Alex Carter, one of the field reps, exit the elevator and step down the hall. She tugs on Russell's sleeve and leans in toward him. He stops talking with the contractors to listen.

"I have to go fire this guy. Keep doing the interior thing," she whispers to him. She quickly catches up with Alex and leads him into the conference room.

After a short while, the conference room door opens and Alex storms out very upset. "I drove all the way from Raleigh to get fired. Thanks for nothing!"

She can't help but feel guilty. She grimaces and mouths the words, "Sorry."

When he reaches the elevator, he turns and flips Rose off. She drops her mouth open. "Oh my god, he's flipping me off!" She returns the gesture but he has already disappeared into the elevator.

Expecting another rep to show at any time, Rose stands by the conference room doors. After a few minutes the elevator doors open to reveal a very large man in a suit. She looks him over, absolutely amazed at his size. She notices his rock hard biceps that are rippling through his shirt. She thinks for a minute about being alone in the room with someone of his stature and having to fire him. When he reaches her, she nervously slides her hand to the conference room doorknob and quickly squeaks out, "You're fired." She rushes inside and closes the door. She throws herself against it fearing he may come in after her.

After a short period, she slowly creeps the door open and peeks out. He's gone. She sneaks out only to bump into a short, dumpy, bald man. She invites him in politely and then delicately breaks the news. He sobs into his handkerchief. Rose puts her arm around his shoulder patting it as she leads him to the door.

Waiting impatiently on the other side is Jack Styles from Georgia. She remembers him from their phone conversation. She knows he's a jerk and wastes no time in firing him. Seconds later the conference door flies open and Rose runs out followed by a very pissed Jack. She scurries down the hall for her life. When she reaches the coat rack she pulls an umbrella from the stand and starts to fence him. She pokes at him with the umbrella until she is able to maneuver him into the elevator. The girls in the office, having watched the spectacle, applaud her bravery. She takes a bow and puts the umbrella back.

Feeling more empowered, Rose heads back to the conference room to prepare for the next victim. She seats herself in the chair at the head of the conference table. Prepared for the worst, she waits with her hands crossed in front of her. When the door opens, she's confronted unexpectedly with a very attractive man. He enters with a smile, sits in the chair closest to hers and winks seductively. Before long he makes his way to her lap where he brushes her hair back, flirting incessantly. She shakes her head defiantly, remembering her position. Although she finds it difficult, Rose manages to say, "You're fired!"

The sales rep steps past her into the hallway, angered and disappointed. She leans on the wall for support, waves good-bye, and sobs.

She gathers herself for the last conference with a middle-aged rep named Carl. After the polite introductions Rose thinks to herself, "Oh, wow. This is getting easier." So without hesitation she confidently let's out, "Carl, you're fired."

Carl opens his eyes wide, the veins on his head pop out and his face turns red. Rose sees the anger boiling and stands to prepare an escape. Before she can reach the door Carl goes after her. He chases her around the conference table. He tries to corner her, but she ducks and crawls between his legs and under the table. As he turns, he sees her edging toward the door on all fours. He slowly creeps up behind her and just as he's about to lunge, she swings the conference door open, hitting him in the forehead. He falls over with a thud.

She drags the unconscious Carl down the hall and rolls him into the elevator. The doors close and she proudly and briskly steps to her office. Exhausted, she decides to call it a day.

The next morning, as Rose exits the elevator, she is confronted with a construction zone. There are workers everywhere. Desks are being moved, walls are being painted, and power tools are humming.

Rose goes to put her bag away in her desk but realizes it's gone, computer and all. She stares at the bare floor confused. She was not informed that the office would be turned upside down in just one day when so much work needed to be done. Ali and Chantelle approach her, noticing that Rose is getting ready to go haywire.

"Don't freak on us," Ali tells her. She and Chantelle each take one of her arms and guide her toward Ophelia's office. They stop at the doorway. Ophelia's office is deserted. "The IT department setup all our PCs in the conference room. Ophelia called in this morning and wasn't feeling well. You can use her office."

Relieved, Rose removes her purse and tosses it in the chair. "Thank God." Rose plops into Ophelia's chair, testing out the feeling of authority. She leans back and puts her feet up. "Get me some coffee. Two sugars and easy on the cream, girls."

Ali starts to go. Chantelle pulls her back. "Get your own coffee."

"Well, I want some," Ali defends herself as she exits the door.

As soon as Ali disappears, Chantelle steps in and closes the door. As she moves to the desk, she pulls out a flyer and lays it on the desk. "You'd better read that."

Rose unfolds it and reads. She lowers it, not understanding the significance. "So, the bottled water supplier is changing. It says a new supplier will be working the building after next week. So?"

Chantelle reaches over and snatches it away from her, folds it and puts it away. "What's numbnuts gonna do?"

"Who's numbnuts?" Rose asks.

"Ali."

"You call her numbnuts?"

"My brother used to call me that all the time."

313

"He did? What kind of brother—"

"You're missing the point here. Who is she madly in love with?" Chantelle asks.

"Oh. Oh, my god. He won't be coming anymore."

"Now you got it. And were gonna have to put up with it. It's the only thing the girl's got. As pathetic as it is."

The door swings open and Ali enters with a big smile. "Hey, someone left some vanilla and spice creamer by the coffee pot. It's really good. You should try it." She takes a big gulp. The girls just stare at her. Her smile disappears. "That's not illegal, is it?"

Chantelle steps to the door, grabs one of her arms and pulls her away.

Rose gets back to work and is busy typing on the computer when Barry steps to the door and begins talking before he realizes Rose is occupying the office.

"Look, Ophelia. I want to call a truce. Even though you're a woman, I do respect you and I've never met anyone like you. After my wife left, I guess I just …" When he finally looks up, he's horrified to find Rose sitting at Ophelia's desk with a bemused expression on her face. "Oh. Rose. Where's Ophelia?"

Rose is still pondering Barry's comment and doesn't answer him immediately. "What? Oh. She's sick today," she finally says.

"Oh. Never mind then." He quickly steps away embarrassed.

Rose stares at the empty hallway, where he stood, struck oddly by his strange behavior.

Ophelia returns to work several days later somewhat rejuvenated. She enters the main lobby and smiles at Will, who is signing in a visitor. "Good morning, Willie," Ophelia offers as she passes.

"Morning, Miss Jones. I hope you're feeling better."

"I am. Do you miss anything around here?" she asks, wondering how he knew she had been absent.

"No ma'am. I try not to. I don't know if you heard, but there's a pool."

"On what?" she asks with curiosity.

"They're calling it the Glass Ceiling Golf Tourney."

Ophelia smiles. "I see." She reaches into her purse to get some money.

"That's OK. I gotcha covered." She closes her purse and starts away. "Don't you want to know the odds?" he asks her with a smile.

"It doesn't matter."

Will watches her enter the elevator and smiles, impressed with her class.

When Ophelia exits the elevator, she stops in amazement. The office has been totally remodeled with new furniture, carpeting, and wall coverings. Walking toward her office, she is met by Rose, Ali and Chantelle. She looks them over and suddenly finds their attire strangely out of date. With the office area newly remodeled, the dated wardrobe and hairstyles are more obvious than ever. At first, the realization almost startles Ophelia, but she recovers before they notice.

"Good morning, girls. I've got to say that this looks pretty fantastic." She walks around with the three trailing behind her. At last she enters her office. It too, has been remodeled and the office furniture replaced. At first, she's pleased, but becomes concerned when she recalls the stash of drugs in her desk. "I thought they were doing my office next week."

"The contractor got ahead of schedule. I hope you don't mind. I had to move some of your things into the new furniture."

Ophelia shoots her a glance to see if she's looking at her any differently. She puts her purse away and seats herself.

"We have a lot of salespeople applying for the rep jobs this week. Ali has a list along with their résumés," Rose informs her without any indication of her knowledge about the medicine.

"Yep," Ali replies.

"Ali, why don't you go run a copy off for Ophelia."

"Sure."

Once she's out of sight, Chantelle and Rose slam the door and rush to Ophelia's desk.

"We need to talk," Rose says, troubled.

"I know," Ophelia says, convinced they have discovered her secret.

Chantelle takes out the flyer, opens it, and lays it on her desk

"You do?" Rose asks, puzzled.

"Did you already see the flier?" Chantelle adds.

Ophelia looks down at it. "Yeah … uh, no. It looks sort of familiar." She opens her drawer, takes out her reading glasses, and scans it. "Mmmmm. Yeah. A new bottled water supplier in the building. That does sound somewhat familiar."

"You know what that means?" Chantelle asks.

Ophelia considers it for a second. "Someone in our office is going to have a broken heart."

Chantelle snatches the flyer and shoves it in her pocket. "See. The woman gets it! I told you."

"You're a mature woman, Ophelia." Rose states.

"Thanks, I think."

"We got to do something, 'cause it's gonna kill the girl. Not that I care, but she'll drive me crazy," Chantelle declares.

"It's really simple girls, she's going to have to tell the water man how she feels before he leaves," Ophelia states.

Chantelle laughs. "Yeah. That'll never happen."

"Sure it will. But it'll take a few changes." Ophelia rears back in her chair and eyes the girls' clothes and hair. "The office got a makeover. How would you girls feel about a makeover-on me?"

Chantelle and Rose grab each other and then jump up and down in joy. The door swings open and Ali enters with the copies. She puts them down and starts jumping along with them.

"Why are we jumping?" Ali asks excitedly.

"We're getting a makeover!" Chantelle and Rose scream in unison.

Ali jumps harder. "To what?"

Chantelle and Rose stop jumping and look at her. Ali starts to slow down until she comes to a full stop. "I was just kidding. When?" she asks smiling.

"Tonight, after work." Ophelia tells them. They grab each other and start jumping again. "Don't you girls have work to do?" They continue jumping their way out of her office.

Later that day, Rose, Chantelle, and Ali set up the conference room to find new sales reps. Photos of the thirty candidates line the walls. Stacks of applications and résumés sit on a table in front of them.

Rose stands in front of the first photo. A good-looking man with a crew cut, dressed in a fine suit, smiles back at them. Ali and Chantelle study his application, and then scan his résumé. They're not impressed. Rose puts an "X" under his picture.

Rose picks up a photo of an Asian woman in her thirties. She looks kind but tough. Rose is intrigued so she grabs her résumé. She flips the page with interest. She reads more then flips the page again. She shows Ali and Chantelle. They nod their heads in agreement. Rose puts a star under the photo.

At that moment, Barry and the men enter the conference room, not realizing that it's occupied. When Barry sees what the girls are up to, he walks around the room to have a look at the photos of the applicants. He picks up one of the résumés. He's impressed with the qualifications. Satisfied with the girls' progress, he motions for the other executives to leave and then follows them out.

Rose lets out a sigh of relief and continues with her search. She reads a résumé of a clean-cut black man in his forties. She likes him and again asks the girls their opinion. They nod their approval. Rose puts a star under his photo.

After looking at all the résumés and corresponding photos, the girls decide to take a lunch break. Many of the photos have stars under them and need further review.

"OK. We're half way there. We just need to call the ones we like and set up interviews. Are you ready to get back to work, girls?" Rose asks as she finishes her sandwich. Ali and Chantelle nod with full mouths.

Later, Rose, Ali, and Chantelle, proud of their accomplishments, enter Ophelia's office. Ali and Chantelle wait as Rose places the final candidate applications and résumés on her desk. Ophelia stops working and looks at the stack.

"That's the best of the best. Ten good candidates. Of course, you or Barry need to make the final decision," Rose tells Ophelia.

Ophelia takes the top one and scans it. She's very impressed. She places it back on the stack. "Good work, girls." She glances at the clock and sees that it is after four. "Wrap it up. Then. We're going shopping."

Ophelia drives up in her rental car and parks at the Village Point Shopping Center. The girls and Henry exit and wait for Ophelia to direct them.

"First stop-hair salon," Ophelia states as she takes a long last look at the pathetic hair styles of her staff. The girls, as well as Henry, jump up and down in excitement.

They sit inside the beauty salon in comfortable adjustable seats, one beside the other. Ophelia gives the beauticians a few suggestions and then waits patiently for the results. Chantelle finishes first. Her hair is straightened and cropped short, which is very reminiscent of Halle Barry.

"It's so wonderful. No ... it's so delicious!" Chantelle smiled big.

Ali is next. Her long frizzy hair is cut and styled. Then Rose appears with a modern bob and highlights. Both were picture perfect. Henry, on the other hand, is too busy giving the stylist tips and in the end agrees to a beautiful wig he saw on the way in.

Ophelia couldn't have been more pleased to see such a big change already. But there is still a lot of work to do. "The next stop is Talbot's for a new wardrobe," she tells them.

Ophelia informs the clerk her plan of action once inside. The young woman immediately attends to their needs. The girls try on and model everything in the store for Ophelia and Henry, who is wearing his wig but no one seems to notice. Henry starts to feel envious of his co-workers and decides to try on some women's wear as well. Everyone claps and nods their approval when he comes out in a sleek skirt and heels.

At the counter, the girls are loaded down with bags and boxes of clothes as Ophelia hands the clerk her credit card. The four of them try to hug her at the same time, but can't because of the packages.

"One more important stop before we leave. We can't show up on the golf course without the proper attire, girls. So we're stopping at The Red Tree Box for some women's golf apparel," Ophelia informs them.

After much success, Ophelia forks up her credit card. The girls try to show their appreciation once more with hugs and shrieks of happiness.

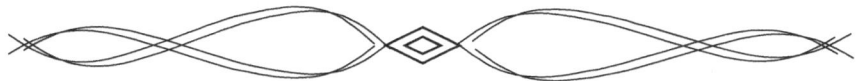

CHAPTER FIVE
ALI GETS A NUMBER

That evening, Ali steps into her bedroom a changed person. She looks around at the old her. The 80s thing is no longer appealing. She goes to the Van Halen poster and rips it down. It felt good. The remaining posters that adorned her walls and doors suffer the same outcome. Laughing, Ali falls onto her bed. The posters, still flying around the room, land on her. She is free at last.

In the morning, Ali's alarm clock beeps. As usual, her door opens and her mother enters to turn it off.

"Come on, Ali," her mother says in a dull voice. She reaches down to pull the covers back and realizes that the bed is empty. She's alarmed at first, thinking that perhaps she's been kidnapped or something just as horrible.

"I'm already up, Mother," Ali says from behind her.

Her mother, startled but relieved, looks up to see a very modern, well-dressed Ali standing across the room in front of her. "Ali, is that you?" she asks, stunned.

Ali smiles a big smile. "Yes, Mother. It's me."

Her mother straightens and smiles proudly. "Edward ... you gotta see this!"

Rose, Ali, and Chantelle, donning their new hairstyles and stylish suits, enter the main doors of H&H Insurance. They stroll confidently toward the elevators. Will, for the first time in his life, is awestruck by the changes. He shakes his head, completely taken aback.

"Looking good, ladies." They smile as they pass him. Unable to believe his eyes, Will stares at them until they enter the elevator. But, when he turns back around, he gets an even bigger surprise.

"Good morning, Will," Henry says with a smile. It doesn't go unnoticed that he is wearing a wig and women's slacks and white blouse.

"Morning, Henry?" Will says, stunned but polite.

"Henrietta, if you don't mind," Henry corrects him.

"Huh? Oh, OK," Will utters.

As Rose, Ali, and Chantelle exit the elevator on the twenty-fifth floor, everyone in the office stops and stares at the ultra-modern women as they make their way to their desks.

The girls look at each other and smile as they sit down. The elevator doors open as they prepare to work. They see one of the applicants for the sales job exit. He's a tall professional man in his forties. Barry approaches him and shakes his hand. As they walk toward Barry's office, he is obviously impressed with the decor and notices how professional the girls look.

"I'm already impressed, Mr. Castle. I hope I can meet your requirements."

Barry looks back over his shoulder at the girls and the office area. Barry is impressed with the change as well.

Ophelia steps out of her office and approaches Rose's desk. She leans toward her.

"Did you talk with Ali and tell her that this is her last chance?" she whispers.

"I told her," Rose says. They both look back at Ali, who is busy typing.

"She looks good. I hope she can do it." Ophelia starts to step away.

"By the way, we weren't sure if we should have brought our golfing clothes. We'll have to go home at lunch to get them," Rose says.

Ophelia steps back to Rose's desk and sits on the edge of it. "I've been thinking. I'm not good enough to teach you girls."

"That's OK, Ophelia."

"So, I made some calls last night. A friend I met at a tournament has agreed to come out for a week and train you girls. She was on the

Women's PGA tour but is between tournaments. She's one of the best. So don't worry about golfing today. We'll pick it up tomorrow when she arrives. Worry about Ali doing what she's got to do." She starts to turn, then stops. "Also, Russell did a fantastic job and I'd like to show my appreciation. Make a reservation at a nice restaurant for dinner tonight. Just the three of us. It's the least I can do. Let him know the time and place."

"Sure," Rose happily agrees. Ophelia leaves. Rose removes the telephone directory from her shelf then looks over at Ali who is now checking her makeup in her compact, then at the new contemporary office clock that shows 8:25. She turns to the restaurant section and thumbs through the pages.

Throughout the entire morning, the women in the office watch the clock with anticipation. Knowing, according to office rumor, that Ali is in love with the water guy and, again according to the rumors, is going to make a final last minute effort to tell him how she feels as soon as he makes his appearance.

When the clock strikes nine the elevator doors open and Luke, the water man, exits for his final visit. He's carrying a water bottle on each of his strong shoulders. Everyone looks at him and then at Ali, who is, for some insane reason, reading her email.

Just then, Henry arrives at Ophelia's door with his mail cart. He's not only wearing the wig Ophelia bought him, but also a brand new shade of lipstick and eye makeup. Just as he is about to speak to Ophelia, she sticks her head out to see what Ali is doing.

"For God's sakes, what is that girl doing?" she asks, frustrated.

Henry looks around the corner and sees her typing on her computer and nothing to attract Luke's attention. "Someone needs to just slap that girl," Henry says, dismayed. He puts his hands on his hips as Ophelia rushes to her PC and types.

At Ali's workstation, an email pops up for Ali from Ophelia. "Ali, get up and go for it. This is your chance!"

At the end of the hall, Luke finishes replacing the bottled water and is now making his way toward the other one near Ali.

Henry is keeping an eye on the events. He steps into Ophelia's office. "He's on the move."

Ophelia types another email. "Girl, if you love this man, get your butt up now!"

Ali reads it and types a response. "Ophelia, what if he doesn't like me?"

Ophelia is steaming. Henry pops back in. "What did she say? He's changing the other bottle now." Henry shakes his hands excitedly. "Ohhhhh. This is so exciting." He fans himself.

Ophelia stands up from her desk and walks briskly past Henry. "Enough of this email crap!" She struts into the office area and up to Ali's desk. She grabs her by the arm, lifts her from her chair, and pulls her around the corner. Ophelia gets in her face. "Now, listen, dear. Life is too short, love too hard to find. Honey, if you love this man, you have to tell him." She escorts her gently back around the corner and releases her.

Luke has finished replacing the water bottle and is now stepping away toward the elevator with an empty bottle on his shoulder.

Ali looks around at everyone in the office. They're all smiling and waiting. She looks at Chantelle, who smiles and motions her to do it. She looks back at Rose and Ophelia. They nod and smile urging her to make her move.

Ali takes a deep breath and takes a step, then another, and another. Before long, she's moving briskly toward him. Everyone stands to get a better look when she finally reaches him. The elevator doors open. When he steps forward, Ali reaches out and touches him on the shoulder. He stops and slowly turns to face her. She takes a deep breath, reaches forward and grabs his T-shirt. Pulling him forward, she kisses him.

Everyone in the office gasps. Ophelia covers her mouth to muffle her shout of joy.

Ali releases Luke and lets out a breath. Everyone is waiting for his response. He's stunned. She forces out the words. "I've always loved you, I think. But I'd like to find out for sure."

Luke studies her and a smile forms. "I've always thought that you were the prettiest girl in the office. I didn't think you liked me."

"Oh, I do, do like you."

He scrutinizes her some more and then moves closer to her face. He reaches up and softly cups her face in his hand. Leaning forward, he gently kisses her. She throws her arms around his neck. Everyone in the office cheers and applauds. Rose and Chantelle wipe their tears.

Ophelia, standing by her office door, has a quiet attack of pain. She turns flush and leans against the wall. She fights the pain back and smiles. Turning, she enters her office and closes the door. Henry's smile fades as he watches the door close. He's not sure what he has just witnessed, but he doesn't like it. He turns his attention back to Ali and Luke who are still embraced and he smiles.

At that moment, Barry steps up behind Henry and looks over his shoulder. "What's going on?" he asks.

Henry turns around. "Romance."

Barry looks closely at Henry, unsure of what he's seeing. "Henry, are you wearing a wig?"

"Don't be silly. Noooo," Henry says in his best male voice. He quickly pushes the cart away.

Ali and Luke finally manage to break away. Luke takes out his pad, writes down his phone number, and hands it to her. He starts to move away, then leans back, gives a quick kiss and enters the elevator. After the door closes, Ali turns, does a little jig and waves his phone number in the air.

"I got his phone number! He likes me!" She gracefully walks to her desk.

Everyone applauds again. Even Barry, who's not quite sure why he's clapping. He shrugs and goes back to his office.

Later in the day at the third hole of the Crestridge Golf Course, Barry and the men notice that the women haven't shown up. Barry glances at his watch as Dale drives the ball. Ed steps up and looks back at the start of the course for the girls.

"Looks like they had enough, huh?" Ed asks, pleased at the possibility.

Barry, surprisingly, doesn't seem as delighted with the idea as he thought he'd be. "Yeah, I guess so."

Ophelia is trying to work, but having trouble focusing. She rubs her eyes and takes a breath. There's a knock at the door. "Come in," she says.

The door swings open and Chantelle stands in the doorway. "I'm ready."

Ophelia and Chantelle exit the elevator with their purses and approach the main desk. Willie is signing out a visitor and putting away his things for the day. They wait for him to finish.

He finally notices them and says, "Afternoon ladies. What can I do for you?"

"I need a favor, Willie. Are you any good with locks?"

He looks at Chantelle. He figures it must be for her, knowing that she's being abused. "Yes, I am. I'm just getting off and am at your disposal, ladies."

In the sparsely decorated apartment, Chantelle sits in the chair, while Ophelia and Willie sit on the couch patiently waiting. Chantelle glances nervously at her watch. "Sorry. He's usually here when I get off work. For some money …you know."

Suddenly, there's a jiggling of keys at the door. Chantelle stands and clasps her hands, fearing what is to come. Willie and Ophelia stand as well. Drey tries to get the key in but it doesn't fit. He pounds impatiently on the door.

"Girl, open this door. What you'd do change the lock? Open the door!" Drey yells.

The door springs open but Chantelle blocks him to prevent him from entering. "We're done Drey. I'm not taking it anymore. Life's too short to be abused by men like you."

Drey looks maliciously at her and readies a strike. "You gone crazy, girl? Move out ta way 'for I hurt you." He puts his hand against the door and tries to push his way in. When the door opens wider, he finds himself facing Ophelia and Willie. Ophelia has a small canister of mace ready.

"You'd better back off before I mace you … Drey," Ophelia says with an attitude.

"Who the hell are you?" he asks angrily.

We're friends. And you ain't welcome here anymore," Willie answers for her.

Drey eyes the mace and Willie, who looks like he'd have no trouble kicking his ass. "Who needs you anyway. I got it going on. I don't need this." He slams the door and then struts down the hall. "You ain't nothin'."

Chantelle closes the door and falls back against it, relieved. "I'm gonna look for a new place. This girl needs a change."

"Sounds like a good idea." Willie says. He goes to the door to leave. Ophelia follows. Chantelle looks at them with tears in her eyes.

"Thanks. Nobody has ever stood up for me before." She moves in closer and gently plants a kiss on both Willie and Ophelia's cheek

Willie opens the door and then escorts Ophelia to her rental car. He looks inside. "Nice car."

Ophelia unlocks the car and starts to climb in. She turns to him. "Willie, would you be interested in having a cup of coffee with me?"

He smiles a big smile. "Ophelia, I'd love it."

They drive to a local restaurant where they sit at a cozy table in the corner. Willie takes a precious sip of the coffee and has a jerk reaction to it.
"Whew. That's good coffee, but hot," he says. He blows on the coffee to cool it. Ophelia sips on hers and gently puts it back down on the saucer.

"When I was a kid, my mother used to pour my hot drink onto the saucer to cool it."

Willie lifts his cup and pours some of it into his saucer. Then he picks her cup up and waits for her permission. She nods. He pours some of hers carefully onto her saucer. "Shall we?" He picks up his saucer then waits for her to take a sip. She carefully lifts her saucer and drinks. He smiles and follows suit. "Hey, works pretty good. Your mother was a smart woman. You must be just like her. Smart, that is."

Ophelia almost blushes. "Thank you."

Willie places his saucer down gently and pours a little more.

"So tell me about the man that seems to know every single person's name in that building. That's pretty remarkable," Ophelia states.

Willie grins to himself. "There's really not that much to tell. I worked the railroad for better than forty years. Started when I was fifteen. Got married young and had one son, Louis. He's a defense lawyer. Good one too."

"I'm impressed," Ophelia says, raising her eyebrows.

"Then the wife got ill. The cancer treatments nearly wiped us out. She passed a few years ago."

"I'm sorry."

"So I went back to work. But I do just fine." He takes another sip and looks at Ophelia as if something were on his mind. "And … I want to thank you."

"For what?" Ophelia asks.

"For lettin' me help tonight. It was beginning to get to me, seeing her come in week after week, knowing that someone was beating up on her and nobody doing anything about it. I kept thinking if that was my daughter, I'd be so damned mad and … well, just thanks."

Ophelia reaches across the table and puts her hand on his. "You're a good man, Willie." Your wife and son would be proud. I know I'm proud to know you."

"And you're a precious woman, Ophelia Jones."

Late in the afternoon the next day, Ophelia enters Barry's office and seats herself. "You wanted to see me Barry?"

Barry clasps his hands and looks down at them. "I just wanted to let you know that I think the new reps that your team selected were outstanding. I think we're gonna have some good reps out there."

"Thanks, Barry. I'll pass that on to the girls."

Barry stands and walks around the room, nervously. "And the girls did a good job with the office. I'm getting lots of compliments. And they look great as well."

"I'll pass that on too." She stands. "If that's all, Barry. I have work."

Barry awkwardly walks up to her, puts his hands on her shoulders and blurts out, "Ah, hell." He plants a kiss right on her lips and doesn't pull back.

Ophelia's eyes open wide in astonishment. She tries to talk but Barry doesn't relent. "My God, Barry, you're kissing me," she says through pressed lips.

"I know," he replies through pressed lips as well.

She pushes him back, but he still has his hands on her shoulders. "STOP!" Ophelia yells.

Barry looks at her strange, not getting it. "What's wrong?"

She looks at him as if he were crazy. "I don't want you kissing me. I don't even like you."

"OK, so we got off on the wrong foot, but—" he tries to defend himself.

She pulls his hands free and pushes him back. "Have you lost your mind?" She backs away, but Barry approaches undeterred. "Don't come near me, Barry. I'm not fooling."

When Barry takes another step, she hits him. He staggers back and plops down on the floor holding his nose. He looks at the blood on his fingers.

"I warned you, Barry. What is wrong with you?"

Barry gets on his knees and starts crawling to her. She backs up toward the door but can't get the door opened fast enough. He wraps his arms around her legs. "I think I'm falling for you. I've never known a woman like you. You make me feel powerless, weak in the knees."

She looks down at him in horror. "You gotta get a grip." She pulls herself free and throws the office door open. There in full view of several employees is Barry on his knees with a bloody nose. Ophelia smiles as if nothing were wrong and quickly steps away. Barry smiles awkwardly and tries to straighten his tie. Then he looks around on the floor as if he had lost something.

"Where is that thing? It was here somewhere." He reaches up with his free hand and closes the door.

At the Crestridge Golf Course that afternoon, forty-year-old Suzy Whaley walks back and forth with a club in her hand as she gives instructions to her new pupils. Rose, Ali, Chantelle, and Henry, who has donned his wig for the occasion, listen intently. Ophelia stands on the sidelines watching with great interest.

"Ophelia asked me to give you golf lessons for the next week. I can't promise that I can make PGA champions out of you, but I can teach you some of the basics," Suzy says as she steps to the tee. She readies her stance and looks back over her shoulders. "One of the most important elements of good golfing is your stance and your body alignment. Notice how my feet are properly spaced apart and my body square." She turns around and leans on her club. "Now I want you to take a stance like you're getting ready to tee off." She steps around to each of them and helps them to stand properly. "Your feet should always be parallel with the target, or where you want the ball to go," she says as she repositions their feet. She returns to the tee and takes her position. "Another important element is the swing." She raises her club back up over her shoulder, then brings it down toward the ball and then stops directly behind it. "The path of the swing is thus." She swings back up and down again. "The angle of approach of the golf club to the ball affects the ball spin rate, trajectory, and distance." She then swings and hits the ball. It gracefully takes to the air several hundred yards out. She holds her pose, then releases.

Ophelia smiles at the perfection of Suzy's swing. The others can only stare in awe. Suzy turns and leans on her club. "Simple, huh? The trick is to just relax and have fun. You'll get your best game that way. Remember, stance, swing, and relax. Now lets see what you got. Rose, you first."

Suzy goes behind Rose and guides her through several practice swings. Then she steps back and lets Rose try it out on her own. The swing is good, but it slices way over to her left. Suzy shows her how to grip and prevent the club from turning. Her next swing is straighter.

The afternoon progresses with Suzy working on each of their swings. Ophelia helps out as well. Henry proves to be a natural; amazing everyone as he nails the ball and sends the ball sailing out of sight with each swing of the club.

Ophelia and Suzy stand back to the side, watching the new and improved bunch practice their drives.

"Well, what do you think?" Ophelia asks Suzy.

"I don't know, Ophy. You say the men they're playing are in a league?"

"Company golf league," Ophelia reiterates.

"Are they as good as you?"

"A couple."

"Even if they give your team the usual handicap, it's gonna be tough. They're pretty green," Suzy tells her.

"I know."

"Now, the tall girl has real potential," Suzy says about Henry.

Ophelia watches him swat another one into space. "Wonderful!" she yells out to him.

Suzy checks her watch. Let's have them do some putting then call it a day. I don't want to overwork them.

On the putting green, Suzy demonstrates the proper way to stand and putt. She then positions each one, corrects their stance, and stands behind them to help them through the first putt.

Rose, Suzy discovers, needs extra help on the putts as she overshoots the hole, again, and again, and again. Chantelle on the other hand is shown how to do it and putts it in the first time. Everyone is pleased except Rose. Ophelia puts her arm around Rose's shoulder and encourages her to try again. Eventually, she gets it and everyone cheers.

Next, Suzy works with Ali and Henry. Ali has a good eye but her nervousness prevents her from sinking the ball. Henry sinks the ball the first time.

" OK. Let's call it a day everyone. I have to say, for girls that have never played before, you all are very good. But we have a lot of work. We'll see everyone tomorrow afternoon."

The girls walk to their cars, ready to leave after a grueling day of golf. Rose approaches Ophelia as she gets into her car. "I set up the dinner with Russell like you asked, Ophelia. It's at the French Café on Howard Street in the Old Market area downtown. I made it for seven. Is that OK?"

Ophelia starts her car. "French Café, Howard Street, at seven. Got it. Thanks, dear. I'll see you there." She pulls away.

That evening at the French Café, Rose sits across from Russell at an off the path, cozy table near the window. Russell takes a sip of wine and waits patiently. Rose looks at her watch. Ophelia is ten minutes late.

"Sorry, Ophelia is usually prompt," Rose apologizes as she looks at the empty chair next to her.

Russell seems relaxed. "That's okay."

Ophelia, who has parked her car just a few stalls down from the French Café on the other side of the street, adjusts the mirror until a view of Rose and Russell comes into view. She puts the phone to her ear and eyes the rearview mirror.

Rose's cell phone rings. "Hello," she answers.

"Rose? It's me, Ophelia. I am so sorry. Something's come up and I'm afraid I can't make it. That's the curse of being management. You understand. But please, you and Russell enjoy the dinner on me. I've already taken care of the bill. So enjoy."

Russell listens astutely, occasionally shooting Rose a smile while she's on the phone. Rose smiles back. "Oh, OK, Ophelia. I understand. Bye." Rose puts the phone away as she explains. "That was Ophelia. She apologizes. She can't make it. Something came up." She nervously takes a drink of her wine, and then tries to smile at him.

He leans forward and studies her eyes, almost staring.

"What is it?" Rose asks, paranoid.

He laughs comfortably. "I'm sorry, Rose. It's just that … I never realized how beautiful your eyes are." Russell looks down, almost embarrassed for having said it and shakes his head. "I'm sorry. That sounds so cliché. I'm sorry."

"Oh, no. That was very nice … of you to say. Really. I'm just not used to it. That's all."

"Really? Successful women like you probably have to ignore such things. Professionalism and all."

"Like me? Ah, yeah, I suppose we do."

"I understand. I have deep respect for women like that. In fact it's a real turn on."

"It is?" Rose asks, almost stunned.

"Oh yes. Men find that very sexy. Russell puts his hand on hers. I find it very sexy."

Rose takes a big gulp of her wine with her free hand.

Ophelia sees that things are going well so she starts the car. Willie turns in his seat to see her take another big gulp of wine. He smiles.

"You're a she-devil, Ophelia."

She backs the car up. "I know. But the girl needs it." She looks at Willie. "We all need it."

He grins. "So, since you sacrificed your dinner in the name of romance, what are your plans for dinner?"

"I was thinking of preparing us something special. I can cook you know."

Willie shakes his head. "Why is it that I'm not surprised that a very special and unique woman like you would know how to cook?"

"Why, Mr. Willie, if I didn't know better, I'd say that you are flirting with me."

He laughs a sincere laugh. "You said it yourself, Miss Ophelia. We all need it."

She laughs as they drive off into the evening.

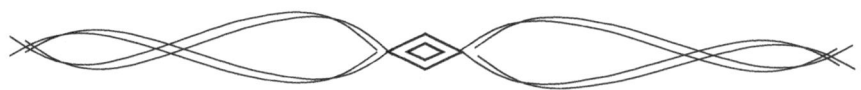

CHAPTER SIX
A TOURNAMENT AND A KISS GOODBYE

The next morning at Harrison & Haney, Willie is greeting employees when Ophelia enters. "Morning, Willie," Ophelia says with a Mona Lisa smile.

Willie smiles back, suggesting that the evening was a memorable one. "Morning, Ophelia."

Rose enters immediately after Ophelia. She appears to be in her own world as she walks obliviously to the elevators. With a smile on her face, she passes Willie without a word. Willie suspects her date resulted in more than expected. He doesn't bother to disrupt her thoughts but just smiles and greets others as they arrive.

When Henry enters there is a noticeable change in him as well. Today, he has done it all. He is wearing makeup, a wig, and a tight black skirt. And under his feminine blouse lay a pair of very womanly breasts, which Henry is caught adjusting on a regular basis.

Willie tries not to laugh. "Morning Henry ... etta."

Henry steps past him smiling as he tries to get his girlish swing down. "Morning, Willie," he says.

Barry steps to Ophelia's open door and taps lightly on the doorframe. Ophelia looks up from her paperwork and removes her reading glasses.

"Yes, Barry?" He starts to close the door. "Leave the door open, Barry. Please," Ophelia asks politely but sternly.

He swings it half closed and approaches the desk. Glancing over his shoulder, he says, "About the tournament try outs this weekend. Since you and the girls haven't been back to the course since ... well, you know, I was thinking that we could push it out a couple of—"

Ophelia interrupts, "That's okay, Barry. The girls will be ready. We're getting some golf time in. Just not when you and the others are there."

"Oh." He starts to leave, then stops. "And about the other day. I was out of line. I owe you an apology."

"You probably owe every female in the building an apology."

"Yeah. Maybe. I'm not real good with women. I just wanted to say—"

Ophelia picks up the phone pretending to have heard a ring. "Oh, yeah, Rose. Sure. I'll be right there." She hangs up, stands, and rounds the desk. "Sorry, Barry. I need to discuss something urgent with one of my employees. We'll have to catch up on our discussion on your inadequacies with women at a later date." As she swings the door open, Henry appears in the hallway with his cart, fully decked out in all his glory as a woman.

Ophelia takes one look at his breasts and is immediately reminded of the cancer that is ravaging her body. She hides it. "Oh, Henry. You have ... " she studies the breasts and sees that one is higher than the other, "lopsided breasts." She readjusts them so they're equal, tries to smile, and then dashes away.

Barry steps to the doorway, leans against it and shakes his head as he scans Henry from head to toe. "Henry, we have to talk," he says, troubled.

Henry looks around then throws one of his hands up as if there were nothing wrong. "What?"

Barry motions with his finger for Henry to follow then moves past him and toward his office. Henry rolls his eyes and follows.

Meanwhile, Ophelia approaches Ali and Chantelle's cubicles and sits on the edge of Ali's desk, her arms crossed. Ali and Chantelle stop working to look at her.

"Is there something wrong, Ophelia?" Ali asks.

"No. I'm just not in the mood to deal with Barry right now," Ophelia responds. Ali and Chantelle shrug and go back to work. "So how are things?"

Ali and Chantelle stop working again.

"Fine. Chantelle and I are looking for an apartment together," Ali informs her.

"That's great," Ophelia says happily. Ali and Chantelle nod knowing it is a good thing. It's an awkward moment. "Could one of you go to my office and make sure Barry is not in there?"

Chantelle slowly stands. "Sure. I can," she says, finding the whole dialogue strange. She leaves to check.

Ophelia checks her fingernails and taps her foot to waste time while waiting for word.

Ali becomes concerned. "Is everything, OK?"

Ophelia looks up, her eyes reflecting a moment of weakness in her armor. It's an opportunity to tell her of a new love in her life, no matter how fleeting her life may be. But Ophelia is supposed to be a strong woman, so she forces the smile and the confident twinkle in her eyes. "Oh, yes. Barry is just being his usual self. You know."

"Yeah. I know. Barry can be a pain sometimes," Ali says.

Chantelle returns to her desk and sits. "He's gone."

Opehlia stands. "Thanks." She walks to her office as Chantelle shoots Ali a concerned glance.

"What was that about?" Chantelle asks in a low voice.

Ali shrugs and watches her turn the corner. "I don't know."

Back in Barry's office, Henry is standing awkwardly on display in the middle of the floor while Barry slowly walks around him, shaking his head. He stops and looks at Henry's breasts. He moves in close to examine them. With his finger, he pushes one in. It pops back out. "Breasts, Henry?"

"They're not real ...yet. And it's Henrietta."

Barry steps back to get the whole picture of the woman standing in front of him. "I don't know Henry. The whole thing just seems ... odd. You know when your sister, Doris, who I hate, hate, hate. Of course you know I hate her." Henry nods. "Well, when we divorced, I sort of promised that I wouldn't take it out on you, with you being an employee and her brother and all."

"Yeah. I know. That was very big of you Barry," Henry says sarcastically.

"Thank you, Henry, or Henrietta."

Henry smiles at him for remembering the name change.

"But this woman thing you're doing—"

"But, I am a woman. I know that now. It's my destiny," Henry states matter of factly.

"Ah, yeah. I see. But it doesn't seem right to me."

"It's a chemical thing, Barry. Haven't you ever read an article or watched educational programming on how sexual identity is determined?"

"No."

"It's like my brain was programmed as a woman, but my body was programmed as a man. It's a glitch."

"A glitch? I don't know anything about that, Henry ... etta."

Henry nods. "When you have those big meetings don't you research everything so you know what the other guy knows?"

"Well, yeah. That's part of the job."

"Well, how can we have an honest discussion about my sexuality, when you haven't done any research?"

Barry rubs his chin, thinking. "I don't know. I guess I can't." Barry sits at his desk and checks his email. "OK, Henry ...etta. Thanks." Barry becomes engrossed in his thoughts.

Henry looks around the room then goes to the door and opens it. Barry, still deep in thought, doesn't notice so Henry shrugs and leaves.

A few minutes later, there's a knock on Barry's door. It takes a second knock to get Barry's attention. "Come in."

Paul Sorenson enters and sits. "Well, it was a little tough, but I managed to get the scoop on Miss Jones through some contacts at corporate."

Barry had totally forgotten that he asked. "Oh. Yeah."

Paul opens the folder. "Did you realize that she's one of the founders, very well educated, top of her class at Harvard Business, and has very substantial holdings in the company? Very."

"Jeez."

"I have no idea what she's doing here. She could easily retire. Easily."

Barry shakes his head. "I don't get it."

"Something else, though."

"Yeah. What is it?"

"She held a very high position at corporate like you said, but there's a very long period of absence from the company. Seemed odd. And well, I'll just say it. It was therapy at a very reputable rehab clinic in New York."

"Rehab? You don't mean like drugs?"

"Cancer. It was a breast cancer rehab clinic, Barry."

Barry is stunned. He eases back, now wishing that he didn't know. "Thanks, Paul. I'm sorry."

Paul stands. "Sorry?"

"Yeah. I should've never asked you to do that. Get rid of it."

Paul turns and leaves.

Barry rotates in his chair and looks out at the overcast clouds beyond his tall office windows. He decides to pay a visit to Ophelia. But when he gets there, her office is dark and the door closed. He goes to the common office area and discovers that Rose, Ali, and Chantelle's cubicles are empty as well. Disappointed, he walks back to his office.

Later that afternoon, Barry pulls up and parks at the Crestridge Golf Course. He exits the vehicle, still dressed in his business attire, and walks to the clubhouse. He spots his new competition practicing their drives so he steps quietly to the corner. He leans against the building and watches the girls, dressed in their new golf attire, getting instructions from Suzy. He doesn't see Ophelia with them. He notices that the girls and Henry are exhibiting some developed skills for golf. It's no longer the chaotic mess that he had witnessed earlier.

Barry is unsure what to think anymore. He goes inside the clubhouse deep in thought when he spots Ophelia's clubs by the ladies restroom door. He steps to the door and listens. He hears Ophelia throwing up so he enters, concerned.

The toilet flushes and Ophelia swings the door open to find Barry standing in the middle of the room with his arms crossed. Ophelia can't believe the audacity. She steps to the sink to wash her hands. She looks up at him in the mirror. "What is with you and bathrooms, Barry?"

"When were you going to tell the girls?"

Ophelia studies him in the mirror, deciding how much he knows and whether or not to evade the question.

"Yes. I know," he tells her.

Ophelia continues to wash her hands and looks down. "I won't ask how. I'm not sure I'd like the answer."

Barry drops his arms. "Just how serious is it? That didn't sound good in there."

Ophelia turns off the water and steps to the towel dispenser. She pulls out a sheet, rips it off and wipes her hands. "Get to the point, Barry. I have to get back to the girls."

Barry shakes his head. "You're a tough one, aren't you, Ophelia Jones?"

Ophelia throws the towel into the trash and checks her hair. "I've had to be. I'm a black woman in a white man's world. You don't have any idea, Barry." She starts to step around him.

"I'm not the enemy, " he says tenderly.

She stops and turns. "You can't have it both ways, Barry." You're either with someone or against, a friend, or not. You can't go through life carefully straddling the fence so it works out the best for you. Men misunderstand power. It doesn't come from you, it comes from the people that believe in you." She looks down. "And to answer your question. No, I won't tell them because I want them to believe in me, not pity me. They need that. I'm sorry I had to hit you. In another lifetime, I wouldn't have."

She leaves and Barry is left standing in the middle of the room facing the mirror. As the door swings shut, he studies the shallow man wearing a suit in the mirror.

The day of the tournament finally arrives and the parking lot is brimming with cars and spectators flocking onto the course to see the Glass Ceiling Golf Tourney. Everyone is eager to see the women take on the male executives.

Barry, Edward, Dale, and Russell, who is subbing for the shipping department supervisor, are standing confidently at the first hole as the women approach. Ophelia, Rose, Ali, and Chantelle smile and wave to the crowd. They are all decked out in their new golf outfits and are looking professional and self-assured. Henry, unable to play officially, serves as the girls' caddy.

Willie, in a worn baseball cap and sunglasses, peeks through the crowd and gives Opehlia a wink. She smiles back.

Tom Tailor, a forty year old man employed by the golf course, serves as the tournament referee. "I'd like to welcome everyone to this playoff tournament between the Harrison and Haney Insurance men executives verses the women executives," he says, laughing. "You all probably know it as the Glass Ceiling Golf Tourney." The crowd laughs congenially. "The game will be played as a four person scramble for eighteen holes of golf. And although normally, we give the men a handicap of twenty six and women thirty three, the women's team leader has asked that we give them a twenty six as well. Therefore both teams are handicapped at twenty six. The men will tee off from blue tees, women red. Each team must use at least two tee shots from each member. After tee off, team members must decide which ball to play. Only three minutes are allowed for ball searching. First ball to go in the hole is counted for the team score. OK, I'll flip to see which team tees off first." Tom flips the coin and catches it. He holds it out, covered.

"Heads," Barry calls out.

Tom opens his hand and shows both Barry and Ophelia that it's tails. "Women tee off first."

All the women in the crowd of spectators cheer as Ophelia steps up to tee off. Putting in her tee, she takes a breath, positions herself and swings. The ball is in flight and a perfect drive out onto the fairway. However, it doesn't make the green.

Barry looks down. He knows that she's better than that.

Rose steps up next and places her ball. "Stance ... swing ... relax," she softly mumbles to herself. Gracefully, she hits the ball. It sails out into the fairway, not as far as Ophelia's, but still good for her. She holds her stance, almost in shock that she did it. She drops her club and steps away.

The men are up and Barry hits the ball out to the green.

Everyone applauds. When he turns, he sees that Ophelia is watching him. She nods her approval. By the end of the hole, the men are in the lead as Dale sinks the ball with one putt.

The women take the second hole even though Rose misses a putt. She is redeemed after she takes a deep breath and putts the ball in on the next try. The women spectators applaud. The girls look at each other and smile.

At the eleventh hole, Ophelia nails a drive several hundred yards and lands on the green. The women in the crowd furiously applaud. Barry smiles at Ophelia and nods his approval.

The game continues with the lead switching between the men and the woman. But things change when Chantelle is teeing up on the fifteenth hole. Ophelia, feeling uneasy, steps to the edge of the green. She goes to a small shaded tree and slides down, resting against it with her head down.

Barry frowns and approaches her, his shadow slides over her, blocking the sun. "You OK?" She doesn't respond. He bends down on his knee and gently touches her on her shoulder. She falls over onto her side on the ground.

"Ophelia, OPHELIA!" he yells in a panic.

Rose, Ali, Chantelle, Henry, and the other men rush over. Willie bursts through the spectator crowd and rushes to her as well. He bends down and places his ear near her mouth.

"Someone call an ambulance!" Willie yells as he lifts her in his arms.

"Willie, what are you doing?" she asks, weakly.

"Shush. I'm taking you to the hospital." He picks her up and walks briskly to the clubhouse.

"We're coming too," Rose, Ali, Chantelle say in unison.

Ophelia protests. "No girls, finish the game, and win. I'll be OK."

The three watch as Willie carries Ophelia away. Barry steps up with his teammates. He removes his golf gloves and picks up his clubs.

"I'm going too," Barry says earnestly.

"But you're our best player," Dale protests.

Barry shoots him a disgusted look. "She was theirs." He trots off after them as Henry steps up and wipes away his tears.

"What are we gonna do?"

"You heard her. We're going to win. We're going to win for Opehlia," Rose says. She turns with a look of determination and heads toward the green.

In the ambulance, Ophelia is on the stretcher with an oxygen mask on her face. Barry and Willie are at her side. Willie is clasping her hand. Ophelia struggles to pull the oxygen mask down. She finally succeeds. "Willie," she calls.

Willie moves close to her. "Yes?"

"I need a pen and paper and then I need you to do something very important for me."

Later at Bergan Mercy Hospital, Willie and Barry are approached by a doctor while sitting impatiently in the waiting room. He doesn't look pleased. They stand anxiously from their waiting room chairs as he nears.

"Well, what's wrong with her doc?" Willie asks anxiously.

"Did you both know that she has cancer?" the doctor asks.

"I knew that she had it, but I thought it was in remission. She was at a cancer rehab clinic in New York," Barry replies.

Willie looks surprised to hear it.

"Her body is ravaged with cancer. I talked with her doctor. It was briefly in remission. But it advanced quickly. I'm surprised that she's alive," the doctor informs them.

"What do we do?" Willie asks.

"There is nothing to do. Her organs are shutting down. I have her on a morphine drip. There's nothing we can do. I'm sorry."

"Can I see her?" Willie asks.

He turns to take Willie to her. "Sure."

Willie enters Ophelia's room and quickly moves to her side. He sees that her eyes are closed and that she looks calm. He lifts her hand and squeezes. Her eyelids partially open.

"Hi, Willie. How'd the girls do?" Ophelia asks weakly.

"Don't worry about them now. Why didn't you tell me?" Willie asks.

Ophelia tries to give him an understanding smile.

"Yeah, yeah. I know. A strong woman like you wouldn't take pity. Would you, Ophelia?" He starts to tear up.

"Oh, Willie. Don't cry for me. I've done everything I've ever wanted to do. I can only think of one thing that would make my life complete."

"Just name it."

"A good-bye kiss."

His tears fall. "But I don't want to say good-bye. I don't want you to go." He pauses. "I was thinking that we could take a romantic trip, just you and me. Anything could happen."

"Why, Mr. Willie, I do believe that you're flirting with me."

"I sure am Miss Ophelia."

He slowly moves to her lips and gently kisses her. Her last breath releases and her eyes close. He lays his head on her chest and closes his eyes.

Willie returns to the waiting room and approaches Barry as he wipes his eyes. Barry starts to step past him to go see her. Willie gently stops him. "She's gone, Barry. Ophelia's gone."

Barry is stunned. "Did she say anything?"

"Yeah. Right to the end she was Ophelia ... right to the end."

Barry almost seems relieved. He sits. "That's good." He breaks down crying. Willie sits down beside him and puts his arm around his shoulder. At that moment, Rose, Ali, Chantelle, and Henry rush into the room. They're excited about having won the tournament, but also concerned about Ophelia.

"Wait until Ophelia hears," Rose says to Ali and Chantelle.

As they approach Willie and Barry, it's obvious that something horrible has happened. Willie and Barry stand and silently approach. The girls can see that it's extremely serious. Rose takes a step back and tears well up in her eyes.

"No. No. She can't be. We won. We have to tell her. She can't be ..."

Henry puts his arms around Ali and Chantelle, who begin crying.

"I don't understand. It can't be," Ali says, shocked.

Willie puts his arms around Rose and the others. "Ophelia had cancer. She'd had it for a while. I'm sorry. There is something else. She wanted me to give this to all of you." Willie presents a manila envelope.

On the front is written "For the Girls" in her handwriting. The girls stare at it.

"Ophelia owned substantial stock in the company. She left it to you girls ... you too, Henrietta." Barry tears up. Rose hands him a Kleenex. He blows his nose. The girls look at Rose, waiting for her to do the honors. Rose tears the envelope and opens it. Stuffed inside are stock certificates and a folded letter. She removes the letter. Stopping to wipe her tears, she reads,

Dear girls,

I'm so proud of each and every one of you. Never, ever take for granted what you have to offer. You're special women and you have made my life complete.

Your Friend,
Ophelia Jones

Barry, Willie, Rose, Ali, Chantelle, and Henry stand at Ophelia's burial site looking down at the covered coffin. A mass of attendees are making their way back to their cars. Rose admires the epitaph on the headstone. She reads it out loud. "'Ophelia Lucille Jones, 1958-2006, The Wind Beneath Our Wings.' Very nice, Ali. Good choice."

Barry starts bawling loudly. Willie puts his arm around his shoulder. "I loved that woman," Barry says. Then he realizes that she and Willie had something between them. "Oh, sorry."

Willie turns him around and begins walking away. The others follow. "That's OK. We all loved her," Willie says gently.

Back at Harrison & Haney Insurance, Rose, Ali, Chantelle, and Henrietta dressed sharply in executive attire walk briskly and confidently down the hall toward the conference room. Henrietta opens the doors wide allowing the girls to enter. The door closes behind them.

Barry sits at the head of the table while every chair on either side of the table are occupied by a male executive. Four empty chairs occupy the other end. A copy of the agenda sits in front of the chairs. The girls sit. As soon as they get settled in their seats, Barry stands and clears his throat. "OK guys." All the men stand. The girls look at them expecting the usual routine of being left alone in the room. But Barry plops back down, followed by the men. "Gotcha," Barry teases. Everyone laughs congenially. "Henrietta, are those new breasts?"

"Yes," Henrietta says proudly.

"They look nice."

"Thank you, Barry. I like your tie. Looks nice on you."

"Thanks. Now, about sales. We're continuing to see improved sales thanks to some new and outstanding salesmen we recently hired. I'm going to turn it over to Rose. She's going to brief us on some new markets that look very promising ..."

The End

Note To Screenwriters

We at Young Films and Publishing do truly believe that screenwriters are the new storytellers of our era. That's how this book series was born. Not only as a screenwriter, but as the manager of a film company, I have seen first hand the abundance of screenwriters from all walks of life trying to get their story out. But when you venture out to tell your story, remember that you are asking to participate in an industry...the film industry. It's a trade like any other with sometimes very high expectations and demands.

Screenwriters must understand that the first expectation of any script reader is that the format be absolutely correct (industry standard). If it isn't, not only is it a distraction from the flow of the story, but it sends a negative signal to the reader that if the screenwriter didn't spend the time to get the format right, what else did they not follow through with; character development, story structure, etc.

My old agent once told me that to attempt to write words on a hundred pieces of paper and sell it to a studio would be one of the most difficult things I would ever try to do in my life. He was right. It's near impossible. I said near, not totally impossible. But simple mistakes in the beginning don't improve your chances.

Fortunately, the screenwriter has vast resources available at their fingertips. The Internet and library contain a wealth of information on screenwriting and filmmaking. Screenwriters (who have honed their craft) may also enter their works in film festivals and screenwriting contest. We've noticed that a very high percentage of screenwriters who have been in contests or film festivals have learned to move past the basics of screenwriting (i.e, format and structure) and put more focus into the content of the screenplays they write.

Screenwriters who attend film festivals can not only make important film industry contacts, but can have dialogue with industry professionals who have been there and done what the beginning writer is attempting to do. Lew Hunter, author of *Lew Hunter's Screenwriting 434,* a must read for beginning screenwriters, attends film festivals in the Midwest and not only offers excellent advise on screenwriting, but holds a pitch session to get the screenwriter tuned in to what a good industry pitch sounds like.

Lew Hunter's website offers some excellent tools and information for screenwriters (beginning or advanced). At http://lewhunter.com/

screenwriters can find links to the WGA website (for registering your screenwplay), contests, software, and other excellent screenwriting resources.

We sincerely hope that someday in our our books series, we will be able to bring your story to the American reading public. Thanks and good luck. Or as Lew Hunter says, "Write on!"

Jackie L. Young
Chief Managing Editor & Manager
Young Films & Publishing LLC

FUTURE BOOKS

The "Movies That Hollywood Didn't Make" and "Movies That Hollywood Made" books are part of the "Read a Movie" book series by Young Films & Publishing LLC. Look for these *"Movies That Hollywood Didn't Make"* In short story format books in the near future at your local bookstores:

◆   "Christmas Movies That Hollywood <u>Didn't</u> Make"
◆   "Action-Adventure Movies That Hollywood <u>Didn't</u> Make"
◆   "Westerns That Hollywood <u>Didn't</u> Make"
◆   "Sci-Fi Movies That Hollywood <u>Didn't</u> Make"
◆   "Children's Movies That Hollywood <u>Didn't</u> Make"
◆   "Animation Movies That Hollywood <u>Didn't</u> Make"
◆   "Horror Movies That Hollywood <u>Didn't</u> Make"
◆   "The Scariest Movies That Hollywood <u>Didn't</u> Make"
◆   "War Movies That Hollywood <u>Didn't</u> Make"
◆   "Dramatic Movies That Hollywood <u>Didn't</u> Make"
◆   "Comedies That Hollywood <u>Didn't</u> Make"
◆   "Romantic Movies That Hollywood <u>Didn't</u> Make"
◆   "Screenplays That Hollywood Should Make Into Movies" (Special Edition, Reader's Choice)

Screenwriters/Writers Biographies and Contact Info

Sheila Brothers & Roxanne Marchand (The Penny)

Sheila Brothers and Roxanne Marchand have been writing together for over nine years. Sheila and Roxanne wrote the horror, *Butchered*, produced by Eleven Bravo Productions. The short film, *I Do?* was written and produced by them as well and should be hitting film festival circuit this year. They are also the head writers for the Video Podcast series, *Port City P.D.,* the first police drama to be made for the internet. They have more projects underway. Check out their web site to get the latest details: wehavenolife.org

Agent:
Barry Perelman
The Barry Perelman Agency
barry_perelman@hotmail.com

Contact:
we have no life enterprises
sheila_brothers@yahoo.com
roxmarch@bellsouth.net

Karen Hicks (Sam's Shadow)

Hicksters30@aol.com

J.L. Chaka (Sheriffs Incorporated & Mr Christmas)

Contact writer via Young Films LLC.

Screenwriters/Writers Biographies
and Contact Info Cont'd

Jackie Young (For The Girls)

Jackie Young, manager of Young Films & Publishing LLC has been a screenwriter for over 12 years and has written over 30 screenplays. Jackie was coordinator of the Nebraskans For Film, a Nebraska screenwriting group, for over 6 years. Jackie wrote, executive produced, and produced a short film (Manimals) in 1997, then wrote and executive produced an independent feature film with Rigtown Pictures titled, Love Wine. Jackie has also appeared in Screentalk Magazine.

jyoung1981@aol.com

Jill Pomerantz (Story Conversions of; Sheriffs Inc, For The Girls, and Mr Christmas, and story editing)

Jill graduated from California State University in 1993 with a Bacholer Degree in Spanish Literature. Because of her life long love for languages (including English) she decided to sell all of her belongings and move to Madrid, Spain. She lived there for six years as an English teacher but family eventually beckoned her back to her hometown of Rockford, IL . She currently lives in Chicago with her husband and two beautiful baby boys. Being a stay at home mom, she has re-found her love of reading and writing, which keeps her blissfully occupied. Previous editing credits includes the book, *Movies That Hollywood Didn't Make, Vol I*, of the *Read-A-Movie* book series. Jill can be contacted via Young Films and Publishing LLC.

"A very marketable picture, with gorgeous scenery, romance, humor and depth."

Stuart R. Wahlin, Movie Critic, The Rock River Times

"Bridget Love returns from the big city to her home on an island to run "Love Wine" Corporation after her Aunt and Uncle die in a boating accident. Bridget soon discovers that she must have sex on the new crop of grapes, a family tradition, to fulfill her contractual obligations or the company will default to her eager and promiscuous cousin."